Friends Like These

By Hannah Ellis

To my amazing mum and dad,
The best people I know

Acknowledgements

I'm so grateful to the people who helped and supported me in writing my debut novel. To those who diligently proof-read and edited, and to those who pushed me to finish it and believed that I could do it.

A huge 'thank you' to: Stephen Ellis, Sandra Ellis, Mario Ellis, Emma Lenze, Jenny Addrison, Dua Roberts and Anthea Kirk.

Chapter 1

I was loitering in the vitamin aisle, staring blankly at the packet of multivitamins in my hands when a high-pitched voice broke my thoughts.

"Hello! Can I help you?"

I looked up to find a short, plump sales assistant in a white tabard smiling at me.

"Oh, no. I'm fine thanks."

And then, just because I couldn't resist, I held up the box and asked, "Do these come with a cape?"

Her smile didn't move from her face but her eyebrows shot quickly in the direction of her hairline and her eyes widened slightly. "I'm sorry?"

"You know, because they're called *Ultra Woman!* And it sounds like they will make me into a pretty awesome specimen of a woman. I'd just need a cape and then I could go and fight crime!"

When her face didn't change I laughed nervously and stuck out my arm, while lifting up onto one foot, wonder-woman style. She didn't react. I settled back into a normal pose.

"I'm okay thanks, just browsing."

She looked at me as though she wasn't sure I was fit to be out on my own before walking away. I returned the box of *Ultra Woman* to the shelf and glanced furtively to my left. A few sidesteps would bring me to the pregnancy tests. I was just waiting for the coast to be clear.

I was paranoid by the fact that anybody seeing me would know more about me than I wanted. They'd know I might be pregnant and would be looking to see if I was elated or horrified. Clearly I wasn't on the elated side of the scale. The way I was feeling, I'd even go one further and say that people would look at me and see someone who caught her ex-boyfriend in bed with a dumb blonde and was now facing the prospect of being a single mother with a permanent connection to a man she never wanted to see again. It was written all over my face, I was sure.

My mind wandered to a few hours earlier when I was still living in the blissfully unaware state of not realising I might be pregnant.

"Morning, Marie!" My co-worker had chirped when I'd walked into work at 9am. Anne was nearly always cheerful, especially in the mornings, and that trait alone meant I would probably never fully understand her as a person. It also made me prone to spending my first hour at work thinking of ways to kill her with office supplies.

That day was different though. I had a feeling of contentment and might even go so far as to say I was cheerful myself.

"Morning," I'd replied, sitting down and shoving my bag into the bottom drawer of my filing cabinet.

I turned my computer on and while it whirred into life I scanned the wall opposite me. It was covered in holiday brochures, all neatly racked up in rows and columns. It was a wall full of promise and excitement. I loved to watch customers stand in front of it and try to decide which of the wonderful places they would visit.

"B6 and F10," I stated, smiling at Anne who was watching me from the desk next to mine. Technically it was the same desk, it curved like a wave down the length of the shop. There were drawers and filing cabinets hidden carefully underneath, with neat gaps for our legs to slip under. More cabinets stood against the wall behind us - lurking below a blissful beach mural - all of them hiding enough paper to bring tears to any tree-huggers eyes.

"One of these days I'll catch you out," Anne said when I got up to return the holiday brochures to their proper places. This was a game Anne and I played. It had started one rainy afternoon when the shop was empty and we'd needed a way to relieve the boredom. I'd long since decided I knew the wall of brochures better than I knew my own face and I'd decided to put it to the test. We developed a 'Battleships' style numbering system for the grid of brochures. Then we would take it in turns to move brochures around and the other person had to say which ones had moved. I was a pro.

"It's too easy," I told her. "It's more annoying than challenging these days. New York, Anne? You should never mess with New York."

I hugged the brochure to me before replacing on the rack.

"So, are you ready for your big night out tonight?" Anne asked as I returned to my desk.

"I certainly am. I'm definitely in the mood to party." I felt like I hadn't had a good night out in forever and I was ready to dress myself up and dance the night away. It was a girls' night with my best friend Grace and a few of her friends from work. I couldn't remember the last time I'd been on a girls' night out and I was excited about it. An evening of drinking, dancing and chatting was just what I needed.

"I'm sure you'll have a great night. You need to get out and enjoy yourself. It's about time you stopped moping around over that idiot of an ex-boyfriend and had some fun. You know, I never wanted to say anything at the time, but I always knew he was no good for you."

I wondered at the wisdom of her deciding not to say anything at the time. A little heads up would have been nice. My good mood took an ebb at the reminder of my ex-boyfriend, Carl.

This was fairly typical of Anne. She had a definite knack of saying the wrong thing. Despite that, I loved working with her. She's fifty-four-years-old and always bubbly and full of life, but there were definitely times (usually several per day) when I just wished she would keep her opinions to herself. This was, without doubt, one of those times. I felt my good mood slipping away from me as thoughts of Carl filled my head.

Carl and I had been together for about two years. He'd always been a little bit mysterious which I'd liked at first. Then the mystery made me paranoid and jealous. I always felt like he was keeping things from me. It turned out I was right to be suspicious because a month ago I found him in bed with some blonde bombshell. And not just any bed: my bloody bed. Well, *our* bed, to be precise. We'd been living together for six months. I packed my things and left there and then. The idiot never even called me.

"You know, you're lucky in a way," Anne broke my thoughts and I looked up, eagerly awaiting the inevitable words of wisdom which were to follow.

"At least you've only got yourself to worry about. When my David cheated on me, I was pregnant and had to face the thought of bringing up a child all alone. At least you can just walk away and get on with your life."

There wasn't much that I could say. She wasn't finished though. I knew her well enough to know there was more coming.

"Anyway, there's plenty more fish in the sea, Marie, especially for a catch like you."

And there we had it: the icing on the cake. What everyone wants to hear after a break up - the old 'there's plenty more fish in the sea' speech. I rolled my eyes while resisting the urge to reach for the staple gun and launch an attack on her. I knew she meant well, but she made me want to scream.

She's quite dramatic too. I'd heard the story of David cheating on her numerous times and the first time I sympathised with her and admired the way she gallantly forgave him and took him back. However, the truth of it is was that a long time ago, a drunken girl on a hen night went over to David in a bar and kissed him for a dare. He didn't have much choice in the matter. Anne managed to turn it into a drama regardless and David has been suffering for it ever since. The man really is a saint.

Anne turned her attention to her computer and I decided she was probably right. I should look on the bright side; at least I wasn't pregnant.

That thought is where my day really started to go wrong. Mainly because it was followed by *When was my last period?* This was closely followed by S*hit, shit, shit!*

My heart raced as I reached into my handbag to find my diary so I could put an end to the panic that was taking over me, and that's when the office door swung open and out walked the boss. Greg's office was tucked away at the back of the shop, beyond Anne's end of the desk. Usually he liked to keep himself hidden away in there for most of the day.

Greg was in his forties. He was friendly, smart and very straightforward. There was never any drama with Greg.

"Morning you two!" he said, smiling.

"Morning!" we replied in unison.

"Marie, I need a quick word with you in the office if that's okay?" He turned and walked straight back into his sanctuary.

I looked at Anne who shrugged and carried on with what she was doing. Usually everything was very informal and things weren't generally said behind closed doors. I walked over to Greg's office with some apprehension, and he waved me in.

"Close the door behind you," he instructed, making me even more uncomfortable. Something was definitely wrong. My eyes wandered the room as I took a seat opposite Greg.

There was a desk, more filing cabinets and an array of office equipment, all of which were hidden in a jungle of photos of his wife and kids and an assortment of kids' drawings. Personally, all I could see were a lot of scribbles, but to Greg they were works of art, all telling their own story. The trick, I'd learned, was to never ask what the pictures were supposed to be, because after lengthy and somewhat boring explanations, you'd be none the wiser. I'd previously turned pictures upside down, on their side, even tried squinting, but those pictures really were a mystery to me.

"So, what's up Greg?" I ventured.

He looked suddenly uncomfortable, shifting his weight in his chair and clearing his throat. "I, erm, the reason that I asked you in here..." He paused and swallowed hard before attempting to continue. "You see, the thing is, Marie, well, Head Office called me and..."

"Oh my God! You're not firing me are you?"

"Oh, no. Nothing like that." I breathed a sigh of relief and waited for him to continue.

"It's just.... you see.... the thing is... well, I'm just supposed to tell you that Head Office called and they said..." He kept looking down as though reluctant to look me in the eye. "Well, they said that as you're a travel agent, it would be good if you actually went somewhere... You know, travelled. So, you just need to take a holiday somewhere. That's all!"

He finally looked me in the eye and seemed to breathe a sigh of relief. I sat slightly dumb-founded for a moment before I found some words.

"So Head Office called and they want me to go on holiday?"

He straightened a brochure on his desk and smiled at me. "Yes, that was about the gist of it."

"Why would they do that?" I asked, trying to get my head around it.

Greg stood up behind his desk and sighed. "Does it matter why? Just go and decide where you want to go and let me know when you need the time off. It's all very simple."

Greg moved around the desk which I took as my cue to leave, but as I stood up I noticed him glance at the window to his left. It looked out into the shop but the glass was frosted so you couldn't really see anything. I followed his gaze and could just make out Anne's figure at her desk. She seemed to be leaning a bit. Actually, it looked like she was desperately trying to see what was going on in here. That would be about right though, she always hated not knowing what was going on. Greg's face reddened slightly when I turned back to him and he looked guilty. I looked back at the window before laughing at the realisation of what was going on.

"Did Anne put you up to this?"

He shifted in his seat again. "No, I don't know what you're talking about. You just need to take some holiday time. You can sit on your couch and do nothing for a couple of weeks if you want, I really don't care. Just take some of your holiday time. Please."

"Head Office didn't actually call though did they?"

He lowered his voice, "Of course they didn't call! This was a stupid idea; Head Office doesn't care if you travel or not. She won't leave me alone though. She thinks it would do you good to get away for a while and she's not going to leave me alone until you agree to it. You can go anywhere you want Marie, and it won't cost much with your discounts. I don't see what the problem is." He was looking in Anne's direction the whole time and I wondered how long she had nagged to get him to agree to this.

"But I don't want to take time off."

He looked deflated. "Fine. Just don't say anything to Anne about this."

I left his office feeling annoyed and lonely. I realised that most people would be over the moon to be told by their boss that they had to go on holiday, but I found it really depressing.

It was all right for Greg and Anne. They had families to take on holidays with them. But not me. All it did for me was highlight the fact that I was alone. I could take a friend, but most of my friends were settled with boyfriends or husbands. My only close friend was Grace but she was all loved up with her boyfriend and busy with work and things. That just left my mother, but to be honest, well… no. I just couldn't bring myself to endure that. It was hard enough spending an afternoon with her, never mind whole days and nights all connected together.

So that just left going on my own, and I'm not the sort of person who would enjoy a holiday alone. Even taking holiday time and not going anywhere wasn't an option. I knew myself too well and if I had time to sit around thinking about my life, I'd be suicidal in no time.

I walked heavily back to my desk and sank down into my chair. Anne was busy at her computer, or at least pretending to be, so I got on with what I was doing. *Right, where was I?*

Shit, shit, shit!

My morning at work went by in a blur after that. I convinced myself that I was pregnant and then that I couldn't be and then back to being sure that I was. I went from absolute panic, to calmly planning my future as a single mother. It was a traumatic morning and by lunchtime I decided I had to put an end to the turmoil.

Taking a deep breath, I turned and walked down the aisle, sticking out my arm and discreetly grabbing a pregnancy test as I passed. I tried to act normal but I could've been walking through the shop naked given how conspicuous I felt. I turned the corner and walked full pelt along the next aisle with my eyes firmly on my goal. All I needed was to get to the checkout and survive the inevitable questioning looks from the cashier and I'd be home - free.

That's when disaster struck in the form of a familiar voice coming from behind me.

"Marie! Mar-ie!"

Oh no! I knew the voice immediately. It was my Aunt Kath. I was fairly sure she could live on gossip alone, and was the last person I would trust with my secrets. She also talks to my mother every bloody day. Basically, she's the person I least wanted to bump into and she was behind me.

"Marieeeee!" I realised there was no escape so I automatically slipped the pregnancy test inside my jacket and turned on my heel to greet Aunt Kath with my brightest of bright fake smiles.

"Aunt Kath! Hi!" I feigned surprise.

"Marie, you must have been miles away, I was calling and calling you."

"Really? I didn't hear you."

"Well, what are you doing here at this time of

day?" she asked. "Shouldn't you be at work?"

"I'm on my lunch break. I thought I'd have a quick browse around the shops."

"Oh that's nice. Shall we grab a quick bite to eat somewhere?"

My heart beat faster and beads of sweat formed at my hairline. "Sorry, I've got to dash. I've already been gone a while. Maybe another day though?"

"Oh, that's a shame. It would've been nice to catch up. I'll see you on Sunday though?"

"Yeah, maybe." I tried to be fairly non-committal when it came to Sundays. Kath always went to my mum's house for dinner and they liked me to go too. I was nervous about it becoming too much of a regular thing, mainly because I felt like I should have something better to do. The problem was, I generally didn't have anything better to do, so I'd drag myself across town so they could interrogate me about my life until I got fed up and thought of an excuse to drag myself back again.

"I hope so. It would be lovely to see you," she said.

"Well I'll try. Promise! Anyway, I need to hurry up or I'll get into trouble at work."

I hurried away from her, deciding that I officially hated the shop and would never return, as I headed for the exit and my freedom.

It was as I was walking through the doors and between the ugly grey thief detectors, that I remembered the offending item lurking in my jacket. Things shifted momentarily into slow-motion before descending into chaos.

The thing with shop alarm systems is that I have innocently set them off dozens of times and no-one has batted an eyelid. I'm fairly convinced that they have two slightly different tones; one being, 'beep for no reason to embarrass people'; and the second being, 'she's stuffed something up her jumper, pounce on her quick, while drawing the attention of everyone in the vicinity.'

I tried desperately to back-track through the alarm system and hopefully through time, but it was useless. The alarm took pleasure in dobbing me in to the uniformed security guard who practically rugby tackled me to the ground.

Okay, slight exaggeration there. In all honesty, once he had me cornered, he was extremely polite and even seemed embarrassed when he asked if he could take a look in my bag.

"No need," I whispered. "It's in my jacket."

I handed him the stupid box containing the stupid pregnancy test and went on the defensive. "This really isn't what it looks like," I told him. "The thing is I bumped into my Aunt and I didn't want her to see it, so I hid it and then I honestly just forgot."

He looked at me, clearly wondering whether or not to believe me so I carried on, talking fast and quietly so that the busy-bodies who were lingering couldn't hear.

"You see I'm having a really bad day. My boyfriend slept with someone else – not today, a few weeks ago - but I just realised I might be pregnant, and I nipped out in my lunch break to buy a pregnancy test and then bumped into my aunt and I panicked because she'll tell my mum and all hell will break loose and I really don't need that at the moment–"

I was interrupted by a loud voice. "What is going on here?" I looked up at Aunt Kath. "I asked, what's going on, Marie? What's happened?"

I looked down at my shoes like a naughty schoolgirl. When I realised there was no other option, I looked up and opened my mouth to confess, but it wasn't my voice that I heard.

"It's nothing, just this bloody alarm system playing up again, nothing to worry about. I'm very sorry about that madam." My knight in shining armour, the security guard, looked at me and I had to fight the urge to hug him and tell him I loved him.

"Is that all? I thought you were stealing, Marie! Right, I better hurry. Bye for now."

"Bye!" I called after her, but she was already gone.

"Thank you so much. You just saved my life!" I said, turning to the very lovely security man.

"Well, we've all got families," he said, cheerfully. "Here - now remember to pay for it this time please."

He pulled the box from behind his back and pointed me in the direction of the till. Three minutes later I was standing outside the shop, the not-so-proud owner of a pregnancy test. Not bad for £9.99 plus all my pride and dignity.

Chapter 2

As it turned out, I needn't have worried about Aunt Kath finding out, because Mrs Turner, Mum's friend from church, happened to be one of the lingering busy-bodies, so while I was wondering what I was going to wear for my night out, I picked up the phone to be assaulted by the following.

"Marie! I just heard the news!" Straight to the point, no 'hello' or anything. "Mrs Turner just called round to tell me she'd seen you stealing from Boots!" She laughed and I'm not sure why. I tried to jump in but she carried on, sounding inappropriately excited.

"AND she said you're pregnant! Well to be honest that was a shock Marie, although when I thought about it, it does make sense, but last time I saw you I really did just think you'd been over-eating. I never even thought you might be pregnant."

"What?" I looked down at my stomach as Mum continued like a runaway train.

"Mrs Turner was very concerned. She rushed off home to start praying for you. She might even call an emergency prayer group! Oh, Marie, it's so exciting! What do you think it is? A boy or a girl? I have to say it was a bit embarrassing to find out that I'm going to be a grandmother from Mrs Turner!" She laughed again and I took the opportunity to jump in.

"I'm not pregnant." I spat the words out. "And I wasn't stealing!"

I sat on the couch in my best friend's house. She'd kindly taken me in after I moved out of Carl's place. It was a cosy two-up, two-down in the middle of a row of terraced houses. The extra bedroom wasn't much more than a box room, but there was room for a single bed, a wardrobe and a small chest of drawers that doubled as a dressing table. I'd been living here before I moved in with Carl, and Grace seemed happy to have me back.

"Well, how many tests did you take? They're not always accurate you know?" There was a definite hint of desperation in her voice.

I really didn't want to have this conversation. "I didn't take any test," I mumbled. "I got my period today."

Yep, that's right! All that humiliation for nothing.

"So, there's definitely no baby then?" Her voice cracked a bit and I almost felt sad for her.

"No, Mum."

"Well that's a shame." She was crying, I could hear it. "You were lovely when you were a baby you know."

"Thanks," I ignored the inference that I'd grown out of that particular trait.

"I better ring round and let people know," she told me.

"Ok, Mum. Lovely talking to you!"

I hung up and sat wondering how many people the gossips had reached and thought of my mum ringing round her friends, telling them I'd got my period.

I sank back into the couch and stayed that way until

Grace got home. I could rely on her to cheer me up. Grace was gorgeous in every way. We met at school and she was always the popular girl. It was a mystery to me how we were friends. I always felt like I'd won the friendship lottery or something. Anyway, since I split up with Carl she'd been the only thing keeping me sane. I don't know how I would've coped without her.

"Hi!" she called as she walked past the living room and went into the kitchen. I followed her and found her putting a carton of milk and some yoghurt into the fridge. "How was your day?"

I took a seat at the kitchen table. "Just the usual. I got called into Greg's office for a "chat", had a pregnancy scare, got caught shop-lifting and then made my mum cry. On the plus side, Mrs Turner is praying for me as we speak, so it's not all bad!"

She looked at me questioningly.

"It's a long story," I told her.

"It usually is," she said, smiling. "What happened at work?"

I'm not sure why she chose that part of my day to ask about. I'd have thought that shoplifting and pregnancy scares were much more interesting.

"Nothing much. Apparently Anne thinks I need a holiday so she got Greg to tell me I had to take some of my holiday time and go away somewhere. I don't actually need to though so it's okay." I saw Grace roll her eyes briefly as she leaned against the work surface.

"Don't you think that maybe Anne is right? It probably would do you good to have a break and it definitely can't do any harm can it?"

I laughed. "Where would I go? More to the point, who with?"

"How can you even ask, where? You sell holidays for a living! If I was you, I would constantly want to explore all the wonderful places that you tell other people they should go to. You should be full of inspiration and enthusiasm."

"But who with?" I challenged.

"Take your mum away with you." I let out a short burst of air and raised my eyebrows to let Grace know my opinion on that idea. She changed tack.

"Okay, then go alone," she said. "Lots of people go on holiday alone. It doesn't have to be depressing. See it as an adventure, you can explore somewhere new and you're bound to meet people along the way."

"I'll have a think about it," I said unconvincingly.

Grace's phone rang, ending the discussion. I headed out of the kitchen when she answered it, but she called me back and I turned and looked at her with the phone buried in her shoulder. "I still want to hear about the other stuff. Just give me a few minutes okay?"

I nodded and she pulled a bottle of wine out of her shopping bag. She handed it to me and then she pulled out two glasses from the cupboard by the fridge. "I'll be quick," she informed me as she moved the phone back to her ear. I headed for the living room and overheard her telling whoever was on the phone that she was out with the girls from work for the evening.

I decided it was probably her perfect boyfriend wanting to see her, or one of her hoards of friends. Not that I was bitter or jealous of all the attention she attracted. Nope, not at all. Well, okay, maybe I was.

Just a little bit though and only because bitter and jealous are two of my many personality traits, along with neurotic, stubborn, pessimistic and moody. It was hardly surprising though when my life played out like scenes from 'A Series of Unfortunate Events', whereas Grace clearly landed the leading role in 'Mary Poppins' for the story of her life. No, like I said, not bitter at all!

She came and joined me on the couch and picked up her glass of wine.

"James?" I asked, (James being the perfect boyfriend). They were one of those sickening couples who just seemed to be made for each other. They'd met at some business function a couple of years before and it'd been plain sailing ever since. Grace probably spent about half the week at his place but I was on alert for the conversation where she told me they were moving in together. I was surprised they'd waited so long. That would mean me being homeless, which was something else to look forward to.

"No. It was Brian," she told me. "He wanted my advice on what to wear on his date tonight."

Brian was Grace's new friend and for six months it'd been, 'Brian this,' and, 'Brian that,' and I was getting to the point where if I heard his name mentioned one more time, I might scream. Instead I gritted my teeth and smiled.

They were working for the same company. Grace worked in Human Resources for an investment bank. I had no idea what Brian did but he'd appeared on the scene about six months before. Apparently they'd hit it off immediately. They'd become firm friends and had lunch dates and he called her for "chats" and asked her for advice on things. Basically he did 'my' things with her - those are the things we did.

I was fairly sure that he was trying to get in her knickers and, to be honest, I admired his persistence. I just hoped that Grace had made it clear that the role of best friend was already taken and I wasn't giving it up without a fight. Not that I was jealous or anything. Well, okay, maybe a bit, but as I said, it's a personality trait. I couldn't help it.

"Come on then, tell me about your traumatic day," Grace interrupted my thoughts.

"Well, you're really not going to believe it..." I began exasperated. I recalled the events of the day for her and she sat and listened and laughed. I put a humorous spin on things for her benefit. I'd hate to drag her into my world of doom and gloom.

We sat chatting for an hour or so before Grace started to glance at her watch. "Right, I'd better start getting ready. I've got to call in at my mum's place so I'll just see you in town. We're meeting at Bar Breeze at 9pm, and then we'll probably head on to a club somewhere later. Is that okay?" She smiled at me and I resisted the urge to back out of the evening and sit on my own watching TV instead.

"It is just girls though, isn't it?" I asked. "I don't want to get stuck listening to Colin tell me about his model aeroplanes all night like I did at that work thing you took me to. Gosh, he was boring!" Something else occurred to me. "Brian won't be there will he?"

"Nope, Brian's out on a date. Although, you'd like Brian. He's great fun. You'll have to meet him sometime." I winced at yet another mention of how great Brian is. "Anyway it's just girls. Actually I think it's only us and Jane and Lucy. It'll be fun. You might even enjoy yourself!"

I gave her a friendly shove. That put me at ease though. I'd met Jane and Lucy several times before and they were always friendly and welcoming.

Half an hour later, I was sitting on the couch eating a bowl of pasta when Grace appeared looking stunning in a little black dress. "I'll see you at Bar Breeze at nine. Okay?"

"Yep. I'll be there," I confirmed.

"Do you think you can manage to be on time for once?"

"I'll do my best," I said as I took a big gulp of wine. In all honestly I was notoriously late for these occasions but, in my defence, circumstances had a habit of conspiring against me.

"Remember, last one to arrive buys a round of shots!"

How could I forget? This had been our ritual for years, and more often than not it was me that had to fork out. Not tonight though. I had plenty of time to get ready and get there. Tonight Grace would be buying the shots. Finally, something I was optimistic about!

I spent an hour getting showered and trying to decide what to wear. Grace had spent ten minutes in the shower, then came out and shook her hair dry. It had settled itself, perfectly styled. She'd slipped into a little black dress and heels, applied the smallest amount of make-up and was ready and looking stunning in less than half an hour total. I spent more than twice the amount of time and I still ended up looking decidedly mediocre.

I tried to make the best of things. Nice fitting jeans that accentuated the bum and hid the flabby thighs; heels to make my legs look longer; low cut top to show off my boobs; a bit of make-up; a half-hearted attempt to straighten my wavy hair and I was all set. I even had time to spare.

I had a bit of a dilemma about when to set off. I really wanted to shock Grace by being early. But not too early, in case I was the first and had to stand on my own. Grace would be on time though so it wouldn't be for very long. It was 8.20pm when I called the local taxi firm and was shocked to hear a recorded message telling me they were closed for the evening. I always used the same taxi firm and that had never happened before. I had to search for another taxi firm.

"You'll have to wait an hour, I'm afraid love. We're really busy tonight," they told me. What? An hour? The usual firm had a taxi with me in ten minutes.

"Okay," I replied in shock. "I'll try someone else."

"The buses have gone on strike, so everyone's busy tonight," he informed me.

He was right. I tried my luck with another firm who told me they could be there in an hour and a half if that was any good. I wanted to scream that of course that was no bloody good, but I held my tongue.

"No thanks," I replied politely. The next number I tried was engaged. That was what I meant about circumstances conspiring against me. Without much thought, I grabbed my bag and headed out of the door. I decided it was probably a forty minute walk into town but if I cut through the park, maybe I could make it in time.

I tottered down the footpath in my heels, cursing the cyclists who flew past me every few minutes. The wheel really was a great invention. They'd be in town in a few minutes and with no effort. I was probably going to fall off my heels in my attempt to be quick and I'd still arrive late.

My phone beeped with a message from Grace: *Just leaving mum's. Be there in 15 mins. Don't forget extra money for shots!*

The thought of Grace beating me riled me up and to my own amazement, when I heard the next bike approaching, I stuck out my thumb. I actually stuck out my thumb like a hitch-hiker!

I turned to see the shocked cyclist swerve to avoid my arm and then come to a stop, looking at me fiercely.

"Any chance of a ride down the hill?" *Oh God what was I doing?* He looked back at me, disgusted, before riding away. Okay, so if I had any dignity left after the whole Boots episode, there went the rest of it.

"Need a ride?" I looked up to see an attractive guy in front of me on a bike. "Hop on!"

"Thanks!" I stuttered.

The trouble with getting a ride on the back of a bike is that there's nowhere to hold on really, except for the person of course, but that's a bit awkward when it's someone that you've just met.

"You'll have to hang on to my waist," he said looking back at me. "Get cosy!"

I gingerly took hold of his shirt and somehow managed to balance myself as he started to pedal down the hill. I couldn't believe what I was doing;

riding on the back of a stranger's bike, holding on to him for dear life, while staring at his bum. Well, it was right in my way. It wasn't like I was doing it intentionally. It was just right there in my face and it was a really nice bum. Fairly close to perfect actually, in my opinion. Not that I was checking him out or anything.

"Where ya heading?" he shouted back at me.

"Into town. To Bar Breeze, but if you could let me off at the bottom, by the main road, that would be great."

"Whatever you want. I aim to please!" I was fairly sure he was mocking me but I didn't feel like I was in a position to say anything back.

He stopped at the bottom of the hill and I de-biked in as lady-like a manner as possible. Which, by the way, isn't easy.

"Well thanks a lot. I really appreciate that. I would have been late otherwise, and then I'd have to buy the drinks." I smiled at him and he looked puzzled.

"So do you often um... hitch-bike?" he asked and then answered my confused look with, "You know like hitch-hiking but on bikes?"

"Oh, right. No, that's the first time actually."

"I'm honoured then," he said with laughter in his eyes. He had quite a cute smile, I noticed. Actually, quite good looking over all. His black shirt complemented his dark hair and his eyes... well it was hard to stop looking at his lovely brown eyes.

"I'd better go." I walked slowly backwards, feeling increasingly awkward at the situation.

"Nice meeting you!" He winked at me then. *Creep.*

I spotted Lucy and Jane straight away, at the opposite side of the bar and I was happy that they'd arrived first. They were friendly and I knew that I could make small talk with them easily. I fought my way over to them through the crowd of people.

"Hi Marie!" They looked genuinely pleased to see me. "How are you? I haven't seen you in ages." Lucy said as she kissed my cheek.

"I'm really good," I lied as I moved to greet Jane.

"So sorry to hear about your boyfriend," Jane said sympathetically. I almost wanted to be annoyed that Grace had told them, but at the same time I knew she would have told them in a concerned way.

"Oh well. I suppose the bright side is that when you walk in on your boyfriend having sex with someone else, it's a clean break. It gets rid of all the 'shall we give it another try' moments!" I smiled at their shocked faces. Grace clearly hadn't mentioned that detail.

"Bloody hell!" Lucy gasped. "I'm getting you a drink."

We chatted easily while we waited for Grace to arrive. I'd been worried that it would be awkward being out and having to pretend to have a good time but I found that I wasn't really pretending at all. I was quite enjoying myself. Grace arrived looking mildly flustered about twenty minutes later. "I had a nightmare getting here. The buses are on strike you know?"

"I know. I had to hitch-bike." I told her. "You know, hitching a ride but with a cyclist?"

Jane and Lucy looked at me with smiles on their faces.

"Are you serious?" Jane asked.

"I'm very serious," I assured them. "Although, I wouldn't recommend it!"

The three of them proceeded to crease up with giggles before Grace finally moved to the bar to buy a round of tequila shots.

By the time we got to the club – some underground hole with cheap drink offers which Lucy wanted to go to on account of a cute barman – we were all a bit tipsy. Lucy decided to prop up the bar and do more tequila shots with the barman, while Grace, Jane and I headed for the dance floor.

I'd lost all inhibitions and was happily dancing away until I saw Grace look over my shoulder and her smile suddenly disappeared. She looked panicked. I turned and followed her gaze, only to see Carl – ex-boyfriend Carl – drinking and chatting with a tall brunette. A brunette this time! So not even the same woman I caught him with! Not that it matters I suppose…

He turned and saw us. I had no idea how to react. He looked momentarily surprised and then he smiled and waved. I waved back automatically. He went back to his date then. The bloody cheek of him. Smiling and waving like we're old friends. I wasn't angry; I was just shocked. Maybe I'd imagined our entire relationship.

"What an idiot!" Jane shouted in my ear.

"Don't think about it!" Grace said. "He's not worth it."

I returned to the dancing but my heart wasn't in it anymore. Bloody men! I decided I was over them. There would be no more men for me. Ever!

And that would be when I looked up and saw Mr. Tall, Dark and Handsome looking at me from across the room. So forgetting my previous thoughts, I put some enthusiasm back into my dancing and pulled out my sexiest moves.

"I'm going to the bar – want anything?" Grace shouted over the music. Jane and I shook our heads and she disappeared into the crowd.

"I really need to pee." Jane yelled a few minutes later. "You coming?"

"No I'll stay here," I replied.

So there I was, alone on the dance floor and amazingly really enjoying myself. I glanced over to Mr. Sexy again but couldn't see him. I scanned the room and eventually found him walking in my direction. I told myself to act casual.

"Hi, I'm Ben," he introduced himself as I continued dancing.

"Marie," I replied, doing my best to play it cool and pretend that I didn't care that this gorgeous man was talking to me. Like this happened all the time.

"I was just wondering if your friend is available... the tall one? She's gorgeous."

What? *Whaaat?*

"No, she's got a boyfriend," I snapped.

"Oh! Right, sorry to bother you then."

"Whatever!" I snapped in reply, totally forgetting my cool demeanour. Like I said, I'm so over men.

I wandered over to the bar and took a seat next to Lucy. "Men are idiots," I informed her.

"True. But they have their uses!" she said, grinning cheekily.

"How's the barman?"

33

"Delicious!" she said with a laugh.

I looked along the bar and noticed Grace chatting to James. What a cheat! She'd invited her boyfriend on a girlie night. James looked up and saw us and the two of them came over.

"Hi, ladies!" James beamed. "I hope I'm not spoiling your party but I wanted to make sure Grace got home safely." He had his arm around her waist and they looked so happy and cute that it almost brought a tear to my eye. Almost.

"Actually, if you guys are heading home, can I share your taxi?" I asked. I'd lost all enthusiasm and my eyelids were feeling decidedly heavy.

"Yeah, of course. We're going back to James' place but we can drop you off on the way," Grace said.

"Great. What about you Lucy? Where's Jane?" I asked.

"She's over there." Lucy pointed to Jane who was dancing away by herself and looked quite happy. "I'm fine here. I'll get a taxi with Jane later."

"Aren't I the lucky one then, taking two beautiful women home tonight?" James commented as we said our goodbyes. Grace rolled her eyes at me and I smiled at James.

I liked James a lot. He made Grace happy which was good enough for me. He was what I would call a 'nice guy', and by that I mean really, genuinely nice. The sort of guy you could take home to your mum, with the only worry being that she would get over-excited and start planning your wedding. Not my type but I could see the appeal and he was definitely what I'd choose for my best friend.

James worked at the same bank as Grace.

Apparently he was a Star Trader, which seemed to mean he had a really good job which he was really good at. To be honest, I was never sure what he did and they tended to do me the courtesy of not talking about work around me.

When I first met James I found him stuffy and serious but as I got to know him I found he was also quite funny, in his own awkward way. I kept thinking they'd move in together and I wouldn't be at all surprised if there was a big proposal on the cards too. I was really happy for her but I couldn't help but compare her life to mine sometimes and have pangs of jealousy. She really seemed to have her life in order, whereas my life? It was just such a mess.

Hannah Ellis

Chapter 3

When my insane day finally came to an end, all I could think was that tomorrow could only be better, and, best of all, it was the weekend and I could lie in bed as long as I wanted. Maybe I'd even have a pyjama day.

That was the blissful thought that transported me to a wonderful, peaceful slumber.

Unfortunately it didn't last very long. The next thing I knew, I was lying wide awake and confused. It was still dark and something had woken me but I had no idea what. I looked at the clock which glowed 4:06 in red neon. I heard a noise and realised that someone was banging on the front door. It stopped, and I stayed as still as I could, listening for sounds. My heart was racing and I realised I was holding my breath. After hearing three more thuds at the door, I slipped out from under the duvet and tiptoed down the stairs into the hallway.

The coats on the rack made creepy silhouettes but I didn't dare turn the lights on and draw attention to myself. I could hear someone moving around outside the front door. Maybe it was Carl, finally coming to apologise and beg me to go back to him. That didn't seem very likely. I reached for the phone and tapped in 999. If anything happened, all I'd have to do is press the dial button.

I tiptoed over to the door and peered through the peephole. A figure was hovering by the road, pacing and looking around. He looked toward the door and I instinctively ducked.

When I braved another look he was walking away from the door and relief temporarily washed over me. I say temporarily because the next moment my gaze lowered and I suddenly found it hard to breathe.

I realised that I knew that bum, that close to perfect bum, beneath those familiar stone-washed jeans. It was bloody bike boy. What the hell was bike boy doing banging on my front door at four o'clock in the bloody morning? I concluded that he must have stalked me all night and I wondered how I'd not noticed him.

"Hello.... hello, is everything okay? Hello?" My thoughts were interrupted by a tiny voice that sounded like it was coming from miles away. I looked around, confused.

"Hello?" I looked down at the phone in my hand. I must have pressed dial without realising.

"Hello," I whispered into the receiver. "I need the police."

"What's your emergency please?"

"There's a man at my door. He's a stalker. I need you to send the police. I'm at 47 Hillside Road."

I looked back through the peephole to see him coming purposefully toward the door. I ducked again and heard him say "Grace?" in a stage whisper. I was confused.

"Is he in the house with you?" the operator quizzed.

"No, he's outside."

"Ok. I'm dispatching a police car now but stay on

the line please. Do you know this man? Has he bothered you before?"

I was staring at the door as he knocked again and called Grace's name.

"I hitched a ride with him today, and I know hitch-hiking is dangerous, and I realise now why people tell you not to do it, but it was just on a bike so I thought it would be okay. I think maybe this guy followed me all night and now he's here at my door. Except he's shouting my flatmate's name which is a bit weird."

"I'm sorry, I'm a bit confused," the operator confessed at about the same time I heard, "Grace! Will you let me in?" coming from the other side of the door.

"Actually, I'm a bit confused too," I said into the phone, and, "Who is it?" into the door.

"Brian. Who else? Now open the door, will you?"

I put the chain on and opened the door to look through the gap.

"You're not Grace. Where's Grace?" he asked me.

"She's not here," I told him. "What do you want?"

"I lost my keys so I thought I'd crash at Grace's place. Did I get the wrong house?" He stepped back and looked up at the exterior of the house.

"This is Grace's place," I told him. "But she's not here."

"Oh, you must be the flatmate! Marie?" he asked.

I yawned as things slotted into place. It would appear that bike boy also happened to be one of Grace's friends.

I realised I should call off the police. "Er, hello?" I said into the phone. "There seems to have been a misunderstanding... it's actually a friend of my flatmate and not a stalker. I don't need the police. I'm very sorry."

I turned back to the door and a puzzled voice asked, "Did you call the police?"

"Never mind," I sighed. "Grace isn't here though. She's at her boyfriend's place."

"Right, can you open the door?" he asked in a tone that people usually reserve for children and idiots.

"No!" I shot back.

"Why not?"

"Because it's four in the morning and I don't know you."

"I'm Brian Connor, Grace's friend... and I lost my keys so I would really like to crash here."

I paused, wondering what to do. I thought I knew all of Grace's friends, or at least any that were likely turn up needing a place to crash. My brain started to wake up and I sighed as things clicked into place. Surely he couldn't be who I thought he was though. That would seem like a horrible coincidence, even for my life.

"You're Brian?" I asked him, unconvinced.

"Yes," he replied slowly, "I thought I'd said that."

"Brian from Grace's work?"

"The one and only!"

My belief in fate was reaffirmed. It conspires against me all the time.

Apparently, I had unwittingly hitched a ride on the back of a bike with my rival, Brian Connor. He's not how I imagined him at all. He was standing at the front door and I couldn't decide what to do; let him in? Or go back to bed and pretend this didn't happen? Or be a grown up and do something rational? Yes, that's what I'd do.

"Sorry. I don't let strangers in, in the middle of the night." I said through the door, feeling very pleased at my maturity.

"Oh, bloody hell!" He sighed, and through the crack I saw him slump to the floor.

"What are you doing?" I asked.

"Sleeping."

"In the doorway?" I clarified.

"I don't seem to have much choice."

Oh great. I was acting like an adult and he just carried on acting like a drunk person. It looked like I was stuck with him. I closed the door and took the chain off. When I opened the door again he landed with a thud at my feet.

"Sexy pyjamas," he mumbled, looking up at me.

He picked himself up from the floor and looked at me for a few seconds before stumbling into the living room and over to the couch where he collapsed in a heap.

"Thanks," I heard before the snoring began.

I took myself back to bed and was comforted by the thought that he at least didn't seem to remember me from the bike incident.

It was late in the morning when I woke and was relieved to find my middle-of-the-night visitor had left. In his place was a note which simply read, 'thanks'. I threw it aside and wandered to the kitchen for some much needed coffee. I put bread in the shiny silver toaster and sat down to wait for it to pop.

Somehow I effectively wasted the day. I managed to do a load of washing and half-heartedly tidied up the place. I also flicked through the TV channels and read a magazine.

I was contemplating watching a movie and drinking some wine when Grace showed up with James in tow.

"So what are you two up to tonight?" I asked, hoping they weren't going out.

"I think we might just stay here and get a take away if that's okay with you?" Grace said. She had a habit of asking if it was okay for them to be there. I always felt a bit embarrassed, what with it being her house.

"Yeah that's great with me, I've spent most of the day killing time... just waiting for wine o'clock to come round!"

James looked a bit unsure of my comment, like he thought I shouldn't really be left alone all day. "Don't worry Marie. We'll stay here and look after you, won't we Grace?"

Grace cringed a little bit at his choice of words. "I'll get the wine, shall I?" She looked at me apologetically as she went to the kitchen.

"So how is the single life treating you Marie? Are you managing to keep your spirits up?"

I smiled at James and was quite sure that Grace was cringing yet again in the kitchen. If anyone else had said it, I might have been annoyed but James had an innocence about him that made him hard to get angry with. I knew he was trying to be nice.

Grace appeared with a bottle of wine and two wine glasses. "James, I couldn't manage a beer as well. Go and grab yourself one from the fridge." He dutifully followed instructions.

"I'm sorry about him," Grace whispered as she poured the wine. "You know he doesn't mean it don't you? He's just got terrible social skills and I'm still in the training process with him, even after two years!"

"Yeah, of course, he's fine." I smiled. "It's your other boyfriend that I'm annoyed with..."

She looked at me questioningly.

"Brian. He turned up here at four o'clock this morning." Grace looked suitably horrified so I carried on. "Actually, I sort of called the police on him but called them off when I realised who it was. He'd lost his keys and ended up sleeping on the couch."

"What? He was out on some blind date. I wonder what happened... I'm going to call him and find out." She reached for her phone and I was about to protest but was interrupted by the doorbell.

I opened the door to find Brian looking at his phone.

"It's Grace calling. We were just talking about you," I informed him and turned to go back inside.

"So you told on me then, did you?" he said, jokingly as he followed me in.

Grace looked at him with surprise. "Your ears must have been burning."

"When you're as popular as I am, Grace, your ears are always burning," he quipped.

James looked delighted to have some male company and reached to shake Brian's hand while offering him a beer.

"So what brings you here on a Saturday night? No date?" Grace asked as he made himself comfy in the armchair. I perched on the couch next to Grace.

"No, I'm having a night off," he said in a tone that I wasn't sure was serious or not.

James handed him a beer and then settled himself

on the other end of the couch.

"So what's this about last night?" James asked.

"Oh yeah. That's why I'm here." He looked at me. "I thought I better come round and apologise. I was a bit drunk and obnoxious. Sorry for that, and thank you for not leaving me on the doorstep."

I don't know what it was about him, but I was completely irritated by him. I felt like he just waltzed in and made everything about him. His whole demeanour oozed cockiness and on top of that, he'd somehow got both James and Grace eating out of his hand – giggling away at everything he said.

"You're welcome. Just don't expect the same hospitality twice." I was aiming for gracious but somehow it came out sounding quite hostile. I have difficulty hiding my emotions sometimes.

"So..." Grace diverted the attention away from me, "what happened, Brian? How exactly did you end up homeless at four in the morning?"

"Well it's not a very exciting story. Quite embarrassing, actually. I somehow ended up stupidly drunk and thought I'd lost my house keys. It turns out they were in my pocket, but I guess I checked every pocket but the right one."

"What about the date though?" Grace asked.

"Well how good do you think it was for me to start on a blind date and end up blind drunk? Not the best date I've had."

"Brian, you never tell proper stories! I want details," Grace said.

"No way. I'm a gentleman and therefore I don't kiss and tell. Although for last night, there was no kissing and definitely nothing to tell."

I sighed and began to wish that it was just me, a bottle of wine and a movie.

"So what take-away shall we get?" I attempted to manoeuvre the conversation away from Brian's date and hoped that he would also take it as his cue to leave.

"Great! I'm starving. Mind if I join you?" he asked, much to my annoyance.

"I'll get the menus," I said and headed for the kitchen. I was busy taking the drawer out to find the menus that had fallen down the back when Brian appeared.

"Need some help?" he asked.

"No, thanks. I'm fine." I didn't even look at him and was aware of the fact that I sounded quite hostile.

"Look, I really am sorry about last night," he said as he hung around behind me.

I was busy trying to get hold of a menu that was jammed at the back of the cupboard. "It's fine." I snapped.

"It's just that you seem pretty annoyed."

"I can't get the menu." I decided to avert my aggression away from Brian.

"Here let me get it?" He moved closer to me.

"No I can do it!" I tugged harder and as the leaflet came loose my arm shot back and my elbow crashed into Brian's stomach.

"Oh shit! I'm sorry!" I said as he doubled over.

"Oh," came a flat voice. We looked up to see James hovering in the doorway. "Am I interrupting something?"

"Yeah! Some sort of primitive, aggressive mating ritual." Brian laughed.

"Oh right!" James laughed nervously and left the kitchen, clearly not sure whether it was a joke or not.

Brian stood upright again. "That is what this is though, right? Sexual tension? I've had women get aggressive with me before and it's usually a sexual thing."

"Oh, get stuffed!" I said, before picking up the menus and marching back to the living room.

Brian followed behind me. "Sorry guys, change of plan. I'm going to head out."

I handed the menus to James and heaved a sigh of relief. Brian smiled politely and grabbed his coat from the arm of the couch.

He'd put me in a decidedly bad mood and all I wanted to do was go and curl up in bed.

"So what did you do to scare Brian off?" Grace teased once he'd left.

"Nothing," I replied sulkily and reached over to the take-away menus.

"Why don't we tell Marie our news now?" James said after we'd demolished a good amount of Chinese food. I looked up and saw him being silently reproached by Grace who was sporting a look I didn't recognise on her.

"What news?" I asked, trying to draw my focus away from my painful belly. I'd eaten far too much.

"Nothing. I'll tell you another time." Her voice had an edge to it and as I looked at her, she looked away and said, "Do you want another drink?"

There was the slightest quiver in her voice that probably no one else in the world would have noticed but it made me glance up at her and that's when I realised something was wrong. Grace was looking at me seriously and I was drawn to her fingers which were rhythmically tapping her thigh.

"No, I'm fine thanks," I told her looking at the full wine glass in front of me. She moved to take the plates and take-away boxes into the kitchen and I stayed put, wondering what it was that she was hiding from me.

Grace was cool and calm and always in control. Fidgeting was her pet hate. I always thought that she saw it as a sign of weakness. So her drumming her fingers was a bad sign. Whatever the 'news' was, it was obviously something big; something she thought I wouldn't like. Probably that they were finally moving in together.

Grace appeared in front of me again about thirty seconds later and after glaring at James briefly, she sat next to me and put a hand on my arm. "I need to tell you something," she blurted, "and you're probably not going to like it, so brace yourself. But I may as well just get it over with and, anyway, I need to tell you before I go crazy worrying about it." She looked at me ominously and I was surprisingly calm as I waited for her to continue.

"The thing is, James was offered this big promotion at work and it's a really great opportunity for him and he just couldn't turn it down."

"Oh well done James! Good for you." He smiled back at me looking pleased with himself.

Grace was looking at me and I looked blankly back. "So the problem is?" I ventured blindly.

"The job is in New York," she began carefully. "The company offered to relocate us both. There's a position for me too. Initially it would be for a year but possibly more permanently if things work out."

She stopped talking and I could see she was holding her breath, waiting for my response. What was my response though? My best friend was leaving to go to New York. I'd be all alone, and what about the house? Could I still live there? A torrent of thoughts washed through my head. Predictably they were all thoughts about how it would affect me. I'm proud to say I quickly moved the thoughts to a far corner of my mind and focused completely on Grace. Well, okay, not completely, but I really tried.

"That's great," I managed solidly, without a hint of the sarcasm that I felt. I'll admit that I briefly thought, *not so great for me though* but I'd argue that it wasn't actually my thought but the mean little goblin that lives in my head, infecting me with selfishness and making nasty comments.

"Really?" Grace asked nervously.

"Well are you happy?" I asked while the goblin screamed, "Of course she's bloody happy, she's going to New York with lover boy. You're going to be stuck here friendless and alone." I ignored him (I'm fairly sure it's male).

Grace smiled cautiously. "I'm really happy. It's such a great opportunity for us but I've been so worried about telling you... after everything with Carl I feel like it's such bad timing..." she trailed off.

"I'll be fine," I said and then tried again more convincingly. "Of course I'll be fine. I'll miss you, of course, but it sounds like an amazing adventure for you and if you're happy then I'm thrilled for you."

"You probably won't be so thrilled when she tells

you that she's selling the house and you're homeless," my goblin sneered.

"Of course, the house is all yours for the time being," Grace contradicted him. "James is selling his place so we want to keep the house for now. I really don't want to sell it and I'll be happy knowing that you're taking care of the place. Depending on how things work out in New York, you might have to get a flatmate further down the line, but for now you can have the place to yourself."

I gave a sigh of relief and banished the goblin back to his dark cave within my head. I spent a while asking all the appropriate questions and being suitably excited for them. It wasn't until I got into bed later that I let my thoughts spin round my head unchecked. My goblin even came back to sneer at me. "You may have somewhere to live but you've got no friends!" he hissed. The trouble was I couldn't really argue with him on that score.

I'd spent the last two years of my life with Carl, and in that time I'd spent time with his friends, but somehow lost track of my own. With hindsight I'd been a complete idiot, not least because I didn't even like his friends.

I needed to find new friends, I realised, and quick. Grace would be gone in a month and I needed some sort of social life by then. I wasn't sure how I would go about meeting new people though, as all I really did was go to work, hang out with Grace, and visit my mum. There didn't seem to be much opportunity for meeting new people there.

I could only really see one solution to the problem. I'd have to join a club. I couldn't think of another option. The only problem was that I'd be surrounding myself with a load of losers looking for new friends, or even worse, people who are actually interested in cooking/ gardening/ knitting/ stamp-collecting. Surely there was another way. *I'll think of something*, I thought positively. I even managed to be quite optimistic. Maybe this was a good thing. Maybe my life was about to take a turn for the better. I would find new friends and have a whole new life.

Maybe.

Hopefully…

Chapter 4

I need to get thicker curtains, was my first thought as I woke on Sunday morning and pulled the duvet over my head to block out the daylight. I snuggled down and decided I would stay there all day, in the blissful cocoon under my duvet. That idea lasted about five minutes before I dragged myself up to get showered and dressed. I grabbed coffee and toast and sat on the couch to eat in front of the Sunday morning cooking show that happened to be on when I switched on the TV.

It was 11am when I reached for the phone and scrolled to the familiar number and pressed dial. The voice that answered was so full of life; it was as though a rush of happiness came at me through the phone.

"Hi Helen! It's me!" I grinned as I spoke my usual greeting to the taxi dispatcher and waited expectantly for the excitement I knew I would hear in her voice.

"Marie!" she screeched excitedly. "Where've you been? I haven't heard from you in weeks. I was starting to worry."

"I called you on Friday but you didn't answer." I laughed. "Where were you in my hour of need?"

"Oh, Marie," she sighed heavily. "You would not believe the day I had on Friday! The phone was going crazy. Dave's dog died. Pat had tonsillitis. Steve was all over the town getting totally stressed. Then he scraped his car so he called and said that as it was such an arse of a day and not getting any better, we should just give up and go home! So I unplugged the phone and had a nice evening in front of the telly with Danny."

She finally took a breath and I laughed. I had an image of her chatting to me on the hands-free kit while she painted her long manicured nails a delightful shade of red. She'd be waving them in front of her face as she gently blew them dry. She's probably wearing a black leather mini skirt and at the other end of her gloriously long legs would be a pair of killer heels that screamed, 'don't mess with me'.

I imagined her in a low cut tank top that stretched over her enormous breasts. Her bleached blonde hair would fall splendidly down her back and her face would be hidden under enough make up to last me a year.

Of course my description of her may have been entirely wrong. I didn't actually have any idea what Helen looked like but that was how I envisioned her when I heard her voice.

"Where are you off to today then? Your mum's?" she asked, finally getting down to business.

"Yeah, 'fraid so!" I replied.

"And you're still at Grace's, I presume?" I could hear her tapping a keyboard in the background.

"Yes, I'm still at Grace's."

"That's good. Please don't go back to that idiot! You can do better."

"Oh, don't worry, there's no going back. Onwards and upwards!" I declared as my smile waned.

"Exactly love, that's the spirit," she said vaguely, her mind on her job for a moment. I pictured her studying her computer. "Well ... Pat's out and about. Looks like he could be with you in ten?"

"Ok," I agreed. Pat was fine, but he didn't talk much and had terrible body odour.

"Oh hang on, if you can wait, Dave can be with you in twenty minutes?" Helen offered cheerfully.

"Great, I'll wait for Dave."

"Thought so! Careful what you say though, he's all devastated about his pooch dying. You'd think he'd lost a limb the way he's going on."

"Oh give him a break. He loved that dog." I was slightly defensive of Dave. He was my favourite, always happy to chat and tell me about his life.

"I know, I know." Helen sounded vaguely sympathetic before erupting into her cackle of a laugh. "It is just a dog though!" I laughed too although I didn't find it funny. She just had an infectious laugh.

"Okay love, you have fun at your mum's and we'll talk soon." She hung up and I was left smiling to myself like an idiot.

"Was that taxi Helen?" Grace's voice made me jump and I turned to find her leaning on the door jamb.

"Where did you spring from?" I asked, hoping to change the subject. Grace raised her eyebrows and ignored my question.

"It amazes me that you can chat away to the taxi dispatcher like she's an old friend."

"Well she is an old friend really." I informed her as I rose from the couch and moved past her to put my breakfast things in the kitchen. I really hated it when Grace got on her high horse about the taxi company.

"There's no need to get defensive," Grace retorted. "I just don't understand why you can't get a bus. It must cost you a fortune to be on first name terms with all the taxi drivers in town!"

"Not *all* the taxi drivers in town. Just three. And is it wrong to want to know the person who is driving you? If I get on a bus I have no idea what sort of person the driver is. They could be half drunk or anything. You just never know."

Grace snorted with laughter as she followed me to the kitchen. I set the cup and plate in the sink and turned to face her. She held her hands up in mock surrender. "Okay, I didn't think about that. Maybe you have a point." She put on her best serious face and I nodded at her. We both knew that I did not have a point; that I had possibly just made the worst point of all time. I wasn't about to admit that though. We'd had the taxi conversation a lot of times over the years and she still thought I was being ridiculous. It was okay with me though. Everyone should have one quirk, I decided, and this was mine. I couldn't stand buses.

"Hi, Dave!" I chirped twenty minutes later as I climbed into the passenger seat of the taxi.

"Hello, love. How are you?" he asked as he pulled away. "To your mum's is it?" he added as an afterthought.

"Yeah, Mum's. I'm fine, nothing new to report really. I was sorry to hear about your dog."

"Oh bloody pets, Marie, they're a nightmare. I

know it's just a dog but honestly it's left such a hole in our lives. I can't get used to him not being there you know?" I nodded and made sympathetic noises and he kept talking about the dog for most of the twenty-minute drive.

"I've never had a dog," I said thoughtfully when we were almost at my Mum's house. "Or any pet for that matter."

"You're better off. They only die and leave you heartbroken. The kids are already asking for another one. We've said no for now but I'm not sure how long before we'll crack." He laughed to himself. "Sorry, I'm chatting away today, aren't I?"

"Oh, I don't mind," I told him honestly. I always liked listening to him talk about his family.

"Do you need picking up later?" He asked as he pulled up outside my mum's house and I got out my purse.

"I'll probably get a lift with my Aunt," I told him, handing him the money.

"Alright love, well give us a shout if not. I'm on until late."

"Will do, Dave. Thanks a lot!" I shouted as I stepped out onto the pavement. I closed the door and watched him drive away. I smiled after him. It was definitely better than getting a bus.

I let myself in and found my mum sitting on the floor in the living room surrounded by DVDs.

"Hi, Mum." I made her jump.

"Is it that time already? I haven't done anything about lunch yet."

"What are you doing?" I asked.

"I'm sorting out the DVDs. Can you believe

they've been lined up in alphabetical order? I can't believe I've lived with such a stupid system for so long! Last night I wanted to watch a thriller. I knew I wanted to watch a thriller but I had to look through all the DVDs to find what I wanted. I'll save myself lots of time if they're organised by genre." She looked pleased with her idea.

She loved movies; watched one most nights. Although she hardly ever bought new ones, I was sure she must have seen some of them hundreds of times.

"Oh, and I mopped the ceiling in the kitchen so watch out for drips."

I stopped being surprised by her a long time ago.

It's hard to remember how old I was when I realised that my mum wasn't like other mums. I presume that at some point in my early childhood I had been blissfully unaware of her 'quirks'. I also know that at some point I must have made a conscious decision to stop having friends over. There's probably a traumatic memory or two locked away deep in my sub-conscious.

I do remember the day that I first heard the word eccentric. I overheard a conversation a couple of teachers were having at school, and for all I know it was my mum that they were talking about. It was the context that they used it in that made me wonder... "Everyone keeps calling her eccentric but in my head it's the words 'mad as a hatter' that always spring to mind..."

I dragged out the dictionary the minute I got home and it was like suddenly having a diagnosis: 'Eccentric: Unconventional, especially in a whimsical way; a person with unusual habits'. I sat on the floor and laughed with relief. It described her exactly. It was like a light had been switched on in my head and my world suddenly made much more sense. There was nothing wrong with my mum, she was just eccentric. That word wasn't so bad; in fact there was something comforting about it.

I started having friends over again and when they noticed Mum vacuuming the inside of the fridge or polishing the tinned goods, I'd just roll my eyes and say, "Don't mind Mum, she's just a bit eccentric". Apparently that was entirely acceptable.

"Hello!" Aunt Kath appeared behind me and took in the mess surrounding Mum.

"Well I think I'll get started on lunch then," she said as she walked back out of the living room and into the kitchen.

"Watch out for drips!" Mum and I called after her. I heard a 'tut,' but definitely no sign of surprise from her either.

In theory, Mum always cooked for us on a Sunday, but in practice it was always Aunt Kath. I was always grateful for that. Mum's eccentricity was much more pronounced in some areas than others. I think the main ones were cleaning and cooking. She was quite logical though, in her own way, and it was difficult to argue with her. "Yes Mum, I do love pasta; and mashed potatoes; and chocolate. Should they ever be together on the same plate? No."

The trouble with Mum was that she could be so childlike. Growing up I often felt like the adult in the relationship; always trying to keep things balanced for her. The particular birthday when I had told her that spaghetti just didn't go with mashed potatoes and chocolate sauce, she looked so hurt that I ended up back-tracking and telling her it was great, and eating every last bit, just to spare her feelings. She was overly sensitive to criticism and sometimes I felt like I was walking on egg shells. She lived in her own little world most of the time and she was happy in it. I suppose we had a completely unconventional mother/daughter relationship but since I'd never known anything different it was hard to complain about it too much.

I left Mum sitting in the middle of her DVD collection and went to help Aunt Kath in the kitchen.

"What can I do?" I asked.

"You do a salad. I'll do pasta... sound okay?"

"Sounds great," I replied as I opened the fridge to rummage the salad drawer.

"Good weekend?" she asked.

"Yeah, it was okay. Kind of strange, but fine," I told her.

"Yes, I heard that you were pregnant from Mrs Burrows but then Mrs Turner told us that was all a misunderstanding and you're not pregnant at all. It caused quite a discussion at book club yesterday!"

"Oh, well, happy I keep you all entertained. How would gossip club keep going without me? Oh sorry, I mean "book club" don't I? Do you even read books anymore or have you finally given up on the pretence?"

"Touché, Marie, touché!"

I returned to my methodical chopping of the salad. "Just to clarify though - it's a 'no' on the pregnancy front, right?" she couldn't resist asking.

I ignored her completely and instead directed my

annoyance at the salad. "I'll take that as a 'no' then shall I...?"

"She's definitely not pregnant," Mum shouted cheerfully from the next room. "She's got her period."

Aunt Kath and I laughed in unison and then carried on preparing the food in silence while I waited for her to ask the inevitable. It didn't take her long. "What about men then, Marie? Got your eye on anyone new?"

"Nope." I responded automatically, as an image of Brian flashed into my head. She eyed me with suspicion before moving on to ask me about work and Grace and my life in general. I tried to see it as her taking an interest and not her gathering ammunition for the next book club.

My thoughts lingered on Brian as I half-heartedly answered her questions. Why had he popped into my head? I didn't fancy him. Definitely not. I didn't even like him. The problem, it occurred to me, was that I didn't have many 'people' in my life. The only reason that my mind had wandered to him was because he was the first new person I'd met in so long.

"Salad's ready." I set the table and called Mum as Kath finished making the pasta. Between mouthfuls, Mum gave us a detailed account of the new DVD categorisation system and Kath and I dutifully nodded along. I'd switched off from the conversation entirely and was thinking about Grace and her move to New York when I was abruptly brought back to the present by the mention of Carl.

I looked up at Mum. "Sorry, what?"

"I said at least Carl's gone." She put a forkful of pasta into her mouth and chewed away as I watched her. I wondered how the conversation had moved from DVDs to Carl. It was most startling because my mother never talked about Carl. She obviously was aware of the fact that I had a boyfriend whom I lived with but we never talked about him. When I told her that we'd split up she'd just shrugged and said, "Oh well."

I looked at Aunt Kath but she was focussed on her food and avoiding eye contact. I smiled at Mum, unsure of what to say.

"Horrible man," she stated. I waited to see if she had any more thoughts on the matter.

"I never liked him. I'm glad he's gone. Now you can find yourself a nice husband, can't you?" She looked at me, clearly expecting an answer.

"Well..." I wasn't sure which issue to address first but I felt a brief surge of protectiveness for Carl. "You never met Carl and you never asked me about him so how can you say you don't like him?"

"He cheated on you," she stated matter-of-factly. I looked over at Aunt Kath who continued to avoid eye contact and started to busy herself clearing the table. I sneered at her, firstly annoyed that she had obviously filled Mum in on details which I had left out and secondly because I had the distinct impression that she was secretly enjoying this bit of lunchtime drama. She'd be getting her notebook out in a minute to take notes for book club.

"He did cheat on me, but one bad deed doesn't make a bad person now does it?" I don't know why I felt the need to defend him. She was right, he was not a particularly nice person and he was a really terrible boyfriend.

"A nice boyfriend would have wanted to meet your mother," she countered, flatly. It was true that Carl had never taken any interest in my family but I'd also never pushed the issue. I was always quite happy that neither my mum nor Carl had suggested that they meet. I couldn't have imagined bringing Carl with me for Sunday lunch. Just the thought of it made me uneasy.

"Anyway," Mum broke my thoughts, "I spoke to Mrs Turner about introducing you to her son but I don't think she'll be keen anymore. Not after the pregnancy and shoplifting."

My jaw dropped as Mum picked up the last of the dishes from the table and moved towards the kitchen. Aunt Kath sat back at the table with me and I slouched back on my chair and sighed loudly. She laughed at me. "You look tired, Marie."

"She exhausts me. I never know what she'll say next."

"Did I tell you about my new dog, Marie?" Mum asked me, as though on cue, as she reappeared from the kitchen.

"I don't think you did." I sighed. Mum took care of some of the local dogs while their owners were at work. I'd seen her once, walking the streets wearing some bizarre outfit and talking loudly to the dogs as though they were small children. She loved it but I guess it caused some amusement with neighbours.

"He's a gorgeous little thing called Rex. You'll have to meet him sometime," she told me. I was sure that the more dogs she had, the crazier she would look. I could imagine her getting tangled in all their leads and making a scene in the neighbourhood.

"I made dessert!" Mum suddenly remembered, and headed back to the kitchen.

Aunt Kath and I exchanged looks of horror.

"I've got to go," I shouted as Kath simultaneously called, "I'm going to drive Marie home."

"That's a shame. It's chocolate cheese cake," she informed us as she reappeared from the kitchen. "I made it with cheddar, Marie. Your favourite!"

I smiled back at her, resisting the urge to laugh and avoiding making eye contact with Aunt Kath. "I'll pack some up for you to take home," she told us as she headed back to the kitchen.

"Lovely, Mum, thanks!"

Chapter 5

"Good weekend Marie?" Anne asked as she handed me a coffee on Monday morning. Needless to say I was not at my most cheerful, what with it being, not only the morning, but also Monday morning; the worst morning of the week.

I pondered her question. Pregnancy scares, shop lifting, seeing my ex with yet another tart, calling the police to report a stalker at 4am, finding out that my only real friend was leaving the country and realising that I had a lack of friends/ acquaintances/ social-life/ reason for being. As far as weekends go I'd say it ranked pretty low.

"It was okay. Pretty average," I said, playing it up somewhat.

"Only average? What about your big night on Friday? How was that?"

"Yeah it was okay. Nice to have a girlie night."

"Meet any nice guys?" She was looking at me with eyes full of hope and it really pained me to disappoint her.

"Nope, no nice men I'm afraid." She looked instantly disappointed and I waited for the inevitable dating advice.

"You know, Marie, I've got this friend and you might not believe this but she actually found love on the internet!" *Oh, God! No. Please! No! Make her stop.* "At first I thought she must be mad. She put an ad on one of those dating sites. You know? But after meeting two Mr Wrongs and one - well one quite scary man really - but never mind that because in the end she actually found Mr Right!"

My fake smile started to hurt.

"So maybe that's what you could do Marie?" she ventured.

"Uh, huh." I was noncommittal.

"Or something else which made me think about you..." She picked up her handbag and started to rummage through it as I waited in suspense to see what she was going to produce.

"Here it is, look. I cut it out of the paper for you." She handed me the small piece of paper and I looked at an advert for a speed dating evening.

"I'm not sure it's really something for me, Anne. Besides, I'm quite enjoying being single. I'd forgotten how much fun it is. I should have split up with Carl ages ago. I think it will do me good to be single for a while." I'm not sure if I was trying to convince Anne or myself.

"But surely being single is fun because you can do things like speed dating! I bet you'd have a great time. Just think about it, won't you? It's not good for you to sit at home alone every evening."

"I'm not on my own. Grace is there," I lied. "And besides, I do go out." I lied again.

Thankfully the shop door opened and I was saved from the conversation. I moved the speed-dating advert to the side of my desk and looked up in surprise at Brian.

"Morning!" he chimed while he looked around the room. "So this is where you work," he stated as he walked over to me.

"Stalking me are you, Brian?" I asked, immediately irritated by him.

He laughed. "Come on, Marie, I think we both know that I'm far too good looking to be a stalker." I glared at him in response. "I mean seriously, have you ever heard of a good looking stalker?"

To be fair he was looking pretty good, but he was wearing a suit. Most men look good in a suit. It was a shame though, that his personality let him down.

"What are you doing here then?" I asked.

"Maybe I came to book a holiday. That's what people do here, isn't it?" He perched on the other side of my desk with an amused look on his face. I had an overwhelming urge to punch him.

I stared him out.

"Okay! You got me. I'm not here to book a holiday. I just I wanted to apologise again about the weekend. I think we got off to a bad start." He sounded sincere and it unnerved me. I reached for my coffee and took a sip, unsure of what to say.

"Can I get you a coffee?" Anne's voice broke the silence.

"Thanks but I'm not staying." Brian smiled warmly at her and she grinned back at him before shifting her gaze and making big eyes at me.

"Sorry, Anne. This is Brian." I offered unenthusiastically. "Brian. That's Anne." They smiled at each other and I felt increasingly awkward at the situation. Why on earth did he come to my place of work?

Brian looked back at me. "Grace said she told you her big news. It's going to be weird without her around the place at work. Same for you at home I guess?"

There was a dramatic intake of breath from Anne. I looked over at her and she took the hint and scuttled off into Greg's office.

"Yes, it will take some getting used to, I suppose." I really didn't want to talk about it at work. Or with him. "I'm sorry but I've got a few calls I need to make now." I decided to put an end to the conversation. The look he gave me as he straightened up from the desk made me nervous, I felt like he could read my thoughts and there was a flash of sympathy in his eyes. As he looked away he glanced at my desk and I cringed as I realised what had caught his eye.

"Speed-dating?" he said with his annoying mischievous grin. His cocky demeanour quickly returned as he picked up the advert. "I didn't really have you down as the type."

I inwardly groaned and grappled with the idea of telling him that it wasn't my advert before deciding that it would only make the situation worse.

"I would've thought that was a bit sociable for you," he went on.

"Excuse me! What's that supposed to mean?" I asked indignantly.

"Well you know, being chatty and meeting new people, getting out there... it just doesn't seem very you."

"Well that just shows how little you know me. It's actually great fun!" I snatched the advert from him.

He immediately snatched it back. "So, where's it at then? Maybe I'll come along if it's so much fun."

"Well, it's not that much fun," I backtracked as I snatched at the advert but he moved it out of my reach as he continued to read it.

"Thursday night. It's a date then!" He grinned and handed me the piece of paper.

"I'll only let the stalking go on for so long and then I'll take out a restraining order... just so you know."

He laughed loudly. "Grace is right. You are funny! Have a nice day, Marie," he said before heading to the door. He winked at Anne who was hovering in the doorway to Greg's office. She blushed. She actually blushed like a schoolgirl. My head dropped to the desk.

"Marie, he's gorgeous!" Anne announced as she went back to her seat.

"He's a pig," I corrected her. "An arrogant, self-centred pig who loves himself."

"I think he's dreamy!" She actually said 'dreamy'. I think she's the only person in the world to still use the word.

"And he's so charming!"

"I'm sorry, Anne, but from which bit of that conversation did you get 'charming'?"

She ignored me. "I think he's perfect for you. I told you you'd find someone else and now you have. It's so exciting! Did you just meet him this weekend?"

"Yes, I did." My mind raced to an image of Brian on his bike and it occurred to me that he'd not mentioned that incident at all. Strange.

"He works with Grace," I told Anne.

"Grace!" Anne suddenly screeched. "What's

happening with Grace? Is she moving?"

"Yes. She's going to live in New York."

Anne moved over to me and put her arm around my shoulder, "I'm so sorry. What will you do?"

I shrugged her off. "What do you mean, what will I do? I'll carry on with my life, that's what! I'm a grown woman. I'm not about to fall apart because my best friend moves away." Again, I wondered who it was that I was trying to convince.

Anne looked wounded as she sat back in her seat. "It was good of her to set you up with Brian before she leaves though, wasn't it?"

My eyes briefly darted to my stapler but I managed to resist the urge to throw it at her.

"She did not set me up with Brian," I growled and then wondered if Anne had a point. Was Grace trying to set me up with Brian? No, surely not. The bike and 4am incidents were totally random and he turned up on Saturday of his own accord. No, the only thing Grace was guilty of was telling him where I worked and I would be having a word with her about that later.

"He does seem like a good catch though." Anne said wistfully as she turned to her computer.

I reached for the pile of mail beside me and didn't look at her. "No Anne, sorry but he is definitely not for me. He's annoying and he loves himself and, well... he's annoying!"

When she didn't say anything I looked up to find her smiling at me, condescendingly. "Me thinks the lady doth protest too much," she chirped.

I wanted to scream.

"You're completely wrong you know," I informed

her, but she was busy tapping away at her keyboard and all I got in response was an irritatingly smug, "Uh huh."

I picked up my phone and called Grace.

"You do realise that you are my best friend?" I fired at her. "Because as my best friend I would argue that you shouldn't be telling arrogant annoying men where I work…"

"Oh, so Brian came round?" she asked innocently.

"Yes. He called in to be rude and obnoxious."

"He said that he wanted to apologise. That he'd offended you on Saturday or something."

"In that case, he's terrible at apologising."

"Wait. I'll call you back in a minute." She hung up and I noticed Greg watching me from his office. "I presume you're hard at work there, Marie?"

I smiled sweetly and he disappeared again.

My phone started ringing and Grace's number flashed on the screen.

"Hi," I managed.

"So Brian said that he came to apologise and you were rude to him before he even said anything, so maybe he responded by being a bit cocky."

"Very cocky, more like. And I wasn't rude." I tried to remember the conversation and who had initiated the sniping. I couldn't remember but decided it wouldn't have been me.

"Well, clearly you two just wind each other up the wrong way so why don't you just stay away from each other?"

"With pleasure," I assured her and hung up.

Hannah Ellis

Chapter 6

When Thursday came around, I collapsed on the couch after work and a few minutes later reached over to my handbag and pulled out Anne's speed dating advert. I sat looking at it and felt defeated. I flashed back to the middle of the afternoon when the phone had rung and I'd answered it cheerfully.

"Hello, *Go Travel.* Marie speaking."

"Hey!" came a breezy voice that I didn't recognise. "I just wanted to check the time for tonight... Was it nine?"

I was momentarily confused. "Oh, it's you." Brian, of course. "Yeah... the thing is I'm not actually going to be able to make it tonight. Lots of things to do. Busy life you know..."

I heard laughter down the phone and then, "Chicken". I opened my mouth to protest but he hung up.

As I sat looking at the advert I could still hear his voice calling me a chicken. I wasn't going to be taken in though. I knew his plan. He thought that if he called me a chicken, I'd have to go, just to prove that I wasn't a chicken. Ha! As if I'd be lured into such a trap. I had nothing to prove to anyone. I was definitely not a chicken and if I wanted to go speed bloody dating then I bloody well would. But I didn't, so I wouldn't, and that was all there was to it.

I sighed and dragged myself upstairs to trawl through my wardrobe for something un-chicken like to wear.

"Wow, I didn't know this place still existed. It used to be a YMCA building you know, a long time ago," Pat informed me as he leant over the steering wheel to get a better look at the building he'd just pulled up in front of. I peered out of the window at the ugly old building that was now apparently used as a venue for all sorts of functions and corporate events. The sign read, 'Manor Brook Hotel', but the name really didn't reflect the dinginess of the place. It was hidden away at the end of a backstreet and was surrounded by a huge car park which I guessed had never been full. I also imagined it didn't get much business on the hotel side of things. You'd have to be pretty desperate to stay there.

"Six pounds, Marie." Pat prompted. "You could've walked this far," he added unhelpfully.

"I don't want you out of business though," I told him cheerfully. His moodiness always brought out the cheerful side of me; I felt like I was correcting the balance somehow. Glancing at the building again, I wondered whether I should ask him to take me back home before leaning forward and handing over the money. I always sat in the back when Pat was driving me. It felt more comfortable and the body odour wasn't as suffocating as when you sat right next to him.

"Work thing, is it?" he asked when I failed to exit the car.

"Oh no, it's a... um... I'm meeting someone. Some people. It's a social thing."

"Have fun then."

"Okay. Thanks!" I finally opened the door and got out. As he drove away, I took a deep breath and marched across the car park and up to the door. I pulled on it but it didn't open. I hoped no one was watching me as I tried pushing it. That didn't work either. I realised that the building looked almost abandoned. Oh well, I'd given it a try. I turned and walked back across the car park, my goal being the main road and into the first taxi I found. Or maybe I could walk home, like Pat had suggested. It was no use ringing Helen; she wouldn't send anyone to drive me home. She'd give me a lecture and possibly call me a chicken as well. She'd been so excited when I'd told her where I was going. Her enthusiasm had briefly rubbed off on me and had given me hope that this was not the worst idea ever. That hadn't lasted long though.

I hadn't gone very far when a car drove past me on the quiet road and I turned and watched it pull into the hotel car park. It drove round the side and I saw someone walk into the building through the side door. Not abandoned after all then. I stood for a minute, trying to decide which direction to walk in.

When I opened the door and walked into the lobby, I noticed a clock on the wall and realised that I was late. That's probably considered very bad form when you're going speed-dating. I'd probably already missed my first 'date' of the evening. So no point really. I'd probably already missed meeting the man of my dreams.

I looked around the dingy hotel lobby and decided this was the worst idea ever and that I could definitely live with being a chicken.

"Excuse me!" I turned to find the smiley guy on the front desk waving at me frantically. "Need some help?" he asked cheerfully.

I didn't reply as I fought the urge to turn and walk straight back out of there.

"I think I know why you're here!" He was using a sing-song voice that people usually reserve for children. He was about my age and if I wasn't so distracted I would have appraised him better and decided he was quite good looking. I was on the verge of a panic attack though, so my radar was a bit off. "Straight up the stairs and turn left. First door on your right. You're a bit late but not to worry. Go on, run along now." He winked at me and, without wanting to, my legs took me up the stairs. I could swear I heard him laughing but I knew that if I turned back to check, there was a good chance I could catch sight of the door and chicken out. I carried on up the stairs, willing myself to stay calm.

I decided, as I walked towards the door, that I just shouldn't think about it. I should walk up to the door and go straight in, head held high, oozing confidence. And, amazingly, that's exactly what I did. I didn't hesitate for a second.

So there I was, standing in a large meeting room. Tables were scattered around the edge of the room, reminding me a bit of my school drama class when we didn't have a proper drama room so we'd just move the tables out of the way and use our best acting skills to pretend we were on stage when we were actually in the Mathematics department.

I was slightly taken aback, because it wasn't at all what I expected. I'd seen movies where people go speed dating and, a) there was usually a bar somewhere and, b) they didn't usually sit around in a circle, on cushions on the floor. Oh well, life isn't always like the movies, I suppose.

I scanned the room but there was no sign of Brian which was a relief. I was suddenly self-conscious as I realised all eyes were on me.

"Hell-oh!" came a voice from the circle.

"Hi!" I said. Everyone was staring at me and I stood frozen to the spot.

I looked round at the group again and decided it was definitely a bad idea. I did not want to date anyone there. For a start there were only three men. One was bald. I'm not being judgemental or anything, and I realise he can't help it but it just really doesn't do it for me. One was average looking but with some weight issues and thinning hair and the other was very tall and skinny with acne scars and a confused look on his face.

I hate to pre-judge people but there was obviously nothing for me in the group. Even if there was, the men were now outnumbered, seven to three. Not that I'd have to worry, I decided; the women weren't much in the way of competition. In fact one of them looked to be in her fifties, and again I don't want to judge but isn't it a bit sad to go speed-dating in your fifties?

"Newcomers are always welcome!" The woman in the circle sounded jolly but looked suspicious. "Grab yourself a cushion and come and introduce yourself." She indicated a pile of cushions in the corner and I went and took one.

I thought that it was strange to refer to me as a newcomer. I didn't know that you got regulars at speed-dating. I guessed it could be speed-dating for people who don't believe in love at first sight. Maybe that makes sense, getting to know people gradually and in a neutral environment. I just hope they don't get reported under the trade descriptions act. Didn't seem like there was anything speedy about it to me.

I plonked myself down, fairly ungraciously and realised again that all eyes were looking at me expectantly.

"Oh! Right, yeah, well, I'm Marie." I wasn't sure what else I was supposed to say but they were all looking at me so I carried on, "I'm twenty eight". The woman who'd spoken to me nodded encouragingly. She had frizzy hair which she'd obviously tried to conceal in a tight bun but it didn't really work. She also wore small glasses which she was looking over the top of and which made her look like a librarian.

"Would you like to tell us why you're here?" she said gently.

"Well..." I wasn't sure if I was supposed to say how I found out about it or some dribble about me being a depressed singleton.

"Um... I... my friend, well not really a friend, a colleague gave me an advert about this... about tonight and then, well to be honest, there was this guy who sort of dared me to come."

Everyone was looking at me with a mix of sympathy and confusion. I was starting to feel decidedly scared and wondered what I could say to get me out of there.

The librarian lady moved towards me on her hands and knees and tapped me sympathetically on the knee.

"A lot of us have been in denial too." Nods all round. "Maybe later you'll be ready to share."

It suddenly occurred to me that of course everyone who goes speed-dating has some sort of story about why they've had resort to it. After all it's not something that anyone with a healthy, active social life does. They obviously all knew I'd got problems and wanted me to share them. It seemed quite like therapy but what the heck, maybe therapy was just what I need.

"I have been having a few problems recently," I jumped in. I didn't want her to think that I was completely clueless. I definitely wasn't in denial. I just wasn't expecting this. "My life doesn't quite seem to be working out quite how I'd like and I feel like I need to make some changes."

"That's great, Marie!" she said warmly. "It's so good that you are facing up to your problems. The first step is always admitting that you've got a problem. Later we'll be able to explore your problems more and help you get back on the right track again. We can help you with your addictions here. It's going to be hard work but in the end it will be worth it." She beamed at me and I panicked. I flashed to the man at the front desk and his mischievous look. That's when I realised that it wasn't speed-dating after all. He'd sent me into flipping Alcoholics Anonymous.

No wonder they'd all looked at me so strangely. I was supposed to be telling them about how I got up in the morning and had vodka on my cornflakes and thought about whether I was going to have wine or whiskey for lunch. Flipping heck! How was I going to get out without being set upon by a load of alco's?

I had, then, what I thought was a brilliant idea. I'd confess and tell them about my terrible addiction. Get them all in tears about my plight. Say, "Thank you very much, I'll be back next week," and flee. It's not like I would see them again. I knew I was making a mockery of AA meetings and to be honest, the way my life was going, I probably wasn't going to be mocking AA meetings for much longer, but it was my only escape. I suppose I could have confessed to being in the wrong room but that would be far too straight forward and just not me!

"Jake, would you like to tell us how your week went?" Librarian lady had moved on to overweight man but I jumped in quick.

"Wait!" I got everyone's attention and ploughed straight on. "I'd like to tell you about my problem." Nods and smiles all round told me I started well.

"I am an addict. I've been an addict for a long time. I'm here because I've hit rock bottom. I know I need to stop but I don't know how. I need help."

Lots of smiling and lots of nodding. I was definitely doing well.

"Was this a sudden realisation Marie? Was there an event that made you admit that you have a problem?"

Usually I was rubbish at quick thinking. Put me on the spot about something and I go to mush, but today I was feeling confident.

"My boyfriend kept trying to tell me that I needed to get help and that he couldn't deal with me and my 'problems' anymore and then one day I came home from work and found him in bed with another woman."

I struggled to keep a straight face at the sight of their shocked faces. There were tuts and sighs, even a gasp or too. I had them all sucked in. And I always thought that those drama lessons were wasted on me!

I put on my best wounded expression as the librarian lady asked, "How did that make you feel?"

"I would imagine it made her feel fat." Overweight man answered for me and rolled his eyes.

I'll admit to being confused by his analysis. I put it down to him being overweight. He probably would think that if he was in the situation.

"Jake!" Librarian gave him what I can only describe as a death look. "Please don't interrupt when Marie is sharing. Only she knows how she felt at that moment."

Jake, quite bravely I thought, answered back. "Well come on, it hardly takes a genius does it? Someone turns up at fatties club..."

"Please don't call it that!" Librarian screeched over Jake.

"Sorry," he rolled his eyes again. "So someone turns up at 'Emily's Encouragement' and tells us that they're addicted to food and the last straw was them finding their boyfriend in bed with a skinny tart. I presume she was skinny, right Marie?" I nodded weakly through my state of confusion. "And you want to know how it made them feel? If the answer's not fat, I don't know what it is!"

Well I'd have thought the answer could have been that I'm a drunk and my boyfriend had had enough of me spending all our money on vodka, wine and whiskey but apparently not.

"Did you or did you not feel fat, Marie?" Jake asked, bluntly.

"Yes, I felt fat," I confessed, thinking I was a complete fraud. Then I felt a bit sad because I'd have thought I should have been immediately thrown out of a 'fatties' meeting on the grounds that I'm not fat. But no one had even mentioned that. I looked round the group with fresh eyes and realised that I wasn't even the thinnest person at 'fatties'. Two of them were thinner than me - skinny girl and very skinny girl. Lady who looked to be in her fifties also didn't look to be overweight. Then there was one other lady who did look a bit bigger but still not the sort of turn out I'd expect at something like this. I guess Librarian lady, who I concluded was in charge and who also was quite petite, was just good at her job. So these people had lost the weight but were still coming to make sure they didn't go back to their old ways.

"I think that's enough for your first time Marie. Well done you!" Librarian said warmly. "Let's move on to someone else shall we?"

As I sat dazed and confused, Jake started to talk about his week. I zoned out for a while and considered leaving. I could just say I had to go to the bathroom and never come back. In the end I couldn't quite bring myself to do it. I'll be honest, I felt like I'd come this far, I may as well stick around for the good bit. The good bit being the weigh-in, of course. That should be fun. Obviously I wasn't going to join in; not with getting weighed anyway. I'd clap if it was called for.

I zoned back in and heard Jake saying he thought he'd had a really good week, only having had four fry-ups, which I thought seemed excessive but he concluded by saying he was sure he'd lost a few pounds. There were some definite sniggers when he said that, which I thought was a bit mean, but Librarian soon put a stop to it with a particularly fierce death stare.

I couldn't help myself then. I thought it was a perfect time to suggest, "Should we have the weigh-in and find out?"

That brought about more sniggers and a full on snort from Jake, "Dream on Marie – this is no Weight Watchers you know!" Really? What was it then? I wished someone would enlighten me.

I looked over at Librarian who looked annoyed. "What I have developed here is a holistic approach to weight loss, Marie. Weighing scales really only serve to create stress and tension."

"Well that, and they tell you how much you weigh, and whether or not you've lost weight," I argued. I was irritated there wouldn't even be a weigh in.

"Very true, Marie," Jake backed me up. Obviously we were met with the death stare which I decided was being a bit over-used. It was definitely losing its effect.

"Weighing scales tell us a number. But what really counts is how we feel," she ploughed on.

"I feel fat." Jake laughed.

"Exactly," replied Librarian, but I'm not sure what her point was.

"The thing is though," came a voice I hadn't heard yet. It was skinny girl and she was chewing gum as she spoke, "None of us actually know if we've lost weight or not, do we? So we don't really know if sitting here and meditating with you for three quid a session is doing us any good at all." Meditating? I hoped that was a joke. She was young and feisty and I liked her. Her jeans were baggy and she was wearing a vest top which revealed bright pink bra straps at the shoulders.

She had a cockiness about her that became more evident the more she spoke. "And it's all right for you to say that if you feel like you've lost weight then you have, but at that rate - if we could think ourselves thin - then we'd all look like bloody supermodels by now wouldn't we? And no offense to the rest of you, but we don't."

"Actually I did weigh myself at home, and I've put on a bit of weight." It was the very gentle voice of lady in her fifties speaking up. She looked instantly remorseful.

I felt like I'd started somewhat of a mutiny as I watched librarian attempt to regain control of the group.

"Let's just move on now shall we? Does anyone else want to share before we begin with meditation?" *Oh god it wasn't a joke. Must get out quick!*

"This has been lovely, but I'm going to leave now, I'm afraid." I got up and gave a little wave to the group as a whole.

Librarian cleared her throat, "Obviously you are free to leave before the end of the session but the fee must be paid first. Ten pounds for the first session and three thereafter."

I laughed. "You have got to be kidding! Ten

pounds? For what exactly? There wasn't even a weigh-in! If I wanted to sit and listen to someone talk rubbish for the evening, I can go and visit my mother for free thanks!" I had no clue what had gotten into me, but this woman had wound me up the wrong way and I just couldn't stop myself.

I pointed at her so there was no confusion as I continued. "You are a fraud. Sitting there taking hard-earned money off good people. If you really want to help them, don't be so cheap! Buy a set of scales and give people the humiliation of being weighed as an incentive to watch what they eat."

With that out of my system, I turned on my heel and marched out. I was feeling, I have to say, rather flipping proud of myself!

I marched all the way down the stairs and out of the building, giving the man on the front desk the finger as I passed.

Stopping in the car park, I heard footsteps behind me. I turned and found skinny girl and Jake beaming at me, and lady in her fifties just behind them looking scared (maybe that was just how she always looked).

"Wow! That was a-ma-zing!" skinny girl squealed.

"Bloody brilliant!" Jake agreed. "You should've seen her face when we left behind you!"

"I wish I'd seen!" I was quite excited, I felt like I'd achieved something, caused a mini revolution or something.

We did quick introductions. Skinny girl was called Sophie and lady in her fifties was Linda, although she introduced herself politely and then scurried away, saying she'd better get home.

I stood with my comrades laughing about Librarian

and her alternative method, until I was hit right on the head with a cushion. The three of us looked up simultaneously to see if it really could be raining cushions, but all we could see was Librarian lady leaning out of an upstairs window shouting, "How dare you come in here and ruin all my good work? How dare you!?" Another cushion came our way and I couldn't help but laugh. She was ranting and raving incoherently and then, all of a sudden, she disappeared under the window. When she came back up she was wielding a shoe. Surely she wasn't about to throw that? There was a hefty heel on it; it could do some damage. She did though, pelting the thing and narrowly missing my head.

"She's actually gone mad!" Jake said.

"She's going for the other one." Sophie laughed as Librarian disappeared from view again.

We looked around but there was nowhere to go. It was an empty car park and we were sitting ducks. I was about to be killed by a librarian's wedged heel.

She appeared back at the window with the other shoe but dropped it before she managed to throw it and bent to retrieve it for the second attempt.

An Opel Corsa pulled up next to us. It was Linda, God bless her. "Get in quick!" she called through the open window. We'd just clambered into our getaway vehicle as the second shoe landed in the exact spot we'd been standing.

"Drive!" instructed Jake, but just as we were pulling away Sophie called, "Stop!" in a voice so high pitched you really couldn't argue with it. We watched open mouthed as she jumped out of the car, picked up the second shoe, got back in the car and yelled "Go!"

I continued to look at Sophie as we drove away. She was laughing so much it looked painful, "Just imagine her getting home now, in one shoe." She carried on laughing and waving the shoe.

After about thirty seconds I realised I was sitting in a car with a bunch of strangers. The only thing I knew about them was where they spent their Thursday evenings and that really didn't say anything good about them. Linda offered to drive us all home, so after some discussion about where everyone lived and, for me, some hesitation about giving these strangers my address, we settled into an awkward silence.

"So why on earth do you go to that bizarre group?" I asked after a few minutes. "And should we be worried about the people we left behind?" Although come to think of it the rest of them had barely moved or spoken so maybe they were well into the brainwash stage.

"Don't worry about the rest of them." Linda said. "The little bald man is Emily's husband."

"Wait! Who's Emily?"

"The leader. You know... it's called *Emily's Encouragement*. She just encourages you to lose weight. I think it's supposed to be something between Weight Watchers and Overeaters Anonymous"

"Okay. And the rest of them?" I asked.

"The little skinny girl is her daughter. The tall lanky boy is her husband's son from a previous marriage and that's everyone I think. Oh, wait, no! There's that big lady, Janet. She's been going to the groups for about six months but she's never spoken and I really don't know anything about her. I'd guess she's another relative."

I was instantly shocked at the fact that someone would have been going to these sessions for six months, and Jake clearly had the same reaction. "So how long have you been going Linda, if you know all this? And why?"

I felt like this could be the most that Linda had spoken to anyone in a long time and we all listened intently.

"I've been going for almost two years." She looked a bit sad as she said that and we all waited in disbelief for her to continue. "You see my husband, George, found an advert for Emily's thing in the yellow pages and he called and booked me ten sessions. He told me about it on my birthday... that was my birthday present, you see. I guess he thought that I'd let myself go a bit."

Linda was clearly trying hard not to cry and we gave her a moment to collect herself.

"But why are you still going after two years?" Sophie asked.

"Well I know it's ridiculous but it's the one place I can go where George won't ask what I've been doing – he's actually happy for me to go, and I just like to have an evening away from him. We don't always get on very well you see." I think the fact that fat club was a nice alternative really gave that away.

"Anyway, why do you all go?" she deflected quickly.

I wasn't sure I wanted to tell them that I was just lost, but Sophie jumped in first anyway, giving me time to think about my story.

"Ha ha! You know why I was there? Because a few

weeks ago, I was gonna go to speed-dating right? But that idiot on reception thought it'd be funny to send me to the wrong room!"

Okay, so she'd stolen my story anyway.

"But then I thought it was alright. I know that Emily doesn't really care but I could say stuff and people would listen to me and it seemed like they care. I still live at my mum's house and I've got five brothers and sisters, so it's not very often anyone actually listens to me. Tonight was the best night yet, that was fun!"

Next was Jake's turn. "Well I go because I'm fat, and I did consider going to a proper meeting after I realised that Emily's way is completely wacko and I wasn't going to lose any weight, but then I thought that if I did go to a proper place then I would have to watch what I eat. With Emily I feel like I'm making some effort to lose weight without actually making any sacrifices food-wise, if that makes any sense. Also I really get a kick out of winding Emily up!"

After Jake had finished talking, all eyes turned to me. On a whim I decided I'd just be honest. "I did the same as Sophie. I was looking for speed-dating." I was finally being honest but even to me it sounded like a lie.

"Yeah, right!" Sophie piped up. "You're just embarrassed about going to a fat club. Nobody's forgotten why your boyfriend ditched you. Of course you'd want to lose weight. That's nothing to be ashamed of you know."

I would honestly say I'm quite an average size. I'm a size twelve for goodness sake, not exactly obese by anyone's standards but I was really starting to feel self-conscious, what with my mother telling me I looked pregnant, not getting kicked out of fat club and now this? I didn't even feel like I could defend myself so I just kept quiet and looked out of the window.

Linda dropped me off first and I felt a bit awkward saying goodbye. We'd been thrown together and I felt a strange closeness with them; I wouldn't be seeing them again though, so I didn't know what to say.

"Bye, then," is what I went for in the end. Then waved as the car pulled away.

Chapter 7

"So how was the dating experience Marie? Meet anyone nice?"

Thankfully my phone rang before I had to answer Anne's questions the following morning. I looked apologetic as I reached to pick it up.

"Hey! How was speed-dating then?" came the enthusiastic voice on the phone. "Sorry I missed it but something came up. A last-minute work thing."

"Hi, Brian." Great, he'd rung to gloat about the fact that he'd set me up. A work thing came up? Yeah right.

"So how was it? Did I miss any good talent?" he asked again. There was no way I was going to give him any satisfaction in this conversation.

"It was great actually, I had a very... surprising evening." That wasn't a lie!

"Really? So you found yourself a man did you?" There was a definite hint of mocking in his voice, as though it was completely implausible that I could have met someone.

"Actually, I did meet someone."

"Really?" He still sounded like he didn't believe a word of it so I expanded on my story a little.

"Yes I left with a guy actually." Not entirely a lie. I just wouldn't mention the fact that I made a quick getaway with a man and two women under a deluge of cushions and shoes.

The line had gone quiet and I thought maybe I'd lost him. "Brian?"

"Yeah, I'm here. Just a bit surprised to be honest. Glad you had fun though. Maybe I'll give it a go next time."

"Okay, well thanks for calling," I said. "I'll see you around then."

"Probably. Bye."

I hung up the phone and laughed to myself before noticing Anne's horrified look.

She tutted loudly and pretended to be busy. I sat and waited patiently, knowing she would have to say what was on her mind.

After straightening the papers on her desk for the third time she finally looked up at me.

"Did you really go home with someone you'd just met? I know that it's all the rage these days for people to have these so called 'one-night-stands', but I would never think that you would do such a thing. I'm actually sorry now that'd I told you about the speed-dating. I feel responsible."

I decided I needed to cut in before she started the lecture on 'being safe'.

"I said I left with someone, not that I went home with someone! And it was actually three people. I made three new friends and it wasn't even speed-dating. It was at a Weight-Watchers meeting, so it was a good evening, all in all."

She smiled at me and looked relieved. "You had me worried there for a minute. What a brilliant idea though. I imagine speed-dating will be much easier after a few weeks at Weight Watchers. What's your target weight?"

I looked down at myself and wondered, for about the fourth time in a week, if I had some sort of disorder where I see myself as much smaller than I actually am.

"I'm not trying to lose weight. I just got lost looking for speed-dating. It's all in the same building you see. It wasn't even really Weight Watchers, it's this thing called 'Emily's Encouragement' and I think it's more of a social club really. They just talk a lot about food."

I wandered across the room to get myself a coffee from little table outside Greg's office. The coffee pot was always ready (thanks to Anne) and there was always milk in the fridge under the table (also because of Anne).

Anne appeared beside me seconds later. "Marie, I think you need to call Brian."

I took a deep breath. "Why's that then?" I was fairly confident I knew what this was about.

"Well, he's going to think that you had a one-night-stand with someone at speed-dating. And men don't like it if they think you give yourself away easily." She was whispering now. "He's going to be put off if he thinks that. But I think if you call him and explain what you really meant, then maybe he'll still go out with you."

Oh how I love getting dating advice from Anne. She thinks she's an oracle when it comes to relationships.

"Yeah, the thing is, I don't care what he thinks. I meant for him to think I'd gone home with someone. I wanted to wind him up. And I'd be quite okay with it if he decides I'm a slut who he wants nothing to do with, because, quite frankly, Anne, I think he's an idiot."

I left her stunned and stalked back to my desk, pausing to swap brochures A1 and F12 on my way. I'm not sure when Anne swapped those without me noticing. She eventually went back to her desk and mumbled something about me never getting a man with a mouth like that.

I made sure she wasn't looking before I stuck my tongue out at her. Childish, but satisfying.

The day dragged on and I was quite glad when it started to rain. It reflected my melancholy mood and made me feel a bit special at the same time; like maybe I at least had a friend in the weather.

It was mid-afternoon and I had my head in a filing cabinet when I heard the door open and then close again. Sometimes I start doodling on a pad of paper or start typing furiously in the hope that the customer won't want to bother me and will look to Anne instead, or at least make sure they know that my time is precious and they shouldn't waste more of it than is absolutely necessary. I'm sure some of the old bids come in for a chat with no intention of ever booking a holiday. They tell me all about their week and want to know the details of my life before they pretend to be interested in a Saga holiday and leave to 'mull over' the brochure.

Anyway, I knew before I even looked up that this customer wasn't our usual kind. It was like his aura washed into the room ahead of him, his effortless cool penetrating everything in its path. I looked up to see Mr Cool, folding away his umbrella and peeling off his coat. He scanned the room as Anne hurried over to him with her eyes agog. He held out his garments for her to take without a word; so arrogant and yet so unbelievably sexy with confidence. Anne stood holding the dripping articles and looking confused as he pulled off his sunglasses and looked directly at me. Never in all my life have I known anyone confident enough to wear sunglasses in the rain. Normally I would've declared him an idiot and a loser right there and then, but there was something about him that made me feel like I was free-falling. There couldn't possibly be anything about this man that I wouldn't love.

His eyes smouldered as he gave me the once over and I tried to discreetly correct my posture and give myself an air of confidence without any sudden movements.

"You..." he said, smiling delightfully while he pointed at me "Must. Be. Marrrie!" He rolled the 'r' and my name has never sounded so magical. I moved towards him with all the grace I could muster and smiled confidently to disguise the fact that I had no idea who he was. He floated over to me whilst saying, "I am Sebastian Featherston. I've been dying to meet you in person! So here I am. Darling! It's so wonderful to finally lay eyes on you!" He air kissed me on both cheeks as I registered who he was.

I'd spent many frustrating hours on the phone with Mr Featherston, attempting to find him the perfect, "fabulous" holidays. I have to admit I'd imagined him to be an overweight middle-aged loser and had been tempted to tell him to get a life on a number of occasions; organising his holidays was the bane of my working life.

I was shocked at how different he was to how I had imagined him. He was gorgeous; thick blonde hair and sparkling blue eyes. He had a body that I would die for. His skinny jeans showed off beautiful toned, lean legs. I felt like I had dreamt of this man and now here he was standing before me calling me "Darling!"

At that moment I realised that somehow, I had to make this man mine, no matter what it took. Clearly, I mean he's going to be my new gay best friend, not my boyfriend. He was far too effeminate and fabulous to be straight. Doesn't every girl need a gay best friend though? Just like the movies!

"And aren't you just gorgeous!" he all but screeched as he wrinkled his nose up at me. I was aware of the fact that a part of me wanted to tell him to sod off and stop being such a sarcastic bugger but the other part of me was overawed by him. I fluttered my eyelashes and somehow I transformed on the spot into a female version of him. For the next hour I was confident and fabulous and to be honest, I gushed and fawned all over him, unashamedly. When the hour was over, I had booked him the holiday of a lifetime in the Seychelles, staying at a five-star resort, complete with his own personal masseur and personal trainer to be on hand 24/7.

"It has been absolutely divine meeting you! Really a treat. I will never be on the phone to you again. From now on we do everything in person! I can't thank you enough, Marie. You are just wonderful!"

"Oh, Sebastian, the pleasure has been all mine. I

hope your holiday is perfect and I can't wait to see you again!"

After a strange farewell ritual full of air kisses and more gushing thanks, I was left sitting at my desk, feeling like an actress coming out of role. It was slightly exhausting being so marvellous for such a prolonged period of time. I very quickly drifted into a daydream where Sebastian is my gay best friend who calls me darling and tells me I'm fabulous and gives me fashion advice.

He also whisks me off on his fancy holidays with him; not just the two of us mind you. No way, if I'm going to dream, I might as well go all the way. There's Sebastian, me and the rest of our eclectic group of friends; a group of stylish young professionals with a variety of interesting jobs and a wide spectrum of different nationalities and sexualities. The 'made in the movies' kind of friends that everyone needs. We spend long evenings together sipping champagne, laughing and chatting into the night.

There I am, lying by the pool of the five-star resort, sipping cocktails and laughing with my perfect friends. Bliss! But wait, who's the gorgeous hunky one that's lovingly massaging sun tan lotion into my shoulders? That would be my sexy, adoring boyfriend who spends his time hanging around me, being attentive and doing whatever it is that perfect boyfriends do.

"Hello? Earth to Marie... Is anybody in there?" I look up to find Anne's grinning face dragging me back to reality.

"Everything okay in there?"

"Yeah. I just need some new friends..." I mumbled.

"What?"

"You know, cool friends? Rich, successful, generally awesome people... Never mind, did you want me?"

She looked completely bemused. "No, I was just thinking, couldn't we all do with a holiday like that?"

She'd well and truly burst my bubble on the daydream front and I was back to myself. "To be honest, I didn't like the sound of it. Why on earth would you go away to a luxury resort and order a personal trainer? That would just ruin it for me. Exercising every day? When you're on holiday? That would negate all the good stuff."

Although, come to think of it, if the personal trainer was some stunning hunk with a sense of humour to match then maybe I could cope. Especially if he just made me do two sit ups and then congratulated me on my effort and took me for a celebratory drink at the bar whilst flirting with me outrageously. Oh but wait, what would my gorgeous boyfriend make of that? Not much probably. I guess they'd end up having a full on punch up over me and everything would be horribly tense and stressful... Oh, wow! This imaginary life is all getting a bit too much for me. Obviously I will do well to avoid luxury holidays and just stay home instead.

"Sorry, Anne, what were you saying?"

"Never mind," she grumbled as she walked away from me. "Sometimes I worry about you, I really do!"

My mind was made up though; Sebastian was my ticket to a great social life. He was going to be my new best friend and I would reap all the benefits that came with that. I was fairly sure he'd be in touch. He'd probably ring me to go out for a drink. If not, the next time he was booking a holiday I would be proactive and create an opportunity for myself. Everything would work out fine, I was sure of it.

Chapter 8

As usual, my optimism didn't last very long. Days went by without a phone call from Sebastian and the doubts started to creep into my head. I had to hush the nasty goblin on several occasions. I'd been so sure that Sebastian would be in touch, wanting to see me socially. Now I was getting insecure about my social life again. Grace would be leaving before I knew it and I absolutely needed to have new friends before then.

I'll be quite honest, by the time Thursday rolled around again, I did actually think about giving speed-dating another try. Last week was very strange but I felt like it was one of those nights that I'd remember fondly and laugh about from time to time. This week I might actually get the right room, or just try a different room and see what happens. I was feeling sorry for myself and speed-dating was appealing in the sense that it had the potential to bring some change to my life. It was all quite irrelevant though, as I wasn't going, but maybe next week.

I picked up the phone and called Grace's mobile.

"Hey!" she sounded like she was on the go. "Sorry I'm a terrible friend. I was in meetings really late last night and I didn't see your message until midnight. I wanted to call you all day but I'm trying to round off some things before the big move so work is hectic and we're trying to organise Visas and things. We're just on our way to dinner with James's parents. I feel like everything is non-stop at the moment. How are things with you?"

"Oh fine. I just wanted to see if you wanted to grab a drink last night but I fell asleep early in the end anyway. I must be getting old!" Wednesday was a bad night for me; there was never anything on the TV. The other nights I have a pretty good TV schedule to see me through, but Wednesday is hard. "Are you coming home tonight?" I sounded desperate and I knew it.

"No, sorry. I was planning on staying at James's place. He's starting to box up all his stuff and I said I'd help. If you need me though, I'm sure he could manage alone."

"No, don't worry. I'm fine." *Except for feeling like a charity case.* "Just wanted to check in. I haven't seen you for a few days that's all."

"I know. I'm really sorry, Marie. I'll make it up to you. Name a day and I'm yours. Promise!"

"It's fine. You're busy. I understand. I'm not a child. I can manage without you!"

"I know. I just worry that you're lonely that's all."

The doorbell rang. "See, there's someone at the door - probably a secret admirer or something. No need to worry about me after all, hey?"

She laughed at me. "Go and answer it then and I'll talk to you soon. I should be home over the weekend but sorting James's stuff is probably going to drag out a bit. I'll give you a call."

I was slightly surprised when I opened the door to

Brian. "I thought you'd be all ready to go," he said casually.

"Hi, Brian." I gave him a puzzled look.

"Speed-dating? I thought I'd escort you. I felt bad about standing you up last week."

"Well there's no need to feel bad about it and no need to go this week. Thanks anyway."

"I thought after the success of last week you'd be raring to go again?" We locked eyes. I wasn't sure whether to go with a lie or a sarcastic comment for a reply, but I seemed incapable of forming words anyway.

"Excuse me, move will you, it's flipping cold out here." Brian looked completely bewildered as Sophie physically moved him to the side and wandered into the house closely followed by Jake.

"Er…hi!" I called after them when they walked into the living room. "Why are you here?" I felt like directness would be my best approach.

"Coz, it's Thursday! *Emily's Encouragement* remember? New location from now on - your place! Nice place by the way." I could almost hear Sophie making herself at home.

I glanced at Brian who mouthed the word, 'Emily?'

"It's speed-dating," I lied. "The official name is *Emily's Encouragement*... because it's organised by a woman called Emily... and she encourages people to meet new people and get into the dating scene..."

"Really? That's a bit weird isn't it?" He didn't look at all convinced. I needed to get rid of him quick.

"Yes, It's very weird. Anyway I made some friends and we arranged to meet tonight so I better go and be a good hostess!" I started to close the door but he leaned into it.

"But why did you ask why they were here?"

"Because... I.... I forgot it was Thursday tonight, that's all! My head is stuck on Tuesday! Thanks for calling round though."

"Marie!" Sophie yelled from the living room. "Shut the door, you're letting all the cold air in."

"Could I maybe stay for a quick drink, since I'm here?" Brian asked. I couldn't think of an answer fast enough and he walked past me into the living room. I closed the door and followed him. So much for a quiet night.

"So how is everyone?" I asked awkwardly, standing in the middle of the living room, looking at Sophie and Jake, who'd made themselves comfortable on the couch.

"This room's very yellow, Marie. Obviously you didn't decorate it, did you?" Sophie said as she looked around the room. "No, it's far too cheerful for you."

"What's that supposed to mean?" I asked.

"I thought I was quite clear." She grinned. "You could do with some cushions though. You should buy some."

I smiled to myself as I thought of the two bin bags full of hand knitted cushions that my mother had made for me over the years. The room definitely didn't need cushions.

"We're not at the hotel anymore, Sophie." Jake said. "We've got a couch to sit on now. What are you talking about cushions for?" He turned to me. "It turns out we're institutionalized," he informed me with a grin. "The three of us - it was Linda as well but she doesn't have the willpower we do. We found each other back at the hotel… loitering in the car park. We didn't want to go in, but we somehow just ended up there and didn't know what else to do with ourselves. Anyway, Sophie and I decided we'd come and visit you. Linda couldn't be persuaded though; she was worried her husband would find out. Anyway, here we are!"

"Who's Linda?" Brian asked.

"Oh, she's another friend who I met last week," I jumped in.

"And she's got a husband?" he asked. I could see where his train of thought was leading. I just nodded and hoped for the best. "And her husband doesn't mind her going to this Emily thing?" Brian continued with his line of questioning.

"Oh no, he doesn't mind at all," Jake said. "In fact he's the one who signed her up for it originally."

"That's very open-minded of him," Brian mused.

I noticed Sophie hadn't taken her eyes off Brian since he entered the room. "Sorry but who is this guy? A newcomer or what?" She nodded in his direction as she dragged her gaze over to me and then returned it to him. "Because, no offence, but you're not fat and you're actually very good looking so I'm not sure you really need to be here, do you?" She was oozing attitude and I was intrigued as to how Brian would react.

"Well on that basis I don't think you should be here either should you?" He smiled at her and it was like her attitude got up and left; just admitted defeat and walked away. She melted a little bit.

"Brian, she's barely legal!" I quickly chastised.

She threw me a look from the Emily school of

death stares, the attitude happily returning for me. "I'm eighteen actually," she told Brian sweetly.

"So I'm a bit confused. What has being fat got to do with anything?" Brian asked.

Sophie rolled her eyes. "Where did you get this one from Marie? He's a bit slow isn't he?"

"Sorry, I don't know who you are?" Jake said as he thrust his hand at Brian. "I'm Jake."

"I'm Brian," he replied and then turned to Sophie. "I gather you're Sophie." He sat on the end of the couch beside her.

Jake looked up at me. "Shall we get on with it then?"

"With what?" I was genuinely unsure.

"Fat club, of course. I thought we'd just do what we usually do. You're just going to have to be the Emily type person, you know? The leader."

I registered the amused look on Brian's face before he spluttered, "I'm sorry, did you just say 'fat club'?"

"Look, I'm sorry, Brian, but if you're the sort of person to insist on calling it *Emily's Encouragement*, then I think maybe you shouldn't be here. Especially since we're not even with Emily anymore. We're hardly going to say *Marie's Encouragement* are we?" Jake was quite firm on his point, having misunderstood Brian completely.

"No, I don't suppose you would," Brian mocked. "Just to clarify, though, is this 'fat club' anything at all like speed-dating?"

Sophie laughed loudly. "Oh God! Did she tell *you* that story too?" She rolled her eyes at me and mouthed, 'loser'. I realised that I should dislike her immensely but there was an innocence to her offensiveness that I found somehow endearing.

I decided to completely ignore the smug look on Brian's face and address the situation head on. "Right..." I started to pace the room as I spoke, "So correct me if I'm wrong, but you want to sit here and tell me how many fry-ups you've had this week? And we'll discuss how much weight you may or may not have lost? And all the while you'll throw insults at me and I'll throw death stares at you. Then we'll meditate for a while before you give me three quid and piss off home?"

"Wow! I really did miss out!" Brian laughed, seemingly unaware of Sophie who was inching closer to him, chest thrust outwards.

Jake looked at me uncomfortably "Well the thing is, Marie, I don't think you can really expect us to pay. You're not a professional after all, are you?"

I found it quite hard to comprehend that this was a real concern.

"He's got a point." Sophie joined in with the madness. "And, really, you do owe us, for getting us kicked out last week. We could be with Emily if it weren't for you."

Was this really happening to me? "But you didn't get kicked out. You left, by your own free will... and..."

Luckily, I was interrupted by the doorbell, because I wasn't sure what argument I could make that would make them see how ridiculous they were being.

As if things couldn't get any stranger, I was now faced with a crying Linda standing on my doorstep. I didn't say anything, just moved aside to let her in. She shuffled into the living room and Brian moved onto the arm of the couch to make room for her. Sophie looked like she might kill her.

She blew her nose noisily and continued to cry. Brian gave her a sympathetic pat on the shoulder and she gave him a look which seemed to say 'thank you,' and, 'who the heck are you?' all at once.

Finally, she managed to get herself under control and told us the problem. "She said that I was a trouble maker and told me that I wouldn't be allowed a turn to speak this week as a punishment for walking out last week." We all knew who 'she' was. Linda started to cry again and we waited patiently for her to finish the story. "So I sat there for a while, listening to her, and then I thought, if she's going to be mean I may as well just stay at home with George. I don't want to spend three pounds for her to be mean. So I just got up and left. But it was too early to go home so I came here." The crying started again.

I admitted defeat and plonked myself unceremoniously into the armchair. "Right then Jake, how many fry-ups this week?"

He looked at me suspiciously. "Are you going to charge me for this?"

"No, there'll be no charge until I've completed the appropriate training!" I grinned at him and he completely missed the mocking in my tone. I was willing time to speed up. Surely, if I just let them talk they'd leave. That was what I was hoping for anyway.

I thought I managed to guide my group through the hour without too many problems, only the debate about what constitutes a fry-up and what counts as half a fry-up (no eggs because he'd run out) got a little heated.

"You'd better be off then," I finally told them. "I've got to be up for work in the morning. I can't be partying with you lot all night." Brian chuckled, Sophie rolled her eyes and the other two missed the irony of my statement completely.

I was happily ushering them all out of the door when Sophie shouted, "See you all next week!"

Whoah! Wait a minute. "Next week? Here?" I asked in disbelief.

They all looked at me as if I was stupid. "The thing is I've got this work thing next week so that's not really going to be possible I'm afraid."

"You're a really crap liar you know," Sophie stated. "You just made that up because you don't want us coming round again. That's quite offensive you know?"

I tried to look outraged but I couldn't quite get it right. "See you next week Marie," Sophie said, grinning at me, and the three of them walked off to Linda's car before I could argue.

I sighed. "Cheeky little cow."

"Yeah! She's definitely feisty." Brian's voice came from behind me, making me jump. I'd forgotten about him.

"Interesting bunch of friends you've got there." Thankfully he had his jacket on and appeared to be leaving.

I laughed at his joke. "They're not my friends. At this point I'm more inclined to call than stalkers than anything."

"I like them," he mused as he walked past me and out the door. "See you next week then," he added casually. I laughed but he was already walking away down the road.

"You're joking right?" He turned and grinned at me. "Seriously? Joke right?" I asked louder as he got further away. He didn't reply, just carried on his way. It was definitely a joke though. Definitely.

Chapter 9

"Morning Anne!" I said cheerfully while I swapped brochures A1 and A2, the next morning.

"Marie, you barely even looked at them. How do you always see which ones I've moved so quickly?"

"It's a talent!" I said and sat down at my desk.

"You're very perky this morning! Did you make it to speed-dating last night?" Anne asked.

"No I didn't. I did have some friends over though. The ones I met last Thursday."

"Oh that's nice, Marie. You'll need friends around you once Grace leaves." Sometimes I think that she's in cahoots with the annoying goblin in my head. At least *she* says things with a happy voice. I was feeling quite up-beat though so I decided to let her words wash over me.

"Oh. Look who's here..." I saw Anne looking beyond me and out of the window onto the main shopping street. There were big posters in the shop window but through a gap I saw Sebastian walking past the shop. He stopped when he got to the door and pushed it open.

"Hello, my lovelies!" He beamed and then moved to air kiss Anne and I.

"Well this is a nice surprise!" I smiled at him. "Surely you don't need to book another holiday already do you? Of course if you do, your wish is my command!"

"Oh no, honey. I was just passing and I wondered if I could take my favourite travel agent out for a coffee? Just as a little 'thank you' for all your hard work. It would be okay with the boss if I steal you away for an hour wouldn't it?" He looked at Anne who blushed.

"Oh, I'm not the boss," she told him. "But I'm sure it would be okay. I can hold the fort!"

"Well, if the boss asks, just say that she's out schmoozing a very important customer!" Sebastian laughed at his own joke.

"I can work through my lunch, Anne," I put in.

"Yes, that's fine. You go and have fun."

I was retrieving my bag from under my desk when my phone rang and I answered it automatically.

"Brian! Hi, how are you?" I mouthed an apology to Sebastian who smiled and waited in the doorway.

"Hi, Marie. Just calling to say thanks for last night. It was fun."

"You're welcome. Sorry, Brian, this is kind of a bad time. Can I call you back later?"

"Oh sure. Quick question though - I've managed to tie Grace down to lunch today. She's becoming a difficult one to keep track of with all this moving stuff and trying to tie up loose ends at work. Anyway, I wondered if you wanted to join us?"

I groaned and bit my lip. "I'd love to Brian, but today doesn't work. I'm just nipping out now so I've got to work through my lunch break. Bad timing I'm afraid. I'm having trouble tracking Grace down too. I'd have loved to have lunch with you."

"Not to worry. We'll try again next week shall we?"

"Yeah, that would be great. Sorry, I really have to go." I looked at Sebastian who was beginning to look impatient in the doorway.

"OK, Marie. I'll catch up with you soon."

"Yeah. Thanks for the invite." As I hung up I felt a pang of jealousy at the thought of Brian spending time with Grace. I focused on Sebastian and the possibilities which lay in this new friendship. "Let's get going then shall we?" I grinned at him as he held the door open for me. He pulled my arm through his as we walked to the nearest coffee shop.

Sebastian ran a finger through the foam of his latte macchiato as I sipped at my Chai tea. The coffee shop was modern and generic and we were seated on a low couch at the back of the shop.

"So what made you want to be a travel agent?" Sebastian asked me.

I tried to think of an appropriate response to the question which I didn't know the answer to.

Sebastian obviously took my thoughtfulness as a sign that I wanted him to guess and here's what he came up with. "You must have travelled a lot as a child, I suppose? I always think that one of the best gifts a parent can give is a lust for travel. I have to say, I was the same. At the time I just saw it as being dragged to all sorts of places that I didn't want to go to, but as I got older I appreciated the experiences I'd had. So what is it that your parents do?" He finally asked.

"My mum is a... flight attendant," I replied

hesitantly, slightly surprised by the words that came out of my mouth.

"Oh, goodness. Don't tell me - your father must be a pilot, right?"

"Got it in one!" I replied with a nervous laugh.

"How very romantic!" he mused. "Do they still work? Or are they retired?"

"Mum's retired. Dad still works. He's always off somewhere. It's hard to keep track!" I was fairly shocked by my own lies here. I just couldn't bring myself to say that I don't know my father; and my mum has a part time job walking dogs.

"So travel really is in your blood then. How fascinating."

"So what is it that you do?" I asked in return, desperate to put a stop to my lying spree.

"Oh, art is my business." He flicked his hand as if to indicate it's not worth talking about. "You might say that's in my blood too. My father got me into it. We have our own gallery now - *Featherston and Son*."

"Oh that's exciting. So are you an artist yourself?"

"No darling. We buy and sell. Do some exhibitions, that sort of thing. It can be terribly dull. Art dealers, you'd call us."

"It sounds fascinating. I find art so intriguing." I didn't really, but it seemed a fitting thing to say.

"Don't get me talking about it, Marie. I'll bore you to death!" He laughed.

"I'm sure you won't. Come on, tell me about your favourite works of art."

"Okay, go on then..." He chuckled and proceeded to describe several pieces of art in great detail while I tried desperately to look interested.

I got to the bottom of my drink and checked my watch, "Sebastian, this has been lovely but I really must get back to work."

"I'm sorry, I kept you too long. I hope you won't get into trouble because of me."

"Not at all. It's fine. I'm sure the place won't fall apart without me for an hour."

"Come on then. I'll escort you back as long as you promise that we can do this again sometime?"

"That would be lovely," I replied as we made our way out of the coffee shop and back to work.

I worked through my lunch break as promised and tried not to dwell on the fact that Grace and Brian were out having fun without me. I thought about the weekend ahead and wondered how I would fill the hours. Anne had nipped out to the chemist on her lunch break so I was alone in the shop when my phone rang and I saw Carl's number flashing up on the caller ID. I had a weird sensation of going back in time. Carl used to ring me at work all the time. It was always such a natural sight to see his number come up. Now it made my heart race. What was he ringing for?

"Hello?" I answered cautiously.

"Hey! Marie! How are you?"

"Fine. Thanks. How are you?"

"I'm good, same old same old, you know? Not much happening really. What about you? Anything new going on?"

This was weird. The last time we spoke I was shouting abuse at him as he tried to cover himself up with the bed covers. Some blonde woman was lying

113

next to him looking not quite awkward enough. We'd been together for two years and he'd not even had the decency to call me after.

"Sorry, Carl, can I help you with something?" I couldn't deal with the chit-chat.

"I just got to thinking about you, after I saw you out the other weekend, and I just thought it would be nice to catch up. Maybe we could go for a drink sometime?"

I couldn't believe he could be so flippant and I was suddenly angry with him. "Have you forgotten that you cheated on me? That I actually found you in bed with another woman? I haven't heard from you since and now you want to go for a drink?"

"Well, I just thought that was water under the bridge now. I know you were probably a bit mad at me, but I think we had a really good time together for two years and you can't just forget that because of one incident, can you?"

"What? One incident? It wasn't that you forgot to take the rubbish out; you SLEPT with someone else! You completely betrayed my trust and you really hurt me. Why can't you see that?"

"Marie, it was one mistake." He sounded exasperated and I hated him for it.

"Goodbye, Carl." I slammed the phone down and felt my body fill with rage. How can a two-year relationship just end overnight? Why was I ever with him in the first place? And how can someone who claimed to love me hurt me so much?

I picked the phone up again to call Grace but it went straight to voicemail. I'd try her again later.

I tried to get lost in my work for the rest of the

afternoon. I was thankful at least that Anne hadn't been present to overhear my conversation with Carl. There was a steady stream of customers throughout the afternoon so I managed to keep my mind off him.

I tried calling Grace again on my way home but I still couldn't get her. I got home and decided to hop in the shower. Maybe I could wash all the problems away. I heard my mobile ringing as the water ran over me. Typical! It would be Grace calling me back. I knew I'd feel better if I talked to her about Carl's phone call. I really needed a sympathetic ear.

I was wrapped in my bathrobe when I picked up the phone to call her back. I perched on my bed while it rang and rang. I'd just decided that we'd missed each other again when a male voice answered.

"Hello. Grace-the-slave-driver's phone!"

"Hello?" I asked confused.

"Marie?"

"Oh! Hi, Brian. What are you doing with Grace's phone?" I asked.

"I'm at James's place helping them lug some boxes around. Got roped into it over lunch." He sounded out-of-breath. "Anyway, Grace just this minute left with James to drive a load of boxes to his parents place for storage. She must have forgotten her phone."

"Oh, right." I was strangely jealous of Brian being included in their plans. I could have helped carry boxes too.

"I'm all finished here now. I was just about to leave if you were looking for company?"

I hesitated, wondering if Brian was also on 'look out for Marie because she's having a hard time' duty. I hated being a charity case.

"I could murder a beer if you have any?" he prompted.

"Yeah, sure." The words were out before I could think it through properly.

"Great. Won't be long."

After I hung up I sat on the bed for a few minutes feeling confused. I wasn't sure an evening with Brian was really what I needed. I barely even knew the guy. It was probably better than sitting alone feeling sorry for myself though.

"Hi. Sorry, I was longer than I thought, but I decided to take the car home first so that I didn't have to worry about drinking." Brian arrived with a six-pack of beers under his arm and gave me a quick kiss on the cheek as he moved past me.

"Did you come on your bike then?" I asked.

"No." He smiled and I thought for a minute that he was going to bring up the hitch-biking incident and have a good laugh. He didn't though. "I got the bus. Biking is far too exerting for me. I know it's eco-friendly and all that, but I see people on bikes in the middle of town and I think they must have a death wish. The roads really aren't designed with cyclists in mind."

That was strange. The way he was talking it sounded like he didn't even own a bike. I was starting to feel like I dreamt the biking episode. Part of me wanted to bring it up, but what if it wasn't him? Maybe he has a double.

Brian made himself at home, handing me a beer before putting the rest in the fridge. We settled down side by side on the couch.

"So how were things at James's place?" I asked.

"Chaotic. There's still a lot of stuff to be moved out. He's trying to figure out what to hold on to and what to sell. I guess it's difficult when they don't really know if they'll be back after a year or if it's going to turn out to be longer. It was a strange feeling helping them move stuff though. I suppose it made me realise they really are moving."

"Yeah. I'm not sure it's properly sunk in for me yet. Grace has always been close by, since school. It's going to be strange to think she's in a completely different country."

"Work is going to be very boring without Grace around," he said.

A silence settled over us and I think I would have been less depressed on my own. Big help Brian was!

"Come on. You're supposed to be cheering me up not making things worse," I told him, jokingly.

He took a swig of his beer and smiled at me. "Sorry, I didn't realise that was my purpose! I can give it a try though. So what's bothering you? Grace leaving? Or something else?"

Carl flashed into my head and I wished I was with Grace so I could replay it all with her. There was no way I could talk to Brian about my ex-boyfriend.

"Okay. So I take it from the hesitation that it's something else." Brian turned his body to face me. "Come on, tell Uncle Brian..."

I laughed at him but said nothing. "Is it work related?" he asked.

"Nope."

"Family?"

"Nope." No more than usual anyway.

"It must be a man then?" He raised his eyebrows. "I'm right aren't I? Come on, just pretend I'm Grace and tell me all about it. We can have a good bitch session and you'll feel better!"

"My ex-boyfriend called me at work today." The words flowed out of my mouth before I knew it.

"How 'ex' is he?" Brian prompted.

"We split up about two months ago."

"Because?"

"I found him in bed with another woman." Saying it to Brian made me want to cry. I felt like such a fool. I didn't want Brian to think that I was worthless; that's how I'd felt after Carl cheated on me.

"Woah..." Brian sank back into the couch while exhaling a long breath.

"Anyway, I've not heard from him since, but a couple of weeks ago I saw him in a club and he just waved like nothing had happened. Then he rang today to see if we could go out for a drink. Again, it was like nothing had happened." Brian looked at me sympathetically and I carried on. "I'm so angry at him because he's put me through so much, but apparently the break-up hasn't affected him at all. He just nudged me out of his life and moved on like two years together meant nothing." I took a breath and swigged my beer and then leaned back into the couch. I looked up at the ceiling and hoped I wasn't going to cry. Why did I just tell Brian all that?

"Okay. So I see why you need cheering up. He sounds like a complete idiot."

"Yes, I think so!" I laughed.

"So, see it this way. You must be better off without him and at least you weren't married by the time you saw his true colours."

"Talking from experience, are you Brian?" I laughed but his face stayed serious. "Sorry." I back-tracked. "Did that happen to you?"

He smiled at me. "Almost. We weren't married. Not quite. But we were engaged, and we'd been looking at houses. As far as I could see, we were going to get married and have kids and live happily ever after."

"What happened?"

"It turned out she'd been seeing someone else. She said that nothing had happened and they were just friends, but being around him made her see that she wanted more. He was some hot-shot businessman living a five-star lifestyle and she wanted in on it." Brian laughed. "The stupid thing is that financially we were okay, but I think she was just attracted to money and power. She never really liked the fact that I wasn't ambitious and power hungry."

"How did you deal with it?" I asked.

He grinned at me mischievously. "I threw myself into my job; became ambitious and power hungry!"

"Seriously?"

"Yep. Not intentionally, but work took my mind off my heartbreak, and since there was nothing to rush home from work for anymore, I worked as much as possible, and when I finally came up for air, I'd turned into exactly what she wanted me to be. I can see the funny side of that now. I can also see that I was lucky that I realised what she was really like before we got married and had kids. It could have been much worse further down the line."

"Okay, so at least I'm not the only person in the

world to get screwed over. That's good to know."

"I'm really glad my heartbreak is useful to you," he said with a laugh. "Here's to getting cheated on." He raised his beer bottle to mine.

I was surprised at how relaxed I became as the evening wore on. I was starting to see what Grace saw. Brian was a nice guy. He was funny and good company. We finished the beers and drank another round before I wished Brian goodnight and closed the door behind him. Maybe it was the beer, or maybe it was Brain's calming effect, but as I got in bed I felt quite content with the world, and sleep arrived without the tossing and turning that had become the norm.

Chapter 10

"They just turned up at the door?" Grace was laughing as I topped up her glass of wine. It was the first time I'd seen her for a proper chat in a couple of weeks but now I had her all to myself for the evening, and was trying to fill her in on what she'd missed. She found my life very amusing as always.

"Yes, they said they were going to have 'fat club' here, and they're not the sort of people you can argue with. I don't know how to get them to stop though. They turned up again last night and it was chaos." I stopped and took a swig of wine.

"Don't stop! What happened last night?" she asked.

"Well, they all arrived and it was okay for about ten minutes but then things just got a bit out of control. You see, Jake, the chubby guy, he had decided to bring a selection of snacks for us to share - crisps and chocolates. I actually thought it was a nice sentiment but Linda started to cry, saying he was making a mockery of the meetings. Linda's older, and seems to be a bit of an emotional wreck most of the time. Anyway then Sophie - she's the young, feisty one - she got angry with Jake for making Linda cry and attacked him with a tube of *Pringles*. Jake got mad and stormed out and Sophie and Linda left not long after him."

"You're not serious?" Grace was going red with laughter. "They sound like a real bunch of crazies!"

"They are. Definitely," I agreed. "It was okay though because Jake left his goodies behind so Brian and I had a lovely feast!"

"Brian? Who's Brian?"

"Your Brian! I didn't tell you that bit, did I? Brian happened to be here the first week when they all turned up and then he came last night too. It's nice to have one other sane person in the room."

Grace's face turned serious and her hands shot up to cover her mouth.

"What?" I demanded.

I saw her trying to hide her smile. "He fancies you!"

"Brian? Get lost!"

"Oh, come on. Why else would he hang out with a load of oddballs? He must fancy you."

"No way," I said adamantly.

"Seriously, why does he turn up then?" she challenged.

"Probably for the same reason as the rest of us... because he's worried about his weight!" We fell about laughing and when we calmed down I noticed the bottle of wine was almost empty. "I'll grab another bottle," I said, and it crossed my mind that there probably wouldn't be many more evenings like this. I pushed the thought to a dark corner of my mind, not wanting to dampen the mood.

"Well I'm happy that you're meeting new people. I'll feel better moving away knowing that you have friends around you." Grace smiled thoughtfully as I refilled our glasses.

I laughed. "Grace, I think you should be more worried if anything. They are probably a bunch of sociopaths. Anyway, I did meet someone new... this guy from work, Sebastian. I've been booking his holidays for a year or so and he finally came into the shop to meet me in person."

"But you know what they say. Never mix business with pleasure."

"I think I'll ignore that rule. Actually he called by the shop again one morning and insisted on taking me for a coffee. I think we really hit it off and he's such an interesting guy. He owns an art gallery and the way he talks about art is just mesmerising."

"An arty person? He doesn't really sound your type."

"Oh it's nothing romantic or anything. In fact he's gay - very gay! I just think he could be an interesting friend to have. He seems like the sort of person to have loads of friends and I really need to meet some new people."

"Yeah. I suppose you've got a point. Are you seeing him again?" she asked.

"He was a bit vague but he said he'd be in touch. He said he'd show me his art gallery sometime."

"I'm glad you're spending time with Brian," she said wistfully. "He's a good guy." She looked at me with a cheeky half-smile and I recognised a hint of matchmaker in her voice.

I shrugged and she laughed at me. "You'll see."

"Don't be such a know-it-all. It doesn't suit you."

"Fine. I'll shut up." She made a zipping motion across her mouth and I couldn't help but laugh at her.

"There is one thing I wanted to ask you about Brian

though," I began. "I was wondering, and don't ask me why, but does he do any sports? Biking maybe?"

Grace laughed. "Are you serious? Brian on a bike? That would be a sight! No I don't think he has a sporty bone in his body. Mind you he does always look good, but he somehow manages to stay in shape without doing any exercise. I asked him about it once and he said he was allergic to exercise! Why on earth would you ask that?"

"No reason really. Just something that he said. It's not important. Tell me how the New York plans are going," I said, changing the subject, "Not that I really want to hear."

"You're such a supportive friend!" We were both laughing and I realised we were both a bit drunk.

"Everything is pretty hectic," she told me, calming down and placing her wine glass on the table in front of her. "I need to pack up here next, then you can move out of the box room. I'll be glad, in a way, when we're all moved, so that I can get back to a normal routine. You'll come to visit me, won't you?"

"Of course I will. Happy to finally use some of my holiday time."

We chatted about all the things we'd do in New York and it was when I was lying in bed later, watching the ceiling spin, that I realised how jealous I was of her big adventure. In just over a week she'd be gone, and I'd be left alone.

I woke to the smell of bacon and followed it to the kitchen to find James standing in front of the stove. "Morning," he said, beaming at me. "I'm on domestic duties this morning, Marie, so just put your order in!"

"A bacon sandwich would be great thanks."

"Coming right up!"

I wandered into the living room and found Grace standing in the middle of it looking thoughtful. "What's up?" I asked.

"Nothing." She turned to me. "I was just wondering if there is anything in here that I need to take, but I realised that there isn't much in here."

I looked around the room and realised that she was right. There was a TV in the corner with a DVD player under it, then the couch opposite that and the arm chair and coffee table.

"Do you remember when I first bought the place and we had to strip that naff green wallpaper?" Grace asked me.

"How could I forget?" I looked at my hands. "I think I have scars to prove it. That stuff really didn't want to come off. Then there was our ever-so-precise paint job!" I laughed.

"There's still a splodge of yellow down the window frame here." Grace moved to trace her finger over it.

"And some on the carpet in that corner," I said. "That one was my fault."

"You kicked over the whole tin of paint and it went everywhere and managed to find its way under the cover sheets."

"It would never have happened if you hadn't left the paint tin in my way!" I protested.

"That was your excuse! I remember now," she teased.

"Two bacon sandwiches, as requested." James interrupted us and deposited breakfast on the coffee table before heading back to the kitchen.

"You know you can change things if you want..." Grace said as I took my first delicious mouthful of my sandwich. "Make the place a bit more you. Re-paint, if you want..."

I laughed through my mouthful of bacon. "I did a bad enough job when I had you to supervise me! I think the place will stay as it is. Thanks though."

Grace looked at me between mouthfuls of her sandwich. "Did I mention that work have organised a leaving party for us on the Friday night before we leave? That's a week on Friday..." She kept reminding me when they were leaving as though I didn't have it ingrained on my memory. I was on the countdown enough already.

"Will you come too?" She asked. It didn't really sound like the way I wanted to say goodbye to her, surrounded by all her colleagues and lots of people I don't know.

"Any chance we could do something a bit quieter?" I asked.

I could see her mind trawling through her hectic schedule, trying to find a space for me. "How about the Saturday before we leave? We could have a quiet drink in the afternoon? I'd have James with me too, as we're having lunch with his parents, but that's okay isn't it?"

"Sounds great... as long as it won't mean that you're rushing around too much?"

"No. It's perfect," she reassured me. "How about I invite Brian along too?"

"Fine by me."

"Great, that's set then." She smiled at me as she jumped up. "Okay I've got work to do!" She headed upstairs and into her bedroom to let the packing commence. I decided to nip into town. I had a feeling it was all going to get too emotional for me and I had been wanting to get Grace a little going away gift, although I had no idea what.

I wandered around town for a few hours and even stopped to wave at Anne and Greg as I walked past work. I was glad they were happy to work Saturdays because the idea of it did nothing for me. It was a short day. The place only opened from 11am until 5pm but I was glad that I didn't have to work it. Greg came out of his office to take my place out front on Saturdays. In theory I was supposed to work occasional Saturdays but I had nice co-workers who were happy to take extra time off during the week instead. I saw Anne's daughter, Millie, swivelling on my chair before she stopped to wave at me.

In the end I went home empty-handed and arrived just in time to help Grace move a few bags up to the attic, before we ordered pizzas for dinner.

I left Grace to finish packing the following morning and headed over to my mum's house. Aunt Kath couldn't make it due to a nasty cold so it was just me and Mum for once. I told her that I'd already eaten to avoid having to eat leftover lasagne with her. It sounds fine but I know from experience that there will be sardines lurking in there somewhere.

I dutifully watched *Midsummer Murders* with her and told her about work and Grace getting ready for the move.

"Oh, I have a present for her!" Mum suddenly remembered and dashed out of the room. She was doing better than me then.

She re-appeared with a hand-knitted cushion with a wobbly blue 'G' set against a green background. I say it's a hand-knitted cushion but that's not technically true. It's a cheap shop-bought cushion with a knitted square sewn onto the front of it. The same as the other twenty or so which live in bin bags in my bedroom stuffed between the wardrobe and the wall.

I was thankful that the house was quiet when I got home. I presumed Grace and James had gone out so I went straight upstairs and pulled a bin bag out from next to my wardrobe, intent on adding Grace's to it.

"Hi!" Grace's voice made me jump and I turned to find her standing in the doorway.

"I thought you'd gone out," I told her.

"No, still packing. James took some stuff to a charity shop. What are you doing?" She moved closer to me. "Did your mum give you another cushion?" she asked.

"Kind of," I said. "Actually it's for you." I held it up to reveal her initial on the front of it.

"That's so sweet! What are you doing with it?" she asked me suspiciously.

"I was just going to keep it in here. You won't want to take it all the way to America with you, will you?"

"Of course I will," she corrected me as she took it from me and hugged it to her. "Your mum is so sweet. I don't know why you hide all those away up here." She indicated the bin bag in my hand.

"What else would I do with them? They're so ugly."

"I think they're homely. I'll have it in my new apartment and every time I look at it I'll think of your mum. It's so nice of her."

Grace went back to her room and I shoved the bag of cushions back where they were. That girl was too nice. She made me feel like a horrible person.

The cushions really are ugly though.

Hannah Ellis

Chapter 11

It was week three of hosting 'fat club' and Brian had just arrived. Grace was out with friends for the evening so she avoided having to meet everyone, even though she said she was dying to.

Brian was in the kitchen helping himself to a drink when the doorbell rang. I sighed and went to let them in. Brian always arrived alone but the other three always turned up together. They were a bit late this evening and I was a bit annoyed about it, although I couldn't quite put my finger on why. I started to wonder if they had decided not to come, in the wake of last week's argument over snacks, and I had mixed feelings about the thought of them not turning up.

I was surprisingly relieved when the doorbell rang.

"I thought you weren't coming," I said as I opened the door. Sophie and Jake looked back at me straight-faced.

"There's a problem," Jake announced solemnly.

"It's Linda," Sophie said as they walked past me. They looked relieved at the sight of Brian.

"We think something has happened to Linda," Jake blurted, taking a seat on the couch.

Sophie hovered in what was becoming her usual manner; waiting to see where Brian would sit before she took a seat. Brian sat on the armchair and Sophie then sat on the arm and dangled her feet in his lap. In fairness to him, he completely ignored her. I found it very off-putting though.

"So what seems to be the problem?" Brian asked as I took a seat next to Jake.

"She didn't turn up!" Sophie said excitedly. "We waited ages. Usually she's there before us."

"Turn up where exactly?" I asked, confused.

"At the hotel." Sophie looked at me like I was stupid and I wondered what it was that I was missing. "You know? At *Emily's Encouragement*? We always meet there and then Linda drives us here."

"But why do you meet there?" I asked.

"Where should we meet?" Jake asked and I noticed Brian smiling to himself in the armchair. He never helped me out when they got like this.

"Well if you make your own way to the hotel then you may as well just make your own way here hadn't you?" Jake looked like he should have thought of that before. "I just always thought that Linda picked you up to drive you here," I told them.

"She does pick us up." Sophie looked confused.

"Yes, but I thought she picked you up from home not from the hotel!" I said, exasperated.

Jake shook his head. "Oh, no."

Sophie laughed. "Don't be stupid! Then we'd have to tell her where we lived. I don't want all you lot knowing where I live." She had a very good point there.

"But... when we first met, Linda drove us all home..." I reminded them.

"No." Jake said as if this was all obvious. "I just told her an address in the same area as me and then walked the rest. I didn't know her from Adam. I wasn't going to give her my address."

"Same here," Sophie said. "What kind of idiots do you think we are?"

Brian cleared his throat, seemingly to hide his laughter. "Yeah, Marie," he echoed Sophie. "What kind of an idiot tells strangers where they live? That's asking for all sorts of trouble, isn't it?"

I looked around the room and sighed. They were definitely right. I should never have given them my address.

"Anyway, what's this got to do with anything?" Jake sounded impatient. "Linda is missing! What should we do? We need a plan."

"Do you think her husband has killed her?" Sophie asked with wide eyes. "She's always making comments about him and he sounds horrible. People are always getting killed by their partners you know."

"Well not *always,* Sophie," I tried to reason.

"They are though," she said matter-of-factly.

"How many people do you know who have killed or been killed by their partner?" I don't know why I always let her drag me to her level but I just couldn't help it.

"Obviously I don't know any. Why would I be friends with people like that? I see it on the news though and the news isn't just made up, is it?" she snapped at me, making me want to scream at her and shake her all at once.

I admitted defeat in the ridiculous argument. "Fine. I'm just saying I don't think that she's been murdered by her husband."

"You don't know that though, do you?" Sophie

fired at me. I took a deep breath and ignored her.

"She might be ill," I suggested. "Or she had something else on tonight. I'm sure she's fine."

"What if she had a car crash on the way?" Sophie changed tack. "Maybe we should split up and go looking for her..." I was fairly sure I knew what's coming next. "I can go with Brian. Marie, you go with Jake, and we'll see if we can find her." I thought so.

"I don't think that's a very good idea, Sophie." Jake said thoughtfully. "I actually don't think there's much we can do. What do you think, Brian?"

"My guess would be that she's sick. I'm sure she'll be back next week. I wouldn't worry too much."

"You're probably right," Jake said.

"She's probably got flu or something," Sophie decided. I thought I might be going mad because I was fairly sure that I'd just suggested this and everyone ignored me. 'Mr Perfect' says it and suddenly it's gospel.

"So, shall we carry on as usual or should we leave it this week?" Jake asked.

"Actually, after all this shock, I feel done in. I just need to go home I think." Sophie was up to something, I would bet my life on it. "I'm a bit nervous getting home on my own after dark though... do you think you could see me home, Brian?" Subtlety really isn't her strong point.

"I thought you didn't want anyone knowing where you lived?" I smiled at her and she sneered in reply.

"Normally I would," Brian said. "But I'm meeting someone in town." I almost felt sorry for Sophie; she looked like she'd been slapped in the face.

"I'll make sure you get home safely," Jake told her

kindly. I think he'd probably missed her motives, bless him.

They put their coats on and moved towards the door. "Is it like a date?" Sophie looked at Brian and I felt a bit sorry for her.

"Yeah," Brian told her, flatly.

"Oh right, okay. See you next week," Sophie replied weakly and moved through the doorway. "Have fun!" Jake called cheerfully to Brian as he followed her.

"Well that was an interesting one," Brian said, moving to sit next to me on the couch. "You really never can tell what's going to happen on a Thursday, can you? They crack me up."

"Why do you let me get caught up in their stupid little discussions and never back me up?" I asked.

"It's too much fun," he said. "You got any beer? I'm parched."

"There should be some in the kitchen," I told him and he headed off to look. I always thought Thursdays would be much more fun if we brought alcohol into the equation but I was fairly sure Linda would veto it in the same way she vetoed snacks.

"I thought you had a date?" I asked as Brian handed me a beer.

"Oh, yeah…that. I hope Sophie gets home safely or the guilt will haunt me forever."

"So you just made that up?" I was quite impressed actually. "I wish I could lie that well."

"It's a skill I've developed over the years. It comes in handy sometimes. Anyway the alternative was that I walk her home and I think I know how that would end up."

135

"Go on," I prompted.

"Well I imagine she would try something. I would reject her and she would get revenge by claiming sexual assault."

I smiled. "You could be right there."

"Or she sexually assaults me and I spend the rest of my life in therapy." We laughed and took swigs of our beers. "She is quite scary sometimes," Brian went on. "She's good fun though... and so full of energy. I really like that about her. But, yeah, she definitely scares me quite a lot." He grinned.

"So you're not attracted to her at all?" I asked.

"God, no!" He looked shocked at my suggestion. "She's a kid."

I smiled, happy at his answer.

We chatted companionably for about an hour, mainly discussing the 'fat club' and the personalities within it. It was good fun until somewhere towards the end of the second beer when Brian changed the subject.

"So this is our last full weekend with Grace in the country. I can't believe she's leaving so soon. It's come around so quick hasn't it?" I wished he'd stop talking about it. I was sick of hearing about it. All I wanted to do was pretend that nothing was happening. He carried on though. "It's going to be weird without her around, even though I don't see much of her these days. It's not going to be half as much fun making prank phone calls when she's all the way over in New York. I might have to phone and annoy you instead."

"Thanks but I think you do enough of that already," I said.

"I suppose we can always fly over and visit her,"

Brian suggested. "Anyway, I'll stop talking about Grace leaving, I'm probably depressing you and..." he checked his watch, "...probably keeping you from your bed." He stood up and put his coat on.

As much as I wanted to bury my head in the sand about it, I knew that Brian was right. I was going to miss Grace so much. The same selfish thoughts niggled me again. I couldn't help feeling that she was leaving me behind. She was starting a whole new chapter of her life and I was being left behind.

Chapter 12

I'd not slept well after Brian got me into turmoil about Grace leaving, so the last thing I wanted when I dragged myself into work on Friday morning was Anne being overly excited and annoyingly cheerful.

"You look tired Marie. I'll get you a coffee. What was it? Were you up late with your new pals last night?"

"No, not really. I just didn't sleep well."

She tutted. "A good night's sleep is so important you know. Anyway..." she flittered over to me with a coffee and then took up position, perching on the edge of my desk. This meant she had something important to tell me. "You're not going to believe what I did last night!" She was so excited she looked like she might burst.

"Tell me then..." I was unenthusiastic as I took a sip of coffee.

"Well, I was thinking about you and how you've made all these new friends by joining a club and I thought, you're never too old to make new friends and it might be nice to join a club of some sort. They do say 'variety is the spice of life', don't they?" I was slightly perturbed by her take on my recent social activities but I couldn't correct her even if I wanted to; she was like a runaway train. "So I was having a flick through the yellow pages to see what I could find and out jumped an advert for *Emily's Encouragement*!" She stopped and studied my reaction.

"Oh, no," I groaned. "You didn't?"

"I did! I thought that if it's good enough for my friend Marie then it's good enough for yours truly!" I wondered whether I should point out that it wasn't good enough for me and that I actually got up and walked out? Probably better not.

"Oh, Marie! I had a great time. Well there were a couple of minor incidents, like when I first got there, the young man on reception accidentally pointed me in the wrong direction and you'll never guess where I ended up?" I think I probably could.

"Only in speed dating! Can you imagine it? Me at speed dating?" Strangely enough I could completely imagine it and I'm not sure how it would go down with the young guys who had turned up in hope of an easy lay.

She continued on. "Well, imagine how David would feel if he thought his wife was out 'dating'!" I had a sneaky suspicion that David wouldn't be overly concerned. "So I had to go back to reception and start again. Then I got the right room and I told Emily that I was there on your recommendation... well that was a mistake! Your name is mud in that place." She laughed and I was actually quite entertained. For once she was managing to lift my spirits.

"Anyway, I quickly explained that you're just a work colleague and not actually a friend at all..."

"Gee thanks a lot Anne!" I said but all I got was a 'don't be daft' slap on the arm and she carried on with the story.

"After that it turned into a lovely evening. Mostly we just talked about food, but I also learnt to meditate, Marie. Now that was fun. And I met this lovely lady called Linda. She was very sweet."

I was shocked. "Linda's been at fatties?"

"Marie, please. That's very disrespectful. It's *Emily's Encouragement*. Don't call it fatties!" She tutted and moved back to her desk. "You know Linda then, do you?" she asked.

"Yes, of course. She's in my gang." I sounded like a school kid, but that's honestly how I felt. How could she have gone back to Emily? I felt betrayed. Why on earth had she gone back to Emily?

It played on my mind all morning. I was quite angry with Linda, I decided. Not only had she ditched us for Emily but she'd let us all worry about her. Poor Sophie didn't even know if she was dead or alive! I had a sudden urge to call Sophie before I remembered I didn't know her number. I picked up my phone and called Brian instead.

"I found out what happened to Linda," I told him after a quick greeting. "She went back to Emily!"

"She did what?" he asked, confused.

"Went back to *Emily's Encouragement*. You know - the original meeting. At the hotel."

"Oh, right." He paused. "I'm a bit offended."

"Me too! I can't believe she left us to go back to that dragon!"

Brian laughed. "Is she really that bad?"

"She's just weird really. Anyway, you'll probably find out for yourself because if Linda doesn't turn up again next week then I vote we go and find her!"

Now he really laughed. "A field trip? I can't wait!"

The weekend was pretty much a repeat of the one before. Grace and James were around the house, packing up the rest of their stuff. Boxing some things up to be shipped to America; putting some into storage in the attic or at James's parents place; and the rest being carted off to charity shops. It was depressing watching all her stuff being taken away or hidden up in the attic but I was trying to stay positive. At least I was looking forward to fat club on Thursday.

When it finally came around, Brian and I were waiting eagerly in the living room when the doorbell rang and I opened the door to the sombre expressions of Jake and Sophie.

"He's definitely killed her," Sophie informed me. "I think it's time to call the police."

They moved to go past me but I stopped them. "It's okay. We know where she is," I told them. "We're going to go and get her back!" I grabbed my coat from the rack and they both looked confused when I turned back to them. "She's gone back to Emily, that's all."

They actually looked more devastated now than when they thought she'd been killed by her husband. "Come on!" I said. "Let's go get her..."

I was all fired up on the way over there. I had a definite sense of purpose and was ready to fight for my cause; the cause being Linda, of course. The four of us chatted excitedly as we sat in Brian's car and made our way over to the hotel. It was only once we were at the hotel and marching up the stairs, that I started to think that it was all a bit ridiculous.

Seriously, what was I doing? How had my life come to this? Mostly, I just started to realise that Linda is a grown woman and if she didn't want to hang out with us anymore then she really didn't have to. Although I was fairly sure we were about to prove that statement wrong.

I was expecting to walk into a scene of quiet meditation, however what I found was not entirely dissimilar to my working day. Anne was standing in the middle of the group – the rest sitting around her on their cushions – clearly deep in the middle of one of her stories. The rest of them sat looking completely bored. Emily was opening and closing her mouth like a goldfish, obviously trying very hard to get a word in. I suspected she wasn't overly thrilled with the latest addition to her group.

Linda looked up at us and then quickly cast her eyes downwards. I cleared my throat loudly as I moved further into the room. Everyone looked at us except Anne who kept on speaking. "Sorry, Anne! Excuse us." She stopped talking and looked over at us.

"Hi, Marie!" She sounded happy to see me which earned her one of those ridiculous death stares from Emily. It was completely lost on Anne.

"Can I help you?" Emily said angrily.

"No, not really. We've just come for Linda," I replied. Linda looked from me to Emily.

"We're in the middle of a session here," Emily growled. "You can't just come barging in and interrupt us. I suggest you wait outside, until the group is finished, if you'd like to see Linda."

"I suggest you shut your big fat mouth!" Sophie yelled. "Linda, let's go!"

I put my hand on Sophie's arm to stop her when she moved forward. I was slightly concerned that she might move in for a punch up with Emily.

"You all need to leave now or I'll call security," Emily warned, getting to her feet. I glanced over my shoulder and Brian gave me a wink. He seemed to be enjoying the show.

"I don't really think there's any need for that," Anne piped up. I wasn't too concerned by the threat anyway, mainly because I wasn't convinced that the hotel had security.

"We've not come to cause trouble," I said, trying to ease some of the tension in the room. "We were just worried about Linda that's all. We'll go now. Linda, do you want to come with us?"

Linda nodded and moved to get up from her cushion. "No!" Emily screeched. "Linda, stay where you are. You're not going anywhere!"

"She can go wherever she likes actually," Jake calmly told Emily while he walked over to give Linda a hand up.

"Fine! but you can't leave without paying the fee," Emily demanded, obviously realising that she was losing the battle for Linda.

We watched while Linda drew her purse out of her handbag. She started to pull out some money and then paused and looked around at us. Finally she looked Emily right in the eye and said, "No. I'm not paying."

"It's not optional, Linda. You have to pay!"

"But I only came and sat on a cushion and listened to Anne talk for ten minutes. Why should I pay for

144

that?" she asked flatly, putting her purse away and linking her arm through Jake's. "Goodbye, Emily," she said as she headed for the door, side by side with Jake. Anne and I exchanged a smile and a wave as we left.

We regrouped in the car park and laughed about Emily and our invasion.

"I hope you're not all mad at me," Linda said, sheepishly. "George started asking all these questions about my nights at Emily's and I felt like he knew that I'd not been going and I felt so guilty. I wanted to come to Marie's house but I was scared that George might check up on me."

"Next time you abandon us it better be because he's got you locked you up or something and not because you've gone back to her again," Sophie told Linda.

"I can see why you all go to Marie's place now," Brian spoke up. "That woman's awful!"

"Speaking of Marie's place, shall we go back for a quick coffee?" Jake suggested. "I actually had something I wanted to talk to you all about." Linda looked nervously at her watch. "Yes, okay. Just a quick one then."

"I wonder what Jake wants to talk about," Sophie mused as we sat in Brian's car on the way back to my place. Jake had gone with Linda in her car.

"Did you notice he had a shopping bag with him?" Brian said.

"I hope he's not going to try and introduce snacks again," I said.

We were settled in my living room when the contents of Jake's shopping bag were finally revealed. "I've been doing some thinking about my life," he told us. "And I've decided that I need to make some changes ... so I bought these..." He pulled out a set of bathroom scales from the bag.

"So you actually want to lose weight?" Sophie asked seriously.

"Yes, I do. I want to make some changes in my life. I'm only thirty-eight but I've let myself go a bit. And I suppose I should really think a bit more about my health. I think I could be an alright catch, you know... if I lost a bit of weight and made some effort."

It was one of the first times I'd heard Jake sound genuine about anything. He seemed almost vulnerable.

"It might be a bit difficult to find someone at your age," Sophie said gently. I suppose he probably looked ancient to her teenage eyes. "Maybe you could find a divorcee or something though." She was clearly making a supreme effort to be helpful.

"Or my mum!" She beamed like this was the best idea she'd ever had.

"Sophie, your mum's married isn't she?" I tried to interject some semblance of rationality.

"Yeah, but she's always on the lookout for someone better. If you did lose some weight..."

"Maybe you could try speed-dating," I suggested.

"Actually, there's someone at work who I've had my eye on," Jake told us. "But every time I look in the mirror I realise no one would ever look at me twice. And I honestly can't blame them."

"It's what's on the inside that counts." I was trying to be genuine but I realised I sounded like Big Bird giving one of his closing statements on Sesame Street. Brian was clearly stifling a laugh and I glanced at

Sophie who was making vomit gestures with her fingers in her mouth. Jake just laughed at me.

"That's easy to say when you're skinny and pretty. When you look like me people tend not to bother getting to know what's on the inside."

"Sorry Jake, did you call me skinny?" I really wanted to rewind to that part of the conversation but Jake rolled his eyes and carried on.

"Now, what I need to do is stop feeling sorry for myself and do something about it. So I've brought this little notebook and I thought that every week we could weigh ourselves and then write it down in the notebook."

"No chance!" Sophie and I said in unison. Jake looked at us blankly. "We don't need to lose weight," Sophie continued. "If Marie and I lose weight we'll fade away." I looked at Sophie with a half-smile as I wondered whether I'd heard her right. I felt like hugging her. That's two weight-related compliments in less than two minutes! "Linda doesn't need to lose any either, do you Linda?"

"I don't think so, no. Not really," Linda replied uncertainly.

"Brian, what about you?" Sophie asked. "Need to lose weight?" She looked him up and down and then answered for him, "Nope doesn't look like it. Sorry, Jake, it's just you. Here's what's going to happen…" She paced the room, grinning like an idiot. "You are going to get weighed every week, not the rest of us, just you. We'll write down your weight and if it's more than the previous week, then we'll be really mean and call you names like fatty and tubby for the whole evening. Okay?"

I smiled to myself.

"What will you do if I've lost weight?" Jake asked.

"I imagine we'll all be encouraging and nice," I said. My comment came out sounding a bit pathetic so there was no surprise when Sophie corrected me.

"Fat chance! If you lose weight we'll just treat you like we normally do."

"So you'll be mean to me either way?"

"Well, yes," Sophie said. "But it'll be far worse if you put weight on. I'm going to call you a useless good-for-nothing slob and a grease-gobbling gargantuan and all sorts of other names. It'll be great fun actually. I'll be disappointed if you lose weight."

"Sophie! This is not the way to go about it," I told her. "You're just being cruel."

"It's called being cruel to be kind!" she replied. "What would you suggest? That we reward him with a Mars bar for every pound he loses?"

"It's okay," Jake said. "I like Sophie's idea; cruel to be kind. I can live with that. It's very 'us' don't you think?"

I sighed and realised Jake was right. It was never going to be a politically correct approach.

"Now, Marie, you grab the notebook and let's get on with this," Jake instructed me as he made a move toward the scales. He gingerly stepped on them and we leaned into him like vultures as we waited for the verdict.

We all winced a bit as the number was revealed.

"Don't worry, Jake, with a bit of work you'll be fighting women off and that lady at work won't believe she's never noticed you before," Linda said kindly. Jake stepped off the scales and returned to the couch.

"Where is it that you work, Jake?" I asked. I really didn't know very much about these people who were occupying my living room.

"I'm a care assistant in an old people's home," he answered.

"That sounds like a rewarding job," Linda said. "Is it enjoyable?"

"I love it. It's nice to get to know the old people and be there for them. Some of them are like family to me. It's nice to feel like I'm doing something meaningful for someone. Of course, there are some things that I don't enjoy, but that must be true of any job. It is very rewarding though. Plus, I work with nice people so that's great too. It's the cook there that's got my eye." He looked slightly sheepish at the mention of his crush.

"It sounds fascinating. I wish I had a job like that," Brian said seriously, "Something where you feel like you actually make a difference."

"Can we get on with fat club?" Sophie smiled mischievously. "All this career talk is fascinating but I'm dying to know how many fry-ups fatty here ate this week? And don't try to con us. We all know you don't get a big fat lardy arse like that eating salads!"

"Hang on a minute!" Jake said. "You don't know what I weighed a week ago so you can't be mean to me for putting weight on."

"I'm doing you a favour!" Sophie told him. "I'm giving you an incentive. You'll work much harder this week if you know what the consequences are!" She looked around the room at the rest of us. "Will you three back me up here? Tell fatty I'm right!" She fell about laughing. "I'm going to enjoy this far too much."

"Well enjoy it while it lasts," Jake said. "Because today is your only chance! From now on it's healthy eating and exercise all the way."

"See I told you it was a good idea," Sophie said. "You're more determined already. Now shuffle your fat arse over. You're taking up all the room on the couch." She leaned into him and laughed wickedly.

Chapter 13

I woke up with mixed emotions on Saturday. I was looking forward to spending the afternoon with Grace, James and Brian, but was not happy about the reason for the get-together. It would be the last time that I saw Grace for a while. If I let myself think about it too much I knew that I could end up wallowing in self-pity.

I decided to focus on getting ready but as I passed Grace's bedroom I glanced inside and was hit by how empty and bare it looked. I went in and ran a hand along the empty dressing table before walking quickly out again. Keeping myself busy was my best option. I had a long shower and as I opened my wardrobe the bag full of cushions fell out from beside it. I growled at it as I tried to fight it back into the small gap.

A thought occurred to me. With Grace's room empty, I could move out of the box room and into her lovely spacious room. It would be nice to have a big bedroom and a double bed. I pulled the bin bag out and dragged it on to the landing before opening the door to Grace's room and throwing it in. I'd wait until Grace was settled in New York before I took over her space but at least I could use it for storage. I'd been tempted to put the cushions up in the attic but I felt guilty at the thought of it. I carried on getting ready and was happy when it was finally time for me to leave the house. I was in need of company.

"Well this is a surprise," Grace said, smiling at me when I approached their table in the trendy new wine bar. "We had bets on how late you'd be," she told me.

"Thanks! I'm glad I keep you entertained. Who won then?" I asked as I slipped into the chair next to Brian.

"Brian did," James informed me. "He obviously knows you better than us these days. He said you'd be bang on time."

"So how is everyone?" I asked. "You guys all ready for the big move?" I silently reproached myself for not even being able to go for two minutes without mentioning the very thing I didn't want to hear about.

"Shh." Brian nudged me. "I made a rule that we're not allowed to talk about it. It's the only way I can get through the day."

"It's not the end of the world. You'll survive," Grace said.

"At least we've got each other," Brian said jokingly as he squeezed my hand. I laughed at him.

"Really, it's a good idea though. Let's just have fun and not think about upcoming events."

"Yes. You're right Marie," James said. "Now I'm going to order a bottle of champagne so that we can toast our new adventure!"

"James!"

"Oh right, yes. I'm not supposed to mention it, am I?"

"Just get the champagne," I sighed. Avoiding the subject obviously wasn't going to be so simple. I was trying to remember to look at it from their point of view. It was all so exciting for them.

We whiled away the afternoon, drinking and eating and chatting. It was all very relaxed and happy. I wished this was just another of a whole string of similar afternoons.

I was on my way back from the bathroom when I noticed a familiar face standing at the bar. It was Sebastian, gesticulating wildly and laughing with a group of people. He spotted me and his face lit up. "Marie! Darling!" he stopped his conversation and rushed over to air kiss me. "How wonderful to see you! I must introduce you to my friends..." he took my arm and led the way.

"Everyone, this is Marie!" he beamed. "Marie is the angel who finds me my divine holidays!" His three friends smiled politely at me. "Marie, this is Carlotta and Cindy..." the two Barbie dolls gave me curt nods and half smiles, while clearly giving me the once over. "And this is Harry." He gestured to the relaxed-looking guy next to me.

"Hi," I smiled, feeling slightly awkward. "Nice to meet you." Harry reached to shake my hand and I was happy he didn't go for an air kiss.

"We were just saying how fantastic this place is, Marie. They've really done a good job with the place." Sebastian waved his hand around as he spoke.

"Yes, it's the first time I've been but I'm sure I'll be back. The food is great too."

"Can I get you a drink, Marie?" Harry offered.

"Oh no, thanks, I should get back to my friends."

"That's a shame, maybe another time?"

"That would be great," I said, hoping I didn't sound

too desperate. I didn't need them to know that I was in the market for new friends and had my sights set on them.

"Oh, you know, you really should come out with us sometime, Marie," Sebastian suggested, "How about dinner one night next week? Does Thursday work for everyone?"

I smiled and was about to accept when I remembered fat club. "Oh actually, Thursday is the one night that I'm not free.... any other night though."

"Well let's make it Friday then shall we? Then we can all get roaring drunk and not have to worry about work the next day!" He laughed and we all agreed on Friday. "I'll give you a call during the week to sort out the details," he told me.

"Lovely, I can't wait. See you all next week!"

I left them and sat back beside Brian.

"Who was that?" Grace asked.

"That guy from work who I told you about." I was pleased with the arrangements for dinner next week and was quietly confident that my social life was about to take a turn in the right direction. Grace discreetly gave Sebastian the once over but didn't comment further.

"How about more champagne?" James offered.

Grace sighed. "I'm sorry but I don't think we have time."

James looked at his watch. "Time flies when you're having fun. Better make a move."

"I'm so sorry, it's hard trying to see everyone before we leave." Grace looked genuinely upset.

It was the moment I'd been dreading. "Can we make the goodbyes quick and painless please?" I asked. "I hate goodbyes."

"Let's just pretend we'll see each other tomorrow, shall we?" Grace suggested.

"Good idea," I agreed as I moved to hug James.

"Look after my friend, okay James?" I said sternly. "Because if you don't you'll have me to answer to. Got it?" James laughed nervously.

"Marie, I'm not sure that's quite how you normally say bye to James is it?" Grace laughed.

"Shut up and come here!" I pulled her in for a tight squeeze.

I watched as she gave Brian a hug and gave him his instructions. "Make sure you look after my best friend, okay? Because if you don't you'll have me to answer to! Got it?"

I laughed as Brian agreed.

The next thing I knew I was sitting silently with Brian watching the pair of them leave the bar and disappear from sight.

"Another drink?" Brian offered.

I was aware of the fact that the champagne had gone to my head but the thought of going home was not pleasant. "Yeah, sure. Whatever you're having."

We drank beers, mostly in silence. The atmosphere was tense and I didn't feel like being there. The place was full of happy people getting into the swing of a Saturday night out and I felt anything but happy. "I think I should probably head on home," I said as we approached the end of beers.

"Will you let me be a gentleman and escort you home?"

"I'll let you," I smiled at him. "I'm not good company though, as you've probably noticed."

"You don't need to be," he said as he helped me into my jacket. "I don't suppose you feel like walking do you? I could do with some fresh air."

"Fresh air sounds good. It might help me clear my head." I wobbled a bit as we headed for the door and could definitely feel the alcohol in my system.

I should've gone to the toilet before we left the bar but I stupidly decided that I could wait until I got home. Amateur mistake.

"Just go in the bushes!" Brian was laughing at me half an hour later as I continued my strange 'I need a wee so badly it hurts' walk up the footpath.

"No! Just hurry up will you," I snapped at him. We were only five minutes from my house but I just couldn't wait any longer. I spotted the grimy little pub and made a dash for it, leaving Brian laughing at me on the street.

"Toilets?" I panted at the barman who pointed to the left of the bar.

I emerged a few minutes later feeling a mixture of relief and embarrassment. Brian was hovering in the doorway waiting for me. "Thanks," I said sheepishly to the barman.

"This isn't public loos," he informed me. I looked around. There were two old men nursing pints in the corner. The barman was probably delighted when he saw the door open. I guess he was disappointed that I only wanted to use the bathroom.

"Right, yes, of course. Well we'll have two pints of lager please." He grinned and I felt like I'd made his day. I'd probably just doubled his takings.

I don't know what made me do it — I'd guess the alcohol in my system made me think it would be a good idea – but I suddenly heard myself saying, "And two tequila shots as well please!"

"Coming right up!"

Brian wandered over and joined me at the bar. "I'm not entirely convinced that this is a great idea but I'm willing to go along with it, but only because I told Grace I'd look after you."

"I hate to break it to you, but I'm fairly sure that Grace's idea of looking after me would be taking me home at this point."

"That's probably true," he mused.

"Let's just drink these, and then head home. That would be okay, wouldn't it?"

"Yes. Just these and then I see you safely home..." Having made such a sensible decision, we got to work on the tequila and then made a start on the beer.

Chapter 14

The moment I woke up I felt like I was trapped in my own body. My eyes didn't want to open, my tongue felt like an intruder in my mouth and none of my limbs were listening to me. It seemed like my body had completely shut down. I managed to get my eyes to open just a slit but they closed again when the sunlight hit them. I tried again and wished I hadn't when I realised I had no clue where I was.

I tried to gather my thoughts. *I was out with Grace and James and Brian, and then I was with Brian walking home. Then what? A bar, yes there was definitely a musty-smelling old pub. Tequila.* The thought made me want to vomit so I tried to remember something else. *More tequila. Oh, no! There were people I think; and maybe dancing; or did I dream that bit? And where the hell am I?*

I made another attempt to open my eyes and forced myself to keep them open. The room came into focus and I was happy that it was somewhere familiar. I couldn't quite put my finger on it but I knew that it was somewhere I knew and that was a comfort. The room was bare, it didn't feel lived in. My eyes roamed around and another wave of nausea washed over me at the sight of the pint glasses standing on the bedside table, with dregs of beer in them. My head started to hurt.

My body was quickly restored to its moving self again at the sound of a snore, coming from somewhere very close. I quickly sat up and saw a half-naked Brian next to me on the bed. *Oh my god.*

Looking down, I was relieved to see that I was fully dressed. I trawled my mind for memories but could only see flashes. I think we must have played pool because there was definitely a pool table floating in my memory bank. However, I could also see birds and a skateboard – in fact it might even be a bird on a skateboard – so my memory probably wasn't to be trusted. The tequila obviously gave me some strange dreams...

"Brian." I nudged him but got no response. "Brian?" I was louder this time but there was still no response. "Brian?" I shouted, nudging him hard.

"Urgh," he grunted and I saw his eyes go through the same process that mine had just done. After a couple of attempts, he managed to keep them open and focus on me. "Where are we?" he asked.

"Grace's room," I informed him after only just figuring out that particular mystery myself.

"Oh right. You wanted to make a toast to Grace," he said vaguely.

"I don't remember. It kind of rings a bell but it's all a blur."

He looked down at his naked chest. "Um, we didn't...? I mean, what happened?"

"I'm fully clothed," I pointed out.

"That's a good sign then." He sighed. "Hopefully I would remember that."

"Was I dancing?" I asked as a memory washed

through my head.

"Lap dancing as I recall," Brian said flatly.

"No! Really?" This was bad.

"It's okay. I think those old guys really enjoyed it." No, surely that hadn't really happened.

"I need coffee," Brian informed me.

"I need a new head," I replied as I made my way unsteadily from Grace's room.

"What did Grace leave behind?" I heard Brian ask and turned to find him with a bin bag in his hand. Mum's cushions! How would I explain this?

"It's nothing. Leave it. It's just..."

"Cushions," he stated holding one up. "That's a lot of cushions. Why are they in bin bags?"

"I'm just storing them here for now," I said vaguely hoping he'd stop nosing through my life.

"You should put some in the living room. They're cute," he said as he returned the cushion to the bag and closed it up again.

"They're ugly," I corrected him.

"No, they're homemade so they can't be ugly. They're definitely cute. Who made them?" He walked out of the room and continued the conversation as we went downstairs. I didn't really want to talk to him about my mum's cushions. Especially not with a hangover.

"My mum," I said.

"They'd look nice in the living room," he said and then thankfully dropped the subject. "I'll get the coffee," he told me and headed into the kitchen while I went into the living room and slumped onto the couch. I stretched my legs out in front of me until my feet bumped into something.

"Marie?" Brian called, as my eyes focused on the skateboard at my feet. "Has there always been a bird in your kitchen?"

"What the hell?" Brian and I stood looking through the bars of a huge birdcage that was on the kitchen table. "There's a skateboard in the living room," I told him.

"Do you remember anything?" I asked after a silence.

"Not really, no." He moved to make coffee.

"Am I dreaming?" I asked him.

"I hope so. Where the hell did we get a bird and a skateboard from?"

We sipped coffee and stared at the budgie that had taken up residence on my kitchen table. I sat beside it and rested my elbow on the table. "Ouch!" I touched my elbow and then rolled up my sleeve to reveal a big purple bruise. On impulse I reached down to my knee and felt bruising there too.

"Any ideas?" I asked Brian.

"I think you fell off the pool table."

"Oh I did, I remember... I was dancing on the pool table. So were you Brian. I fell off it."

"Sounds about right." He looked thoughtful. "Yeah you started pole dancing around a pool cue and then climbed up on the table and pulled me up with you."

I groaned. "You were supposed to be looking after me."

"I don't think I did very well there, I'm afraid."

"What are we going to do about the bird?" It suddenly occurred to me that someone might be missing it, and even if they weren't I had to get rid of it. What would I do with a bird? They're the worst kind of pet ever.

"I've no idea," Brian said. "Have you got any food?"

"What do they eat? Seeds? Of course I don't have any bird food. Why would I? I could give it some bread I suppose..."

"No! I meant for me, you idiot. What do I care about feeding the bird?" He got up and went to the fridge. "I need hangover food. I can't think straight." He closed the fridge door again. "I need to look for my shirt and then I'll make breakfast." He walked out of the kitchen.

"If you happen to see my dignity while you're looking for your shirt, I'd really like it back..." I called after him.

I forced down some of the bacon, eggs and toast that Brian made but this was not the sort of hangover that could be cured by food.

"We need to figure out how to get rid of the bird," I said, trying to focus on something other than how terrible I felt.

"I guess we could just release him into the wild," Brian suggested.

"We can't do that! We need to figure out where we got him from and take him back. It must have been the pub right? That's the only place we went... wasn't it?"

"Yeah. I guess you're right, Sherlock... so we just take him and give him to the barman?"

"No! I can't show my face in there again, especially not with a bird that I don't know how I acquired. We just take the bird and leave him outside, then sneak away."

"Okay. What about the skateboard?"

"I don't know. I'm not very concerned about the skateboard. I just want rid of the bird."

I took one side of the birdcage and Brian took the other and we lifted it off the table. "It's heavier than it looks," I said. We manoeuvred it out of the kitchen and into the hallway before it got too much for me.

"I have to put it down," I groaned. It was deceptively heavy and awkward to carry. We lowered it to the floor and stood looking at it.

"How the hell did we get it here?" Brian sighed. We suddenly looked at each other. "Skateboard!" we said at once. The birdcage was balanced precariously on the skateboard when we set off, pushing it out of the door and down the street.

It was a beautiful day, the sky was a bright blue and there wasn't a cloud in sight; the sort of weather that drew people outside. Not really ideal conditions for wheeling a bird down the road on a skateboard. Luckily, we were treated to a typically English response. The people we passed greeted us cheerfully but no one questioned what on earth we were doing. As we got to the end of the road and the pub came into sight, I was fairly devastated to see a couple of people sitting outside on one of the crumbly old picnic tables. There went my plan of dumping it on the doorstep.

"Brian, let's just keep walking past and take it somewhere else."

"Like where?" he hissed as we got nearer to the pub.

"I don't know but we can't leave it outside the pub

with people watching us. We'll take it to a police station or something."

"You're kidding, right?" he said as we slowed down outside the pub.

"Ahoy!" We turned and looked at the two old guys sitting outside the pub. They looked quite familiar. "Brian! How are ya?" the one with the flat cap asked.

Oh no!

"Marie, you've brightened up my day - just the sight of you!" the other one said. Brian and I stood there grinning like idiots as the door opened and the barman walked out.

When he looked at us a smile lit up his face and he marched over and flung his arms around me.

"Marie! I almost didn't recognise you with your clothes on!" he said. I waited for some horrible memory to storm into my head but nothing came. "It's a joke Marie! Don't look so worried." He laughed. "Good morning, Brian!" he reached over and shook Brian's hand. "What can I get you both? The usual is it?"

"Actually we can't stop. We just wanted to return the... um..." Brian pointed at the bird.

"Oh, hello, little Timmy! I didn't notice you there!" He poked a finger through the cage and the bird flew around in a frenzy. The barman looked up at me. "Come on then Marie, show me what you've done...."

I wondered what I was supposed to have done and felt like a complete idiot. "Well the thing is..." I tried to remember his name. Glanced up, I read the sign above the door, stating the name of the proprietor. Gerry - that was it. It was all coming back to me... kind of. "The thing is, Gerry, last night I think I was a bit drunk and I'm not sure I remember why I have your bird..."

"You took him home to train him!" he told me. Of course I did. I was going to train his budgie. "You were going to teach him to talk and sing and dance! Little Timmy here was going to be the star attraction at my little pub. You said you'd have people flocking here to see 'The Great Timmy Bird'. You were going to turn this place around. You were going to make me a rich man with this little bird... or so you said!" He laughed and the two other guys joined him. The joke was most definitely on me.

"Come on, Marie! Make him sing a Michael Jackson number!" The guy with the flat cap shouted, provoking more laughter. Brian even joined in with them.

"Let's see some break dancing!" Gerry said. I slumped onto a bench and hung my head in shame.

Gerry patted me on the shoulder. "Come on, Marie. We're only winding you up!"

I looked up and smiled. "I'm sorry but there's a slight chance I might have over-estimated Timmy's abilities."

We all looked at the bird, who was sitting on his perch doing nothing. I finally started laughing and the others joined me.

After promising to return and visit our new friends soon, Brian walked me back home and I immediately collapsed on the couch and fell asleep.

The phone woke me a few hours later and I reached an arm out and answered it without even opening my eyes. "Hello," I grunted.

"Marie? Are you alright? You sound strange?"

"Oh, hi, Aunt Kath..."

"I just wanted to check you're okay?" she said. "Your mum and I thought you'd be coming over today."

I heard Mum's voice in the background. "Ask her if Gracie liked her cushion?"

"She loved it," I said. "Said it would be lovely in her New York apartment." I heard Aunt Kath relay the message before she asked. "Are you okay? You sound ill..."

"Yeah, I am a bit ill. I think it's flu or something. I was going to give you a call earlier but I must have fallen asleep." Technically, I wasn't even lying. I just didn't mention the fact that it was 'Tequila flu' and not regular flu.

"Poor you. Do you need anything? I could come over if you want?"

"No, I'm fine thanks. I just need to rest. I'll be okay." The last thing I needed was Aunt Kath fussing over me.

With a quick goodbye, I hung up and went back to sleep.

No more tequila for me.

Ever.

Chapter 15

The hangover lasted until about Wednesday, which wasn't entirely a bad thing. All I could think about was making it through the day so I could get into bed and sleep which meant that the week went quickly and I barely registered Grace's absence. Before I knew it, it was Thursday and I was opening the door to the cheerful faces of Sophie, Linda and Jake. I'd set the weighing scales up in the middle of the living room in preparation.

Sophie saw them and immediately started chanting, "Weigh in! Weigh in! Weigh in!"

Linda clapped her hands excitedly. Jake looked nervous and shuffled his feet as he moved towards the scales. "Wait!" I stopped him. "Brian's not here yet. We can't start without Brian, can we?"

Three disappointed faces looked at me. "She's right," Jake finally said glumly. "We'd better wait."

"Anyone want a drink?" I offered.

"Not for me thanks," Jake said. "Nothing is going inside my body until after the weigh-in. I've worked hard all week. I don't want it wasted because I drink a pint of water before getting on the scales."

The other two shook their heads at my offer too so we sat in a nervous silence for a few minutes until the doorbell made us jump.

"Brian!" I hissed as I let him in. "We've been waiting for you. It's the first proper weigh in."

"I know. I'm sorry. My conference call went on late. Sorry," he repeated to the others when he walked into the living room.

Jake approached the scales for the second time. I was ready with the notebook as he hesitated in front of the scales. We all crowded around him again and I found that I was nervous for him. "Last week you weighed 17 stone 4 pounds," I said. "This week..." he stepped on and closed his eyes, "17 stone...5 pounds."

Jake looked upset as he slouched into the couch. "I tried really hard. I really did."

"Never mind, Jake. These things take time. Stick at it and I'm sure you'll see some improvement next week," Linda gently encouraged him. Brian sat down in the armchair and I perched next to him on the arm. There was a definite air of melancholy in the room. I'd really wanted Jake to do well.

Sophie was sitting on the edge of the couch next to Jake, saying nothing.

"Go on then, Sophie. You may as well get on with it. Cruel to be kind isn't it? I can take it."

I looked at Sophie who bit her lip and was quiet for once. Jake looked up at her. "Come on, don't be shy," he prompted.

"Your belt!" Sophie suddenly shouted, making me jump. "It's your belt!" she said again. "You didn't have that big belt on last week did you? It must be the belt..."

Jake looked down. "Take it off," Sophie said. "Take the belt off and let's weigh you properly. That wasn't fair last time. Not with a great big belt like that on." She looked at the rest of us with desperation in her eyes.

"She's right," I backed her up. "Let's give it another go."

Jake dutifully removed his belt and, holding his trousers up, went for another attempt at the scales. We all held our breath as he stepped on again, "17 stone 4 pounds!" I squealed.

"I told you it was the belt!" Sophie went to high five Jake but he didn't move. Linda was happily clapping her hands and Brian slapped Jake on the back.

"I still didn't lose weight," Jake said, forlornly.

"You stayed the same though Jake. That's a good thing. Especially in the first week," Linda told him.

"You did great," Sophie told him cheerfully. "Just keep at it, okay?"

"Okay," he finally agreed with a hint of a smile. "Next week I'll do better. I spoke to my friend at work today, only chit-chat but it's a start."

"How is work?" Linda asked politely.

"Good thanks," Jake replied.

Linda looked thoughtful for a moment. "I wish I had a job. I'm so envious of all of you with your lovely jobs. It must make your lives so interesting. I'd love to have a little job and earn a bit of money. It would be lovely."

"Why don't you get a job then?" Sophie asked.

"I don't think George would like it if I had a job. I have to make sure the house is nice and tidy, and do the washing and the cooking. He likes me to be around the house."

"You could just get a part-time job though, couldn't you?" I asked innocently.

"No. I don't think that would work out. It's okay though. I'm used to things the way they are." We smiled at her awkwardly as she deflected the conversation away from herself.

"Tell me about your job, Marie, it must be so exciting?"

"Oh well, it's okay I guess. I'm not sure it's exciting really. Although, tomorrow one of my big clients is taking me out to dinner with a couple of his friends as a 'thank you'. That might be fun."

"Where are you going?" Brian asked.

"Some place called DeLuxe." Sebastian had rung me at work that morning with the details. I was meeting them at 8.30pm and I'd never been to the place before so I was quite excited.

Brian let out a low whistle. "Nice! Very fancy."

"Really?" I asked anxiously. I hoped I wouldn't be out of my depth in some fancy restaurant.

"It sounds so exciting Marie," Linda smiled. "You're so lucky!"

"Actually, I'm a bit nervous," I confessed. "They're all very sophisticated and I'm not sure how well I'll fit in with them."

"You'll be fine," Jake said. "They're the ones who're lucky to have your company for the evening. Just think of it like that and you'll be fine."

"Yeah and if you have a crap time, just get up and leave," Sophie suggested helpfully.

I felt a little better but I was still nervous, not just because I mightn't fit in with them, but because I had such high hopes for the effect they would have on my social life. If they didn't like me, I was back to square one.

Fat club continued as normal but after I'd mentioned Sebastian and my big night out, I found it hard to concentrate. I had a lot of concerns about how the evening was going to go but it wasn't until I got home from work on Friday afternoon that the major dilemma hit me. I had no clue what to wear and getting ready was definitely going to require a second opinion.

I really wanted the night to go well and first impressions are always important. Plus I'd seen how dressed up Cindy and Carlotta were in the bar last week. I didn't want them to be embarrassed to be seen out with me.

I scrolled through my phone to find Grace's new US phone number. It was depressing that I had to call New York just to ask a friend for fashion advice. I desperately wished she was here so that she could trawl through my wardrobe with me and tell me what would look good. I was puzzled when I found Grace's name on the screen because right after it I noticed it said Jake. I only knew one Jake and to my knowledge I didn't have his number. I scrolled some more and found Linda and Sophie's numbers in there too. Strange. On impulse, I called Sophie's number. She was young and into fashion, surely she could help. If it was even Sophie's number.

"Sophie?" I said as she answered her phone on about the fifteenth ring, when I'd almost given up on her. "Why do I have your number?"

"I put it in your phone," she replied with a sigh. I

had more questions but they didn't seem that important. "I need your help." I sounded desperate, but let's face it, I was.

"Oh, really?" she replied smugly.

"Yeah, I have this thing tonight. The dinner thing I mentioned. It's with one of our biggest customers and it's a posh place and I've no clue what to wear." I felt a bit guilty about the fact that really I was lying to her. It wasn't strictly a work dinner but I knew that if I told her the truth that she'd see it as an insult. She'd want to know why I needed new friends. She'd ask why she wasn't a good enough friend; and Jake and Linda too. She'd probably start shouting at me and I really didn't need it.

"Okay, I'll be over in a bit," she said and hung up, leaving me wishing she'd been a bit more specific about timing.

I needn't have worried. Sophie appeared at my door about half an hour later with a large holdall draped over her shoulder.

"How long have we got?" she asked, as I opened the door.

I looked at my watch. "About two hours until I have to be there... It's not far away, just in town."

She cocked her head to one side and wrinkled her forehead. "That should be okay."

I followed her to the living room and wondered what was in the bag, and why she sounded dubious as to whether two hours would be long enough to make me over.

"Right, so what are my specifications here?" she asked me seriously.

"Well it's a work dinner but..."

"Male or female?"

"Male but he'll have some friends with him - professional people, probably all in their late twenties/early thirties"

"Got it. We need you to look sophisticated and stylish? Hot, but not too hot. Classy, right?"

"Exactly!" Somehow, she'd gotten it spot on.

"I don't know what to wear. I don't want to look over the top, just kind of...."

"Effortlessly chic?"

"Yes!" She was good at this game.

"Right well, there's going to be nothing effortless about it, but I'll do my best. Let's start with the nails, then hair – that could take a while – then we'll do make-up, and finally clothes."

"Maybe we should go through my wardrobe first.... I don't know what I'll wear..."

"Don't panic, I will create you a look!"

I was slightly worried. This could have been a bad idea. "Sophie..." She looked up from her holdall and glared at me impatiently. "This is quite important to me..."

She stood up straight and sighed. "You know this is a favour, right? That I have better things to do than give you a makeover on a Friday night?"

For a moment, I thought she was going to walk out. She looked annoyed and once Sophie gets annoyed I know from experience it usually means trouble. Suddenly, her face relaxed. "What is it that you think I do during the day from Monday to Friday?"

I was completely taken aback by her question "Well... you... um…" I should definitely have known. "School?" I ventured. Her half smile told me this was wrong. "College?"

She laughed. "I'm a trainee at a health farm. We specialise in making over rich, bored housewives who have nothing better to do than get manicures and pedicures and all sorts of weird treatments to try to make themselves look 'effortlessly chic'... so if you wouldn't mind having a little bit of confidence in me on this occasion?"

"Sorry," I mumbled.

She delved back into her bag and starting pulling out the tools of her trade. "Do you want curly or straight hair? Because, to be honest, that in-between look is a disaster."

I stroked my hair protectively before throwing myself at her mercy. "You're the expert, Sophie. Do your thing."

She grinned and got to work.

Chapter 16

I stood at the entrance to the restaurant feeling a million dollars. Normally, I'd feel completely out of place and worry that I'd be asked to leave on the basis that it was a fancy place for fancy people and I didn't fit the bill. Sophie had done an amazing job though. I was still reeling slightly from the change in her. The minute she got to work she was like a different person, full of confidence and self-belief. She made me feel completely relaxed as she plucked, scrubbed, polished and styled me. Even the parts of me that weren't on show were groomed to perfection, making me feel completely renewed.

I was wearing a pair of black trousers – ones that had previously been 'interview' trousers and had spent a good few years lurking in the back of my wardrobe. Sophie said that you couldn't go wrong with classic black trousers – and a glittery top that clung to my boobs but billowed slightly to hide the stomach. Sophie had produced a pair of killer heels from her Mary Poppins bag and the overall effect was unbelievable.

My hair was straight and sleek and my nails were French-manicured. I would've been happy to stand in front of a mirror all night checking myself out. It'd been fun with Sophie too. I was surprised at how much I'd enjoyed myself. She regaled me with stories of her family and all her little brothers and sisters, and I'd laughed more than I had in a long time.

"Marie! Darling!" I saw Sebastian waving at me as I crossed the room. "Darling! You found us!" He beamed as he air kissed me on both cheeks. "Come, meet everyone again. You remember Cindy, and Carlotta..." I received fake smiles from both girls. "And Harry, of course." He stood and kissed my cheek. I enjoyed the physical contact. I really wasn't a fan of air-kissing. I took the spare chair between Harry and Sebastian. "We've all started on champagne, Marie. Would you join us?" Sebastian asked.

"Champagne sounds lovely," I replied, sending Sebastian into action, clicking his fingers at the passing waiter who smiled and poured me a glass of champagne. The waiter was very professional; I think I'd have bashed Sebastian around the head with the bottle at that point. I didn't realise there were people who actually clicked their fingers at waiters; I always thought it was just a TV joke.

Harry turned to me as I took a sip of champagne. "Sebastian says that you do a brilliant job finding him his holidays. I'm not quite sure why he can't get on the internet and do it himself, but I guess it's good for you that he doesn't." I liked Harry's relaxed manner.

"Now, now, Harry! Be nice," Sebastian admonished. "Some of us have demanding jobs you know. I can't spend the whole day surfing around the internet."

Harry smiled at me. "Which is basically all I do working in IT."

I smiled and tried desperately to think of something witty or intelligent to say. Nothing sprang to mind.

"And yes I am a computer geek," Harry told me. "But people only tease until their computer crashes, and then they're all smiles!"

"He really is a whizz," Sebastian said. "He makes me feel completely stupid when it comes to computers."

"Well I know who to call next time I have a computer problem." I made an appropriately impressed face and realised I was feeling self-conscious. It felt like I was at an interview. I really wanted them to like me. Cindy and Carlotta were opposite me on the round table and I could feel their eyes burning into me as they tried to size me up.

"Carlotta, your nails look a-mazing!" I said in a bid to break the ice. "Where do you get them done?"

She beamed at me before launching into a rant about how terrible the local beauty salons were and how long it took her to find a good one. Cindy jumped in too and they were both in fully-animated mode in no time. I nodded and forced myself to look interested.

"Your nails are beautiful too, Marie. Where do you go?" Cindy asked.

"Oh..." I looked at my nails to stall for time. Where the heck did Sophie say she worked? "A lovely place called The... Eden Day Spa." I remembered at exactly the right moment. "It's a lovely place, and there's a fantastic young girl that always looks after me... she even does house visits for me if I don't have time to get to the spa during normal hours." I perked up as I dragged Sophie into the conversation. "She's great

179

actually." I smiled at the thought of her.

"Sounds wonderful. You'll have to give us the details of the place."

"Okay, that's enough girlie talk," Harry cut in. "What are we going to eat?"

I opened the menu and scanned through, trying not to wince while I read through the array of fancy foreign foods, most of which I had no idea what they were.

"I was thinking we could just go with the taster menu," Sebastian suggested. "It's eight courses. I always enjoy a bit of variety."

"Sounds great," I put in, as the others also voiced their approval. I was really happy to eliminate the process of choosing from the absurd menu.

"Let's order then, I'm starving," Harry said which immediately had Sebastian clicking his fingers again. I cringed as another waiter appeared.

We finished off the champagne and switched to wine and chatted politely until the first course arrived. I was totally amused to see five waiters file out of the kitchen carrying one plate each. Only when there was a waiter standing uniformly beside each of us, did they place the plates in front of us.

The food was concealed under old-fashioned silver domed plate covers.

"A pea and mint soup for you this evening," one of the waiters announced. The five waiters removed the silver domes with a flourish, all at the exact same moment and with a white glove-covered hand. They then filed back to the kitchen and left us to it.

I sat looking slightly bewildered at my plate. In the middle of the large plate was a spoon with a spot of something green on it about the size of a fifty pence piece. The rest of my party didn't bat an eye lid and picked up their spoonful of soup. I use the word 'spoonful' pretty generously - the spoon wasn't even full. I guess the waiter was being literal when he said it was "A pea and mint soup". You could definitely make this with just 'a' pea. I hesitantly followed the others in eating my soup. It wasn't even enough for me to be able to tell if it was nice or not.

Sebastian suddenly started a discussion about which new car he should buy. I feigned interest and tried not to get too distracted by the bustle of the restaurant. I loved people-watching.

Carlotta mentioned an old school friend she'd bumped into and the four of them reminisced about their school days for a while. They did their best to include me and describe events to me but their anecdotes were generally of the 'you had to be there' variety.

At various points throughout the somewhat dull conversations, the five waiters would file out with more food. I couldn't help but think that with a bit more training they could surely manage more than one plate each.

The food was nice, but I wasn't keen on this taster menu concept where each course just left me wanting more. I actually felt like I was getting hungrier the more the evening went on. I was shocked when one course arrived and the waiter announced it to be cow's cheek with caramelised onion and a jus de something or other. Cow's cheek? It actually turned out to be really yummy; basically a nice tender mouthful of beef with one tiny piece of onion and a swirl of gravy going round the plate.

The low point of the meal was definitely the steak tartar with quail egg. If I'm honest my brain only seemed to register the words 'steak' and 'egg' so imagine my horror when the silver dome was removed to reveal some raw minced beef with a tiny raw egg balancing in half an egg shell on top of it. To me this was the food of lazy chefs. Cook it, for goodness sake!

I sat staring at the raw meat and wondering what to do about it. I slowly picked up my fork as I watched everyone else tuck in. I was actually going to have to eat it and I was surely going to die. I'm from the salmonella generation of kids that grew up not being allowed to eat raw cake mix because it might kill you. Every fibre of me screamed "NO" as I filled my fork with raw meat and egg. I tried to pretend that it was just a tiny hamburger with fried egg. I even found myself discreetly breathing on it before I put it in my mouth in the vague hope that the warmth from my breath might cook it slightly.

Four terrible, torturous mouthfuls later and I relaxed as the ordeal came to an end. I decided that I needed to have a fun evening because I would definitely wake up in the night with horrific stomach pains and be dead by morning. No doubt about it. I washed it down with plenty of wine and hoped that the alcohol might kill the germs.

I suppose the evening was successful. The atmosphere was slightly tense but that was probably just because I was still getting to know them. I couldn't help but think of my fat club evenings, where things were about as relaxed as could be. I imagined them in this setting though and cringed. They couldn't really be taken out in public.

It was as Sebastian was paying the bill that I suddenly started to panic a bit. What if I didn't pass the interview and they never invited me out again? I wondered whether I should take the initiative and suggest something but Harry saved me the trouble.

"Hey, Marie. Seb got us VIP passes to some new nightclub next week. You should come with us, it'll be fun."

"That sounds great," I said with a sigh of relief. The girls were wearing their fake smiles again and I was sure they hadn't really warmed to me. I could make up for that next week though.

"You should definitely come with us," Sebastian chimed in. "The more the merrier. I'll give you a call in the week."

I said goodbye and exchanged air-kisses with my new friends.

Walking away down the road, I realised that my stomach was rumbling. Those eight courses had probably added up to about ten mouthfuls of food. I'm also unimpressed with anywhere that counts coffee as a course. I always feel cheated by it. I was glad that Sebastian had paid for the meal because I'd be really disgusted if I'd had to pay a fortune for uncooked food and find that I wasn't even full at the end of it. I was quite tipsy as I headed down the road and into the nearest kebab shop.

Chapter 17

I answered the door at 9am on Saturday to find Linda looking nervous. I wiped the sleep from my eyes and tried to focus, wondering what good reason there could be for Linda to be at my door, outside of her usual visiting time. "Is everything okay?"

"Yes, sorry..." She eyed my pyjamas and I checked my watch – it was only nine; definitely still pyjama time. "I've got you out of bed. I thought you'd be up." It was before midday on a Saturday so I have no idea why she thought I would be up, but never mind.

"It's fine. Come in," I told her.

"No. I'll just go. It's not important."

"Just come in, will you? I'll put the kettle on."

She followed me into the kitchen. "I just realised that I didn't really thank you properly, for coming to get me from Emily the other week. It was kind of you to come and fetch me."

"Oh, it was nothing. Good fun actually."

"Well, it's just that I've not really had friends for a long time..." she trailed off and there was an awkward silence. I wasn't sure that I actually considered her a friend. She was just someone who I'd been thrown together with. Fat club was okay. The three of them kept me amused and I'd accepted the fact that for the moment Linda, Sophie and Jake were in my life. I just wasn't sure that 'friends' was an accurate description.

"Anyway, I always go shopping on a Saturday and I thought that maybe you'd like to join me? Sometimes I get a bit bored on my own." I wondered why she bothered going if it was boring but thankfully I realised what the answer would be before I asked; George, of course.

"Are the shops even open at this time?" I asked but she clearly thought I was joking and just smiled politely. My brain wasn't working and I couldn't think of an excuse. "Um, yeah. Okay." How bad could it be anyway? "You make coffee then and I'll get dressed."

I jumped in the shower and threw on some clothes and before I knew it I was sitting in a car with a fifty-something-year-old woman, on my way to a fun-filled day of shopping. I soothed myself with the thought that I was well on the way to having young trendy friends and then resigned myself for the day ahead.

"So where do you want to go?" Linda asked.

"I don't know... the High Street? Where else is there?"

She tutted and it was clear I'd said the wrong thing. "The High Street's fine I guess, if that's where you want to go shopping..."

"Actually, I don't care Linda. Wherever you want to go is fine."

"Good. I like the little boutique shops or sometimes I head out to the outlet stores. I feel like looking round the boutique shops today."

"Okay, well just lead the way. Aren't those shops expensive though?"

"Yes I suppose so, but it's much nicer and you can

find some really unique things. I never really buy anything anyway."

My brain tried hard to comprehend this. "You go shopping every week, but you don't buy things? What's the point?"

"Well it's just nice to have some time to myself." I knew it. Shopping is like fat club - an excuse to get away from George. "George doesn't like me buying lots of things. He's always asking what I've bought and how much everything costs. It's nice to look though."

I sighed and decided against discussing this with her. I didn't get it though. What exactly did she spend money on that George begrudged so much? And how the heck is shopping fun when you don't buy anything?

Linda took me to a part of town that I never knew existed, and dragged me round a lot of shops which were out of my price range and also out of my age range. There was a definite whiff of middle age in these shops. It felt a bit like when I was a child and Aunt Kath used to take me out some Saturdays and I'd drag my heels while she visited every shop in town. The only good bit was when she bought me McDonalds before she took me home.

As we stopped outside the millionth shop of the day – well okay, it was maybe the fourth, but I already felt like the day might never end – Linda stopped and stared at the mannequin in the window.

"Oh wow, Marie, look!" I followed her gaze to a very elegant cocktail dress.

"Yeah, very nice," I mused without any enthusiasm.

I followed Linda into the shop and was surprised to

hear her speak confidently to the shop assistant.

"My friend would like to try on the dress in the window please." I looked around for this mystery friend, but there was no one there.

"Certainly," the shop assistant said, looking at me. The dressing room is at the back. I'll just see if we have it in your size... about a twelve are you?"

"Um, yeah," I said. Linda pushed me to the back of the shop and I tried to protest. "I didn't want to try it on. What do I need a dress for?"

"Just try it. It'll be fun!" This was something that I didn't understand. I just couldn't see how it was fun to try things on if you knew you'd never buy it.

The smiley shop assistant handed me the dress and closed the curtain to the dressing room.

I squeezed out of my clothes in the small space and slipped into the dress, feeling quite stupid and fraudulent. The poor shop assistant probably thought there was a possibility I would buy it.

"How does it look?" Linda asked from the other side of the curtain before sticking her head in to look at me. She opened the curtain and I moved backwards, out of the dingy cubicle light.

I looked in the mirror, then looked some more, before turning to look from a different angle. Linda was beaming with what I could've sworn was pride. "You look amazing. I knew it would suit you!"

Surprisingly, I had to agree with her. It did suit me and I actually felt amazing in it. For a moment I was almost swayed to her way of thinking: that trying things on was fun. I admired my reflection once more before returning to my clothes. I felt a bit like Cinderella when the clock struck midnight.

"So are you going to buy it?" Linda asked, as I emerged from the changing room.

"No, I can't afford it." Actually I'd not even bothered to check the price tag but I was fairly sure it was out of my price range.

"You should buy it. It looked so good on you!"

"Linda, it's a cocktail dress, and a red one at that! When will I wear a red dress?"

"It's classic though, and sometime you will be invited to a fancy party and you'll think about this dress and kick yourself. You will. I promise! You'll regret it if you don't buy it."

I gingerly checked the price tag and my heart started beating faster. "Don't think about it, just buy it," Linda urged.

"No way," I told her. "Definitely not! I'm not buying an expensive dress that I don't need. Stop trying to bankrupt me!" I handed the dress to the shop assistant and moved towards the door.

When we finally arrived back at my apartment, almost seven hours after leaving it, I was exhausted. It was more tiring than a day at work. I did have quite a good time though. Once I'd gotten into the swing of things, it wasn't too bad at all. I also felt better after making a few purchases, just a couple of tops and a scarf; those fancy shops give you fancy shopping bags so I started to feel a bit like Julia Roberts in *Pretty Woman*.

I collapsed on the couch and dropped the shopping bags at my feet. "Thanks Linda. That was fun!"

"Look at the time though. I need to go. George will want his dinner soon." She'd been almost relaxed while we were shopping, so I was disappointed at her shift back to her usual, anxious self.

"Okay. Don't forget your shopping." I'd actually convinced her to buy a new jacket and some nice boots that she'd been admiring.

"I'll have to leave them at your place for now. I don't want George to see them."

"Linda!" I was shocked at her again, but wasn't sure it was worth getting into a discussion about. "Fine, leave them here," I sighed. To me, her situation was quite obvious: she should tell her idiot of a husband where to go.

"Won't he wonder about the money?" I asked, suddenly interested.

She looked sheepish. "I used my separate account to pay for it. If I'm careful with the housekeeping money then I can keep a bit for myself and I set up an account to put it into."

I laughed. This shy little lady was quite surprising at times. "So are you going to leave him one day then?" She looked confused. "Surely if you're siphoning off money, you intend to leave him. Why bother otherwise? So you can buy clothes to hide at my place?"

"I don't know really." She was starting to look like she might cry so I decided not to quiz her anymore.

"I'll see you on Thursday," she whispered.

I sat thinking about her situation. "If I were you, I'd leave him. Just tell him to bugger off and get out of there."

"Really?" she looked at me intensely and I regretted saying anything.

"Easier said than done I suppose, isn't it? I just don't know why you stay when he makes you miserable. You could get a part time job in a shop or something and live quite happily." I should definitely have kept quiet. It's really nothing to do with me and I'm not sure I'm really in a position to be offering marriage advice.

She smiled at me and left without a word. I finally managed to get up from the couch - completely oblivious as to how that conversation would come back to haunt me - and went about unpacking my shopping bags.

Chapter 18

I was gripping the notebook too hard, my finger crumpling the pages slightly. "Last week 17 stone and 4 pounds..." I did the build-up. "This week... 17 stone... 2 pounds!"

A cheer went up around the living room and Jake looked very proud of himself. "I've been very good you know. I only had two fry-ups this week and I've tried to cut down on snacks. I even walked to work one day instead of getting the bus."

"It worked, Jake. Well done," I praised him. "Keep it up next week, won't you?"

"Definitely. I might try to cut out the fry-ups altogether. If the weather's nice, I'll walk to work again too." I was surprised at his dedication and hoped that it would last.

"Just don't go all anorexic on us will you?" Sophie laughed as she and Jake slumped into the couch side-by-side. He nudged her playfully and laughed along with her.

"Everything okay, Linda?" Brian asked from the armchair. I was sitting on the floor by the coffee table and looked across to Linda who was also sitting on the floor.

"Yes. I think so," she replied, wringing her hands.

"What's wrong?" I asked.

"It's probably nothing," she answered quietly. "But George has started asking questions again about my Thursday evenings. He was asking me the names of the other people who go to Emily's, and asking what everyone is like. I'm sure he's suspicious. I'm worried he's going to find out that I've not been going and that I've been lying to him all this time." She looked at us nervously.

"What would happen if you just told him the truth?" Sophie asked. Linda shuffled nervously on the floor and Sophie back-tracked. "I'm not saying that you should tell him the truth. I just wondered what would happen if you did?"

"Well I'm sure he'd be very angry and..." She stopped unsure of herself.

"Does he shout at you?" Brian asked.

"Well no, up until now, he's never actually shouted at me, but he likes everything to be just so. I have to have the dinner ready at a certain time and the house always has to be spotless. If I'm home late from fat club he'll always want to know what I was doing."

"But do you never think about just not having dinner ready on time?" I asked. "Just to see what happens. Maybe he wouldn't be as mad as you think."

Linda smiled at me condescendingly. "We've been married for over thirty years and we've developed routines. I can't just start changing things. As long as I stick to the routine, everything will be okay. I shouldn't really complain. I have a nice house and some nice things."

"But wouldn't you like a bit more freedom?" I went on, angry on her behalf as I watched her feebly talking about her life in the same flowery calf-length skirt and blouse combination that she always wears. "Wouldn't you like to buy new clothes and come home half an hour later than you told him? You could order a take away when you didn't feel like cooking and leave the washing for tomorrow. You could get a job like you talked about. Wouldn't you like to try?"

There were tears in her eyes and I felt guilty for my rant. "It's not that easy though. I don't want to cause trouble," she whimpered.

Sophie knelt down beside her and put a protective arm around her shoulders. "Don't worry Linda, you've got us. We'll look after you." Linda smiled at Sophie and dried her eyes.

The evening was fairly sombre after that. I think everyone was thinking about Linda's situation and I was relieved when it was time for them to leave. It had been an emotionally draining evening and I was ready for bed.

"Is it okay if I hang around for a quick beer?" Brian asked once the others had left. "I feel like I need one after all that stuff with Linda. It was a bit heavy wasn't it?"

"Definitely," I said, following Brian into the kitchen. "Poor Linda. I don't suppose she'll ever do anything to change the situation though. It's really sad." My mobile started to ring. "It's Grace!" I said excitedly and Brian moved closer to the phone as I answered it.

"What? Grace? I can't hear you properly... Grace?" She was talking but I couldn't make out what she was saying. "Is everything okay, Grace? You sound strange." Brian moved to listen at the phone with me.

"I said, we're getting married!" she suddenly

yelled, making me move the phone away from my ear. "James proposed! We're engaged!" It was so unlike Grace to let her emotions go unchecked and it was so nice to hear her so excited. Brian and I grinned at each other.

"Oh my God! Congratulations!" I squealed. "How did he propose?"

"It was in one of those horse and carts in Central Park. It was so romantic! Marie, I have to go. I'm on my mobile and I've got lots of people to call. It's going to cost me a fortune. I'll call you from the office tomorrow, okay?"

"Of course. I'm so happy for you!"

"Congratulations!" Brian called down the phone.

"Great, Brian is with you. I was going to call him next. I'll talk to you both tomorrow on company time!" She laughed and Brian and I shouted our congratulations into the phone again before hanging up.

"Wow!" I said when Brian gave me a beer. I was excited for Grace. Everything was working out perfectly for her.

"Big news," Brian smiled at me. "They're such a great couple."

"Yes they are," I agreed. "I've been expecting it for a while but it's still strange to think that my best friend is going to get married." I leaned against the oven as Brian took a seat at the table.

"Jealous?" he asked and looked straight into my eyes. He'd know if I lied.

"Yes!" I smiled. "But also no. I'm happy for her. It seems like she has everything she wants, and I used to think that she had such an easy life and everything seemed to fall into place for her. I used to compare my life to hers a lot, and I spent a lot of time being jealous of her."

"But..." he said with a smile.

"But it's not really as simple as that. If I could have the things she has, I probably wouldn't want them anyway. I think I realised, listening to Linda, that I'm pretty lucky. My life might not be quite what I'd like it to be right now but at least I have options. It's more of a blank canvas at the moment and maybe that's something to be excited about rather than something to worry about."

I looked at him smiling at me and laughed. "Sorry. I guess all the emotions of the evening have got to me. I'm not usually so soppy."

He smirked. "Or so positive."

"What's your point?"

"Nothing. It suits you, that's all. Maybe you should try it more often."

"Maybe I will," I said. "I can't promise anything though. People don't just change overnight!"

When I finally crawled into bed, I was still feeling positive. I was really happy for Grace and I realised that comparing my life to hers was completely unhealthy and not good for our friendship. Plus, my life really wasn't so bad.

Chapter 19

I was having some serious problems. In fact, on a Friday night in the VIP section of a fancy nightclub, I don't think problems got much worse than this. You see, I was feeling self-conscious and completely out of place. For a start I had completely overestimated how much clothing I should wear. What I thought was sleek and sexy at home, suddenly felt decidedly nun-like. The girls around me must've been freezing. Some of the outfits were more revealing than what I wear to go swimming.

My awkwardness started when the bouncer looked me up and down, clearly deciding whether or not to let me in. I was cast back to being fifteen and praying the bouncers wouldn't tell me to come back in a few years. Now I was concerned they would tell me I was a few years too late and really not hip enough. Thankfully, Sebastian put his arm through mine and marched me in, giving the bouncer a wink as he went.

I decided that to get through the night, I needed some Dutch courage. I wasn't going to get really drunk, but just drink enough to give me some confidence. The problem was that, as I stood next to Carlotta and Cindy at the bar, I jumped on their vodka martini bandwagon.

I realised my error as soon as the barman placed the drink on the bar in front of me. I eyed the ridiculous glass like it was my nemesis. I was wearing a white shirt (with skinny jeans, super high heels and a wide brown belt – I thought I looked hot until I got to the room full of anorexic model types!) and I knew that the chances of me manoeuvring that glass to my mouth without spillage were fairly slim. I saw Carlotta pick her glass up and hold it out beside her with her elbow on her hip. She was gesticulating with the other hand and chatting away to Cindy and somehow the liquid didn't move. Where the heck did she learn that trick?

At this point I was already struggling to balance my own body on my stupid high heels; add a cocktail in a stupid shaped glass and I'm a one-man balancing act. I checked that no one was looking, and then bent down and sucked up as much of the martini as I could through the barely-there tiny straw without moving the glass an inch. It was all gone in about ten seconds and as I stood up I came face to face with an amused-looking barman.

"Could I get you anything else madam?"

"Yes, I'll take a vodka cranberry please." I smiled at him. "And if you could put it in a normal glass I would appreciate it!" He smiled warmly back at me and moved to get my drink.

I took my second drink and edged my way into Cindy and Carlotta's conversation, thinking that I should try and make friends with them. They stopped talking as soon as they realised I was there and looked at me like I was a snot-nosed child. It was a mix of sympathy and wishing I would go away. I tried to tell myself I was just being paranoid, even though I knew I wasn't. I would make them see my sparkling personality and they'd be fighting over the role of my best friend before the night was over. I was determined.

"So..." I wished I was good at small talk. "This place is nice, isn't it?"

Cindy moved her eyes down to her drink and Carlotta sniffed. "It's alright, I suppose." She looked around the room. "It's a bit... you know... obvious."

"Oh! Well, yeah, of course, it's definitely a bit... obvious. Obviously!" I had no clue what she meant but wanted to be agreeable.

"She means it's just like everywhere else. Nothing unique about it. Probably won't last very long," Harry mused as he swept his gaze around the room. I relaxed with him by my side. Sebastian was chatting to some people at the bar, laughing loudly and generally making his mark on the room.

"We just have to go to the bathroom," Carlotta declared and she turned and walked across the room with Cindy at her heels.

"Don't mind those two," Harry said. "Carly's a bitch through and through, and Cindy is her lapdog. If you can get them apart Cindy is quite nice but they're pretty much joined at the hip so you'll probably never see that side of her."

"They don't seem to like me very much," I told him.

"Don't take it personally. They don't like other girls in general. They see them as a threat, I guess. I don't think they really like me either and I've been friends with them for over ten years now." He laughed like he was telling a joke. "Funny the people you end up with, isn't it? You know the saying 'you can't choose your family, but you can choose your friends'? I think it's completely wrong. If I could choose friends, I don't think I'd choose friends like these!"

My mind drifted to my fat club gang. I always thought of them as the people that I'd been thrown together with but maybe that's all that friends ever really are. Maybe Harry's right and I don't get to choose my friends. Maybe friends choose us.

The very exuberant Sebastian shimmied over to us. "I'm going for a dance! You two coming with me?" He strutted his stuff over to the dance floor when we declined his offer. He was the only person dancing and was causing quite a scene. The confidence he radiated was amazing and he was mesmerising to watch.

As Carlotta and Cindy emerged from the bathrooms, Sebastian moved to the edge of the dance floor to drag them out with him. I watched them laugh and join him, making a stunning threesome, before the dance floor gradually filled up.

My relations with the girls didn't get any better. They took a break from dancing and I made another attempt at chatting to them. I felt like I was fighting a losing battle though.

Carlotta did make an effort to talk to me at one point.

"So, Seb told me that your dad's a pilot?" she said, cocktail in hand.

"Yeah."

"That's cool," she said flatly.

"Yeah, it's pretty cool." I agreed. At least I guess it would be.

"Can you get free flights then?"

"Well... yeah, of course." I replied automatically.

"So maybe we could all go away somewhere, sometime? That would be fun. You could book us a hotel as well, right? You can probably get lots of discount through work, can't you?"

"Yeah. Maybe."

She gave me a half-smile and I had the horrible feeling of being at school and trying to please the school bully. Harry was right. Carlotta was a bitch. I didn't know why I was even bothering with her. She seemed intent on disliking me and I got the impression that when the two of them had excused themselves to the bathroom earlier, it was only so that they could go and talk about me.

Carlotta was obviously trying to see what she could get in return for a fake friendship. The other three were okay. Harry was lovely and Sebastian seemed harmless, as did Cindy. It was probably worth hanging around for them. I just wished that Carlotta would disappear.

When another awkward silence encroached, I decided to take a breather and made for the quiet comfort of the bathrooms.

It was on my way back from the bathroom that I saw *him*. By him, I refer to the lovely-looking man who I was positive that I knew, but I'd forgotten some vital information, such as his name and where I knew him from. This actually happened to me a lot and it usually turned out to be someone who I'd booked a holiday for.

Normally I remembered the attractive guys though, and this one was exactly my type. He was walking straight towards me with a deliciously easy smile on his face. I wished I could remember something about him. I was going to have one of those horrible conversations where I had to pretend I knew who he was.

I decided I'd just do what I always do in these situations and wing it.

"Hi," I said cheerfully as he got near me. The fact that his gaze shifted to me from somewhere just over my right shoulder and he looked slightly confused should probably have been a sign to me, but once I've started on a path there's just no stopping me. He did a kind of half smile, half nod thing so I blundered on. "How are you?"

"I'm good. Thanks. And you?" I got the feeling that he was also trying to figure out where he knew me from. I decided to be kind and give him a clue.

"Fine, thanks! Did you enjoy your holiday?"

"It was great! Thanks. Yeah, we had a really good time." He still looked a bit puzzled, bless him. I hoped that he would suddenly figure things out. Anytime would be good because it was starting to feel awkward. That wouldn't stop *me* though.

"Nice to get some sunshine, I'll bet? A nice change from all this drizzle we've been having..."

"Definitely. Sun, sea and sand! Always nice!" He looked almost nervous as he spoke.

I grinned like an idiot. I'd got myself into a bit of a weird situation, what with him clearly not remembering me. I wasn't actually sure I booked his holiday at all. Maybe I went to school with him? I definitely had to bail on the stagnant conversation. It was a shame though because he really was quite edible looking.

"I better be getting back to my friends," I gestured in their direction and noticed them all grinning like idiots. "It was lovely to see you and I'm really glad you enjoyed your holiday!" A professional service to the end with this travel agent.

"Thanks. Have a good night then."

"You too!"

I directed my attention back to Sebastian and his gang and walked into a bubble of excitement. It was radiating out from Carlotta and Cindy. They squealed and drew me into them, both of them talking at once.

"Oh my God!" one or both of them screeched.

"How do you know *him*?"

"What did he just say to you?"

"You have to introduce us. You just have to!" My eyes moved from Carlotta to Cindy and back like I was watching a tennis match.

"This is amazing!"

"Seriously, tell us how you know him..."

They eventually fell silent and I wondered what the appropriate response was and why it was so amazing that I knew a hot man.

"Well, I just see him around sometimes. I suppose we just happen to go to a lot of the same places."

"Oh wow, Marie. He's so gorgeous, I can't believe you know Dermot O'Leary!" Carlotta was on the verge of hyperventilating as her cold bitchy persona vanished.

"Ha-ha. Yeah I wish!" I looked over and finally figured things out. Yes, that's who it was! It was Dermot 'hottest man in Britain' O'Leary. Now they'd said it, it was glaringly obvious where I knew him from. His loveliness has spent many hours in my house thanks to the magic of television. I have to say it was a relief to figure out who it was. Slightly embarrassing though, at that point. However I was proud of my chat-up line: genius if you think about it, because I suppose that most celebrities *have* just been on holiday.

"What?" Carlotta demanded "You do know him, don't you?"

"Of course I know Dermot! Phff! I mean, I know him. I don't *know* him. Obviously!"

They clearly had no idea what I meant and quite frankly neither did I. I forced myself to ad lib.

"I've never slept with him," I whispered conspiratorially.

"But you are friends?" Cindy clarified.

Am I friends with Dermot O'Leary? I'd definitely like to be. I guess it might be stretching the truth a bit.

"He's not so much a friend per se, but when I see him we always stop and say hello. More of an acquaintance I suppose."

That seemed to be acceptable to them. "So how did you meet him?" Cindy was curious.

I decided that an obnoxious flick of the hand would be fitting. "In the travel industry you really do meet all sorts of people," I told them.

The rest of the evening went by quite pleasantly. I got lots of attention from Cindy and Carlotta, who finally seemed to be warming to my presence in the group.

Eventually I dared to look in my friend, Dermot's, direction and he gave me a nervous smile. Oh, how I loved that man. If only I'd realised earlier who it was, I could've just snogged him, like a normal person. I'll bet he gets that all the time. He'd have thought it was completely normal. Trust me to be so inappropriate that I ask him about his holiday and talk about the weather. And I still don't even know where he went!

Chapter 20

"I never did hear from Grace after her engagement announcement on Thursday," I told Anne on Monday morning.

"Well it's such an exciting time for her, she probably just forgot. She'll call you when things calm down again, I'm sure."

So she's having such a good time that she's forgotten all about me. *Thanks for the insight, Anne.*

I looked up at the brochure wall and was surprised to see D3 and E5 had been switched. I went and moved them back to their proper places.

"Marie!" Anne looked at me with concern. "I swapped them last week! I thought you were never going to notice. That's not like you."

"No. It's not, is it? I've got a few things on my mind, that's all."

"Why? What's going on?" She asked.

"Nothing much. Just Grace moving and things."

"Well I hope you're keeping yourself busy and not just moping around at home now that Grace has gone. You can always come over to our place on the weekends if you're lonely."

I looked over at Anne and smiled and then looked away quickly as I felt my eyes involuntarily well up. The thought of feeling lonely enough to visit Anne on the weekends was a depressing one, but I was genuinely touched by her concern.

"Thanks, Anne. I actually had a busy weekend though. I was out with Sebastian and some friends on Friday night..."

"Not that Mr Featherston?" Anne rolled her eyes dramatically. "He's a funny one. Very odd. I don't know why you're hanging around with him. He's bad news if you want my opinion."

"I think I can choose my own friends thanks." I remembered my conversation with Harry on Saturday night and wondered if my statement was true. At the very least I didn't need Anne choosing my friends for me.

"I know you can, Marie. I'm just saying that you should choose carefully."

I sighed and decided to change the subject and avoid letting her increase my anger levels further.

"I saw Linda on Saturday too," I said. "We went shopping together."

"Oh lovely. How is she?"

"She's fine. She has a few problems with her husband, but that's nothing new." I was surprised to see Linda on my doorstep for the second Saturday in a row. She'd at least done me the courtesy of waiting until 10am this time.

"Oh the poor love; an unhappy marriage is a terrible thing. She's lucky to have you to keep her spirits up."

"How's Emily?" I asked.

"Oh her!" She sighed. "She's fine. Well, she's a bit odd actually, isn't she? I enjoy my evenings there though."

"Losing any weight?" I asked with a smirk.

"You're such a tease! That crazy woman says we shouldn't weigh ourselves. Some silly ideas she has." She smiled over at me. "I've lost eight pounds but don't tell Emily!"

The door opened and our conversation was interrupted. I smiled at the young couple who came and sat in front of me wanting to book their honeymoon. We had a steady stream of customers after that and I was winding down for the day when Grace called.

"I'm sorry I didn't call on Friday," she said. "Everything got hectic but I haven't forgotten about you, I promise."

"It's okay. I understand. So tell me all the news. What's going on? Have you set a date?" I asked.

"No date yet. We're going to wait and see how things go over here. The big news is the engagement party! The company are throwing us a huge party. It's two weeks' on Friday and I know it's short notice but I want you and Brian to come over for it. Do you think you can?"

I had the feeling she was holding her breath waiting for my reaction but she'd caught me off guard and I wasn't sure how to react. "It sounds great. It might be difficult to organise so quickly though."

"Marie! You're a travel agent for goodness sake."

"I know, but it's getting the time off as well."

"But you told me you have loads of time you need to take and you could just come for the weekend, couldn't you?" she said.

"I guess I could, but won't it be a bit hectic? Especially if it's a big party. Everyone will want a piece of you. Wouldn't it be better if I came at another time, when I can stay for longer and have you all to myself?"

She sighed. "Maybe you're right, but I know you, you're going to keep putting it off. I feel like you'll never get around to visiting and I thought if there was a specific reason, maybe you'd actually get your bum over here! And I'd really love to have you here for the party. It would be much more fun if you were here."

"I'll think about it," I told her. "But I really think it might be better to wait and come for a whole week."

"Okay. Think about it, and I'll call Brian and tell him to nag you about it, okay?"

I laughed at her. "Sure! You do that!"

"Okay. I have to get some work done. It's only 6.30am here but the office is already busy..." Then she whispered, "These Americans take work far too seriously!"

"Okay, I'll talk to you soon then."

"Yes. And I can't wait to see you at the party!" She laughed and we rung off.

"What was Grace saying?" Anne's voice made me jump. I'd forgotten she was there.

"Oh, she was just telling me her plans for her engagement party."

"Ooh! How exciting! You'll have to fly over."

"I might wait actually. It will be better to spend a bit more time planning a trip and then I could stay for longer too."

"It's your best friend's engagement party! Of course you have to go. Don't be so silly!"

"Well it sounds like it's more of a business 'do really. I'll have to think about it. Anyway look at the time Anne. Let's get out of here!" There was a lot of eye rolling and some remarks about me avoiding the subject but I grabbed my bag and made for the door.

The engagement party played on my mind all week. I ended up really frustrated with myself. Anne was right, I should go and I knew that getting time off wasn't a problem and nor was the cost. All I could really think was that deep down I just didn't want to go. It didn't make sense though. It would be great to see New York and to spend time with Grace and James.

Maybe it was because I'd never travelled anywhere before. The fact that my mum never took me anywhere as a child should have left me dying to get out and see the world but it seemed to have had the opposite effect. The more I thought about it, the more I leaned toward blaming my mum.

By Thursday, I'd gone over things a million times and I knew that I wouldn't go to the engagement party. I also knew that Brian was going to ask me about it and I didn't know how I'd deflect his questions.

We were alone in the kitchen and I was waiting for Brian to bring up the party and New York. I glanced at the clock on the wall above the kitchen table and realised that the others were a bit late. The doorbell would ring any second so it seemed that Brian had missed his chance to persuade me to go to New York.

"Grace said you probably weren't going to make it to the engagement party?" he finally asked.

"I don't think so, no. It's a long way to go for the weekend. I think I'll go another time when things aren't so hectic for Grace."

I was surprised when he nodded along with me. "You're probably right."

"Are you going?" I asked, praying he'd say no. I didn't want to be outdone on the friendship stakes. If Brian was going I might have a re-think.

"Maybe," he said vaguely. "I'll wait and see how things are at the office. It's all pretty busy at the moment. James said they were only really having a big 'do because the company were organising it. More of a business thing than anything so I don't think we need to feel too guilty for not going." I was surprised Brian had spoken to James about it. I never really thought of the two of them as proper friends.

"I would have gone if you were going," he continued. "But I'm not sure how much fun it will be on my own. Maybe we can go another time."

I was a little bit disconcerted by the way the conversation had gone. I was expecting some resistance from Brian. I thought he'd be set on the idea of going to New York and wouldn't take no for an answer. It had all been a bit easy.

"Where the heck are they?" Brian suddenly asked, looking at his watch. "They're really late now."

We moved to the living room and peered out of the front window. There was no sign of them.

About ten minutes later there was a frantic knocking at the door and I opened it to find Sophie looking red and out of breath.

"What's wrong?" I asked.

She took a deep breath and then grinned at us. "You have to come see this! Come on... run..." She turned and ran down the road in the direction of the pub.

Brian and I followed her round the corner, then she stopped and crouched with her hand on her knees. "You're not going to believe this!" she told us laughing.

"Sophie? What's going on?" Brian asked, slightly out of breath after our little jog.

Sophie stood up straight, still grinning. She looked along the row of terraced houses; a street almost identical to my own. At the end it joined a busier road which eventually led into town. The street was completely empty though and I had no clue what she was looking for.

"Look!" she finally pointed and I saw a red car turn the corner. I watched it crawl along for a moment. "Is that Linda's car?"

"Yes!" Sophie threw her head back laughing.

Linda's car crawled down the street towards us and then noticed a figure beside the car. "Is that Jake?" I asked in disbelief.

"Yes!" Sophie told us. "He's jogging. I found him in the hotel car park, doing his stretches! Linda said she'd follow him in case it was too far. I drove with Linda and then ran ahead to get you."

"Go, Jake!" I laughed.

It was fairly slow going but when he got near us we started to cheer him on. He didn't pay any attention; he was so focused on his goal. We jogged along with him when he reached us and let out a huge cheer at my front door.

He was starting to look like he might collapse and I went to get him a glass of water. He smiled as I passed it to him, still trying to catch his breath. He flopped into the armchair and we waited for him to regain the power of speech.

"I did it," he finally gasped through a grin. "I actually did it."

The room was suddenly animated as we laughed and offered praise and encouragement.

I pulled the scales out from under the couch when Sophie suggested we have the weigh-in, but Jake made no effort to move and when I looked at him he shook his head.

"I don't think I will today."

We looked at him waiting for the explanation.

"I think I might finally understand a little bit about what Emily was talking about. I had a really good week. I only had one fry-up and the rest of the week I had muesli for breakfast. I've been trying to do some exercise and I feel really good. I know that I've achieved something and I don't need to weigh myself to prove that. So this week I'll leave it."

I pushed the weighing scales back under the couch and Jake laughed. "You're all very quiet. I hope I haven't ruined the evening for you!"

Sophie sighed. "All right, fine. Next week you're getting weighed though, whether you like it or not." She glared at him to make her point until he stretched out his foot and gently kicked her over. She rolled dramatically from sitting to sprawled out on her back and then exploded into laughter. "I can't believe you ran here," she told Jake between bouts of laughter.

"Me neither." He grinned and then roared with laughter and it was infectious. It was the kind of laughter that just won't stop. Even when you want it to. Even when your face hurts and your stomach muscles have had enough.

It was the best evening I'd had in a long time.

Hannah Ellis

Chapter 21

I was walking out of work on Friday when I bumped into Jake. The previous evening's fat club had left me in a good mood and I was humming to myself when I closed the shop door behind me and then turned to find Jake looking at me.

"Marie! What are you doing here?"

"I work here." I gestured the shop.

"Oh, right. Well I was just... well... we..." He glanced beside him and I noticed that he had a little boy with him. Well, not that little but definitely a fair way from fully-grown.

"Hi!" the kid said cheerfully and held out his hand to me. "I'm Callum."

I shook his hand which seemed to be a strange formal gesture for a kid. "I'm Marie. I'm a friend of Jakes." He smiled sweetly. I'm not good at guessing people's ages, especially kids but I'd say he was around seven maybe. I was also frantically trying to guess who he could be. Surely Jake didn't have a child. I was fairly sure he would've mentioned that.

"Nice to meet you," he said. I was impressed by how genuine his smile was and briefly wished I had a more cheerful disposition. "Jake's my Uncle," he added.

"Well it's nice to meet you too." I felt a sudden and irrational annoyance at Jake because he'd never mentioned any of his family to me. Jake was hovering awkwardly and I realised that he seemed almost embarrassed around me. Clearly, he had never mentioned me to Callum, and it didn't seem like he wanted him to meet me now. He happily comes over and ruins my peace every Thursday but doesn't want to be seen in public with me!

"What have you two been up to then?" I asked in a bid to clear the tension.

"We've been out buying computer games," Callum told me and held open his shopping bag to show me his treasures. "I'm staying at Jake's tonight and he lets me stay up as late as I want, so we can play PlayStation all night!" His excitement was obvious.

Jake patted his head affectionately. "Perhaps not all night."

"We're going to get dinner now. Do you want to come with us?" Callum asked.

Jake shifted his weight and gave a nervous laugh. "I'm sure Marie has something better planned for her Friday night."

"Really?" Callum asked. "What's better than having dinner with us?" He grinned and nudged Jake with his elbow. I was mesmerised by his cheeky-chappy routine and didn't even think about my reply.

"Actually, I can't think of anything better. I'd love to come."

"Really? That's great." Jake didn't even try to hide his surprise. I wasn't going to let him keep me hidden away for his Thursday evening entertainment. I was also quite happy that he thought I would have something better to do. We obviously don't know each other very well at all.

We ended up in an American-themed place and I ordered a burger with curly fries.

"Not a word about this at fat club, okay, Jake?" I said when the food arrived and looked over at his 12oz steak with chips.

"I won't tell, if you won't."

"I thought you didn't go to that anymore?" Callum jumped in.

"I don't really," Jake said. "We go to Marie's house instead. It's just a bit of a joke we have."

The food was great and I marvelled at what a difference it made when minced meat was cooked.

"I'm full," I stated after my last mouthful and slouched back into my seat.

"I think I better go and wash my hands," Callum told me while he waggled his barbecue sauce covered fingers. I have to say that I was impressed at how many spare ribs such a small person could eat.

We watched Callum walk across the restaurant before turning to each other.

"So what was all that about, Jake?" I asked. "It seemed like you were embarrassed to introduce Callum to me?" I spat the words out in a low growl. He tried to interject but I wanted to have my say before Callum returned. "I think if you'd have noticed me earlier you would have kept walking and pretended you hadn't seen me!"

"No, it wasn't like that," he started to protest.

"And why have you never mentioned Callum?" I demanded, cutting him off. "He's obviously a big part of your life. He stays at your place and you seem really close and yet you've never even mentioned him

221

to us."

"I would never be embarrassed to be seen with you," he told me while I took a deep breath. "I thought you wouldn't want to see me outside of fat club. It often feels like you would rather be somewhere else. I didn't really know how to act. We never see each other apart from on Thursdays. I never mentioned Callum because we don't tend to talk about our personal lives. We just tend to talk about food and tease each other. I don't know anything about anyone's family apart from Linda's husband."

"Oh." I sank back into my seat, realising he was completely right.

"I didn't think you would be interested in my life, or coming out for dinner with me and meeting Callum." I didn't know how to reply to Jake. Not long ago if he'd have asked me to go to dinner with him I would have been mortified by the idea. At that moment though, all I could think was how much I was enjoying myself.

I saw Callum walking back towards us. "He seems like an amazing kid," I uttered without looking at Jake.

"He's the best," Jake replied and I could hear the smile as he spoke. "He hasn't had the easiest of times but he's always cheerful and never lets things get him down. He amazes me all the time."

"He's lucky to have an Uncle like you," I turned back to Jake but he looked away, embarrassed. We smiled at Callum as he re-joined the table with a mischievous grin on his face.

"Think you can manage dessert, Marie?" he asked.

"I think I can probably squeeze a sundae in

somewhere," I replied.

Callum laughed. "They're huge! You'll never manage one. Why don't you get something girlie like a sorbet?"

"Hey! I can always eat sweet stuff."

"But you said you were full already!" he said with a grin.

"Don't you know? It's a different stomach for sweet stuff. I thought everyone knew that!"

His bright smile lit up his face. "I bet I can eat more than you!"

"Challenge accepted Callum. You're on!" I held out my hand and we shook on it.

Twenty minutes later, I had learned a valuable lesson; don't make bets with a ten year old (Yeah it turns out I was only three years out!)

"I'm going to be sick," I groaned, holding my stomach. "Take it away!" I begged the waiter, pushing aside my leftovers.

Jake and Callum were laughing at me, Callum still happily tucking into his chocolate sundae which was probably as big as his head.

"Well that was fun," I said when we walked out of the restaurant. "The best Friday night I've had in ages."

"Told you!" Callum piped up. "Want to come and play computer games with us?"

"Callum, all I can think of now is collapsing on my couch, my stomach feels like it's going to explode thanks to you."

The boys were going to catch the bus but I decided I definitely needed a taxi, and they waited with me until one came by. We said goodbye and I climbed into the car.

Callum looked suddenly vulnerable. "Can we go out again sometime?" he asked.

"I hope so," I replied but he looked unconvinced. "I'll arrange something with Jake, okay?" He smiled and I looked up at Jake who nodded and mouthed his thanks.

Chapter 22

I opened the door at 10am on Saturday with sleepy eyes. "Hi, Linda," I said without surprise and turned in the direction of the kitchen.

"I woke you again didn't I?" she asked as she followed me inside. "I'm sorry."

"That's okay. I needed to get up anyway," I told her.

"Have you got plans already because I wanted to ask you if you felt like coming shopping again...?"

My mind wandered at the sight of Brian's iPod sitting on the kitchen table and remembered him taking it off as he arrived on Thursday before all the jogging commotion. I'd give him a call later in case he was looking for it.

"Actually, it's my Aunt Kath's birthday so I'm going to my mum's house for a little celebration. I've got a bit of time though, so maybe we could go for a coffee or something first."

"That would be nice, if you're sure you have time?"

"Loads of time. Make yourself at home while I jump in the shower."

The quaint little tearoom was apparently Linda's favourite and I could see why. It was really small, but it had a charm about it. I felt like I'd stepped back in time. The tables all had beautiful lace tablecloths with little jugs of wild flowers in the centre. We ordered a pot of tea for two and a scone to share, and when it arrived it was served in a matching delicate bone china tea set. We spent the first ten minutes people-watching in a relaxed silence.

"How are you doing without Grace around the place?" Linda asked me as she poured us both a cup of tea.

"To be honest, I've hardly noticed she's gone," I told her. "I've been pretty busy the last couple of weeks so I've not really thought much about it."

"Do you think you'll visit her?" she asked. "It'd be lovely to go to New York, wouldn't it?"

"I don't know. I mean of course it would be lovely and I'm sure I will go, but I'm just not sure when. Grace wants me to fly over with Brian for the engagement party but it's very short notice so I think I'll wait a while."

"I didn't know they got engaged!" Linda looked genuinely excited by the news. "How lovely. You should go; it would be so magical to be there for the engagement party. And it'd be great fun with Brian. He's such a nice guy and I think he's got his eye on you. Maybe there could be a little holiday romance!"

"Linda!" I laughed with surprise at her thoughts on Brian. "I don't think so!" She grinned at me. "What on earth makes you think Brian has his eye on me?" I asked.

"Well I can't think of another reason for him to come to fat club every week!" We laughed together. That was exactly what Grace had said too.

Linda looked so dainty taking sips of tea from her

cup and saucer. I became aware of the clumsy way I was holding my teacup with my hand wrapped around the whole cup and the saucer abandoned on the table. I replaced the tea cup on the saucer and tried again, lifting the saucer and then gently taking the cup between my thumb and index finger. I automatically sat up straighter and then stuck out my pinkie finger as I took a sip of tea. I smiled to myself, amused by my life.

"How's George?" I asked casually. Since Linda seemed comfortable chatting about my love life, I felt like I could dig a little into hers.

"The same as always," she said with a shrug.

"Were you ever really in love with him?" I asked.

"Oh, yes!" Her eyes lit up and she smiled at some secret memory. "He was my first love. I was the happiest girl in the world when I met George! We were so in love and so happy. We were fifteen when we met at a youth club disco." I watched her take a bite of scone and waited for her to continue.

"I liked him from the first moment I saw him, but we were both a bit shy so it took us a while to get together. My best friend, Jill, started seeing one of his friends and there was a group of us that used to hang around together. After a while, the gang moved on and got jobs and did different things, you know, just drifted apart. There was always me and George though. We used to have so much fun. He'd take me to different places for day trips and we laughed so much." She stopped and took a sip of tea, a silly grin on her face.

"We got married when we were twenty-one," she told me. "I was working in a restaurant back then. We bought the house and then, once we'd paid off some of the mortgage, George said that I should just work part-time. We wanted to have children but it never happened. Eventually I stopped working all together. I don't know when we stopped being in love. It just happened gradually. We stopped laughing; we stopped doing anything really, we hardly talk anymore. That's sad isn't it?" she asked me.

I nodded, not sure of what to say to her. It was really sad and it made me angry. I didn't want that for Linda. I wanted the story of her life to be a happy one.

"Can't you do something about it?" I said. "Talk to him maybe? If he knew how you felt then maybe things would be different, like they used to be."

Having always thought of George as being a bit of a bully, her story made me feel he wasn't so bad after all. Whatever happened to the fun, happy George that she'd fallen in love with all those years ago?

"I don't think so," she said thoughtfully. "I shouldn't really complain. I have a nice enough life really. George looks after me and he's not really unkind. Anyway, I've got you and the rest of the gang so things really aren't so bad are they?" She perked up and smiled at me. "Finish your tea. I'd better get you over to your mums, hadn't I? You don't want to be late to the birthday party."

I had a sudden urge to invite Linda to my mum's house but had an internal struggle over the idea. I was swaying between the thought of it being weird and awkward for me, and then thinking that Linda would probably enjoy it and get on well with Mum and Aunt Kath. They definitely wouldn't mind a party crasher.

I finished my tea in one gulp and pulled on my

cardigan. "My treat," I told Linda as I headed to the counter to pay.

The idea of inviting Linda to my mum's house played on my mind the whole drive over there. I don't know why I was making it such an issue.

"Do you want to come in for cake?" I blurted as we pulled up outside of my mum's house.

Linda looked fairly shocked by the invitation. "I don't think so. It's a family thing. I don't want to intrude."

"You won't be intruding, it's fine. Come on." I got out of the car and didn't leave room for discussion.

"I'll just say a quick hello, Marie, then I'll get off." Linda muttered as I opened the front door.

"Happy birthday!" I hugged Aunt Kath as I entered the living room. "I brought a friend. This is Linda."

"Hi, Linda!" Kath beamed at her.

"Happy birthday. I hope I'm not intruding." Linda looked lost and I felt guilty for dragging her in without warning.

"Not at all!" Aunt Kath reassured her. "It's lovely to have you here.... now we only have to eat a quarter of a birthday cake each instead of a third!"

Linda seemed to relax a little and moved further into the room. "Linda, this is my mum, Eleanor." I winced slightly as I looked at my mum and tried to see her from a stranger's perspective. She was dressed in a well fitted, knee length, green dress with buttons down the front. Nothing remarkable about that. In fact it was a nice dress and looked good on her. She'd accessorised it with a bright pink head band that had two springs sticking out of the top, each with ping pong ball eyes on the top, which bobbed as she moved. She was also wearing a happy birthday banner as a sash draped from her shoulder to her hip.

"It's lovely to meet you, Eleanor. I do like your outfit," Linda said with a straight face.

"Thanks!" Mum beamed at her. "It's a birthday party so I thought I'd add a bit of fun!" She shook her head and the boppy eyes bounced above her head. I rolled my eyes and laughed at her.

"So how do you two know each other?" Kath asked as we sat around the coffee table ten minutes later, each with a slice of cake in front of us. We'd sung 'Happy Birthday' which I always found awkward in a small group. I was poking my slice of cake nervously with my fork. Mum had made it, so although it looked like a delicious chocolate cake, I was fairly sure that there would be some surprise element to it.

"It's a long story," I started since Linda had a mouthful of cake. "I was going to a speed-dating event..." I registered the shocked look on Aunt Kath's face and tried to decide if she was shocked that I would go speed-dating or if she thought that I'd ended up with Linda as a date.

"She didn't actually go speed-dating," Linda jumped in, which I was glad of, because I wasn't sure how to tell this story to Mum and Kath. "I was at my social club in the next room and in walked Marie, not realising that she had the wrong room. A few of us got chatting to Marie and somehow we all just clicked. A real little gang we've got now, Marie, haven't we? Firm friends we are!"

I laughed at Linda's version of events. "Yes, something like that, Linda!" I risked a mouthful of cake and Linda did the same.

Linda's face was suddenly serious. "Is that a... there's something.... pineapple? Is there pineapple in the cake?"

"Yes!" Mum smiled proudly. "Do you like it?"

"Pineapple?" Linda swallowed the mouthful of cake. "Yes I do like pineapple. I've just never had it in chocolate cake before. It's certainly an interesting combination."

"Very diplomatic!" Aunt Kath laughed. I breathed a sigh of relief; at least pineapple was easy to pick out. It could've been much worse.

"It's Kath's birthday and she loves pineapple," Mum declared.

"Your fault then!" I looked at Aunt Kath with a grin.

The time at Mum's went much quicker with Linda there. It was surprisingly relaxed. If Linda found my mum odd, she never showed any sign of it. She stayed for the cake and two cups of tea and then excused herself to get back to George.

I didn't stay much longer and instead of calling Helen for a taxi or getting a lift with Aunt Kath, I decided to have a walk into town. It was a beautiful sunny day and the world felt like a happy place. I could feel the sun tingling my skin and the warmth and the brightness made me buzz with happiness. Despite my leisurely speed I was in town before I knew it. I headed for the taxi rank but when I passed the bus stop, I saw the number 75 just sitting there, as though it was waiting for me. Without thought or hesitation I stepped onto the bus and paid the driver.

I took the ticket and then turned to find a seat. That's when I remembered why I hate buses. The air was thick and sticky. And what was that smell? It was like stale alcohol and cigarettes mixed with sweat and feet. I gagged and turned back to the door but I was too late. I lurched as the bus pulled away.

I stood at the front of the bus looking down the aisle for a place to sit. I always found it hard figuring out where to sit on buses. I once ended up next to a man who spent the whole journey snorting up phlegm and spitting it into the aisle. I ended up getting off the bus five stops early just to get away from him.

I looked at the front of the bus, which was full of old people, and decided that I didn't belong there. I moved unsteadily down the aisle, grabbing at a hand rail as I went. I looked to the back of the bus and saw school kids sitting with their feet up and listening to iPods so loud that I could hear the buzz from the front of the bus. I couldn't venture back there.

That left the middle of the bus. I came to the conclusion that I had a choice of two seats. One was next to a seemingly normal looking woman, who I judged to be in her forties, maybe a housewife. She wore that dishevelled look that people with too many children have. The other seat was behind her, where both seats were free and I could sit alone.

Sitting alone was tempting, but that meant giving up the ability to choose who I sat with. I decided to sit by the woman and smiled at her as I got close, but she looked out of the window and made a noise that was something between a hum and a squeak so I bottled it and slipped into the seat behind her. Crazy lady!

I took a deep breath and tried to relax. I got nervous when the bus pulled into a stop and more people got on. I tried to discreetly eye the new passengers while hoping that they wouldn't sit by me. I toyed with the idea of humming or maybe singing a nursery rhyme out loud. No one would sit by me then. They'd think I was crazy and give me a wide berth.

The bus pulled into another stop and a young guy sat next to me. He seemed normal enough at first but after a couple of minutes I could feel him looking at me; he was going to talk to me, I knew it. I stared ahead and contemplated getting off at the next stop.

"Sorry," he finally said. "I don't mean to stare but I feel like I know you from somewhere." You'd think he could've thought of something original to say.

I turned with the intention of telling him politely to get lost, but when I looked at him properly I realised I knew him.

"Great! First time in years that I get on a bus and I end up sitting next to a complete idiot!" I huffed and turned away from him. I registered his puzzled look at the edge of my vision.

"I'm sorry, but how do I know you?" he asked meekly.

"You don't!" I snapped. "But apparently you think I'm fat!" He gave me another bemused look and I decided I'd better tell him. It wasn't that much fun having a go at someone when they didn't know why.

"You work in the hotel. You sent me into fat club instead of speed dating. You caused me all sorts of trouble."

His face changed. "Shit! I'm sorry. It was just for a laugh." He seemed genuinely apologetic and I was tempted to let him off the hook. "Honestly, you have no idea how boring it is working there. I stand at that desk for nine hours a day, and nothing happens. So I get bored and sometimes it just seems like a laugh. I promise I won't do it again, and I really never meant any harm. I definitely don't think you're fat. I send fat people into speed-dating."

I felt bad for having a go at him. It was quite funny - when the joke wasn't on me of course.

"It's okay. It actually didn't turn out that badly. I made some friends. So maybe I should be thanking you. Although who knows what I missed out on at speed dating? I could have a gorgeous boyfriend by now if it weren't for you."

He laughed. "Actually, most people just realise they're in the wrong room and walk out again." I guess that would be the normal thing to do.

"This is my stop," I told him, registering where we were.

As he got up to let me out, he looked outside. "It's actually my stop as well."

We stepped off the bus together and he turned to me. "I'm going that way," he blurted and pointed down the road. "Just in case you're going that way too. I don't want you to think I'm stalking you or anything." He looked concerned and I laughed.

"I'll have to go the other way now so you don't think I'm stalking you!"

"I'm Jeff," he held his hand out.

"Marie," I said, shaking his hand.

"I feel bad about the speed-dating thing," he told me. "How about I take you out to eat tonight as an apology?"

"Yeah, sure. Why not?" I said automatically.

"Great! I know a really good steak place. You're not vegetarian are you?"

"No." I laughed, "Steak sounds good."

"How about I come to your place and we can go from there? Say eight o'clock? Promise I'm not a crazy stalker!"

I nodded and I looked at my watch, impressed by his directness. I scribbled my address on a scrap of paper and then we headed off in separate directions.

I decided that maybe buses weren't so bad after all.

When I got home, my thoughts turned to what I would wear for my night out. I longed for the times when I could just shout to Grace in the next room and ask her advice. I trawled through my wardrobe, wondering why I didn't have anything nice to wear and missing Grace all the while.

I finally settled on my 'going out' jeans and a tried and tested black top of the low-cut variety. Nothing spectacular but I was comfortable and almost confident in it.

It was when I was all dressed and ready to go, pacing the place, waiting for the doorbell to ring, that the nerves set in. It wasn't like it was a date or anything, but in my head it suddenly felt like it. What the heck would we talk about? I didn't even know the guy.

The goblin in my head was being his usual cheerful self and telling me that Jeff would turn out to be a boring loser and I'd end up waiting for him to go to the bathroom so that I could employ my 'grab coat, down contents of drink, fling bag over shoulder and run' manoeuvre. I was doing my best to ignore the annoying goblin and trying really hard to be positive when the doorbell rang, making me jump. I took a deep breath and answered it.

"You look nice," Jeff said.

"Thanks. You too," I replied quickly. He was looking rather casual actually in jeans and a t-shirt but it put me at ease. The fact that he wasn't making much effort banished my thoughts of this being a date.

"So, this steak place I know is great, but it's nothing fancy. I hope that's okay with you?"

"Sounds lovely," I said and smiled as an image of my last fancy meal popped into my head accompanied by a taste of raw beef. 'Nothing fancy' was definitely okay with me.

"Let's order a taxi then shall we? That way I get to nosy at your place while we wait."

I ushered him into the living room while he rang a taxi. Thankfully it wasn't my usual taxi firm. I didn't really want twenty questions from Helen about Jeff.

"Five minutes," he informed me as he hung up the phone and sank into the couch. "Cute place." He had an easy smile that made me relax.

"My friend owns it but she just moved to New York so I have the place to myself for now."

"That's cool. I live with an old school friend, which used to be great, but he got a girlfriend and she's around a lot now. So we have to tidy up now and again or she goes a bit crazy." He rolled his eyes. "Maybe I'll get my own place. Is it lonely on your own?"

"No, not really," I answered automatically and then corrected myself. "Maybe sometimes." My mind wandered and he looked at me with a half-smile. "Well, Grace only just moved to New York a few weeks ago so I'm not really used to it yet." I smiled back at him.

"Have you ever been to New York?" He asked.

"Nope."

"I went once." He grinned. "Craziest week of my life!" He laughed but we were interrupted by a car horn before I could question him about it. He was still smiling to himself as he held the taxi door for me.

"Tell me about New York then..." I prompted once we were settled in the taxi.

"I honestly wouldn't know where to start," he said. I laughed at him and leaned back into the seat for the ten-minute drive.

Chapter 23

By the time we'd ordered steaks and taken the first sips of beer I was feeling content with the way that the evening was going. I was definitely seeing this as a meal with a friend rather than a date. Jeff didn't seem my type and there were no sparks between us. He seemed like a nice, easy-going guy though and I was happy in his easy company.

"So I take it you don't fancy me?" He broke my thoughts as though he was reading them and I looked at him to see him smiling to himself. "Ordering onion rings was a giveaway. People only order onion rings when they have no intention of doing any kissing, so I'll take that as a signal."

A laugh escaped me. "You're quite straight-forward, aren't you?"

"Yeah. And it's okay. I don't see any romance between us either; hence I ordered garlic bread." I watched him with a smile on my face, aware of the fact that I should be offended.

He grinned as his eyes stopped roaming the room and landed on me again. "I reckon you're a bit old for me actually."

I laughed. "Are you kidding me?"

He squinted at me. "How old are you then?"

"Twenty-eight."

"You see, you've got four years on me. Cradle snatcher!" I couldn't help but laugh again. I was surprised though. He looked older.

"Come on then, tell me about yourself," he said and I had an awkward moment where I didn't know what to say. There wasn't much to say really. "Your subjects are work, family, friends. In that order. Go!" he prompted.

"Okay. Well I'm a travel agent..."

"Oh, no! Wait, sorry, first tell me what happened that night that I sent you into Emily? I've been dying to know. I bet that's a good story?"

"That is a good story...." I smiled at the memory and then launched into what I intended to be a brief overview but ended up being a detailed account. It became a vicious cycle of him laughing and me adding more details.

After that, the evening went by in a blur of laughter and anecdotes. With all thoughts of romance gone, we relaxed into a rhythm of easy conversation. We swapped stories of drunken nights out and embarrassing dates and I was surprised when I looked at my watch and found that three hours had passed. We'd eaten our steaks almost without noticing. The beer kept flowing and I suddenly realised that I was well on the way to being drunk.

"I think they're gonna kick us out soon," I commented as I looked around at the almost empty restaurant. The waitresses were sweeping the floor and tidying up for the night.

"I think you're right. Shall we hit the town or are you too old for that?" My brain whirred. Go home or go out? I could happily have stayed there chatting to

Jeff but the thought of going into town was unappealing. Maybe I was getting old!

"I think I should probably get home. I reckon I've had enough to drink for one night."

"No problem, grandma! I will escort you safely home."

I ignored the jibe and smiled when he stood up and swayed as he took a step. He reached for the back of a chair to steady himself. "Maybe I need to go home too!"

We made our way out of the restaurant and stumbled into a taxi. Jeff paid the driver and got out at my place.

"Are you sure you can manage to walk from here?" I asked.

"It was the restaurant that swayed, not me, okay?"

"Oh, right, yeah, got it." I winked at him while I searched my bag for my keys.

"You're not going to try and kiss me goodnight are you?" I said with a laugh.

"No chance. I don't kiss grandmas! Especially when they stink of onions!"

He leaned against the door frame as I fumbled with the key in the lock. "I had a really good night," I told him.

"No need to sound so surprised!"

I pushed the door open and shrieked in surprise at the sight of Sophie in my hallway. "Oh my God, Sophie, you nearly gave me a heart attack!"

She looked past me at Jeff. "Hello, I'm Sophie." She glared at him. "It's been lovely meeting you. Hope to see you again sometime!" She pulled me over the doorstep and slammed the door in his face.

"Sophie! What on earth?" I nudged her out of the way and grabbed at the door. "I'm so sorry, Jeff."

"You never mentioned you had a sister," he said with a lopsided smile. "I better get home. Take care." He waved as he turned and wandered away down the road.

I closed the door again and looked at Sophie who had her hands on her hips. "You can thank me later!" she said.

"For what?" I demanded, following her into the living room. "Why are you here? How did you get in? And why are you wearing my clothes?" I got gradually louder with each insane question. I collapsed on the couch and waited for the explanations.

Sophie glanced down as though she'd forgotten she was dressed as me.

"That's a bit creepy actually," I told her.

She grinned at me. "I already called my mum to tell her I was staying here so I just wanted something comfy to sleep in."

"And why are you staying here?" I asked.

"That's Brian's fault." She looked suddenly panicked and reached for her phone which was lying on the coffee table. "She's here," she said into the phone. "Yes. She's fine." Her voice got suddenly louder. "I don't know, Brian, ask her yourself! Goodbye." She turned to me as she hung up the phone. "He can be so annoying!"

I raised my eyebrows questioningly.

She put her phone back on the table. "Brian called me a couple of hours ago looking for you and he was being all weird and secretive so I said I had no clue where you were and hung up. But he rang back later to ask if I knew where you might be and then he dropped in the conversation that he was at your place. He claimed he'd come to pick up his iPod but I'm not sure, I think maybe he's a stalker. Apparently he has the spare key from your friend and thinks it's okay to let himself in. I think that's totally out of order, but then I was thinking about it and I think if he's got a key, then maybe you can give me a key too?"

She finally stopped talking and looked at me with her big eyes, as I tried to take in what she'd said. I definitely remembered Grace saying that she would leave a spare key somewhere but I thought she meant with her parents.

"So, can I have a key?" Sophie interrupted my thoughts.

"What? No! You're right though; it's not okay for Brian to let himself into my home. And you! How did you end up here?"

She looked hurt that I wouldn't let her have a key. "Brian mentioned he was here and I didn't want to miss out so I came round. Then he left and told me to call when you turned up."

"So what did Brian need me for so urgently?" I asked.

Sophie smirked. "He turns up on a Saturday night with a flimsy excuse about his iPod. What do you think he wants? You're quite innocent really, aren't you?" She looked thoughtful for a moment. "Actually, it was when I suggested that you were probably on a date that he suddenly left."

"What did you say that for?" I asked, not quite sure why it bothered me so much.

"We were just discussing where you might be, and since we know you don't have many friends, I had to get creative!" She shot me her mischievous grin. "If I'm honest, I didn't actually think you were on a date. Where did you pick him up?"

I shook my head. "I need to go to bed. You can sleep on the couch. I'll throw you a blanket down." I could've offered her a bed but I was nervous of making her too comfortable. She might decide to never leave.

When I headed for the stairs, I grabbed my handbag from where I'd dropped it in the hall and pulled out my phone. I looked at the screen and registered the missed calls, remembering that I'd switched it to silent. I was a popular girl: one missed call from Mum, four from Brian and eight from Sophie. I wondered again what Brian wanted and decided I would figure it out after some much-needed sleep.

Chapter 24

My head was foggy when I woke up. Brian popped into my head and I checked my phone. No new calls or messages. *Why had he been so keen to get hold of me?* I wondered again. I was also feeling a bit weird about the fact that he had a key and had let himself in. I decided to call him later and get some answers. I dragged myself out of bed and went down to the living room, quietly poking my head around the door to check if Sophie was still sleeping. I found her lying on her back with her eyes wide open, staring at the ceiling.

"Do you know Brian likes you?" she asked drearily, without moving.

"What do you mean *likes* me? Because he's my friend, and usually friends like each other. I think that's fairly normal."

She bent her legs up as I walked into the room and I sat in the space she'd created at the end of the couch.

"I don't mean as friends," she said. "I mean he really likes you."

I wondered where the conversation had come from, and where it was going. Sophie wasn't her usual happy self.

"It's just that I kind of hoped that he might like me," she told me, all trace of attitude gone. This was definitely not the same Sophie who spent so much time teasing me. I stayed quiet hoping that she would let me in on the full story eventually. "Then last night he called my mobile."

"Why does he have your number?" I jumped in. It suddenly occurred to me that maybe they had a whole different relationship that I didn't know about where they called each other and did things together. My heart was beating faster.

"I've got everyone's number. I took people's phones and called myself. I put my number in everyone's phone too like I did with yours." She paused and I wondered why none of us had ever suggested swapping phone numbers.

"Anyway, he was just asking about you when he rang. He couldn't find you and he was worried. He sounded weird on the phone, like something else was going on. I came over here and he said he'd called Jake and Linda and no one knew where you were. Then his phone rang and he wouldn't tell me who it was. He said he had to leave and told me to call him if you turned up."

My mind whirred, trying to process the information. It didn't sound like Brian at all. He was always so cool and calm. I couldn't figure out what could have gotten him so wound up.

He obviously thought I had such a sad life that if I wasn't sitting around the house in my pyjamas on a Saturday night, something must be seriously wrong. In fairness it was quite an unusual night for me but I think it was quite presumptuous of Brian to immediately worry.

"You should call him," Sophie suggested.

I reached for my phone and found his number in my recent calls but he didn't answer.

"I thought he seemed worried but do you think he's actually mad at you for something?" Sophie asked.

"I don't know. Why would he be mad at me?"

"Are you sure you hadn't arranged to meet him last night and then you forgot and went on a date instead? By the way, you haven't told me about your date yet... Who was that guy?"

"That was just Jeff," I answered automatically. "And it wasn't really a date. He's just a friend. At least he might have been until you scared him off! And I'd remember if Brian had asked me to do something. I definitely had no plans to see him."

"But you do like him?" Sophie asked.

"Brian? No. Not like that," I told her adamantly.

"I've gone off him too," she told me. "He's actually far too old for me and he's quite annoying sometimes."

"I wonder why he was so worried," I said.

"Well, just go round to his house if he won't answer the phone." Sophie actually sounded like she was trying to help.

"I don't know where he lives." It was a bit strange; he was one of my closest friends and he spent so much time at my place, but I had no clue where he lived and before then it had never occurred to me to wonder.

"I can show you if you want!" Sophie looked excited, as though she was hatching a plan for a Sunday morning adventure.

"Did you steal his address too?" I was a little bit in awe of her.

"No!" She started laughing. "I followed him home one day!" Her eyes lit up as she said it and I laughed at her joke.

"Good one, Sophie! I'm not completely gullible." Her laughter subsided and she was left with a silly grin on her face. My eyes got wider. "Are you serious?"

"Don't ever tell him. I'll show you where he lives if you promise never to tell him?"

I didn't think I could be surprised by Sophie anymore... but stalking? She was staring at me, waiting for a reply.

I wasn't sure though. I mean, what would I do when I got there? What would I say? I was over-thinking it. "Okay, then. Let's go."

We got dressed and hurried out on a surge of adrenalin which dipped when I realised our little adventure meant getting on a bus. I would've suggested a taxi but I knew that wouldn't go down well with Sophie. At best she'd call me a stuck up snob, and probably a lot of other things too. At least I had Sophie as protection, safety in numbers and all that.

It turned out to be entirely painless. We only went five stops, away from the city, and then we were off again, deposited into a part of town that was entirely different from where I lived. Instead of apartment buildings and rows of terraced houses the street was lined with tall, old Victorian houses. It was all leafy and homely looking.

"This is where Brian lives?" I asked dubiously.

"Yep." She led me along the street a little way and then came to a stop outside a house with a green door, a brass knocker in the middle of it.

"Wow!"

"I know. He must be loaded, right?" Sophie asked with wide eyes.

"I guess so," I replied.

"What now then?" Sophie asked.

"Maybe we should just go home…" I suggested feeling suddenly nervous.

"No chance!" Sophie said as she reached up for the doorknocker. It was loud and drowned out my protests. I felt like a teenager again. What the hell was I doing? We stood waiting and when it became clear that there was no one home I breathed a sigh of relief.

"Come on then, let's go…" I suggested but Sophie was already bending down to the letterbox.

"Sophie!" I hissed.

"Hello, Brian!" She held the letterbox open as she shouted through. "Mr Connor. Come and let your girls in. We want to be your sex slaves!" She giggled and I was reminded of how simple life is when you're eighteen.

"Sophie! Stop it!"

She peered into the house through the letterbox. "You should see this, Marie… it's nice in there…"

Curiosity got the better of me and since it was clear he wasn't in, I bent down and gently shoved Sophie out of the way. "Let me see".

"Hey!" Sophie shouted as she shoved me back. We were shoulder to shoulder, tussling away when a voice interrupted us.

"Ladies, I'd appreciate it if you didn't fight on my doorstep. It lowers the tone of the neighbourhood."

I jolted upright and tried to look casual. "Hi,

Brian!" He raised his eyebrows as he moved between us to put his key in the lock. He had a take-away coffee in one hand and a newspaper tucked under his arm.

"You coming in?" he asked as he held the door for us. "What was that about sex slaves?" he called to Sophie as she dashed into the house to explore.

"You wish!" she shouted back.

"I'm not sure I want to know how you found out where I live," Brian said as I followed him through a beautiful dining room and into a large but cosy kitchen.

"No, you don't." I replied while I looked around in wonder. Everything about the place had the 'wow' factor. I'd always imagined him living in a bachelor pad full of black leather and fur, but it couldn't have been further from it. It was classy and full of charm. It felt like a family home and I could just imagine it full of kids and a lovely old Labrador roaming around the place.

"Something to do with Sophie, no doubt?" he asked.

"I really wouldn't like to say," I replied lightly.

"Tea?" Brian offered.

I nodded and was amused as I watched him turn on the gas stove and move an old-fashion kettle over the flame. I pulled out a stool and took a seat at the island in the middle of the kitchen, pots and pans hung overhead.

I suddenly remembered why I was there and felt strangely self-conscious. "I tried to call you earlier..."

"So you did," he said, lifting his phone from the sideboard and unplugging it from the charger.

"I was wondering about last night. Sophie said you were at my place looking for me? I didn't know you had a key."

He looked unsure of himself. "Sorry, I thought Grace told you, she gave me a spare key for emergencies. I thought you wouldn't mind if I ran in and grabbed my iPod."

"It's fine," I told him, not wanting to make a big deal out of it. "But why were you so desperate to find me?"

"I should probably just confess," he said, looking sheepish. "When I was at your place, the house phone rang and it was right next to me. I picked it up automatically." He looked nervous, as though he expected me to be mad at him.

Reaching for the newspaper, I flicked through the pages to give my hands something to do. Not many people called the house phone so I was fairly sure I knew who he'd spoken to.

"Who was it?" I asked nervously.

"Your mum."

That's what I thought. I tensed, wondering what she'd said to him. I was trying to look casual by shifting my gaze between Brian and the newspaper.

"She was surprised that you weren't home," he told me. "She said she'd seen you earlier and that you were heading home for the evening. She was really worried so I told her I'd wait while she tried to get you on your mobile. She called back even more worried because there was no answer and she said that you always answer your mobile. So I told her I'd ring around and see if anyone knew where you were."

"Oh." I wasn't sure what to say. My mind went into

overdrive with thoughts of my mum on the phone to Brian. Did she just sound like a caring, worried mother or was the craziness conveyed down the phone?

"So that's why I was looking for you. To be honest, your mum was so worried that it made me worry." His sheepish smile made him look adorably vulnerable. "It was stupid, you're a grown up, you can look after yourself, right?" He looked apologetic as he spoke.

"Yeah," I agreed. "I can take care of myself." It was nice though, to think that someone was worried about me.

"Where were you, by the way?" Brian asked suddenly, as the kettle began to whistle. He turned his back to me to make the tea.

"Just out for dinner with a friend," I answered casually. "Nothing special."

He turned and smiled at me. "We thought that you might be on a date?"

There was a look in his eyes that gave me butterflies. I opened my mouth to answer but Sophie chose that second to come bounding into the room and the moment was lost.

"This place is huge!" She was so hyperactive and happy that it was almost infectious. I was dizzy just watching her.

"It's a lovely place," I commented, looking around the room.

"This house is far too big for you," Sophie told Brian. "You must be lonely. I thought I could do you a favour and move in... and before you ask - no, I won't pay rent and I don't do cleaning. I want the bedroom with the big window seat. Deal?" She held out her hand for him to shake and grinned up at him.

"No," he said with a grin. "But thanks for the lovely offer." He took her hand and pulled her to him, ruffling her hair as he held her in a headlock and she squealed with laughter. He relaxed his hold and draped an arm over her shoulders. She leaned into him, her face a picture of contentment.

It felt like someone had stabbed me in the chest. I was jealous of the affection between them. I'd never really had a tactile relationship with anyone other than boyfriends and even then it didn't sit naturally with me. I guess it came from being the only child of an unconventional, single parent.

All I wanted to do was shout "group hug" and jump in with them. The moment passed and Sophie bounced back out of the room, intent of putting some music on.

"I have a question about last night..." Brian said cautiously. "It's just that I spent quite a lot of time talking to your mum..."

"Yeah - so?" I tried to sound casual but my whole body tensed.

"Is she always so... irrational?" His voice was deadpan.

My eyes darted to the newspaper. "She's a bit eccentric sometimes, that's all." My eyes unwillingly filled with tears and I longed for a way to jump into the newspaper and escape the conversation. I didn't want Brian to know about my crazy mother and I definitely didn't want to talk to him about her.

The awkward silence was killing me when he placed a cup of tea in front of me. I could feel his eyes on me but I kept my head down, poring over the newspaper without reading a word. He lingered beside me and then pulled my head in his direction and kissed my forehead. Right on the hairline.

He moved away from me and out of the kitchen. "Sophie, if you break my sound system, I'll break you!" he called teasingly as he went.

A teardrop splattered onto the pages of the newspaper and I forced myself to breathe.

Once I'd pulled myself together I joined them in the living room. We drank tea and chatted idly for an hour before my phone rang and I moved into the kitchen to answer it.

"Hi, Mum," I greeted her as I paced the kitchen.

"Are you coming over? I've been waiting for you." She sounded flustered.

"No, Mum, I saw you yesterday. I thought you knew I wasn't coming today." I sighed as I answered her and let my eyes explore Brian's very impressive kitchen. It almost looked like a show home.

"Well, I thought you might come today as well. And after I spent so much time worrying about you last night, I wanted to see you."

"I don't know why you were so worried. My phone was on silent that's all. I was having dinner with a friend."

She didn't reply.

"Anyway, I'm just at a friend's place," I told her. "Can we talk later?"

"Which friend?" I was surprised to hear her ask. She was never usually so interested in my life.

"Just a couple of friends. I'll tell you about them when I see you."

"Fine," she said and hung up.

I followed the sound of laughter back into the living room. Sophie was regaling Brian with stories from the beauty salon where she worked.

Brian's phone began to buzz on the coffee table when I took a seat on the couch. He picked it up and looked at the screen, hesitating for a moment before pressing a button to end the buzzing without answering it. He put it down beside him but the buzzing started again almost immediately.

"Someone loves you," Sophie commented.

"Sorry," he looked suddenly serious. "I better take it... work..." he mumbled as he left the room to answer it. Sophie and I stayed quiet, trying in vain to listen in.

"I think that was a lie," Sophie told me. "Work wouldn't call him on a Sunday, would they?"

"I was thinking the same. He looked suspicious."

"Do you think he's seeing someone and doesn't want to tell us?"

I shrugged, uncomfortable at the thought.

Brian reappeared in the doorway. "Anyone want a drink?"

"Why were work calling you on a Sunday?" Sophie asked bluntly.

"The boss is a slave driver." he answered easily. "Drinks?"

Sophie eyed him suspiciously and he ignored her completely. The atmosphere had changed and I decided to get out of there.

"I'm fine thanks, I'm going to head home," I told them, standing up.

"What are you gonna do at home?" Sophie asked and looked at her watch.

"Washing, tidying up."

"Boring! I don't want to do that," she informed me. I wasn't sure why she thought she was invited. "Brian, can I stay and hang out here? I don't want to go home yet." She looked at Brian with big eyes and he laughed at her. "Sure, you can finish telling me how you torture women for a living!"

She stuck her tongue out at him as I walked past her. "See you soon, Sophie."

"Bye," she shouted after me.

"Sure you don't want to stay?" Brian offered at the front door. "We could get a take-away later?"

I hesitated. "No thanks, I really need to do some washing or I'll have no clean clothes for work. Thanks, though."

"Need a lift home?" he offered as I opened the front door.

"No, I'm fine." I lingered at the door unsure of myself. "See you on Thursday?" I asked.

"Yeah."

I moved slowly away from him. I was suddenly angry at myself. Why was I annoyed with him over a phone call? For all I knew, it was just a work call, and even if it was a woman calling him, why did I care?

I didn't want to leave. I wished I'd accepted the offer of a take-away, or a lift home even. I really didn't want to spend the afternoon sitting on my own and doing my washing.

I pulled myself together and moved quickly down the front steps. "See you soon!" I turned and waved up at him, desperate to look like a normal, sane person. He stood on the top step and waved. When I walked down the street, I had an urge to turn and see if he was watching me. I finally glanced back but his door was closed. He'd gone back inside and was no doubt laughing with Sophie.

I walked to the bus stop with absolutely no intention of getting on a bus. Pulling out my phone, I rang Helen and asked her to send me a taxi. She let out a low whistle when I told her where I was.

"You're certainly going up in the world," she said. "Tell me you've found yourself a man who lives in one of those lovely big houses?"

I laughed and took a seat on the bench at the bus stop. "Just a friend," I told her.

"Well keep hold of that one. Or if you don't want him, introduce him to me!"

Pat arrived ten minutes later and drove me home. He was my least favourite driver, but I wasn't bothered. I didn't have to chat to Pat and I could sit on the back seat and have some time to think.

My mind was all over the place. I kept thinking about Brian asking me if I'd been on a date, and the way he'd kissed my forehead. I was suddenly unsure of how I felt about him. He'd been a really good friend and I really liked spending time with him, but that was all.

I couldn't understand why the thought of him with someone else made me nauseous all of a sudden. Everyone else seemed to think that he had feelings for me. I'd never really believed it though, at least not until today. Was he jealous that I'd been out on a date? My brain went over everything but I couldn't make sense of any of it.

I was home before I knew it. I paid Pat and said a curt goodbye, my mind still elsewhere. I resisted the urge to sit on the couch and wallow. Instead I put a load of washing on and then got to work on cleaning the house from top to bottom. I put some music on and it was quite satisfying. I even made up the bed in Grace's old room and moved some of my things over. It suddenly seemed silly that I was still sleeping on a single bed in the little room when I could be in the double bed.

I was happy at how productive I'd been and suddenly realised that I was hungry. I settled for cheese on toast and a cup of tea and then treated myself to a long hot bubble bath. I managed not to think about Brian for the whole afternoon, but as I crawled into the satisfying comfort of the big double bed with fresh sheets, my mind wandered to the morning after Grace left. I'd woken up in that bed with Brian beside me.

"Get out of my head, Brian!" I said aloud before turning out the light.

Chapter 25

It was a hectic weekend and the rhythm of the working week came as a relief. I was tapping away on my computer on Wednesday afternoon when a knocking drew my eyes to the shop window. The view was restricted with the posters and a huge cardboard aeroplane and I couldn't see anything except for the usual bustle of shoppers wandering by. I'd just turned back to my computer when I heard the knock again.

"What was that?" Anne asked.

"No clue," I told her while I got up and moved to the window. "I can't see anything," I told Anne when I turned back to her. I jumped as the knocking returned, much louder and more frantic this time.

I turned and laughed at the sight of Jake and Callum, sticking out their tongues and pulling faces through the window. I beckoned them in and opened the door for them.

"This is a nice surprise." I ruffled Callum's hair. "Even though you did nearly give me a heart attack!"

"I hope it's alright to call in?" Jake asked. "I picked Callum up from school today and he was asking about you, so I thought we'd call in."

"Of course. You're always welcome."

Anne cleared her throat.

"Anne, come and meet my friends," I told her. "This is Jake, who I met at *Emily's Encouragement* and his nephew, Callum."

She came over and greeted them both warmly. "Did Marie tell you that I go to Emily's group now?" Anne asked. "She's a funny one that Emily isn't she?"

"She's a bit odd," Jake agreed.

"Anyway, it's always nice to meet Marie's friends but I better get back to work." Anne moved back to her desk.

"We should probably let you get back to work too," Jake said.

"Do you want to come and have dinner with us at Jake's place?" Callum asked.

I smiled at him. "I've got some work to finish here and then I need to do some shopping. Maybe we could do something at the weekend instead?"

Callum looked up at Jake. "How about a movie night on Friday?" Jake suggested.

"Sounds good to me. Come to my place and I'll cook something," I said and high-fived Callum who looked pleased with the arrangements.

Callum hugged me and Jake patted my arm affectionately as we said goodbye. They both waved frantically through the window, before disappearing from view.

"What a lovely pair," Anne said as my phone rang. I returned to my desk to answer it.

"Marie, Darling! How are you?" said the flamboyant voice.

"Hi, Sebastian. I'm great thank you. How are you?"

"Oh you know. Surviving! I was just thinking about you and wondered if you were free on Friday night. I thought we could go for a nice meal again."

"I already have plans for Friday night. Sorry."

"Oh don't worry, how about Thursday evening?"

I winced. "You won't believe it but I have plans for Thursday night too?"

"Well I can't make Saturday night, but how about we grab lunch on Saturday?" he suggested.

I winced again. I didn't have definite plans but after I didn't have time to go shopping with Linda last week, I'd had it in mind that I would reserve that time for her. "Sorry, that doesn't work either."

"Well what a hectic social life you have!" He laughed. "I hope you're not just avoiding me!"

"Of course not. We'll find a time soon, I promise. Let's talk again next week and try and arrange something then, shall we?"

"Marvellous, Darling. Let's do that. Have a wonderful week won't you?"

As I put the phone down I felt a sense of relief. I wasn't sure I could face another night out with Sebastian just yet. So far it had never turned out to be a relaxed experience and a night with Jake and Callum seemed much more appealing.

I'd just helped a lovely retired couple pick out a cruise when my mobile rang again. I answered it hesitantly after I saw it was Mum.

"How's Brian?" she asked immediately. I'd been trying not to think about the fact that she'd been talking to him on Saturday night. I was hoping that would never be mentioned again.

"He's fine," I answered calmly and waited to see where the conversation would go.

"You didn't tell me you'd got a new boyfriend,"

she snapped.

"He's not my boyfriend," I told her calmly. For most people that would put a stop to the conversation but not my mother.

"I'd like to meet him. You can bring him over for dinner one day." She sounded serious but the thought of bringing Brian round to have dinner with my mother made me snort with laughter.

I tried to be patient with her. "Mum, I'm not going to bring him for dinner because he's not my boyfriend." And even if he was I wouldn't subject him to such an ordeal. In fact especially not if he was my boyfriend. I'd never once brought a boyfriend to meet my mother. I always felt that would be a sure-fire way to get rid of them.

"You never let me meet your boyfriends," she said, sulking.

"You never wanted to meet them!"

"Only because I didn't like any of the others, but I like Brian. Why can't I meet him?"

"How did you know you didn't like them when you never met them?" I shot at her.

"Grace didn't like Carl, so I knew that I wouldn't," she explained.

"What did Grace say about Carl?" I asked, intrigued. Grace was the only person who'd I'd let near my mother but I was surprised that they'd spoken about Carl.

"She didn't say anything. But if she liked him she would have said so." I looked at my watch; I should get on with some work. "Brian was very nice to me on the phone on Saturday and he said that he knew you through Grace. He must be nice if he's friends with

Grace." I couldn't fault her logic but it irked me that she trusted Grace's judgement over mine.

"So when can I meet him?" Strangely, it was Mum who seemed to be getting frustrated with the conversation.

"The problem is that he's really not my boyfriend. He's just a friend."

"Fine. It's because you're embarrassed by me isn't it?" I was confused. Never in my life had she acknowledged that her behaviour is peculiar or that she was aware of me being embarrassed by her.

"That must be the reason," she sniffed. "I know he's your boyfriend because he was at your house when I rang you. Why else would he be in your home and answering your phone? And why was he so concerned if he's not your boyfriend?"

I liked to think that he could also be concerned as a friend but I was starting to realise that arguing was futile. I decided to go for a different tack; one that would get me off of the phone sometime in the near future.

"Well, yeah okay, you're right, Mum, but it's still early days. You can definitely meet him soon, it's just that he works away a lot, so I will have to find out when is good for him."

She squealed with delight. "Of course. You just ask him and then tell me when you can both come over and I can think of something yummy to cook. When's his birthday, Marie? So I can make him a cushion."

"I can't remember but I'll find out and let you know in plenty of time." I hated myself for getting her excited about nothing. I was clearly going to be making up excuses from now until the end of time. It was nice to hear her so happy though, even if it was under false pretences.

Chapter 26

The doorbell rang early on Thursday and I looked at the front door suspiciously. My fat club friends were becoming quite unreliable when it came to timing. It used to be that I could set my watch by them on Thursday evenings.

My stomach went all fluttery when I realised it might be Brian arriving early. Thoughts of him had been popping into my head frequently in the last few days.

I ignored the fact that I was suddenly nervous about seeing him and plastered a smile on my face when I opened the door. It was Linda, and she had a suitcase which made me uneasy. I checked her face but she wasn't crying, nor were there any signs of recent tears.

"I got a taxi here," she told me happily. "I never take taxis. And I left George," she announced when she moved past me, dragging her suitcase behind her. I followed her into the living room where she sat on the couch and smiled up at me. "I actually left him!" She laughed and it made me nervous. "You won't believe what I said to him." She looked excited. "I told him to bugger off!" she said, giggling.

I snorted a bit. "Linda!"

"I did! Just like you said I should. I actually told

him to bugger off. You should've seen his face!"

"Linda, stop it!" The change in her was unsettling me.

She looked over at her case. "I thought I'd stay here for a while," she said confidently as she got up and walked to the kitchen. "Tell me you've got wine. I definitely need wine."

I stood open-mouthed wondering who the woman in my house was. "What have you done with Linda?" I called after her but she only laughed in response. The doorbell rang again and I checked my watch; still not time for fat club.

This time it was Sophie, also with a suitcase. She heaved it into the living room.

"I thought I'd move in here," she said. "Since you've got a spare room and my mum's place is so full..." She stopped abruptly at the sight of the rival suitcase in the room.

Linda returned from the kitchen with a glass of wine in her hand. "Sorry, Sophie, you're about five minutes too late. I believe the couch is still available though."

"Get lost, Linda, Marie doesn't want to live with an old fart like you!"

"Sophie! Linda just left George," I said.

"Oh, right. Sorry, Linda. I've brought my stuff all the way over here though. Do you think you'll be staying for long?"

"I've no idea how long I'll be staying," Linda told Sophie. "But since I was here first I'm afraid you're going to have to make do with the couch. Or bugger off home, I don't care which." Linda's voice was calm and authoritative.

Sophie's bottom lip was twitching and I wondered how the universe could alter so drastically in such a short space of time. I threw the box of tissues in Sophie's direction.

"Don't be so pathetic," Linda snapped at her. "Stop blubbing and get yourself a glass of wine."

I followed Sophie into the kitchen, thinking that I could use some wine too.

"Everything okay at home, Sophie?" I asked.

"Yeah," she sniffed. "It's just a bit crowded and Mum's annoying me"

"Well, you're a teenager and she's your mother, that's just what they do I'm afraid."

"What's happened to Linda?" she changed the subject.

"Apparently she left her husband and developed an attitude."

The doorbell rang again when Sophie and I returned to the living room. "What's wrong with you all this week? Did we change the time and no one told me?"

I wasn't at all surprised to find Jake standing on my doorstep. "Sorry I'm early..." he said.

"Not a problem," I jumped in, overly-cheerful due to the absence of any worldly possessions, until I noticed the carrier bag in his hand. "Unless there's a toothbrush and undies in that bag, because I'm afraid this inn is well and truly full!"

"What? I just wanted to..."

"Come on in," I interrupted him again and he followed me into the living room.

He looked surprised at the sight of Linda and Sophie. "I thought I would be the first." He checked his watch.

"Don't worry Jake, your watch is right, but apparently everyone wanted to be early this week," I told him.

"I see," he said nervously.

"Have you brought presents?" Linda asked, eyeing Jake's shopping bag.

Jake looked a little unnerved by Linda. It wasn't just the attitude earlier; she was too cheerful and talkative. It wasn't like her at all.

"Not exactly," Jake replied.

"For goodness sake!" Linda said impatiently. "What's the matter Jake? Just spit it out will you?"

"What's gotten into Linda?" Jake looked from me to Sophie but we just shrugged. "It is a gift actually," Jake said cautiously. "But it's for Marie. To say thank you... for letting us come round every week."

Jake pulled a snow globe out of the bag and handed it to me. I tipped it up and then watched the snow fall down around a New York scene.

"It's lovely," I whispered.

"Well I know that your friend moved to New York and I know how fascinated you are with other places because of your job, so I thought you might like it."

I felt a lump form in my throat and tears stung my eyes. "Thanks, Jake."

"Oh yeah. Thanks a lot Jake!" Linda laughed. "You could have told the rest of us you were bringing a gift! You've made us look like bad friends now."

We all looked at Linda. "Give me your wine please," I demanded and moved to take her glass. I really didn't think that she needed alcohol. I took the glass into the kitchen and Jake followed me.

"I wasn't expecting anyone to be here," Jake said.

"Really, I wanted to say thank you for taking an interest in Callum. It means a lot to him and he's having a tough time at the moment..."

"Who's Callum?" Sophie's voice cut in as she joined us in the kitchen. I looked at Jake.

"He's my nephew."

"How come Marie's met him and not me?" she demanded.

"Oh you can meet him, Sophie, it's only that we happened to run into Marie in town," Jake told her.

"That's okay then. I thought you had a favourite for a minute!"

"He's coming round here tomorrow night," I told her. "So if I let you stay here for the weekend, you'll meet him then."

"Excellent!"

"What's all the business with people moving in here?" Jake asked.

"I'm trying to get away from my mum and Linda is getting away from George," Sophie filled him in.

"Just for the weekend though, Sophie." I said as we went back into the living room.

Linda was looking a bit peaky. "Do you know, I'm not feeling myself at all," she told us before getting up and hurrying toward the bathroom. I sat looking at Jake and Sophie as we tried to ignore the sound of Linda throwing up. She returned looking pale and embarrassed.

"I'm so sorry," she muttered. "I think I'm a bit drunk. I just wanted a bit of Dutch courage before I spoke to George. I'm so ashamed. Sophie, of course you can take the bedroom. I can sleep on the couch."

"That's alright, Linda; age before beauty, as my

mum always says. I can top 'n tail with Marie anyway." Sophie winked at me.

"You can do what?" I asked.

"Top 'n tail. You know, head to toe?" I had no idea what she was talking about.

"I don't know what that means, Sophie, but you're not doing it!"

She smiled condescendingly. "You're such an only child!"

Sophie's phone beeped with a new message. "It's Brian," she said. "He's stuck at work. Can't make it tonight."

My heart sank and I hoped the others couldn't read my thoughts. Sophie glanced at me but obviously decided she had better things to do than wind me up. She went for Jake instead. "Can we please have a weigh-in this week?" she begged.

"Go on then!" he agreed.

There was some delight in the fact that he'd lost another four pounds but the evening wasn't quite the same without Brian. Having sobered up a little, Linda was now even quieter than usual, apparently lost in her thoughts and occasionally voicing her concerns about leaving George. I kept thinking that she might change her mind and flee back to him. Once Jake left, I switched on the TV.

It was late and we were about to head off to bed when the doorbell rang.

"It's him," Linda gasped. "It's George. He's come for me!"

I couldn't decide whether it was elation in her voice or fear. "It can't be," I said. "He doesn't know where you are and even if he did, he doesn't know where I live."

"I left him a note," she confessed. "But I didn't really think he'd come after me."

"Are you mad?" Sophie asked. "You told him to bugger off and walked out on him, but on the way out you stopped to write him a note telling him where you'd be?"

"Don't be silly!" Linda said. "I wrote the note first."

The doorbell rang again.

"Someone answer it," Linda instructed.

I looked at Sophie. "No chance," she said. "I'm not going – he might be a complete psycho who's come to kill us all, chop us up and hide the pieces!" It was always nice to hear Sophie's calm voice of reason.

"I don't think he'd do that," Linda attempted to reassure us. We looked at her. "Of course he wouldn't! Just answer it."

I still wasn't convinced but headed towards the door, hoping that this would turn out like a scene from a fairy-tale or a romantic comedy rather than a scene from CSI.

"Hello?" I said to the man standing on my doorstep. He was short and bald, with a moustache and his eyes were small and squinty. He wore a brown knitted waistcoat over a shirt which was probably originally white. He definitely didn't look like a threat.

"I'm looking for my wife, Linda," he told me. "I believe she's here?"

"Um yes, she's staying with me... Linda," I called. "Your husband is here to see you." I decided they could have it out on the doorstep, just in case Sophie was right about him being a crazed axe murderer.

"Bring him in," Linda shouted, thwarting my plan to keep him out of the house.

"This way," I motioned and he moved past me into the living room.

I was surprised to find Linda sitting on the couch with an air of defiance about her. I would be tempted to say she'd been drinking again if I didn't know better. "Hello, George," she said curtly without looking at him.

"Hello, Linda," he said sheepishly, trying desperately to make eye contact. "I was just wondering if... or when you'd be coming home?"

"Oh," she said, feigning surprise. "Well as you can see, I'm the middle of a girl's night at the moment. These are my friends, Marie and Sophie." She waved a hand at nothing in particular and George smiled awkwardly at Sophie and me.

"It's just that, I'd really like it if you came home," George muttered.

"I suppose you want me to come and make your dinner. But as I said before, I'm in the middle of something." Sophie and I exchanged a look and I wondered at how George had ever been the dominant party in this relationship. She was certainly bringing him down a peg or two now.

"I didn't want you to make me dinner," he said. "I just, well I missed you, that's all." She finally made eye contact with him and held his gaze as though assessing whether he was telling the truth.

"Well I'm certainly not going to make your dinner tonight... and I may not feel like it tomorrow either." She was testing the waters now.

"That's fine. I could take you out to dinner... or maybe I could try to cook something..."

"Well, it would be nice to go out to dinner now and again, but it's not just the cooking, George. You realise that, don't you?" I almost felt sorry for George, standing with his head bowed like a naughty school boy.

I felt increasingly awkward at being witness to the scene. "I think Sophie and I will just wait in the kitchen," I pulled Sophie into the hall by her arm.

"Marie!" she hissed. "What did you do that for? We'll miss everything! You can go in the kitchen but I'm staying here to listen." She sat herself on the bottom of the staircase and turned her ear in the direction of the living room. I sighed and joined her.

"Actually, Linda," we heard George say. "I am a bit confused because I always thought that you liked cooking."

"I don't mind cooking. I just don't like doing it every night, that's all."

"Well that's fine." George sounded genuine. Maybe he was a good actor.

"There's something else. I don't go to fat club... I mean *Emily's Encouragement* anymore. I come here, to Marie's house instead, and sometimes I might want to go to other places with my friends. I don't want to have to lie about where I'm going, but I don't want to have to ask your permission either."

"Of course you should go out with your friends, Linda. That's why I wanted you to go to that Emily thing in the first place. I thought it would do you good to get out of the house and meet some new people. I was a bit concerned because you never seemed to want to go out."

"But, George," Linda jumped in, "Whenever I go out you always ask me so many questions about where I've been and what I've been doing, and if I'm late you always ask me why." She sounded tearful and I felt guilty for listening in. I was too involved to move now though.

"But that was only because I wanted to show an interest in what you were doing. I just wanted to know that you were having a good time. And if you were late, I never minded. I might have worried, but I was never angry." Now George sounded tearful and tears welled in my eyes. "Is there anything else that's been bothering you?" George asked.

"Well I know you like me to stay at home and look after the house but I need to be able to buy my own things without you always questioning it. I would actually quite like to get a part-time job."

"Of course you can get a job, you silly woman!" He laughed. "You don't have to though. You're more than welcome to spend money. What's mine is yours. I never understood why you didn't buy anything on your shopping trips."

"Because you always asked me what I'd bought and how much it cost. I thought that you didn't like me spending money."

George laughed again. "I think we've had our wires crossed for rather a long time. I don't know what to ask about your shopping trips or about women's clothing. I was just trying to make conversation!"

Linda half laughed and half cried. "I've been so unhappy. I thought that you just saw me as a maid; there to keep the house nice and do the washing and cooking for you. We don't talk anymore. I felt so trapped and then I made some friends; the girls and Jake and Brian reminded me what it was like to have fun! I laugh with them and talk to them; they reminded me what life is all about."

"But that's what I want for you Linda." George was speaking quietly; we had to strain to hear him. "That's why I wanted you to go to Emily, so you'd make friends and have fun and be happy! I knew you weren't happy with me anymore. I just wanted to make you smile again, but I didn't know how. Get a job, if that's what you want! Go shopping and spend all our money! Go out with your friends! Do whatever makes you happy!"

I imagined them hugging as I sat on the stairs not daring to look at Sophie because she'd tease me for the tears that were falling down my face.

"I would do anything to make you happy," George told her. "I just want you to come home. You are coming home, aren't you?"

"Of course I'm coming home!" Linda sounded ecstatic.

"I think we have a lot of talking to do," George said. "Why don't I put your suitcase in the car while you say goodbye to your friends."

Sophie and I automatically leaned back on the stairs so he wouldn't spot us from the hallway.

"Girls!" Linda called as she rushed out of the living room. She stopped when she saw us on the steps. "You heard, didn't you? Haven't I been a silly fool?" She was laughing as tears streamed down her cheeks and I finally looked at Sophie whose eyes were also full of tears. She fanned her face with her hand as if to waft them away and Linda leaned down and put her arms around us both. "Will you look at the pair of you," she said with a laugh. "You're worse than me, you big soppy girls! I better go. My George is waiting for me and we've got a lot of catching up to do." She turned and headed confidently for the door.

"Well, at least we don't have to share a bed now," Sophie broke the silence and I turned to smile at her.

Chapter 27

I'd given Sophie a spare key and it was nice to hear her wander in after work on Friday. "What time are the boys getting here?" she called from the hallway.

I came out of my room, where I'd been changing into comfy clothes and looked down the stairs at her. "I guess they won't be long. Jake said he was working until 5pm and then he'd pick Callum up and come straight over."

"I thought I'd cook, if that's okay?" Sophie said, holding up a shopping bag. "Nothing fancy, just sweet and sour chicken with rice."

"Sounds great to me," I told her and she headed for the kitchen.

"I hope it's okay, but I brought the PlayStation with me," Callum told us when he and Jake arrived. He looked up at me for approval.

"Of course. It's fine by me."

Sophie peered into Callum's bag of treasures. "I can beat you at all of those games!"

"Careful now, Sophie," Jake warned. "Callum here is a pro."

"We'll see," Sophie fired back. "I've got three younger brothers so I'm fairly up-to-date with PlayStation games. We need to eat first though.

Who's hungry?"

We ate on our knees in the living room and then Callum set up the PlayStation with Sophie while Jake and I headed to the kitchen to clean up.

"Did she cook in here or have a food fight?" Jake asked when he looked at the sauce that was splattered up the wall behind the stove.

I smiled thinking how nice it was to have some signs of life around the house, never mind the mess. We got to work cleaning up the kitchen and my smile stayed fixed at the sound of Sophie and Callum laughing and chatting in the living room. I enjoyed having the gang round and it occurred to me that I should have invited Linda and Brian too. Although Linda was probably busy re-building her marriage and Brian seems to be avoiding me. Maybe I was just being paranoid. Perhaps he really was busy at work. I should just call him but something was holding me back.

When we went back into the living room, Sophie cheerfully had Callum in a headlock and he was trying to fight his way out, laughing all the while. "Just admit that I'm better than you..." Sophie said to him as she dragged him affectionately around the room.

"No way!" Callum giggled. "You're just a girl. Let me go! Someone help me!" I stood laughing at them before shoving them so that they landed in a heap on the couch.

"Thanks, Marie!" Callum laughed and straightened his t-shirt. "Do you want to play?" he said offering me a PlayStation controller.

"No thanks. I'm more of a board game type of

person myself. I'm not really up on computer games."

"We could play a board game," Callum suggested. "Have you got Monopoly?"

"Yes, somewhere." I went upstairs to find it.

"Right, before we start..." Jake said once we'd set up the board. "I would just like to make it clear which rules we're going to play by..." There was a groan from the rest of us. "The rules are... there are no rules! You can lie, you can cheat and you can steal... so long as you don't get caught! Got it?"

There was a cheer of approval and the game began.

Two hours later, I was close to tears. "This isn't fair! You're picking on me. You can't all just gang up on me like a bunch of bullies!" They had though, and I was losing badly. "I give up! You win!" I threw my remaining pitiful amount of money on the board as they all fell about laughing. "You can all get out of my house now, you bunch of cheats!" I sulked for a moment before joining in with the laughter.

"Come on, Callum, we'd better get home, it's way past your bedtime." Jake said when the laughter died down.

Callum looked disappointed but dutifully moved to find his shoes and coat. "I'll see you again soon though, won't I?" he asked when he hugged me goodbye.

"Yes you will," I confirmed. "We're never playing Monopoly again, but we'll do something soon."

I had no idea how soon I would see Callum again. The next day in fact, although it wouldn't be quite such a happy occasion as the evening had been.

Chapter 28

Sophie was still fast asleep in bed when I left to go shopping with Linda the following morning. Linda was in a fantastic mood. She was full of excitement about how things were working out with George and at how things had changed so much between them in such a short space of time.

"I know it sounds silly," she told me in the car. "But we actually talk now. We've been making polite conversation for years but it's so nice to actually tell him about my life. I told him all about fat club and all of you, which he thought was very funny, of course. We've actually been laughing. I can't believe the change." She was smiling away as she chatted and it was nice to see her so relaxed.

"I bet you wish you'd left him years ago now don't you?" I said.

Linda looked suddenly serious. "I couldn't have done it years ago," she told me. "I could never have done that without you. Apart from anything else, I never had anywhere to go before. I only did it now because I have you, and I knew that if things didn't go to plan that I could stay with you and I'd have friends to help me out."

The sentimental talk made me uncomfortable so I switched the conversation to shopping and Linda told me her plans for the next few hours. I think she wanted to make up for all the times when she'd felt that she couldn't buy things, so we ended up laden down with shopping bags full of her new purchases.

I arrived home in the middle of the afternoon to find a note from Sophie telling me that she'd gone to visit her mum. The kitchen was a mess, even though it looked like she'd only eaten cereal. My feet crunched on cornflakes on the floor and there was a splash of milk and crumbs all over the table. She'd forgotten to put the milk back in the fridge and her cereal-encrusted bowl was sitting next to the sink. *That's what I get for letting a teenager stay with me.* I ignored it and headed for the comfort of the couch.

I'd been lying peacefully, with my eyes closed, for about an hour when the doorbell rang.

I was surprised to find Jake and Callum standing on the doorstep, and my mouth broke into a smile. It quickly disappeared. Callum managed a weak smile but he looked like a different child. All hint of his youthful energy had disappeared.

"Sorry, Marie, I didn't know where to go. Could I leave Callum with you? Just for a couple of hours? I wouldn't ask but I'm a bit stuck..." I'd never seen Jake like this. He was so serious and stressed.

"Of course it's fine." I held out a protective hand to Callum. "Honestly, Jake, it's fine," I attempted to reassure him.

"Why don't you go and set up the PlayStation?" Jake suggested to Callum. "I'll be back for you as soon as I can."

Callum said nothing and went into the living room.

Jake switched to hushed tones. "His mum was

supposed to pick him up from my place this morning but she didn't turn up. I have a shift and I really have to go in. Normally, I'd just take him with me but one of the old ladies had a heart attack and it sounds like it's chaos today. I'd leave him with his gran but I can't get hold of her."

"I'm happy to have him," I said. "But what about his mum? Should we be worried about her?"

He shook his head. "No, Carol will turn up eventually. She always does. Unfortunately this isn't that unusual. I'm really sorry about this, Marie. I'll be back as soon as I can."

I found Callum sitting on the couch with the PlayStation still in the bag.

"Sorry," he apologised to me with his eyes fixed firmly on his feet.

"Don't be sorry. I was bored here on my own so you're doing me a big favour. You okay?" I asked. He nodded and sat in silence.

"I hate my mum sometimes," he eventually said. I nodded but he wasn't looking at me. I could definitely sympathise there. Poor kid.

"I used to hate my mum too," I confided, more to kill the silence than anything.

"Yeah?" he asked with a sniff. He looked up at me with bloodshot eyes and I wondered what I should say.

"She's kind of crazy."

"Yeah?"

"Yeah. I usually say that she's eccentric because it sounds better. And I don't even know who my dad is." I'm not sure whether I kept talking for his benefit or mine but he seemed to want to hear it so I carried on. "I love my mum, but sometimes she made me so mad. I got teased at school because I was the one with the crazy mother who would turn up at the school gates in a fur coat in summer or shorts in the middle of winter. And we never did things that other families did. Like, we never went on holiday, not even once. I used to go to the travel agent and take travel brochures and spend the summer imagining what it would be like to go to all these places. Sometimes I'd even make things up when the other kids asked what I did in the summer holidays." He looked interested so I kept talking, nervous of the silence.

"The worst thing was that if I had a problem, I always had to deal with it myself because my mum couldn't cope and she'd just get stressed and upset about things."

"That's like my mum," Callum jumped in. "Sometimes I feel like I'm the one who's looking after her. My friend's think she's really cool because she lets me stay up late and eat whatever I want. But I she doesn't care like other mums do. She'd rather I eat pizza and chips all the time because it's easier for her. She's not really interested how I do in school. She never notices when I need new clothes. She forgets to pick me up from places, like today..." He sighed and sank back into the couch. "I don't know what would happen if Uncle Jake wasn't around. And I feel bad for Uncle Jake too," he went on. "I know that he has all this stress because of me and he always pretends to be really cheerful, but I know it's hard for him."

"I don't think you need to worry about Jake," I told him. "He loves you and I'm sure he'll always be around to look out for you. This isn't your fault, you know?"

"I know but she's my mum. I always feel responsible for her." He looked so sad and tired, I felt like giving him a big hug and never letting go.

I thought about my mum. "You know, my mum was crazy but she was always there and she definitely liked to cook for me." I smiled cheekily in an attempt to lighten the atmosphere.

"What's so funny?" he asked.

"I just remembered the time she made me a carrot cake," I laughed at the memory. "She thought that since carrots go really well with peas, she would put peas in the cake too!" I snorted and looked at Callum who seemed suspicious of my story.

"She didn't know how to make carrot cake so she made a sponge cake with carrots and peas in it!" I couldn't stop laughing.

"No way," Callum said smiling. "Really?"

"Yes! And she'd gone to so much effort, so I had to sit and eat a whole slice so I wouldn't hurt her feelings. It was disgusting!"

Callum started to seem like his usual self and was setting up the PlayStation when the mobile phone in his backpack started to ring. "It's my mum," he told me as he pulled it out of the bag.

I listened as he answered the phone and explained where he was.

"It's okay, Mum. I'm fine here. You don't need to get me," he told her.

"She wants to come and get me," he said me. I didn't know what to say.

"It's up to you... you can stay here if you want..." I

said.

I could hear her talking on the other end of the line. Without thinking, I told Callum my address when he asked and he repeated it down the phone before hanging up.

"She said she'll come and get me," he told me. "She was angry that I wasn't at Jake's and said he wasn't allowed to just leave me with people that she doesn't know. I think she's been drinking." He looked upset and my heart started beating faster.

"I might just give Jake a call. Why don't you finish setting up the PlayStation and we can have a game before your mum gets here." I tried to sound casual and moved into the kitchen to call Jake. There was no answer so I left a stuttering voicemail asking him to call me back.

I was worried about what would happen if Callum's mum turned up drunk and wanted to take him. I couldn't let him leave with her if she was drunk. But what could I do to stop her? She was his mum after all. I should never have given her my address.

I picked up my phone again and called Brian. He didn't answer and it made me angry. I needed some help.

I went back into the living room. "Did your mum say what happened? Why she didn't pick you up this morning, I mean?"

"She works in a bar. That's why I stay at Jake's so often, but sometimes she goes out to parties after work and then doesn't wake up in time or something. She's got a new boyfriend at the moment so she's with him a lot. I don't think he's a very good influence."

I nodded and tried to disguise my worry and rising panic about the situation. "I'm going to make a cup of tea. Do you want anything?" I asked.

"Can I have juice please?"

"Sure." I headed back to the kitchen and got us drinks, while frantically trying to call both Jake and Brian again to no avail. I don't know what Brian would do, but I needed some moral support and he was good with people. He'd know the right thing to say and do.

I took the drinks into the living room and watched Callum absorb himself in some mysterious Treasure Island game on the PlayStation. I really couldn't see the appeal of making a little man run around, looking for hidden doors, weapons, secret codes and all sorts of random things, but Callum seemed to enjoy it and at least I had something to focus on so that Callum wouldn't notice that I was a nervous wreck.

Jake finally called me back half an hour later. I explained the situation and he sounded stressed. "Sorry to put you in the middle of this, Marie. You'll probably just have to let him go with her. I don't know what else you can do. It's crazy here and I really can't leave yet but I should be able to get out in a couple of hours. If she turns up obviously drunk, then call me back."

"Okay," I answered unsure of what else to say. "See you later."

When the doorbell rang a couple of hours later, Callum was fast asleep on the couch. The emotions of the day had finally gotten to him.

I was happy to open the door to Jake and not have

to deal with Callum's mum. He was such a strong kid. Neither of us had made any reference to the fact that she had failed him for the second time in one day by not coming to pick him up from my place. I was happy that she didn't but also really sad that she'd let him down.

"Poor kid. He deserves a lot better," Jake told me as he looked at his nephew asleep on the couch.

"Well at least he has you," I said, trying to be positive.

I saw Jake's shoulder's rise as he tensed at my words. He walked out of the living room and into the kitchen. I followed him in. "Jake?"

"Sorry," he managed. He was standing at the sink with his back to me and I could tell he was fighting his emotions. "I'm so angry with Carol. I don't know how she can treat him like this." He took a deep breath. "He's such an amazing kid and he just deserves better."

"Jake." I put a hand on his arm, not knowing what to say.

He took another deep breath and then laughed. "I'm sorry. This is all you need on a Saturday night, me blubbing in your kitchen!"

He turned and smiled at me. "We'll get out of your hair. I really can't thank you enough for today."

"Do you want to stay here?" I offered as we stood looking at Callum fast asleep, "Then you don't need to disturb him...I could make you a bed on the floor..."

"Thanks but I think it's better if we go home. I'm trying to keep things as normal as possible."

"You're probably right," I agreed.

Jake collected Callum's things and then gently

nudged him awake. "Come on! Time to go," he told him.

"Thanks for having me," Callum said to me politely as he moved groggily out of the house.

"See you soon," I told them when I gently closed the front door behind them.

I sat down on the couch feeling drained and exhausted. Two things occurred to me: firstly, Sophie hadn't come home yet; and secondly, Brian hadn't called me back.

Sophie was old enough to look after herself, I decided and my thoughts moved to Brian. I wasn't interested in a relationship with him; I just wanted him to be a friend. I hated that I was suddenly spending so much time wondering if he liked me and why he didn't come to fat club on Thursday and why he didn't call me back today. The second-guessing and over-thinking things was exhausting and I wanted to go back to the times when we'd just hang out and have fun. I looked at my phone as though willing him to ring. I was pretty pathetic, I decided.

Chapter 29

"Oh, Marie, that's a lovely cushion!" Anne complimented on Monday morning.

"Thanks. My mum made it for me." I smiled. Mum had been excited at the realisation that she'd never made me a cushion to have at work. This creation had a wobbly white aeroplane on a blue background, and it was kind of cute in a childish way. Obviously, the most amazing thing was that it was actually at work with me and not hidden away like the rest of my collection.

"Isn't she clever? I wish I was a bit more creative."

"I can get Mum to make you one if you want. She's always on the look-out for someone new to make them for."

"Oh, that'll be lovely, if she has the time..."

"I'll ask her. Did you have a good weekend?"

"Yes it was good. We went to David's parent's house for dinner yesterday so that was nice. Other than that it was quiet. How about you?"

"I had a crazy weekend," I told her. "I don't know where to start... Sophie has been staying with me. Jake and Callum were over on Friday evening, then there was a shopping trip with Linda on Saturday, and of course I was at my mum's house yesterday... I'm exhausted thinking about it all."

"You have been busy. It's nice that you've got some company in the house now. What about Brian? You haven't mentioned him recently? Romance not blossomed yet I take it?"

"Anne!" I laughed at her. "How many times do I have to tell you that we're just friends?"

"I understand that you're just friends. I just keep hoping that will change. He's a lovely man."

"I've not seen him for a while actually. He's been busy with work." When I thought about it, it was only a week that had gone by without seeing him, but it felt like longer.

"I'm sure he'll pop up again soon, don't worry about it."

She was wrong though. When Thursday rolled around, Brian was a no-show yet again. In fact it was a disappointing fat club all round. Sophie was still staying at my place. She'd not mentioned moving back to her mums and I didn't have the heart - or the nerve - to ask her to leave. Now she was in a bad mood with me because I'd asked her to clean up the mess she'd left in the kitchen. It was becoming more and more apparent that she thought of me as her maid; either that or she thought fairies came and cleaned in the night, I'm not sure which. Anyway, she was sulking in a fairly impressive teenage way.

Linda was also being quite teenage-like and giggling about things that George had said and done. I was pleased she was so happy but it was a bit sickening at the same time.

Jake had lost three pounds but no one seemed overly-enthusiastic - not even Jake. The stress of recent events was obviously taking its toll on him and he seemed distracted. I managed to get him to myself for a few minutes in the kitchen.

"How are things?" I asked.

"Not great, to be honest," he said. "Carol seems to be going through another bad patch. I think it's this new boyfriend. She's even more self-obsessed than usual and it's hard on Callum."

"I hope things get better for everyone's sake," I told him.

"I've asked her to move in with me for a while. I've got enough room for the two of them and I think it will make things easier on everyone. It will be a bit more stable for Callum, so hopefully things will improve."

"That's amazing, Jake. You're so good to them." I was fairly amazed by his generosity.

"They're family, so of course I help them out where I can. Carol might drive me mad but she's still my sister and I want the best for her, as well as Callum. I just wish she would sort herself out. Anyway, thanks for stepping in when you did. Callum's really fond of you and I know that he was glad to have you around."

"He's a great kid. I was happy to help." I could see why Jake would always jump in to help Callum out, but I was slightly concerned that Carol would take advantage of his kindness. I was an only child though so I had no insight into the sibling bond. It seemed like he would always try to help his sister out when she needed it, even if she didn't really deserve it.

On Friday I found myself sitting behind my desk, thinking about Brian. He'd missed two fat clubs in a row and I was starting to think I may never see him again.

The phone rang at midday and I saw that it was Grace.

"Hi!" I said excitedly at the sound of my best friend's voice. "How are you? How's New York?"

"It's good." She sounded tired and unenthusiastic.

"Are you sure?"

"Yes! Everything is fine. It's just that it's 6am and I'm already in the office. I wasn't even the first one here this morning. "

"Wow! That's dedication."

"Yeah! At least I get to leave early today. It's the big party tonight."

"Oh! I completely forgot. How exciting."

"Are you sure you won't change your mind and hop on a plane? You could still make it..."

"I'll come and visit soon," I told her. "I need to check up on you."

"What's new with you then? Anything exciting going on? How are your crazy friends?"

"Not so crazy these days, but they're fine. Sophie is staying with me at the moment. I moved into your room so she's in the box room."

"Oh, okay. That's nice." She sounded hesitant and if I didn't know her better I would have sworn that there was a hint of jealousy in her voice.

"I'm not sure how long she'll stay for. I think she's realising that there are rules wherever she lives and it's not just her mum being mean. It's nice having the company, though."

"That's great. How's Brian? I haven't heard from him in ages."

"I think he's fine. I haven't seen him for a couple of

weeks but I think he's okay. Busy at work I guess."

"I thought for sure that you two would end up getting together," she mused and I was strangely annoyed that she seemed to think that that wouldn't happen now.

"So why aren't you excited about your party?" I changed the subject.

"I suppose I should be excited but I feel like the company just took over and arranged everything. I had nothing to do with the planning. They said they wanted it to be completely stress-free for me but I feel like they took the fun out of it. I also think it's more of a corporate event than an engagement party. It's mainly business people who are probably only coming to rub shoulders and make contacts."

"I'm sure you'll enjoy it, once it gets going," I told her.

"Maybe. Sorry, Marie, I need to go. The office is filling up and I need to get some work done before I go home and get ready for the party."

"Okay. Well I hope you have a great time and I expect to hear all the details."

"Yes, I'll talk to you soon and tell you all about it." She sounded deflated and it was worrying. She didn't sound herself at all.

I put the phone down and looked at Anne who'd been listening in on the whole conversation.

"Everything going well for Grace in America then?" she asked.

"Yeah, fine."

"Don't worry about Brian. Things will work out fine." I realise that the room is fairly small so she can't help overhearing but sometimes it would be nice if she could at least pretend not to listen in. I looked over to find her staring at me and grinning like a Cheshire cat.

"What?" I asked her impatiently.

"Nothing." She laughed and then her eyes moved to the window. "Oh speak of the devil!" She nodded towards the shop front and I saw Brian pushing open the door.

"Hey!" he greeted me with a smile.

"Hi!" I said, unable hide my surprise and trying to ignore the fact that my stomach flipped at the sight of him. "What are you doing here?" I asked.

"I missed you!" he replied with a cheeky grin. "Any chance you can take an early lunch?"

"I'm not sure," I answered hesitantly. I looked over to the office and saw Greg standing in the doorway. He nodded a greeting to Brian and then looked to Anne. "I'm sure we can manage without her for a bit, can't we, Anne?"

"I should think so, yes," Anne agreed.

"Are you sure?" I asked, as I gathered up my jacket and purse.

"Take your time," Greg told me and disappeared back into his office.

"Have fun!" Anne was grinning and waving like a crazy person as we walked out of the door.

"Hop in," Brian instructed as we walked out of the shop and straight into his car which was parked illegally with the hazard lights on.

"You know this is a pedestrian zone, don't you?" I asked as I got in the car.

"Yes. But we're in a rush."

"Where are we going?" I asked, smiling. It was nice

to be in his company again.

"For lunch," he replied vaguely, as the car pulled away.

"Can you be more specific?"

"It's a surprise. Just relax and enjoy the drive." He turned on the radio and concentrated on the road.

"How far is it?" I asked.

"You're not very good at relaxing are you?" he said and then added, "Half an hour," when I glared at him.

"Half an hour? I have to go back to work this afternoon."

"Your boss just said you could take your time."

"I don't think he meant two hours!"

"It'll be fine. Don't worry so much." He turned the radio up louder as though trying to drown me out.

I sat back in the seat and sulked. I was annoyed at him. I couldn't believe that I'd been missing him and then after five minutes I wanted to shout at him. I hated it when he was like this; when he acted like the world revolved around him. I thought we were just nipping out for a quick lunch in town. If I'd known he was taking me off for a drive to who-knows-where I wouldn't have agreed.

I huffed loudly but said nothing as we pulled onto the motorway. I was not amused.

"Brian? Where are we going?" I asked cautiously ten minutes later, as we pulled off the motorway and I leaned forward to watch an aeroplane flying low in front of us.

He kept his eyes on the road and didn't answer me.

"Brian?" I snapped.

"Yes?" he asked innocently.

"Are we going to the airport?"

"Maybe."

My heart started to beat faster. "Brian, what do you mean 'maybe'? Are we going to the airport?" He pulled onto a roundabout and then exited it, following the direction of an airport sign.

"Why are we going to the airport?" I asked, trying not to panic.

"For lunch," he replied.

I kept quiet until Brian parked the car. "Come on then," he said getting out of the car.

"Brian, I'm not getting on a plane," I told him as I watched him take two medium-sized suitcases and a suit bag out of the back of the car.

"I didn't say you were!" He laughed. "Just come and have lunch with me before I fly."

I glared at him, annoyed and bewildered. "How am I going to get back if you're getting a flight?"

"Could you do me a massive favour and drive my car back for me? It costs a fortune to park here." He threw his car keys at me and started walking away. I wanted to punch him.

"Brian!" I chased after him. "I can't drive!"

He stopped and looked at me with a smirk on his face. "Are you serious?" he asked.

"Yes, I'm serious. I never learnt."

"Wow. Okay, sorry about that. Maybe you can get a train then or a taxi." He took his car key back and kept walking. He was being all cool and annoying. This is just how he was when we first met and I remembered how much I used to dislike him.

I felt like crying and was tempted to walk away and find my way home, but in the end I followed him.

"I take it you're going to New York?" I asked as we

sat in a booth at the airport bar.

"Yep. I decided I couldn't miss out on the party of the year." He got the attention of a passing waiter and ordered two beers and then handed me the food menu.

"I'm not hungry," I told him.

"Why don't you come with me?" he asked. "Since you're here, you may as well."

He sounded cool and confident but when I looked him in the eyes I saw his confidence waver. I didn't reply to his question and leaned back in my seat as the waiter placed a beer in front of me. I looked around and the buzz of the airport excited me. I drank my beer quickly and ordered another.

"Ok, I'll come," I told Brian suddenly. I'm not sure who was more surprised by the statement, me or him.

"Really?" he asked and I nodded in reply.

He reached into his inside pocket and handed me my passport and a boarding card. My heart raced.

"That's your bag," he motioned to the case nearest me. "Sophie packed it. I take no responsibility for its contents!"

I nodded and tried not to freak out as things started to sink in. This had all been planned behind my back. I wondered who else was in on it.

"I guess Anne and Greg know that I'm not coming back today?" I asked.

"Yeah. They know. They're not expecting you back until Tuesday."

"When do we fly back?"

"Monday."

"Does Grace know we're coming?"

"No, I didn't tell them. I wasn't sure I could get you to come." He looked nervous. "I'm still not

299

convinced. Are you really going to come?"

"Yeah," I told him without emotion and took a long swig of beer.

"You know they might not let you on the plane if you're drunk," Brian said.

"I'm not drunk," I assured him.

"Are you scared of flying?" he asked gently.

"No," I said. "I don't think so anyway."

"What does that mean?" he laughed.

"Well it means I'm not sure yet but as soon as I know I'll let you know."

"You have flown before, haven't you?"

"Well, not exactly, no."

Now he really laughed. "So you're a travel agent who's never been on a plane?"

I glared at him in response.

"Sorry. It's just a bit unusual. Anyway, you'll be fine. There's nothing to it. Come on, boarding will start soon." I sighed nervously. "Don't worry, I'll look after you," he promised and squeezed my hand.

"Well, Brian, if I'd known it was like this, I'd have gotten myself on a plane years ago." I laughed and took another sip of champagne. "I always hear people complaining how cramped the seats are but I think this is loads of room." I splayed my arms out to the sides to make my point.

Brian laughed from his seat beside me. "It's called business class, Marie."

I smiled at the stewardess who handed me a fancy looking little bag which I hastily unzipped.

"Ooh! Brian, look, I've got an eye mask. And a toothbrush and toothpaste... and a tiny little hair brush... and socks. Brian they even give you socks!"

He was looking amused beside me. He'd tucked his little bag into the seat pocket without even looking in it.

"Can I get you another glass of champagne madam?" the stewardess asked as I finished the first one.

"Yes please, that'd be lovely."

"Just remember it's an eight hour flight, Marie. Don't overdo it. You'll need to try and sleep once we're in the air. It's going to be a long day. We'll be partying late into the night New York time don't forget."

"Be quiet, Brian! I'm just enjoying myself a little bit, if that's okay with you?"

"That's fine with me," he said with a smile.

"Here's your champagne, madam, and we'll be taking off shortly so if you could buckle your seatbelt there... thank you."

I looked out of the window as we waited at the end of the runway and then all of a sudden the engines roared into life and we were off.

"Wow, Brian, look at the clouds... we're actually in the middle of cloud now... oh wait, now we're through them. They're so fluffy! It's amazing, Brian look..."

I turned and caught him looking at me with a coy smile on his face. "What?" I demanded. "It's beautiful out there... you should have a look."

"I'm glad you're not scared of flying, Marie."

"You're right! I'm not, am I? What's to be scared of?"

I turned back to look out of the window again,

concerned I might miss something. Brian, however, seemed intent on interrupting my cloud-watching.

"What did I miss at fat club then?" he asked. "Sophie told me that she'd moved in with you?"

I'd completely forgotten that he still didn't know about all the crazy goings-on of the past weeks. I snapped my head around to face him and laughed. "Linda almost moved in too!"

I spent the next hour talking non-stop, and telling him all about the night of the girls turning up to live with me, and how sweet it was to see Linda sort things out with George. Then I told him all about Jake and Callum. At some point a drink trolley came around and I indulged in a cheeky little vodka and orange. I was on my holidays after all!

"I really did miss out, didn't I?" Brian laughed. "So Sophie's still living with you? How's that working out?"

"It's great actually. She's messy but it's so nice to have someone else around. I've realised that I'm not really suited to living alone. I like company. Oh look! Here comes food. How cute! It's all on one little tray."

Once the food trays had been taken away, Brian pressed a button which turned his chair into a bed. "I think I'm going to get a bit of sleep," he told me.

"Cool!" I pressed the same button and lay down beside him.

"Brian?"

"Mm...Hmm." He'd covered his eyes with his eye mask and pulled his blanket over him so that he was all cosy. I, on the other hand, seemed to be on a bit of an adrenalin high. I was also probably a little bit drunk. I was losing my inhibitions at an alarming rate.

"Why haven't you been at fat club?" I asked.

He lifted one side of the eye mask up and looked at me seriously. "I was busy at work."

"I thought you were avoiding me."

He pulled the eye mask off his head and turned on his side so he was looking right at me. "I was trying to organise this weekend and I thought that if you suspected anything, you'd freak out and wouldn't come. I wasn't sure I could get you to come at all."

"You're lucky I did come," I jumped in. "You were such an idiot on the way to the airport."

"I know," he said quietly. "But I had this whole weekend planned and it was all pointless if I couldn't get you on the plane. So now you know my one flaw..." He pulled the eye mask over his eyes. "I act like an idiot when I'm nervous.

"Yeah. You do." I recalled the first few times I'd met him and wondered if the arrogance was just a cover for nerves then too.

I smiled and watched him turn away from me.

"What else have you got planned for the weekend?" I asked him, suddenly excited.

"Go to sleep, Marie!"

I couldn't sleep though. I was far too buzzed on excitement and alcohol to be able to sleep.

"Brian!" I was still excited when he finally woke up. "Look there's a TV in the arm of the chair!"

"Have you been watching movies the whole flight?" he asked.

"Yes." I yawned. "I think we're nearly there. I can't wait to see Grace's face!"

Hannah Ellis

Chapter 30

When we pulled up outside the hotel, I followed Brian up the steps and through the revolving door with my jaw hanging somewhere near the ground. The concierge took our bags and escorted us into the hotel. I'd been expecting America's equivalent of a Travel Lodge but this definitely wasn't that.

Brian chatted away to the man on the check-in desk as I looked around the lobby in awe. The place was amazing.

"Mrs Connor?" I laughed as the concierge addressed me as Brian's wife but I didn't bother to correct him. "This way please."

Brian linked his arm through mine and we followed him into the lift and then along a wide corridor until he stopped at a door saying 'Imperial Suite'. Inside the room I stopped at the sight of the biggest bed I had ever seen. I glanced quickly around the room as a thought occurred to me: there was only the one bed. It was big but it was definitely only one bed.

My mind lingered on the thought of sharing a bed with Brian before my eyes darted round the rest of the room trying to take everything in. An intricately carved wooden desk stood in the corner next to a matching armchair; an antique lamp complemented the most comfortable looking couch I have ever seen;

beautiful heavy velvet curtains framed an open door leading to the balcony. I wandered out and admired the view while Brian tipped the concierge.

I walked back into the room and looked at Brian. I started laughing and couldn't stop. "Oh my god!" I squealed as I took a running jump onto the bed. Brian landed beside me seconds later.

"I hope this bed comes with a map or I'll never find my way out in the morning," I said before bouncing back up and heading for the bathroom. "I have to see how big the bath is," I called behind me. I was so excited, I couldn't stay still. I landed back beside Brian moments later beaming with delight.

"So does it meet with your approval Mrs Connor?"

"Oh, my God, yes!" I told him. "The bath is huge, and it has jets, and there's a double shower!"

"Well I'm glad it meets your standards. Now run along and swim in the bath or dance in the showers and then get your glad rags on. We've got a party to gate-crash, remember?"

I jumped up and went over to my suitcase. "I wonder what Sophie packed for me." I was nervous as I unzipped the case. "She knew I needed something for the party didn't she?"

My eyes scanned the case. Everything looked neat and organised. On the left I noticed a bag with a post-it note attached. I was filled with relief as I read the words, 'for the party'.

"She knew about the party!" I said excitedly, without looking up.

I lifted out the bag and pulled out its contents: a pair of heels, a clutch and a little make-up compact.

"Linda sent you a little present as well," Brian said

but I barely registered him. I was frantically digging through the case for my party clothes. I was starting to worry that she'd forgotten to pack the clothes. I imagined them hanging in my bedroom back home. I knew she would've found me something nice. I got to the bottom of the case and panic set in. "I think she forgot," I said as I went through the case again.

"Marie." Brian was louder this time. "Linda sent you this...."

I looked up and my hands shot to my mouth and my eyes filled with tears at the sight of Brian holding a red dress.

"Oh wow!" I bit my lip.

"She assured me that it will fit you perfectly."

"It does." It was the dress that I'd tried on the first time I went shopping with Linda. I wouldn't buy it because it was expensive and I thought I'd never wear it. "I can't believe she did that," I whispered, full of emotion.

"Come on then," he prompted holding out the dress. "We haven't got long."

I jumped up and took the dress from him before running into the bathroom. I could feel the excitement flowing through me as I got ready. I was alternately singing and dancing and laughing or doing all three at once. I came out of the bathroom and stood in front of the mirror. I felt like a whole new person in a whole different life. I ran my hands over the silky material of my dress and felt like a princess. *Thank you Linda!*

I looked up and noticed Brian standing behind me. My stomach flipped at the sight of him in a perfectly fitting tux.

"Wow," he said softly. "You look beautiful." My

stomach flipped again at his compliment and I felt like I was on a rollercoaster. I'm not sure how much more my stomach could take. "Let's get going then shall we?" he suggested before I could say anything.

We got another cab to another fancy hotel for the party. I spotted Grace as soon as we walked into the lobby and I couldn't believe I'd been willing to miss this. Thank goodness my friends had more sense than me. When Grace looked over at us, she looked confused before she burst out laughing and rushing over to us.

"I can't believe you're here! I never thought it would happen." She hugged me tightly and then turned to Brian. "Brian, you're amazing! I can't believe you actually pulled it off. Thank you." She gave him a big hug as James came over and kissed me on the cheek, looking equally as happy to see us.

"Wait," I was distracted. "Sorry, what did Brian pull off? Am I missing something? I thought you didn't know we were coming."

"I told Brian weeks ago that it was his mission to make sure you were here. He said it wouldn't be a problem but I didn't believe him. Then he went quiet and I couldn't get hold of him, so I had no clue what was happening. I'm so glad you're here!" She hugged me again.

"Brian got me to the airport under false pretences and then sprang it on me."

"I was on the phone to you this morning," Grace said. "Didn't you know then? I can't believe it's still the same day."

"No, I had no idea. I thought Brian was taking me out for lunch and he took me to the airport. I didn't even pack, Sophie did it for me."

"Well she did a great job... you look stunning." She stood back and looked me up and down "You really do look unbelievable, Marie. That dress is amazing." She was smiling but there was a look in her eyes that I couldn't quite read.

"Linda bought it for me," I told her.

Grace smiled but she looked tense. "Come in. The firm went really over the top and organised a formal meal and then a live jazz band for the evening." She led me into an elegant room with round tables perfectly set at one end, and at the other end a four-piece jazz band played beside a spacious dance floor.

"This is amazing," I told her.

"Yeah! The thing is..." I heard something like concern in her voice. I glanced around at the people and decorations. Then I stopped and looked again as Grace continued. "It's America and you know what Americans are like. It's not really a party without a theme..."

"Black and white?" I murmured

"Obviously I never mentioned it. I'm sorry. But it doesn't matter." She spoke quickly.

I'd never worn red before. I was not a red person. The one stupid time I wore red and it was a bloody black and white party. If ever there were a time for the ground to open up and swallow me; that would've been it.

Brian took my arm and tugged me into the party. "You know what? You look stunning. You're beautiful and you'd stand out no matter what you were wearing. Let's just have a good time."

"Charmer," I said, glancing up at him while the

smile spread over my face.

"He's right," Grace said appearing at my other side. "Anyway you only came to see me, so who cares what anyone else thinks? I have to mingle I'm afraid, but you two take advantage of the free bar and I'll be back in a while."

We grabbed some champagne and found a quiet corner to hide in. "So how long have you been plotting to get me here?" I asked.

"Not that long. I just thought you might find the surprise approach easier to handle. You're not angry, are you?"

I had the feeling that he'd set me up. I hated it when people thought they knew what was best for me and didn't bother to ask my opinion. He'd been right though; if he'd tried to talk me into coming I don't think I would have. Leaving it until the last minute, so that I didn't have time to think about it had been the best thing to do. It would have been a shame if I'd missed out because I was worried about stepping out of my comfort zone.

"No, I'm not angry," I told him. "I'm glad that I'm here." We smiled at each other and it suddenly hit me that I was tired. I'd been full of excited energy for the whole of the trip. I'd not slept and I'd drunk too much and all I'd thought about was the look on Grace's face when she saw us. I didn't think any further than that. The thought of having a formal meal with a bunch of strangers and then dancing the night away did not appeal to me at all. All I wanted to do was curl up in bed and sleep.

"I can't stop thinking about that huge bed and all those pillows," Brian said, interrupting my thoughts.

"Stop it," I said through a yawn. "How long before we can politely leave?"

"I reckon we've got a while yet."

My mind drifted to the huge bed and I wondered what Brian had been thinking when he booked a double room. Was he being presumptuous about my feelings for him? What were my feelings for him? I looked around the room and tried to push the thoughts from my mind.

Soon there was an announcement that dinner would be served and people started to move towards the tables. Our table was made up mainly of men. If I hadn't been so tired I would have been quite excited by the prospect of an evening with young, good-looking (a couple of them anyway) business men.

As it was, the only person I felt I could bear to talk to was Brian. With him I didn't need to make any attempt at intelligent conversation. The way I was feeling it would be difficult to string a sentence together, never mind make any decent attempt at polite conversation. Unfortunately, Brian had jumped straight into a conversation with the woman on his right. I glanced around him to get a look at her. She was gorgeous. All glossy and smiley and she seemed to be making intelligent conversation. I hated her.

It looked as though I would have to make some small talk. I pasted on a smile and turned to face the man taking a seat next to me. He grinned at me and then laughed loudly.

"You won't get lost in the crowd with that dress will you?" I managed to keep smiling but I was crying great big sobs on the inside.

"Hi. I'm Marie." I extended my hand which he

pulled to his lips and kissed, and somehow miraculously my fake smile stayed fixed.

"Nice to meet ya, Marie. I'm Duke." He had such a distinctive American accent. I think they call it a southern drawl and an hour ago it probably would have excited me. Now it sounded like nails on a blackboard. And Duke? Never in my life had I met anyone called Duke, but this guy was so clearly a Duke. Describing him as a big guy was a major understatement. And I don't mean tall. I guessed he was in his fifties. I also guessed that, a) he was loud and overbearing and, b) he was going to make me want to kill either him or myself before the end of the evening.

"So, Marie. You make sure you save a slow dance for me tonight, okay?" He was grinning and leaning into me, but turned and aimed a wink at the other men on the table. I was physically repulsed and my fake smile was replaced by a sneer that made him back off slightly.

I leaned towards Brian but he was completely engrossed with the hot girl next to him. Trust Brian to end up next to a gorgeous woman while I got stuck with Duke. It seemed like I only had one option; I'd have to drink copious amounts of wine.

I reached for my glass, sticking it out for the passing waiter to fill and took a big gulp. After that the meal wasn't too bad. The food was fantastic and I managed to avoid having to talk to Duke very much by answering his questions monosyllabically until he got bored of me. Brian even tore himself away from Claire (yeah I actually introduced myself and it turned out she was very nice) enough to keep me vaguely amused.

After the four courses were finished, the band got into full swing and people gradually started to dance. "Come on lady in red, let's have a dance shall we?" Brian took my hand and I reluctantly followed him to the dance floor. I wasn't in the mood for dancing. "At least pretend you're enjoying yourself," Brian said as he lifted my arm above my head and spun me around. I couldn't help but laugh.

He spun me around the dance floor for a couple of songs and I was enjoying myself when James and Grace appeared next to us and James demanded a swap.

"Are you having fun?" James asked as we danced together.

"Yes, it's great, but the jet-lag is setting in, and I'm a bit drunk. I don't think it's a great combination!"

"Oh, well! Tomorrow will be much more chilled out; just the four of us. I had an idea that you might turn up so I made sure we had the rest of the weekend free. It means so much to us that you came. You made Grace very happy."

"It's great to see you both. And it's New York. I can't believe I was thinking of missing this!"

When the song ended I excused myself to the bathroom and then decided I would convince Brian it was time to leave. I scanned the room and saw him dancing with Claire. I didn't want to interrupt and I couldn't face going to sit down next to Duke so I hovered at the edge of the room and watched the dancing.

I caught Grace's eye and she came and joined me. "I am so sorry," she said. "I've hardly seen you all night. I have to make small talk to all these business people and all I really want to do is chat to you."

"Don't worry, we'll catch up tomorrow. I'm not good company now anyway. I'm jet-lagged and fed up."

"You'll feel better tomorrow. Why don't you go and get some sleep?"

"Yeah, I will. I'm just waiting for Brian to finish flirting with Claire and then we can go."

She looked at me sympathetically and then turned and watched Brian. "You know he's in love with you, don't you?"

A chill ran through my body but I didn't comment. I had an overwhelming urge to cry.

I felt Grace's eyes on me. "Why else would he spend all his spare time with you, talk about you constantly and pay for a trip to New York just so he can spend time with you?"

"He used to spend so much time with me because we're friends but actually I barely see him these days. And he didn't want to come here for me. He came for you and James." I was getting quite upset. "And if he was in love with me he wouldn't have spent all night with Claire."

"He hasn't spent the whole night with Claire. He's just being nice because she doesn't know many people." We were both watching him glide around the dance floor and suddenly I was angry with him; angry and upset and jealous.

"How do you feel about him?" Grace fired without looking at me.

"He's my friend." I paused. "I don't know, Grace, but it doesn't really matter. He's just Brian. I got used to having him around as a friend, and that was nice. Then all of a sudden he stopped turning up and I started to think that maybe I felt something more for him. But I only started to think about it when he stopped showing up in my life..."

She looked back at me and I hated the fact that she knew me better than I knew myself.

"I'm tired," I told her. "And I don't want to talk about this now. I don't know what's going on."

An elderly couple waved to Grace and she went over to say goodbye to them. I was left alone, watching people chat and dance and have fun. I was at a fancy party in New York and I was miserable; and that thought made me even more miserable. I stared ahead, seeing nothing until Brian came into focus in front of me.

"Had enough partying?" he asked.

"Yeah, I think so," I replied as tears sprang to my eyes. "That is, if you've had enough fun with Claire? If I'm going to spoil your night then I can get myself a taxi." I could hear how horribly passive aggressive I sounded, but I couldn't stop myself.

Brian sighed. "Let's just go. I'm tired. You're tired. It's time for bed."

"I didn't like you dancing with her," I confessed as more tears appeared. The alcohol and lack of sleep had tipped my emotional balance way off kilter.

"Okay, I understand that, but at this moment you just need sleep, so let's focus on that please."

"But—"

"No," he interrupted me firmly. "You have to sleep and then if you still want to have this conversation, we can, but I am not having this conversation with you now. Let's just go." He wiped tears from my face and I tried to compose myself. "Okay," I nodded.

Outside, we got straight into a taxi and while Brian directed the driver, I rested my head on his shoulder and closed my eyes. Brian nudged me awake as we pulled up in front of the hotel and I managed to drag myself up the steps and into the lobby but that's all I could manage. I stopped and Brian turned back to me. "What's wrong?"

My bottom lip twitched as I whispered, "I'm so tired."

He smiled as he came towards me. He lifted me effortlessly off the ground and carried me through the hotel lobby. I rested my head on his shoulder as he carried me up to the room and deposited me on the bed.

"Why did you only book one room?" I suddenly slurred.

"I didn't know if you'd come. Then today I just didn't really think about it."

"Okay," I mumbled.

"Sorry," he said. "If it bothers you I can go and see if they have another room."

"It doesn't bother me."

I saw the cheeky grin spread over his face. "I'll try and keep my hands to myself."

He disappeared into the bathroom and I wriggled out of my dress and crawled under the covers in my underwear. I was asleep within seconds.

Chapter 31

The throbbing in my head was terrible and I did not want to be awake. The digital clock by the bed told me it was just after four and I could hear Brian's rhythmic breathing beside me. Dragging myself up, I got some water and when I looked at myself in the bathroom mirror, my head filled with memories of the previous evening and I groaned. I recalled telling Brian that I was jealous of him dancing with Claire. It seemed ridiculous now.

I slipped back into bed and lay watching the time tick by. At 7am, I got up and pulled on some jeans and a t-shirt. Moving the heavy curtains aside, I slipped out onto the balcony to look down at New York below. The green of Central Park was visible and the busy streets moved with cars and people. I watched for a while, fascinated, and then sat down on a sun lounger and finally fell back to sleep.

"Good morning, beautiful!" Brian's cheerful voice interrupted my peaceful slumber.

"Morning," I whispered and squinted at the sun when I tried to open my eyes. "How long have you been watching me sleep?" I asked as I sat up and stretched. Brian was sitting opposite me reading a newspaper and drinking coffee.

"A while. I ordered you a coffee but it's probably

cold now."

"It'll do," I murmured and reached to take it from the table. As I leaned over, Brian's phone began to ring on the table and I automatically glanced at the screen. Apparently someone called Ellie was calling him.

Brian took the phone, looking guilty as he glanced at me. He obviously thought I was going to turn into a jealous wreck again like the previous evening.

"It's nothing important," he told me. "I'll call back later."

"No problem." I dragged myself out of my chair. "I have to shower so I'll give you some privacy." My voice was calm and casual and somehow I managed to stifle the jealousy that bubbled inside me.

As I showered, my head was all over the place. The fact that a woman was ringing him shouldn't really have mattered to me. It was the look on his face and his awkwardness that bothered me more than anything. Whoever was calling obviously meant something to him, or he wouldn't be acting so cagey. I decided I would just ask him.

I tried to act casual as I came out of the bathroom and I intended to just start a normal relaxed conversation but as I opened my mouth, my emotions took over and the conversation didn't go to plan.

"New girlfriend on the phone?" It didn't come out sounding as breezy as I'd intended.

"No." He looked at me with a blank expression, "Not a girlfriend."

When he didn't say anymore, I had to fill the silence. "Ex-girlfriend? Someone you're dating? Give me a clue…" I was trying my hardest to sound casual but I'm not sure I pulled it off.

"We're meeting Grace and James downstairs in half an hour." He completely ignored my questions. "How did you end up sleeping out here?"

"I woke at four and was wide awake. I'm not keen on jet-lag."

"How's the head?" he asked.

I thought again about the things I'd said to him at the party. "Not the best," I told him and he walked past me and into the bathroom.

We got ready in silence and went downstairs to find Grace and James waiting for us in the hotel conservatory. It was beautiful and elegant and I fleetingly wondered at the price of everything.

"I think I'm getting too old for all this partying," James said through a yawn, as we relaxed around a table laden with croissants, bagels, muffins and a huge selection of fruit. It looked divine but I'd lost my appetite. I picked at a croissant and drank coffee but I suddenly felt self-conscious.

"I still can't believe you two showed up," Grace said. "You really made my evening. It was the best surprise ever."

James picked up his coffee and looked at Brian. "You were the envy of all the men last night, sitting between two gorgeous single women. What did you think of Claire? She just joined the company so I don't know her well, but she seems lovely."

"She was really nice," Brian replied without emotion.

I realised that my heart was racing. My conversation with Brian about Claire the previous evening flashed through my mind yet again. I was jealous that they were dancing together and now I was paranoid that the jealousy was written all over my face. I occupied myself picking over the brunch selection.

"You know, if you want me to play match-maker, I could try and get her number for you," James offered. "I definitely think she took a shine to you."

My stomach was doing somersaults as I waited for Brian to react.

"Long distance isn't really my thing," Brian told him.

"Oh but it's easy these days. She flies to you, you fly to her. Very romantic I'd say."

I waited for someone to change the subject and wished I could shut James up.

"Sounds like a lot of hassle to me," Brian replied, flatly.

I was practically holding my breath waiting for the conversation to end.

"How is the dating scene these days, Brian?" At that point all I could think about was how I was going to kill James.

"Good question, James. I'm well out of it these days. Ask Marie though." He looked at me coolly and the other two followed his lead. "How is what's-his-name? The hotel guy... Jeff isn't it?" It seemed like my passive aggressive tendencies were rubbing off on Brian.

All eyes were on me. "How do you know his name?" I asked.

"Sophie told me about him," he said casually.

"Tell us everything Marie... You're seeing someone are you?" James asked.

"No, I'm not. Can we change the subject please?" I glared at Brian trying to figure him out. He picked up his coffee and ignored me.

"Yes, will you two leave Marie alone?" Grace came to my rescue. "We've got lots to do so let's eat up and get going. I thought that we could take a trip on the Staten Island Ferry – that way we get a good look at the Statue of Liberty and the views of the city are great from the water – then we could go up the Empire State Building. Does that sound okay?" Grace asked, ignoring the awkward atmosphere that had surrounded us.

"Sounds great to me!" I decided to be overly cheerful to hide my annoyance. I couldn't believe that Sophie had told Brian about Jeff, and wondered at her motives.

"I just need to run up to the room and grab my camera," I said, really just needing to have a moment to myself. I walked through the hotel getting angrier while I thought of how Sophie had betrayed me. She'd obviously been making up lies about Jeff and me. I thought about all the times I'd talked to her, and how all those times she was probably just storing up everything I said so she could gossip to Brian about me.

I took a deep breath as I got to the hotel room. I couldn't let Sophie ruin my weekend. I'd deal with her when I got home. Picking up my camera, I turned and jumped at the sight of Brian in the doorway.

"Everything okay?" he asked.

"Yep fine. All ready for some sightseeing!" I adopted my happy tone again.

"Sorry about before. I shouldn't have said anything

about your dating. It's got nothing to do with me."

"It's fine. Don't worry about it." I even waved my hand around to show how little I cared.

"You're annoyed though, aren't you?" he asked.

I sighed and dropped the cheerful routine. "To be honest, I am a bit annoyed. I just don't like the thought of you two gossiping about me behind my back. You're supposed to be my friends."

"Who's gossiping?" he asked with surprise.

"You and Sophie. I can't believe I actually thought she was my friend."

"She is your friend! No one was gossiping about you."

"So what exactly has she been telling you about Jeff? She shouldn't be telling you things that I tell her in confidence."

"Marie!" He had the exasperated tone that he used when he thought I was being dramatic. "Sophie wouldn't go behind your back. She idolises you. I asked her who the guy was that you'd been out with. She said she didn't know but I pestered her about it until she told me his name was Jeff and he worked at the hotel. That you'd only been out with him once and that she didn't think you were interested in him."

"Oh."

"Yeah, 'Oh!' And after she told me that, she shouted at me and told me that next time I wanted information I should ask you and not her. She felt bad for even telling me that snippet."

I had a horrible feeling in my gut. I was a really bad friend. Thank goodness I hadn't had time to talk to Sophie. It suddenly seemed obvious that Sophie wouldn't do anything to hurt me, and I couldn't believe I'd been so quick to jump to conclusions.

"Well, she was right, anyway," I told him. "I'm not interested in Jeff."

Brian looked at me intensely and I thought he was about to say something, until his phone rang, interrupting us. He looked at the screen and his face flashed with the same guilty look as earlier. "Sorry, I need to take this. I'll just be two minutes. Can we meet in the lobby?"

"Yeah, okay." I smiled weakly and walked out of the hotel room.

I heard him answer the phone from the other side of the door. "Ellie! Hi, how are you?"

I walked along the corridor and then backtracked, unable to resist eavesdropping on his call. The door hadn't shut fully behind me and I lingered outside as I heard the warmth in Brian's laugh. "I don't know, I'll think about it. I'm just not sure I can pull off superman! I'm not comfortable with that much lycra!" I could imagine him slouched on the couch, his smile lighting up his face. He sounded so happy and relaxed. I moved away from the door, unable to torture myself anymore.

Chapter 32

"What was all that about at brunch?" Grace asked, when she got me alone for a few minutes. We were leaning on the rails of the Staten Island ferry, watching the impressive Manhattan skyline recede as we pulled away. We were enjoying a wonderful combination of sun on our faces and wind in our hair; a perfect day in New York.

I glanced at Brian and James who were chatting on a nearby bench. "I'm not sure," I told her quietly. "Everything was great between us, he was such a great friend after you left and we were seeing more and more of each other, but then I went out for dinner with Jeff. It wasn't even a date but it seems to have annoyed Brian, and now he's being all weird, which I think is cheeky since he's seeing someone."

"Is he?" Grace asked, surprised.

"Yeah. I think so. Some woman called Ellie keeps calling him."

Grace rolled her eyes. "Why don't you keep things simple and talk to him? He's a pretty straight-forward guy. Just be honest, tell him how you feel and see what he says."

"I tried to talk to him this morning. It didn't work out very well though. Anyway, I'm not sure how I feel about him so it's not that easy."

"Oh, come on!" Grace laughed.

"What?" I asked.

"Last night you were jealous of Claire and today it's Ellie. He doesn't like you going out with Jeff. He obviously likes you and you clearly like him! Can't you just get together without all the drama?"

I smiled at her analysis and turned to look at Brian and James. They were sitting with their legs stretched out, looking beyond us to the Statue of Liberty which was coming into view. On a gorgeous day on a ferry easing past the New York harbour, I suddenly agreed with Grace; Brian and I should be together. I turned back to the sun and closed my eyes. Everything suddenly felt crystal clear.

We walked along the waterfront on Staten Island and squeezed together on a bench to eat ice-creams. The salty breeze and sunshine relaxed us and we laughed easily. Brian cheekily painted my nose with ice cream and I chased him around the bench trying to get my revenge. He grabbed both my wrists when I caught him and I pretended to cry as the remainder of my ice-cream fell to the ground.

"Poor Marie!" Brian said with a grin. "I'll buy you another one later if you're good!" He casually snaked his arms around my waist and rested his chin on my shoulder.

"I'm always good," I informed him as I wriggled to get away.

He moved with me, trapping me with the weight of his arm draped over my shoulder. I relaxed into him when we started the walk back to the ferry. Grace and James walked ahead of us, hand in hand. I looped my arm around Brian's back and hooked my thumb on his jeans.

"One day we should bring the whole gang here," Brian said as he looked out across the water. I looked up at him as his face broke into a grin. "Can you imagine them loose in New York? Sophie would have the time of her life!"

I smiled back at him, amused that he was thinking about Sophie, Linda and Jake. "You really care about them, don't you?" I asked.

He looked slightly wounded. "Of course I do." It immediately felt like a stupid question. "You do too," he said, nudging me. "You just don't like to admit it!"

I smiled and nudged him back.

He removed his arm from my shoulders as we reached the ferry. It was busy at the terminal and as we moved with the crowd to embark, I glanced around, nervous that I would get lost. I felt a hand move into mine and I turned to see Brian behind me. He moved beside me and squeezed my hand, keeping a firm hold of me.

He led me onto the ferry and up to the top deck. Grace and James had found seats in the sun and waved us over. Brian released my hand as I took a seat next to Grace. He stood looking at the view for a minute before sitting next to me, his knee touching mine.

We walked through Manhattan, Grace being a wonderful tour guide and pointing out all the sights along the way. I felt like a wide eyed child as I took everything in.

As I browsed the souvenir shop at the top of the Empire State Building, I found a mini snow globe that I decided I had to buy for Jake. I picked out a pen for

Linda, a key chain for Sophie and a baseball cap for Callum. Just silly little gifts, but I decided that Brian was right; they would love New York. I'd give them the souvenirs and promise that we'd all come together one day.

Wandering back outside, I marvelled some more at the view and walked around until I finally found Grace and James.

"There you are!" James said. "Have you seen Brian?"

"No," I told them. "Not since we first got up here."

We looked around some more before James's phone beeped with a message from Brian saying he was waiting for us on the ground. We took the elevator back down and laughed at the idea of Brian being scared of heights.

We found him on the street, smiling away with a hotdog in his hand.

"Are you scared of heights?" Grace asked him through a laugh.

"No." He shook his head as he took a mouthful of hotdog. "I just smelled food and followed my nose!"

"Come on," Grace said, taking James' hand and turning to walk up the street.

I grinned at Brian, moving closer to him. "I can't believe you're scared of heights!"

"Me?" He raised his eyebrows. "I'm not scared of anything!"

There was that look of vulnerability lurking behind his smile that made me want to kiss him.

He pulled me towards him as a group of tourists walked behind me. My hand moved to his chest and I felt his heart beat as I looked up into his eyes.

"Hurry up, you two!" James's voice interrupted us.

"Hotdog?" Brian offered, laughing. I took a bite before we moved to catch up, hand in hand.

As we walked through Times Square and craned our necks to the lights, I felt a pain between my temples and realised I'd barely drunk anything all day. Grace led us to the Hard Rock Cafe and I gulped down water hoping I'd feel better once I was hydrated. We shared a huge platter of ribs, chicken wings, potato skins, onion rings and fries. I thought we'd never get through it all but we managed most of it, mainly thanks to James and Brian. I tried to keep my spirits up but the headache only got worse and my eyes felt heavier by the minute.

Brian looked concerned. "You okay?"

"My head's killing me."

"You don't look great," Grace informed me. "Are you going to be able to come for drinks?"

The plan was to meet a few of Grace and James's friends for drinks in the evening. I desperately wanted to go. It had been such a great day and I really didn't want it to end. I wanted to go out and drink cocktails and dance and flirt with Brian. There was no way I could manage it though. My body was screaming at me for a dark room, painkillers and sleep.

"I think I'm going to have to head back to the hotel," I told them. "I'm really sorry."

"Don't worry," Grace said gently. "We've got tomorrow night too. It's the jet lag, it's horrible. You'll feel better once you've slept. We can get a cab and drop you back at the hotel."

"Shall I come back with you?" Brian offered as James hailed a cab.

"No, I'm fine. You should go out," I told him.

"Are you sure? I don't mind."

"Honestly, I just need to sleep and then I'll be fine. I'm just annoyed I'm missing out on the fun."

"I promise we won't have any fun without you." He looked at me solemnly. "No fun at all."

"You better not," I told him seriously before breaking into a smile.

We climbed into the yellow cab which took us the short distance to the hotel. "Are you sure you'll be okay?" Brian asked again as I stepped out of the cab. "You don't need me to carry you up to the room again or anything?" He gave me his cheeky smile and I blushed at the memory of the previous night.

"You're telling me about that tomorrow!" Grace said as I closed the door and waved them goodbye.

The bed was a relief and I was asleep within minutes of falling into it.

When I woke I felt refreshed and the headache was gone. I looked at the other side of the bed and was surprised to find it empty. Brian must have had a fun night. I wondered if he'd ended up crashing at Grace and James's place.

I drank water from the bathroom tap and looked at my watch. I was amazed to find I'd slept until 9am. As I stepped out onto the balcony, I checked my watch again. Why wasn't the sun up yet? It took me a few minutes to figure out that I'd only slept for a couple of hours and not the whole night. It was only 9pm but I felt like I'd slept all night.

I called Grace on her mobile. "Is it too late to catch you up? I had a nap and I'm all recharged!"

"I'm so glad you're feeling better," she said. "Brian

just left. He turned all boring after you left and he wanted to go back and check you were okay. Why don't you wait for him and then see what you guys want to do? Maybe you want some alone time!" I could hear the teasing in her voice and at the same time felt butterflies in my stomach.

I hung up the phone and went down to the lobby. The hotel really was magnificent. I surveyed the place as I walked into the lobby. A grand piano was situated in the middle and a suited gentleman sat tinkling away. To the right, I saw the staff working away on the reception desk. I headed left, to the bar. There were a variety of seating options and people were dotted around, quietly chatting over drinks or tapping away on laptops and other electronic devices. I perched on a bar stool, ordered a lemonade and then watched people come and go while keeping an eye on the door, waiting for Brian to arrive.

I hadn't been waiting long when my eyes glanced to the door and I saw Brian walk in. My face lit up and I raised my hand to wave him over. I lowered it again as I saw his face break into a laugh. He turned and held the door while a familiar face followed him in. It was Claire, the girl from the party.

They slipped onto a couch at the opposite side of the lobby. A waiter approached them and then headed over to the bar. I saw them laugh and flinched as Claire touched Brian's leg. I decided that I'd seen enough.

Turning when I reached the lift, I noticed her leaning into him, her body language telling me all I needed to know.

I crawled into bed with a crushing feeling in my

chest. It should be me sitting down there with Brian. He should be telling *me* stories and making *me* laugh. I thought that after today, everything would just fall into place between us.

When Brian slipped into bed beside me I was still awake. I lay on my side with my back to him. I heard him whisper my name and then felt his hand on my shoulder. A part of me wanted to turn and shout at him, tell him that I knew he'd been with her. I resisted the urge and pretended to be asleep. He said my name again and then his hand gently stroked my hair before he moved back to his side of the bed.

I waited until I was sure he was asleep before picking up my phone and slipping out onto the balcony. I loved the balcony, it was small but there was something magical about overlooking New York with the bright moon overhead.

I called Sophie, who answered quickly. I ignored the sleepiness of her voice and launched into an account of everything that had happened and how much of an idiot I felt.

"He's the idiot," Sophie corrected me. "I don't understand him. It doesn't make sense. Should I talk to him? I could call him and find out what's going on?"

"No," I said. "Please don't say anything. I need to sort this out myself. I just wanted to talk to someone. I'd better go. Did I wake you, by the way?"

"Yes!" She laughed. "But it's okay. Try and have fun and let me know what happens with Brian."

"I will," I promised. "Thanks, Sophie."

"You're welcome. You can always call me."

"Not just for that," I told her. "For packing for me."

"Ooh!" she squealed. "It was so much fun. I did a good job, didn't I?"

"The best," I told her. "You're amazing."

We said goodbye and I sighed as I hung up the phone. I felt so much better after talking to Sophie. It had really cleared my head. I slipped back into bed and fell fast asleep.

Chapter 33

I sneaked around the room early in the morning. I wanted to be out before Brian woke. I left him a note saying I'd gone for a walk and would meet up with Grace to go shopping. I'd see him back at the hotel at lunchtime. Grace had already told us that she planned to take me shopping in the morning, so the note wouldn't surprise Brian. I could avoid him until later in the day and try to figure out what to say to him in the meantime.

I walked until I found a coffee shop to hide away in and sat in the window watching the world go by. I messaged Grace to tell her where I was and she joined me an hour later.

"So?" she asked, when she sat down beside me. "What happened with Brian? Tell me everything."

"Nothing," I waved the conversation off. "I was fast asleep again by the time he got back."

Grace looked at me sympathetically before growling in frustration. "I don't like all this uncertainty. I thought last night was the night."

I shrugged. "Maybe it's just not meant to be."

She looked sceptical of my indifference but took the hint and changed the subject. She talked about the shopping areas and places she wanted to show me. I nodded along but struggled to muster any enthusiasm. I found myself thinking of Linda and our shopping trips together. I hoped things were still going well for her and George.

"Let's get going then," Grace prompted. "We've got lots to do. I can't believe you're going home tomorrow."

I followed Grace around what felt like a hundred or so shops and waited while she tried on outfits. I dutifully gave my opinion when called on, and tried to have a good time, but I wasn't really enjoying myself. My feet hurt and my mind was elsewhere. There was a time when I would have told Grace everything, but I found myself keeping my thoughts to myself.

We arrived back at the hotel to find Brian and James waiting in the lobby. My heart raced at the sight of Brian and I felt immediately self-conscious. He looked happy to see me as he kissed me on the cheek and asked me about our morning. I was vague and pleasant and tried my best to act like nothing was wrong.

We'd ordered a picnic from the hotel and left for Central Park loaded down with a hamper and picnic blankets.

"You must've been up early," Brian commented as we walked. "Are you feeling better today?"

"Yeah, fine thanks. I guess I was just tired and dehydrated. Did you have a good night?" I tried to sound casual and didn't look at him as I waited for a reply.

"Yeah, it was okay. Nothing special. You didn't miss much," he answered flatly and we walked in silence from there.

James picked out a spot in the park and we spread out two picnic blankets and distributed the contents of the hamper onto them.

"Don't forget to drink today." Brian handed me a bottle of water as I moved my empty plate away from me and kicked off my shoes. The food was divine but I didn't have much of an appetite.

"Thanks." I took the water from him and drank a few mouthfuls before handing it back. He smiled and tried to hold my gaze but I ignored him and lay down to watch the dozens of kites soaring above us. I felt Brian's hand graze my knee and moved purposefully away from him, closing my eyes to the sun.

I dozed for a while and when I came around I found that James and Brian had gone and it was just Grace and me on the picnic blankets.

"It's amazing here," I said when I sat up.

"Sleepy head!" she teased.

"I'm just so relaxed here. Do you think you'll stay forever?"

"No." She sighed. "At least I hope not. It's not always like this."

"What do you mean? Aren't you happy here?"

"Not really, no. It is an amazing city and there's so much I love about it, but I'd like to be like you; just here for a visit. When you're here for a few days, everything seems to sparkle. It's like one big movie set and there's a buzz about the place. I hate the job though; no matter how hard you work and how many hours you put it, it's just not enough. This is the first full weekend off we've had since we got here. It's exhausting and when I'm tired the city loses its buzz. It becomes like any other big city; dirty and busy and unsafe."

"I'm sorry," I put my hand on her arm. "I had no

idea. I thought you loved it here."

"I'm probably being dramatic. Maybe it's just seeing you and Brian. It reminds me of home and all the things I miss."

"Why don't you take a holiday?" I suggested. "Fly back home and see your family and friends. Recharge the batteries a bit."

"Americans don't seem to understand the concept of holidays or taking a break. It's survival of the fittest." She seemed suddenly wiped out and I felt sorry for her.

"Where are the boys?" I asked.

"Over there," she pointed behind me. "They got roped into a soccer game."

"Grace!" I admonished her. "It's football. You really do need a trip home!"

I turned and watched Brian and James run around the pitch with a bunch of strangers. "That's not a bad view!" I commented cheekily. "The guy in green shorts is very easy on the eye."

Grace laughed. "I thought you only had eyes for Brian?"

I winced and kept my eyes on the football game. "I like to keep my options open," I told her lightly.

"Just don't miss the boat. Brian's a catch. Who knows how long he'll be on the market for."

Her words stung and I had to bite my tongue to stop myself from snapping at her. It seemed like she thought I was lucky that Brian showed any interest in me at all.

"I just haven't decided yet if he's good enough for me," I finally told her flatly, never taking my eyes off the football game.

James and Brian jogged over to us a few minutes later, breaking the awkward silence. Brian reached over me to grab a bottle of water and I turned my nose up.

"Brian you stink! Get away from me!"

He laughed and moved away, shaking his head so that beads of sweat flew from his hair like a dog. "You're disgusting!" I told him and he smiled at me.

"I might need to nip back to the hotel for a shower and a change," he told us.

"I'm not as fit as I used to be," James said as he bent over with his hands on his knees, breathing hard. "I need a shower too. Why don't you guys head back to the hotel and get cleaned up and then grab a cab over to us. You can come and check out our place and we can cook something for dinner later?"

I looked over to Grace who just shrugged.

"Sounds good to me," Brian replied as he finished the bottle of water and flung it back onto the blanket. He lay on his back at the edge of a blanket and closed his eyes, breathing heavily, legs bent up at the knee. As I watched his chest rise and fall, I suddenly felt sad. I definitely had feelings for him and I could see us in a relationship together, but at the same time I knew that I was still vulnerable after Carl. He'd treated me so badly and I just couldn't risk letting anyone do the same. I was in such a good place at the moment and I wanted it to stay that way. I needed to look after myself for a change. As long as there was a chance that Brian was seeing someone else or being secretive about things, I just couldn't let myself get involved.

My gaze shifted to his face and I realised that his

eyes were on me. He gave me a puzzled look and I felt like he was trying to read my mind. I attempted a smile and tried to shake the thoughts from my head.

"Let's get this cleared up and head off," I said and moved to clear the picnic things away. "I can't be around these sweaty smelly men for much longer!"

"Is everything okay?" Brian asked when we got back to the hotel room.

"Yes, fine," I replied. "I think I'll have a shower too but I'll let you jump in first."

"Thanks," he said while he moved into the bathroom. I sat on the bed and waited. When Brian re-emerged from the bathroom it was with only a towel around his waist. After glancing at him I averted my eyes and decided that the universe was trying to torture me.

I took a long shower and when I turned off the water, I could hear Brain's voice as he chatted on the phone. I wondered who he was talking to as I tried in vain to listen in, and then realised that this was exactly the reason I should not get involved with him.

He looked in my direction as soon as I opened the bathroom door and quickly ended his phone conversation. I went out to him on the balcony and poured myself a glass of champagne from the bottle sitting in an ice bucket on the table.

"I thought we should celebrate our last night in New York." Brian raised his glass to mine. I wanted to ask him who was on the phone but knew I couldn't. It was none of my business.

"Cheers." Our glasses clinked together and I stood to look over the edge of the balcony, admiring the view.

"You're quiet," Brian commented after a few minutes.

"Yeah," I replied, not sure what else to say. I drained my glass of champagne. "Shall we get going?"

"Okay, I'll put this in the fridge for later," Brian told me as he lifted the champagne from the ice bucket and wiped the drips from the bottle.

I was surprised by the size of Grace and James's apartment. It was tiny. Grace gave me the tour and I managed a few compliments but really I found it quite depressing. Brian made himself comfortable flicking through the TV channels, ignoring James' protests that he wanted to watch some baseball game.

"It's not going to happen," Brian called to James who was busy cooking in the kitchenette at one end of the small living room. "There are about a thousand channels and I'll flick through them all before I watch a three-hour game of rounders!"

We laughed as James grumbled away in the kitchen.

"It smells good, James," I shouted my encouragement. "Keep up the good work."

Grace sat next to Brian on the two-seater couch and I opted for a spot on the floor, leaving room for James on a comfy-looking chair at the other end of the couch. He joined us a few minutes later and handed us plates of fried rice with chicken. We ate from our knees and Brian relented and let James put the baseball on. It turned out to be quite entertaining, mainly due to James' enthusiasm for the game and his insistence on trying to explain the rules to us.

Grace handed me a glass of wine after we'd eaten and I felt my face flush the more I drank. I relaxed and enjoyed the company. Brian and I pretended to get really into the baseball game and cheered on the Chicago Cubs, much to James's disgust as they were playing his favourite team, the New York Mets.

I was well into my second glass of wine and feeling merrier by the minute, laughing and playing around with Brian again as though I'd never seen him with Claire.

"It's a shame we didn't manage a crazy night out in New York," Grace laughed. "You'll have to come again!"

"Which reminds me," Brian said looking at his watch. "We have a flight to catch tomorrow. Maybe we should call it a night?"

He glanced at me and I nodded my approval.

"I half thought that you'd re-appear last night after Marie rang and said she was revived after her nap," Grace carried on as if she'd not been interrupted. "I can't believe you fell asleep again! You must be getting old." She laughed and I registered Brian's puzzled look.

I put my wine glass down and stood up. "Come on Brian, let's make a move." I took his hand and pulled him up from the couch.

"I'm so sorry we can't come and see you off tomorrow," Grace frowned. "We have to be in the office early."

"It's fine," I told her. "It's been amazing. Thanks for having us and for being such a wonderful tour guide."

I saw her eyes well up as I moved to hug her. "We'll see each other soon," I promised and squeezed her tight.

I handed her over to Brian for a hug and smiled up at James as he embraced me.

They saw us into a cab and waved us off. I looked back at Grace with mixed emotions. I'd miss my friend but I mainly felt sad for her. She didn't seem like the happy, together person she was back home. Some of her shine was missing and I hoped that she'd find a way to make things better for herself.

Brian and I sat in the cab in silence. He didn't speak until we were back in the hotel lobby. "Do you want to get a quick drink at the bar?" he asked.

I hesitated, thinking of the previous evening, before agreeing and perching myself on the bar stool that Brian pulled out for me. I'd just taken a sip of wine when Brian looked at me. "What did Grace mean about you having a nap last night?"

I placed the wine glass carefully on the bar. "I woke up after a couple of hours and called Grace to see if I could catch you up but she said you'd already left."

He looked at me without commenting so I carried on talking. "I came down here to wait for you."

He sighed and rubbed his eyes with the palms of his hands. "So that's why you were upset today? You saw me with Claire?"

I didn't bother to answer, just gulped at my wine.

Brian downed his beer. I waited for the excuses and apologies but none came. "I guess there's no point even talking about it," he finally growled at me. "If you cared enough to want an explanation, you would've asked earlier."

343

He picked up his jacket from the back of his stool and headed for the lift. I finished my wine in one long gulp and followed him.

"Why are *you* angry?" I finally snapped at him when we walked into the suite.

He pulled the bottle of champagne from the fridge and poured himself a glass. "Because you could have mentioned this before and we could have discussed it but it doesn't matter what I say, I'm going to be the bad guy. I'm in the wrong no matter what. So it's a pretty pointless conversation."

"Yesterday things were great with us," I blurted. "But when you spend the whole day flirting with me and then you come back here in the evening flirting with someone else, what am I supposed to think?" I was getting steadily louder and angrier.

"But you always assume the worst of me," he shot back. "I just bumped into her by the hotel and she asked if I wanted to get a drink. It wasn't a big deal."

Tears stung my eyes and I picked up my pyjamas and ducked into the bathroom to get changed. Maybe it wasn't a big deal to him but it was to me.

He was sitting on the edge of the bed, head in his hands, when I came out of the bathroom. "I'm sorry," he said quietly. "I didn't plan to meet her, I just bumped into her outside and we got chatting. It didn't mean anything to me. I had one drink with her, that's all." He sounded upset and I had an urge to wrap my arms around him but resisted.

"What about all the mysterious phone calls?" I asked.

He closed his eyes and sighed in frustration. "The phone calls are nothing! It's just a friend. It's nothing for you to worry about."

"If you could talk to me about it, instead of being so secretive, then I could decide for myself whether it's nothing."

"I can't." He looked at me. "It's complicated. Can't you just trust me?"

"No," I told him honestly. "I can't."

"Fine." He forced a smile and moved out onto the balcony with the bottle of champagne. I crawled into bed and let the tears flow freely down my face.

Chapter 34

There was no sign of Brian when I woke up. His bag was packed and standing by the door. I jumped in the shower and got dressed before packing up my things. I didn't want to leave. The thought of going back to real life was depressing.

I parked my suitcase next to Brian's and did a quick sweep of the room to check that nothing had been forgotten. Then I headed down to the lobby in search of Brian, determined to clear the air before we left. He was sitting at a little round table, reading a newspaper and sipping a coffee. Breakfast items were spread out in front of him.

He didn't notice me until I was standing over him saying good morning.

"Morning," he replied. "Are you all packed?"

"Yep. All ready to go."

"Great. Help yourself to breakfast and I'll get someone to bring the cases down." He headed over to the reception desk and I helped myself to coffee and a bagel.

"Are you okay?" I asked when he returned and sat opposite me.

"Yeah. I couldn't sleep," he told me. "Sophie messaged me last night and told me how upset you were when you saw me with Claire. I feel terrible, so even if you don't want to hear it, I need to explain

347

things to you." I was annoyed that Sophie had spoken to him when I'd specifically told her not to, but I kept quiet.

"When I went out with Grace and James, I missed you as soon as the taxi pulled away. I went for a drink but I just wanted to leave and come back to you. Then I got back to the hotel and Claire was there, waving at me. She lives just around the corner and was walking home. I didn't think anything of it when she asked if I wanted to get a drink. To be honest, I was nervous about seeing you and wondering what I'd say, so I was happy to stall for time. When I realised that she was flirting with me, I told her I wasn't interested and she left. When I went upstairs, you were fast asleep. I know that you don't trust me but I honestly wanted to be with you and not her."

The concierge suddenly appeared behind Brian and told him there was a car waiting to take us to the airport whenever we were ready. Brian nodded at him and then turned back and looked me in the eye.

"I was never interested in Claire. I was only interested in you. I've only been interested in you since the first time we met. The phone calls are nothing. I can't explain it now; it's a strange situation that I have to sort out when we get back home and then I can tell you all about it. It's not that I'm seeing someone else though."

He stood and picked up his jacket. "We better get going," he told me and headed for the door.

I felt like an idiot. I should've said something but I didn't know what. My heart was racing as I got up and hurried to catch up with him, trying to figure out what to say. I moved through the hotel doors and found him waiting at the top of the steps.

"Brian," I called, pulling him to face me.

"You don't have to say anything," he said. "It's okay."

It wasn't okay though. I did need to say something but I had no clue what. On impulse I leaned in, put a hand on the back of his neck and kissed him. His arms moved around my waist and he pulled me closer. I closed my eyes and wished the moment would never end.

Eventually we drew apart and he led me down the few steps and into the waiting car. I kept my eyes on him as he leaned his head back on the seat, looking at me with a sly smile. "You exhaust me."

"And that was just a kiss," I told him coyly.

I felt on top of the world as I turned to look out of the window. I wanted to feast my eyes on New York one last time.

"I told Sophie not to say anything to you. I might have to watch what I say to her in future," I said as we sat in the departure lounge waiting to board.

Brian looked at me condescendingly. "I knew you'd be upset about that."

"I just think it's a bit rude of her to tell you things when I've asked her to keep out of it."

"She's my friend too," he said. "So sometimes she's going to interfere whether you like it or not. If you tell her you're upset because of me, she'll probably always call me and shout at me, even if you ask her not to. It's only because she loves you and wants you to be happy. That's the kind of friend you want in your life. They don't come around very often," he added as we were called to board the plane.

Brian fell asleep as soon as we were settled on the plane. I flicked through the movie channels but I kept thinking back to kissing Brian and I couldn't concentrate on anything. Occasionally I looked over to steal a glance at his sleeping form. I wanted to kiss him again. I was so happy. All my fears about being in a relationship with Brian disappeared and I was excited about what was to come.

I thought about my fat club friends and realised that I missed them. I couldn't wait to tell Sophie about the weekend and I could imagine her squealing with delight as I told her about Brian and me. I realised as soon as Brian said it, that he was right about Sophie. She was only trying to help.

Brian took my hand as we walked through the airport to baggage claim and I was filled with nervous excitement. We were waiting for the luggage to arrive, laughing about James' newfound obsession with baseball, when Brian's phone rang. He pulled it out of his pocket and looked at the screen before silencing it. I felt him tense but said nothing. It rang again a minute later and he answered it without looking at me.

"Hi," he said quickly. "I'm just at the airport waiting for the cases to come through. Can I give you a call back later?"

He hung up and said nothing. My stomach felt like it was one big knot. I'd believed him when he said it was nothing, but now I was back to being paranoid and jealous. He was acting suspicious and there was an atmosphere between us again.

Brian grabbed the cases and we walked in silence to

the car. The silence continued on the drive home and when we arrived outside my place Brian switched off the engine and turned to face me.

"I can't do this," I told him as tears filled my eyes. "I've been here before and I don't want to be in a relationship with someone who can't be open and honest with me. Carl was secretive and he always fobbed me off with stories and told me to trust him. I shouldn't have blindly trusted him. I don't want to go through that again."

He took my hand in his. "I'm not going to hurt you."

I smiled at him as the tears spilled down my cheeks. "I want to believe you but I don't. I think that I need to be single for a while."

I pulled his hand to my mouth and kissed it before leaning over and hugging him. Finally, I pulled away and opened the car door.

Sophie appeared in the hallway as soon as I walked in the house. "You're home!" she said excitedly before seeing my tear-soaked face.

Her face fell and she wrapped her arms around me.

"You can do better than him anyway," she stated once she'd led me into the living room and settled me on the couch. "I always thought that he wasn't good enough for you. You're better off without him."

I smiled at her attempt to cheer me up.

"I'm serious though," she looked me in the eye. "You shouldn't be with someone who makes you cry."

I smiled at her and wiped my eyes with a tissue.

"Hey!" She looked at me seriously. "I'll take you for a night out. We'll find you someone who deserves you. We could go speed-dating!"

I laughed and put my arms around her. I squeezed her so hard that she had to peel me off, fighting for breath.

I went to bed feeling terrible but appreciating the fact that I hadn't come home to an empty house.

Chapter 35

"Tell me everything!" Anne demanded as I walked into work on Tuesday. I'd hardly slept and felt horrible. I'd spent all night questioning whether or not I'd made a massive mistake. I'd even considered calling Brian and telling him that he could be as secretive as he wanted as long as we were together. I'd barely fallen asleep when my alarm woke me and I resisted the urge to take a sick day.

I smiled dutifully at Anne as I dumped my bag in the bottom of the filing cabinet and turned my computer on.

"Was it amazing?" she prompted. "How was Grace? How was the engagement party? What happened with Brian?"

"Slow down!" I laughed. "Yes it was amazing. We had a great time. Grace is doing well. She hates her job and wants to come home, but she'll be fine. The engagement party was lovely. Everything was lovely." I was transported back to New York as the highlights of the weekend flashed through my mind: Brian flicking ice cream on my face and the weight of his arm around me as we walked in the sun; him carrying me up to bed on the first night; his hand finding mine in the crowd by the ferry; kissing him on the hotel steps.

"And what about Brian?" Anne practically shouted at me. "Are you two together now? Was it really romantic? What happened?" She looked like she would shake the information out of me if she had to.

"It was nice and it was all very romantic," I told her. "But we're going to stick to being friends." As I said the words, I suddenly felt like I'd been punched in the stomach. I'd been so upset about Brian and me not being together, that I'd not even thought about our friendship. Would we still be friends? Could we go back to how things were? The thought of not having him in my life at all, made me feel physically sick.

Anne sighed and perched at the other side of my desk. "Poor Brian." She looked genuinely upset.

I screwed my face up at her. "Why poor Brian?"

"He went to such effort. He wanted to sweep you off your feet. What went wrong?" she asked drearily. "And all that money!" she added as an afterthought.

I put my elbows on the desk and leaned towards her. "What are you talking about?"

"That beautiful hotel cost a small fortune. Not to mention flying business class." She clucked and I shook my head trying to figure out how Anne knew so much.

"Oh, didn't he tell you?" She perked up. "I booked it all!"

My eyes widened and I told her to keep talking.

"Oh, Marie, it cost an absolute fortune! But Brian didn't even bat an eyelid; just said he wanted the best." She paused for what I can only assume was dramatic effect. "It was a few weeks ago, one Saturday morning when you were off. In he walked, looking as handsome as ever. I told him you weren't here but he said that he wanted to see me, well me and Greg really. He told us that he wanted to surprise you with this weekend away in New York for Grace's engagement party. He asked if we'd book it all for him and make sure you had the time off work. Of course we were under strict instructions to keep it all a secret." I smiled at her, thinking this was the best story she'd ever told.

"Anyway what on earth happened?" she asked. "I thought for sure that this would make you realise how you really felt. He obviously adores you. And the price of it all! You honestly wouldn't believe... I could show you the bill!"

I didn't know what to tell her. I wasn't sure why things weren't working out between us. I felt like crying. I tried to keep it together as I looked across at Anne. "It was a lovely weekend... but I think it's bad timing. Maybe it's just too soon after Carl."

She sighed and looked at me sympathetically before moving back to her desk, looking almost as disappointed as I felt.

The next couple of days were a blur. Brian filled my every thought and I wondered if we would remain friends after everything. I wasn't even sure I could be friends with him now. I was in pain without him around but I had the feeling that seeing him could be a whole lot worse. Sophie spent the evenings distracting me with movies and TV shows. She put food in front of me and insisted that I ate. She never mentioned Brian.

I was on my way home from work on Thursday when my phone rang and I felt my heart rate rise at the sight of Brian's name on the display.

"Hi," I said nervously.

"Hey. How are you?" It was so nice to hear his voice.

"I'm okay," I told him. "Still fighting the jet-lag but I'm fine. How are you?"

"I'm good."

"Are you coming over tonight?" I asked cautiously.

"That's why I was calling. I'm totally snowed under at work. I didn't manage to wake up in time for work on Tuesday so now I have loads to catch up on. So I won't be able to make it but I wanted to let you know. I didn't want you to think I'm avoiding you."

"It's fine," I told him. "I understand."

"I'm sorry. Say hi to the gang for me. I have to run. I'll talk to you soon." He hung up before I even said goodbye.

It took a lot of effort not to cry. I'd lied when I said it was fine; it wasn't. And regardless of what he'd said, it felt like he was avoiding me.

Sophie greeted me with a cup of tea when I got home and I told her about Brian's phone call. She was surprisingly quiet about it and just gave me a hug and told me everything would be okay.

My spirits lifted at the sight of Jake and Linda who were eager to hear all about my New York adventure.

"Thank you so much for the dress," I told Linda and gave her a hug.

"Oh it was nothing." She blushed.

"It was one of the nicest things anyone has ever done for me," I corrected her. "I wish you could have seen my face when Brian gave it to me." I smiled at the memory and wished that I could jump back in time, to that moment.

"Brian's stuck at work," I told them. "But he says hi. I have presents for you all," I told them and dashed upstairs to grab the souvenirs.

I spent the next hour telling them all about Grace and New York and answering their questions. It was bittersweet to re-live the weekend with them. It had gone too fast. No one asked about me and Brian. I guess Sophie had filled them in and warned them to tread carefully.

"How's the healthy lifestyle going Jake? Have you been sticking to it?" I asked as I exhausted all talk of New York.

"I've been trying. How about a weigh in?" Jake looked keen and I dragged out the weighing scales.

"Ready when you are," I said with my pen poised over the notebook. "Last time you were 16 stone 10 pounds... so let's see where you are today..."

"16 stone and 4 pounds! Wow Jake! You're doing so well."

"Did anything happen with the woman at work, Jake? What's her name?" Linda asked.

"Well actually, we've been out for drinks a few times. I didn't want to say anything because I don't want to jinx it, but fingers crossed, everything seems to be going really well."

"Wow! You kept that a secret," Sophie said. "Come on, we still don't even know her name!"

Jake looked decidedly nervous. "Actually, I still feel like I might jinx things. I think I'll keep it to myself a little while longer; see how things go."

"Very mysterious, Jake!" I said with a laugh.

"You realise that I'm going to annoy you until you give me a name don't you?" Sophie told Jake.

"Yes, I believe that, Sophie, but be patient. All in good time."

"Look at the time. I better get going," Linda suddenly piped up. "George will be missing me." I watched her smiling to herself as she busied herself getting her coat on. Jake followed her lead and they headed for the door. Sophie and I waved to them from the living room window as they got into Linda's car and drove away.

"I think I'm going to head up to bed," I told Sophie.

"Marie?" she called as I reached the doorway. "Is it okay if I'm still friends with Brian?"

She looked sad when I asked her what she meant.

"Well what will happen if he keeps avoiding you and doesn't come to fat club anymore? Can I still see him or will that be weird for you?"

"Of course you can still see him!" I told her. "He's your friend. Anyway, he's just busy at work today, he's not avoiding me. He'll be here next week."

"But you said it was awkward on the phone, so it will be awkward when you're face to face and that's going to be weird for the rest of us." She paused. "I'm sorry, I'm not trying to be mean, it's just that I liked it when it was the five of us."

"Me too," I told her. "I'm sure it'll be fine. It might just take some time."

I didn't know what else to say to her. "Goodnight," I called as I turned towards the stairs.

Chapter 36

I was with Linda on Saturday afternoon, trawling through the fancy boutiques when I stopped outside an art gallery. I noticed the words 'Featherston & Son' neatly tucked into the corner of the window.

"Something wrong, Marie?" Linda asked.

"No, it's just that I think I know the son, in Featherston and Son."

"A friend of yours?"

"Yes. Kind of," I answered vaguely.

"Hi, can I help you? Feel free to come in and have a look around." The voice trailed from the doorway which I hadn't noticed was open. I looked over to a pleasant-looking man smiling at us. I guessed he was around fifty but looked to be in good shape. He was good-looking and well-groomed in suit trousers, shirt and tie.

"Actually I just noticed the place and was being a bit nosey. I'm a friend of Sebastian Featherston. Is he here by any chance?"

He laughed as though I'd told a joke but his eyes were kind. "No, I'm afraid he's not here today. Like most days. You say you're a friend of his though?"

"Yeah, I—"

"Come on in then and have a look around. I'm Paul, by the way, Sebastian's dad, for my sins!"

I introduced myself and Linda, while we walked into the large white-walled room and took in the artwork dotted around the place.

"Paul, what did you want me to do with... Oh... hi..." I was surprised to see Cindy appear from a back room.

"Hi, Cindy"

"So you know my assistant too, do you?" Paul looked amused.

"Yes we know each other through Seb," Cindy filled him in. "I haven't seen you in a while though, Marie. How've you been?" This was perhaps the most Cindy had ever spoken to me.

"I'm really good thanks," I told her. "I just got back from a trip to New York. I've been quite busy lately." I was glad that I managed to drop New York into the conversation.

"This is my friend, Linda, by the way." I glanced at Linda who was looking slightly uncomfortable by my side.

"Nice to meet you," Cindy said. "Would you like a drink? Tea? Coffee?" I was taken aback by how friendly she was.

"No thanks," I replied. "We're just out doing some shopping. We should really get on."

"We'll have to get together soon, Marie." Cindy said.

"Has Seb invited you to our exhibition next week?" Paul asked. "It's probably going to be a very boring stuffy affair but it would be great if you could stop by."

I liked the sound of an art exhibition and Paul was so friendly it was hard to refuse. "It sounds lovely.

When is it?"

"Monday night. Eight o'clock. You're welcome to bring friends... we could actually do with boosting the numbers a bit, so you'd be doing me a favour."

"We could bring the whole gang," Linda said eagerly.

"Great! A gang sounds good." Paul said with a smile.

"It's just a little group of us that meets up sometimes," Linda told him. "Five of us, if that's okay?"

"Great! Cindy, grab the guest list and add Marie and Linda to it... and the rest of the gang!"

I panicked slightly at the thought of a fat club outing to a fancy art exhibition. I supposed it might be okay though, and maybe Brian would come and we could show Sophie that we could actually be in the same room together.

The weekend seemed to go very slowly. Sophie made a great effort to keep my mind off Brian but he sneaked into my thoughts even as I nodded along to another of Sophie's long-winded stories.

I was even glad to visit my mum on Sunday, hoping that might be a nice distraction but she was in a strange mood and seemed annoyed with me. I had no idea what I could've done to upset her. No doubt she would eventually let me know and it would almost certainly be something ridiculous. At least Aunt Kath was cheerful and asked me all about New York.

By Sunday night I was starting to worry about my sanity. I missed Brian and I was starting to think that Sophie was right: we wouldn't be friends anymore and the awkwardness between us would remain. I kicked myself for agreeing with Linda when she said that she would let everyone know about the exhibition on Monday. I could've used that as an excuse to call him. I wished he would call me. I wanted to chat and hear about his week. I wanted to know that he wasn't out of my life completely.

As I lay in bed unable to switch my thoughts off, I decided that I'd send him a message. I tapped out a long apologetic text message, telling him that I hoped we'd still be friends. Then I deleted it all and started again. I sighed as I read and then deleted my second attempt.

Friends? I typed quickly and hit send without stopping to think about it.

Always xxx he replied immediately. I sighed with relief as a smile spread across my face and I felt my whole body relax. I turned and pulled the covers up around my chin.

It felt like a huge weight had been lifted from my shoulders when I walked into work the next morning.

"Morning," I greeted Anne cheerfully while I threw my bag onto my desk and headed for the coffee machine.

"Morning," she replied. "You seem better. Did you have a nice weekend?"

"Yes thanks," I replied. "You?"

"Oh I had a lovely weekend..."

"Hang on a minute," I said as my phone started to ring.

"Hey!" Brian's voice came down the phone.

"Hey yourself!" I replied.

"I felt bad last night after you messaged me." He

paused. "I don't want you to question our friendship. I'll always be your friend. I should've called before, I just needed some space."

"It's okay," I told him.

"It's not really," he told me. "But it will be. Eventually."

I turned as I heard a faint knock on the window. Brian had his phone pressed to his ear, looking through the window. "I didn't want to come in and talk in front of Anne," he explained. I turned, but Anne was busy searching for something in a filing cabinet on the back wall.

"Linda invited me to some art exhibition tonight, so I'll see you there," Brian said while I looked at him through the window.

"Okay," I said, grinning at him. "I'll see you later."

We hung up and he waved before walking away.

"Go on then Anne, tell me about your weekend..." I listened half-heartedly to her telling me every detail of her uneventful weekend and wished that time would speed up. I was excited about the evening ahead.

Chapter 37

It was mid-afternoon when I really started to wonder if it would turn out to be a mistake to take Linda, Jake and Sophie along to the sophisticated event. I had a nagging feeling that it would end in disaster. Sebastian and his friends occupied a different world and I was fairly sure that my two sets of friends would clash. I couldn't back out though; I'd already invited them, so there was no escaping it.

Sebastian rang late in the afternoon and told me how pleased he was that I was coming and that he couldn't wait to meet my friends. I tried to be enthusiastic but it was a struggle.

When the evening came around I was pleasantly surprised. Jake had a suit on and Sophie had a lovely A-line black dress which was cool but conservative. Linda had opted for a long black skirt and simple blouse and looked less frumpy than usual; I think it was the heels that did it. I'd decided on a navy blue wrap-around dress with a pair of heels, and a sparkly clutch to finish the look. I felt good and it was nice to see my friends all dressed up. It didn't quite quell my fears that Sophie was probably going to offend someone and embarrass me but I definitely felt better.

Linda drove us into town and Brian said he would meet us there.

In the art gallery, a young girl took our coats and

gestured a waiter who brought a tray of champagne. It was busier than I expected, and Paul was right about the atmosphere; it was somewhat stuffy. Lots of older looking businessmen and their trophy wives drifted between sculptures and lingered over some very strange paintings. Barely a smile to be seen anywhere; apparently it was a serious affair.

I spotted Sebastian deep in conversation with an older woman across the room. She was stroking his arm and his head was thrown back in laughter. Carlotta and Cindy quickly noticed me and came over for air-kisses, demanding to be introduced to my friends. I'd just made the introductions when Sebastian waltzed over and I had to start over again. He gave them the once over and said a quick hello to them before taking my elbow and pulling me away from them. I heard the others making polite conversation as we moved away and I prayed that they would all get along.

"So glad that you could make it, Marie!" Sebastian purred. "And don't you just look divine!" He held me at arm's length and looked me up and down, making me feel self-conscious. I resorted to the comfort of my old friend the fake smile. "And what interesting friends you have..." His voice was condescending and it annoyed me. I struggled to keep the smile on my face as I changed the subject and congratulated him on such a lovely exhibition.

I was happy when Harry appeared and embraced me in a big bear hug.

"I have to mingle," Sebastian told us, moving away. "I'll see you later."

"How are you?" Harry asked, his warmth putting

me at ease.

"I'm good. I've not been to anything like this before."

"I only called in for the free drinks!" he confessed. "I hate these events. Most of the people are so fake; everyone should lighten up."

"I wanted to ask you..." I felt like I could actually talk to Harry without watching what I said. "What's the deal with Sebastian and this place? His dad implied that he didn't really work here..."

He smiled and lowered his voice to a whisper. "Sebastian has barely done a day's work in his life. He only comes in here to raid the till or schmooze with wealthy women. I don't know how his dad puts up with him."

"Paul seems nice," I said.

"He's great. I see you brought friends?" he said, changing the subject. "And you left them with Carlotta and Cindy? That's brave!"

Linda and Jake were chatting to each other while Sophie was obviously being given the once over by Carlotta and Cindy. I tuned into the conversation.

"Nice handbag," Carlotta was saying to Sophie. "I had one a bit like that last season but it was Prada." I winced and waited for Sophie to bite her head off and tell her what she thinks of people who pander to designer labels.

"Oh really? Lucky you," she said. "I'm only eighteen so I can't really afford designer things but maybe one day." She smiled sweetly, to Carlotta's obvious annoyance. I felt like going over and high-fiving Sophie.

"Let's go rescue her," Harry said.

I went back to my little gang of friends and introduced Harry. Carlotta and Cindy excused themselves to go and mingle and I waited for Sophie to comment on what a pair of bitches they were. She didn't say a word though and it unnerved me.

Harry stood beside me, sipping his drink. "Do any of you have any interest in all this arty-farty stuff or are you just here for the free drinks like me?" He lightened the atmosphere and I was glad of his presence in the group.

"I'm with you," Jake agreed. "It's just a shame they don't serve beer."

"We can always head out in search of a pub later if any of you feel like it?" Everyone nodded their agreement and Jake and Harry broke off into their own conversation about where was good to go locally.

"I've never been to anything like this before and it's all rather fascinating," Linda commented.

Sophie was unusually quiet as she scanned the room. I thought she was probably looking for Brian. He should have been there by now. "I'm going to look around a bit," Sophie said and wandered off into the crowd.

"What's wrong with her?" I asked Linda.

"I think she probably feels a bit out of place here, that's all. It's not really her sort of thing is it? I know she got all dressed up, but she's still the same old Sophie underneath."

"Didn't she want to come?" I asked.

Linda shrugged. "She wanted to come because we were all coming and she likes to spend time with us, especially you. I know that she seems really tough but she's so young and a big softie really. I think she feels uncomfortable with new people, that's all."

It dawned on me that I spent a large portion of waking hours being a complete idiot. I was worried that Sophie would embarrass me with her loud mouth. I'd never even considered how she would feel. I thought I was doing them a favour, bringing them, but in reality they were doing me a favour. Sophie had only come for me and she had to deal with Cindy and Carlotta.

"Linda, I need to go and check Sophie's okay. Will you be all right with Jake and Harry?"

"I'll be fine. It's lots of fun just watching all these people." At least Linda was enjoying herself.

I made my way through the crowd to where Sophie was standing, looking up at a painting hanging on the wall. Next to her, Carlotta was schmoozing a group of older men, chatting away about the same picture that Sophie was focused on. I was just within earshot when I heard Carlotta drag Sophie into her conversation.

"So what do you think about this piece, Sophie? Is it a decent representation of how the abstract is indicative of a departure from reality?"

She'd questioned Sophie loudly so there were now a number of people listening for her response. She was deliberately trying to embarrass Sophie. I silently prayed that Sophie secretly had a vast knowledge of art so that she could make a string of fascinating, intelligent comments and put Carlotta firmly back into her place. I knew Sophie far too well though so I waited for her to tell Carlotta that she thought it was all a load of crap and she couldn't care less.

"I'm sorry but you've asked the wrong person," she

said with a smile. "I don't know anything about art. All I can tell you is that if I was going to hang a painting in my house – if I ever have a house – then I'd want the picture to tell a story. I'd like to look at it and it immediately say something to me. I don't like this because I have no clue what it is supposed to be." She stayed focused on the painting the whole time. A few people murmured their agreement or at least accepted her point of view.

"It's just my opinion though," Sophie said and turned to walk away. I decided to fight Sophie's corner and tell Carlotta exactly what I thought of her.

I'd just opened my mouth to speak when Cindy waltzed over to us.

"Check out the hottie who just walked in. I saw him first so he's mine!" I followed her gaze to the door and saw Brian arriving. My heart started pounding in my chest and my stomach filled with butterflies. He was looking particularly yummy in a dark shirt and tie.

"That's my friend, Brian," I told them.

"Really?" Cindy asked unable to hide her surprise.

"He's delicious," Carlotta said. "You'll have to introduce us. What's the deal with the other people you brought with you? Are you doing some charity work or something?"

The pair of them cackled with laughter.

"What did you just say?" I asked.

"Come on, Marie," Carlotta said. "They're a bunch of oddballs! Surely even you can see that..."

She'd gone too far. I didn't stop to think, just threw my drink over her. I'd like to say that I felt much better, looking at her dripping wet, and giving her a piece of my mind. I didn't feel better at all though. Mainly because champagne is served in quite small amounts and I'd already drunk half of it. So I splashed her face – hopefully ruining her make-up at least – but that was about it. It didn't cause a scene; I don't think anyone else even noticed.

"Bitch!" Carlotta shot at me as Sebastian appeared at her side.

He looked at me. "What's going on?"

"She called my friends oddballs," I told him, outraged.

He laughed and raised an eyebrow. "Well let's be honest darling..."

"No! Stop. You don't know them so you don't get to say anything about them, okay?" I glared at them, each in turn, but none of them dared to say anything so I turned on my heel and headed for the door. I needed some air.

I waited outside feeling sorry for myself. If I'm honest I was waiting for someone to come after me; surely someone would come looking for me. Brian would be wondering where I was. I hadn't even said hello to him. Although I wasn't sure I'd know how to act around him anymore. Just the sight of him made me a nervous wreck.

I peered in through the window, trying to spot my friends. When I heard laughter behind me, I turned to look, sure that I knew the woman's distinct laugh. It was a couple who I didn't recognise but when she spoke I was sure I knew her.

"Excuse me," I uttered automatically.

They turned and I decided that I might be going crazy. I felt like I knew them, but I didn't remember their faces at all. "Sorry," I muttered. "I thought you were someone else."

"You all right?" the woman asked me and I had a strange feeling of deja-vu.

"Yeah, I'm sorry, I just feel like I know you from somewhere."

She grinned at me and she was quite intimidating. She was short and stocky with wild red hair. Her front tooth was chipped making her look quite scary.

"Sorry, love, I don't recognise you." She cackled loudly and suddenly clicked into place.

"Helen?" I asked when she turned to walk away from me. "Taxi Helen?" She turned and looked at me. "It's me!" I told her. "Marie!"

She roared with laughter. "So it is! I don't know why I didn't recognise you!"

She moved quickly, pulling me in for a bear hug and I hugged her in return. I laughed when she pulled away.

"Danny," she called to the man she was with. "This is my good friend, Marie. This is the first time we've met in person," she told him with a grin. It was all very surreal.

"What are you doing here then?" she asked.

"I'm hiding for a minute because I just threw a drink over someone in this party." I pointed to the art gallery behind me.

She raised her hand and I high-fived her. "Found yourself a new fella yet?" she asked.

"I had my eye on one, but I don't think it's going to work out." I pulled her to the window so I could point out Brian.

"Nice!" she said. "I wouldn't kick that one out of

bed! You go for it."

"Do you think we'll get to the pub before close?" Danny asked impatiently.

"All right, all right!" Helen replied. "I better get on, Marie, but good luck with that one." She nodded in Brian's direction. "And give me a call if you need a ride!" she shouted as she wandered away, laughing loudly.

Harry appeared beside me a few minutes later. I was still grinning away from my little encounter.

"Hi," I smiled at him.

"Seb told me that you threw a drink over Carly?" I shrugged. "Well done! There have been so many times when I felt like doing that."

"She deserved it," I told him.

"I know. Anyway, I like your friends. They seem really cool."

"Yeah they are," I said, smiling. How did it take me months to figure out what Harry had seen in five minutes? I'd been trying to make friends with a bunch of people who didn't even know what friendship was, and the whole time I had the most loyal friends right under my nose.

"Coming back in?" he asked. I looked through the window and saw my little gang of friends. They looked like they were having fun. I guess Linda was right; it's who you're with that counts and not where you are.

"Yeah, okay."

As we moved back inside I noticed Carlotta move in close to Brian and start whispering in his ear. He glanced up at me and pulled away from her.

He beamed as he gave me a hug. "Sorry I was late.

You look great."

"I missed you," I told him, impulsively.

"Can we grab a drink later?" he asked. "Just the two of us? I need to talk to you."

"Yes," I told him. "I don't want things to be awkward between us."

He smiled at me and I glanced over his shoulder.

"Hey!" I screeched without thinking. Carlotta was moving in for another chat with Sophie and it made me angry. I marched over to her.

"Get away from her!" I grabbed Carlotta's elbow and turned her away from Sophie. "Do not talk to Sophie. Do not look at Sophie. Stay away from Sophie. Do you understand?"

"What is your problem?" Carlotta asked, wriggling out of my grip. "Why do you have a problem with me talking to Sophie?" She looked at me with defiance and I knew what she was up to. She wanted to make it seem like I was crazy. She turned to Sebastian and rolled her eyes, which just made me angrier.

"You're a bully," I told her loudly. "And you're jealous of Sophie who is young and beautiful and has more personality than you'd know what to do with."

She laughed but I could see I'd gotten to her.

"You're fake," I went on. "Everything about you is fake; including your friends. I feel sorry for you. It's very sad."

Sophie took my arm. "I think maybe we should go..."

"Why should *we* leave?" I snapped.

"Because you're making a scene and it's a bit embarrassing," Sophie whispered in my ear. I looked up and noticed the dozens of pairs of eyes that were watching me around the room.

"Oh, okay. Let's go." I turned and headed for the door and came face to face with Paul. "Mr Featherston, I'm so sorry about that. I didn't mean to cause a scene and ruin the evening."

He patted my arm kindly. "No harm done. I always did think that we were missing some entertainment on these evenings. Enjoy the rest of your evening!"

"Thank you," I said, continuing on my path for the exit.

"Well you certainly livened up the evening," Harry laughed once my gang was assembled outside.

"I'm so embarrassed. I don't know what came over me." I sighed. I couldn't believe that I'd been worried about Sophie embarrassing me.

"Shall we go somewhere else for a drink?" Jake asked.

"I think I better head on home to George," Linda said, looking at her watch.

"We should probably get home too, shouldn't we?" Sophie looked at me.

"I guess so," I replied hesitantly, glancing at Brian.

"Boys night then?" Jake suggested.

"I'm in," Harry answered.

All eyes were on Brian who looked unsure.

"Come on Brian," Jake said. "A quick drink with the lads won't do you any harm, will it?"

"Okay, why not?" he answered finally.

While everyone said goodbye, Brian came over and casually kissed me on the cheek.

"Sorry," he whispered with a shrug.

Linda drove Sophie and me home and we were barely in the door when Sophie flung herself at me.

"Thanks so much. You're amazing. I can't believe you just started shouting at her for me. You're the best!" She let go of me and headed up the stairs. "Sleep tight, Marie!"

"Sleep tight, Sophie," I said, smiling after her.

Chapter 38

"You need to apologise this minute!"

"Actually I don't have to apologise because I've got nothing to apologise for," I said bluntly.

"You have got to be kidding? Last night was a very important evening for us and you turned it into a farce!"

"It was a farce long before I got there, Sebastian. If anyone is owed an apology it's Sophie."

"Don't even bother bringing your hideous friends into this, Marie. If you hadn't brought them for an outing in the first place then none of this would have happened."

"Excuse me?" I shouted, standing up behind my desk.

"You heard me!"

"I think you'll find it's your friends who are the problem. Now get out! Go on! You weird, self-absorbed, pathetic man!"

"How dare you speak to me like that?"

I glanced at Greg who was casually leaning against the office door while he watched the scene unfold. He gave me a discreet nod.

"Get out and take your business with you; we don't need it. In fact, you're barred! Never step foot inside here again, do you hear me?" I spat the words at him and he marched out of the shop without a backward glance.

I breathed in until my lungs were full and then slowly breathed out. I was trembling slightly when I sat down.

"Well that was an interesting start to the day." Anne grinned at me, as she and Greg moved closer to me.

"I'm sorry about that. Sorry I told him to stick his business, Greg."

"It's okay. He always was a demanding prick anyway, and I think you put up with him for long enough. He can find another travel agent to annoy for a while."

"What happened last night then?" Anne asked. "It sounds like it was very entertaining!"

I laughed as I thought back on it and then regaled the pair of them with the story.

"What about Brian?" Anne asked once Greg had returned to his office. "Any developments there?"

"No, I'm afraid not. But I'm not too worried. I've got great friends so I can't complain about my life, can I?" I smiled happily to myself.

"As long as you're happy, Marie." Anne sighed. "But could you do me one favour?"

"What?" I looked at her questioningly.

"Put the brochures back into their proper places! I keep swapping things around but it's been ages now and you've still not noticed. You must have your head in the clouds."

I laughed. It was nice that I had more to think about these days than a wall of holiday brochures. I grinned like an idiot as I skipped over to swap them round.

I went through the rest of the day like Little Miss Cheerful and I was still smiling away to myself when

I got home and found Brian sitting on my doorstep.

I was surprised and very happy to see him. "Sophie not home yet I take it?"

"Nope, no answer," he told me, standing up. "I just thought I'd wait for you..."

"Great, come on in. Everything okay?" I asked.

"Yes, everything's fine. I just really wanted to talk to you."

I moved to open the door but he put a hand on my arm to stop me. "Fancy going for a drink? I thought we could pay Gerry a visit."

"After last time?" I hesitated. "I'm not sure."

"Last time was fun!"

"Okay," I agreed.

We were greeted like old friends by Gerry and after declining 'the usual' - which was apparently a pint of lager and a shot of tequila - we took our drinks to a far corner of the bar to hide ourselves away. I relaxed, happy to be in Brian's company again.

"Last night was fun," he said. "You standing up for Sophie like that."

"Carlotta needed to be told. I wasn't just going to stand by and let her upset Sophie."

He smiled at me. "I'm glad you finally see who your friends are."

"Don't be smug," I told him, taking a sip of my drink. "I always knew who my friends were." It wasn't a complete lie. I just hadn't always appreciated my true friends.

He was grinning as he took a swig of beer.

"What's so funny?" I demanded.

"Sorry. Nothing." I glared at him until he continued. "Well it's just quite funny how you never really saw the true picture."

"What's that supposed to mean?" I asked.

"Nothing, it doesn't matter." He was stifling a smile and it annoyed me.

"Just spit it out!"

"Well, you spent the whole time thinking that Jake, Sophie and Linda were a bit odd and a bunch of misfits, but you never noticed that you fit right in with them. You don't need cool friends because you're not cool."

I hesitated, unsure how to react to his revelation.

"Don't start looking all offended!" he said. "It's not an insult."

"Telling someone they're not cool is a compliment these days, is it?" I asked with raised eyebrows.

"I'm just saying you can be a bit quirky."

"I am not quirky," I told him adamantly.

He smiled. "Let me give you an example..." He thought for a moment. "You went out to a posh restaurant and stopped to get McDonalds on the way home?"

"It was a kebab actually..." I shrugged and he carried on.

"You bumped into Dermot O'Leary and chatted to him like an old friend..."

I shrugged again and winced a little at the memory. I guess I could concede his point there.

"You accidentally go to a fat club, cause a mutiny and end up hosting fat club in your own home..."

"That was not my doing!" I jumped in indignantly. "That was just a series of bizarre events..."

"Yes, but that doesn't happen to normal people, Marie."

I thought he was finished with his little speech and I took a long swig of my drink, certain that he hadn't really made a very good point.

"Who else do you know that would thumb a ride on the back of a stranger's bike?"

"Now, wait a minute... that was one time and there were mitigating circumstances and..."

"And the stranger was gorgeous with an arse you couldn't keep your eyes off so that makes it all okay?"

"The bum was at eye level so..." It was this far into the conversation that I realised that the only reason he knew about this was because he was the one on the bike. When he hadn't mentioned it, I'd convinced myself that it hadn't actually been him at all.

"It was you! I mean I knew it was you, but you never mentioned it! And you told me that you don't have a bike. I thought I was going mad."

"Sorry, I was just amused when you asked about my bike. You looked at me like I might have just forgotten about it. As if I could forget that! It's not every day I get thumbed down for a lift on my bike... It makes a fairly lasting impression!"

"So you do have a bike?"

He laughed. "No. That part was true. I needed to get into town and my car was in the garage. I couldn't get a taxi so I borrowed my neighbour's bike. The one time I've ridden a bike since I was about twelve and I get some nutter hitching a ride!"

"Hey!" I punched his arm playfully while my mind raced back in time and I smiled at the memory of hanging onto the back of Brian on the bike. "In my defence, the buses were on strike and you couldn't get a taxi for love nor money."

"Yes, but as you clearly can't see, other people would have been in the same situation and I think it's safe to say that no one else ended up climbing onto the back of a stranger's bike... which brings me to my original point - you are a bit quirky."

I laughed and leaned into Brian. It felt good to be with him again. I looked up at him and we stopped laughing at once. He moved his hand gingerly into mine. I was torn. The situation hadn't changed in a week.

Slowly, I pulled my hand away. "Brian I meant everything I said last week. Nothing has changed."

He took a deep breath. "What if I changed things?" I gave him a puzzled look. "Every time my phone rang, I wanted to explain everything to you. But I was worried about how you'd take it."

"Well if you want to explain now, I'm listening," I told him, slightly annoyed.

He pulled his phone from his pocket, looking nervous. "Just try to keep an open mind and don't freak out until I've told you the whole story."

"Okay," I said hesitantly while he pushed buttons on his phone. He placed it face up on the table and I leaned in to read the display; he was calling Ellie. I had no clue what was going on.

"Hi," came a muffled voice.

"Hi, Ellie. Everything okay?" he asked, glancing up at me.

"Yes, fine," came the reply. "I was just knitting a jumper for Rex. I've done it in red but now I'm not sure it's his colour. I might start again in blue. Do you know any dogs that would suit red?"

I stayed still, trying to figure out why Brian had

called my mum.

"I don't think I do, but I'll keep it in mind in case I meet any," he told her casually. "I'm just out for a drink with Marie at the moment."

"Oh, how nice."

"Hi, Mum," I said, utterly confused.

"Why are you ringing me if you're out?" she asked.

"We just wanted to see how you're doing," Brian told her.

"That was nice. You two have fun. I'll talk to you tomorrow."

Brian ended the call.

"That was weird," I told him. "My mum's name is Eleanor by the way. No one calls her Ellie."

"She introduced herself as Ellie," he told me.

"So it was my mum who was calling you?" I asked sceptically.

"She calls me a lot."

I didn't say anything and Brian leaned back into the seat. "It started the night when I answered the phone at your place. I gave her my number because she was so stressed, but then she started calling me all the time. I didn't want to say anything because I thought you'd be embarrassed and freak out about it. At first I found it weird and didn't know how to get her to stop and then I just sort of got used to it."

He was right about me being embarrassed. I was mortified. I'd stopped being surprised by my mum a long time ago, but this had caught me off guard.

"You should have told me," I said. "I could've told her to stop. I'll talk to her. I'm sorry." I sighed and closed my eyes briefly.

"Don't say anything to her," he said quietly.

I was annoyed at him for his sympathetic look. I didn't need him to be embarrassed for me. I could manage that one all by myself.

"I'll call her later and it will stop," I told him.

"Don't," he said again. "I don't mind it."

"Well I mind it! She needs to know that it's not okay. You don't have to put up with her just because you're worried about me being upset."

"I like her calling me," he said, looking at me intensely. I raised my eyebrows at him. "Not in a weird way," he said with a laugh. "It's just nice to have someone taking an interest in my life or just calling to see how I am. My mum died when I was a teenager, so I don't really have that."

I winced as I realised that I didn't know anything about his family. It was never a subject I wanted people to ask me about, so I tended to pay others the same courtesy.

"I'd been wondering how to get her to stop calling so often, then a couple of weeks ago I spilled pasta sauce over my couch and found myself calling her to ask her advice on getting it out."

He smiled and I had to ask. "What did she tell you?"

"She asked for my address and promised to send something to fix it."

"And?"

"Well you can't see the stain anymore." He grinned. "She sent me a cushion. Covered it up completely."

"A homemade one?"

He nodded. "It's got a 'B' on it."

I shook my head and took a drink.

Brian's expression turned serious again. "Can I make a suggestion without you getting mad at me?"

"Go on," I said.

"Maybe you could give your mum a break. Stop being so embarrassed by her. Just accept her for who she is and stop worrying about it. It might do you good as well as her."

He moved his hand over mine as a silence fell over us and I fought the sudden urge to cry.

"Need another drink, you two?" Gerry asked. I was glad of the interruption; my thoughts were all over the place and I seemed to have lost the power of speech.

"I think it's time we went home," Brian told him, finishing his drink.

We walked slowly back to my place.

"I'd like to meet your mum sometime," Brian told me. "I was thinking we could talk to her about not calling me during work hours... and maybe we could teach her to text. A text message might be less intrusive sometimes."

I looked up at him and nodded. "Okay, I think we could do that."

"She's pretty upset with you actually," he told me. "So maybe we could fix that too..."

I thought back to the last time I saw her and how she seemed annoyed with me. I had no clue how to feel about her confiding in Brian.

"What did I do to upset her?" I asked as we reached my front gate.

He paused and looked at me with a smirk on his face. "You never bring your boyfriends home to meet her."

I shook my head in disbelief and then smiled up at

him. "Well maybe I should do that sometime then."

"Maybe you should," he told me, with a huge smile on his face. He turned to walk away. "Goodnight, Marie."

"Good night, Brian." I called after him. He turned and casually walked backwards for a couple of steps. He gave me a quick wave and the smile never moved from his face.

Chapter 39

Fat club was in full swing when my phone rang. I sighed when I saw it was my mum and moved to the kitchen to answer it, pulling the door shut behind me.

"Hi," I greeted her, still grappling with the revelation that her and Brian were best phone-buddies.

"Hi! I have a question about your birthday? I was wondering if we should have a party. Maybe a fancy dress party? I could make you a costume."

I took a deep breath and tried to be patient, Brian's advice about giving her a break was playing on my mind.

"I already had my birthday." Surely she hadn't forgotten when my birthday was? That would be worrying, even for her. "It was four months ago, remember? You made me a cheesecake with tomato ketchup on the top..."

"I know that, silly! I was talking about your next birthday!"

"My next birthday, which is eight months away?"

"Yes! Costumes take a long time to make so if we're going to do fancy dress we need to start planning..."

I re-joined fat club five minutes later and Sophie asked who I'd been talking to. "I tried to listen through the door but I couldn't hear properly," she told me.

"It was just... it was..." I sighed. "It was my mum... she was asking if she can throw me a fancy dress party for my birthday next year. She wants to make me a Little Bo Peep costume." I slouched onto the couch as I carried on talking with everyone's full attention. "She's quite unconventional. I've spent my life being embarrassed by her and her funny little ways, but she's just unique and special... and she's my mum; I'm stuck with her. She is who she is and I should have embraced that a long time ago."

I took a deep breath and swallowed the lump in my throat. I looked around at their sympathetic faces and decided I may as well carry on with my confessions. "And there's something else too... I really enjoy going shopping with Linda; and I love spending time with Jake and Callum; having Sophie live with me is great and I like it when Brian calls round for no reason. So I guess my point is that you've turned out to be great friends and... well... thanks."

Predictably, it was Sophie who broke the silence. "I hate to tell you this, Marie, but it's actually Thursday today... fat club? I think your therapy session is on Tuesday, isn't it?"

Linda cleared her throat. "Do you know, I've fallen in love with my husband all over again. After thirty years of marriage! I never thought I could be this happy." She blushed bright red and I smiled at her, happy that things had shifted for her.

Sophie slapped her hand to her forehead "It's confession time! Who's up next? Brian? Jake?"

"Well, I'd like to tell you that I'm dating someone,"

Jake admitted. "It's getting quite serious."

"I was actually being sarcastic," Sophie said needlessly. "But if everyone's telling secrets I may as well tell mine. Although after what Marie said this is a bit awkward... but I don't really like living here." She went suddenly shy and I loved her for it. "I miss my mum and my bags are already packed. I just felt bad leaving Marie alone." She turned to me. "I thought you'd have kicked me out by now."

I smiled at her and it took about ten seconds for the vulnerability to disappear and be replaced by the loud, sarcastic Sophie that we knew and loved. "Your turn, Brian... tell us what's on your mind..."

Brian grinned at her and then shifted his gaze to his feet. I thought he was going to keep quiet but he finally looked up at me and whispered, "I'm in love with Marie."

I was so shocked, I wasn't even sure that I'd heard him right.

Sophie's voice cut through the silence. "Brian, I don't think you really understood the point of the exercise... we're telling *secrets*. You know? Something that people don't already know..."

My heart was beating far too fast and I didn't know what to say.

"Actually," Jake jumped in. "I wasn't really finished..." He was bright red and sweat was trickling down his temples. "The person I'm seeing, well, like I said, it's getting serious and we're at the point where we want to meet each other's friends and since you're my friends, I'd like you to meet..."

"Oooh, Jake's got a girlfriend," Sophie sang. "Can you finally tell us her name then?"

"Yes, well, actually…" His voice was shaking. "His name is Michael." He exhaled loudly and looked round at us. It's hard to believe but Jake had actually found a way to shut Sophie up. Someone needed to say something but I was in a state of shock.

"That's lovely Jake," Linda said kindly and he smiled at her. I realised he was so nervous because he didn't know how we'd react. He desperately needed our approval.

"Good for you, Jake. I look forward to meeting him." Trust Brian to know the right thing to say.

I wanted to say something heartfelt and genuine, and amazingly the words were out of my mouth before I knew it. "I always wanted a gay friend!" I smiled at Jake and he beamed back.

He visibly relaxed and then looked at Sophie. She had that vulnerable look that she got when someone caught her off guard. True to form, it disappeared pretty quickly and she was back to being sure of herself. "Didn't I just explain about *secrets...* do you really think that I didn't know you're gay? Give me some credit; I spotted that the first time I laid eyes on you... I only said that stuff about a girlfriend for a laugh." She gave him a wink as the room filled with easy laughter.

I'd been grinning like an idiot since Brian had announced that he loved me. We'd barely lost eye contact and as the revelations came to an end, I couldn't help myself any longer.

"I think you're all going to have to leave," I said with my eyes on Brian. I felt all eyes on me so I clarified things for them. "Sorry. But go on, get out."

"Everyone?" Brian asked cheekily.

"No. Not you. Everyone else though." I got up, hoping the rest of them would follow suit. Only Brian stood up and we locked eyes as I took the few steps over to him.

I turned to the rest of them and raised my voice, "Go!"

"So this is how it's going to be now, is it?" Sophie asked with a laugh as they finally started moving. "I have to get my bags! I'm going home to Mum!"

She thundered up the stairs and then ran back down just as fast and re-entered the room with a black bin bag in each hand.

"What's happened to your suitcase, Sophie?" Linda asked.

Sophie looked at me with laughter in her eyes. "I just keep thinking that this room could do with cushions." She tugged at the bottom of the bags and lifted them up in the air scattering my mum's cushions all over the room.

"Cushion fight!" she screamed.

I gave up on ever getting them to leave and stifled a laugh as I put my hands in Brian's hair, kissing him lightly on the lips as cushions flew around us.

Epilogue

Eight months later...

I was standing in Brian's kitchen smiling to myself while I watched my mum at the other side of the room having an animated discussion with Brian. I knew that she was telling him to marry me and he was calmly discussing the idea with her. It had been going on for a while now and I loved the fact that Brian never lost patience with her. His easy smile made me think that he even quite enjoyed it. I loved how fond they were of each other.

My smile suddenly turned into a snort of laughter. I couldn't help it; the whole scene was hilarious. You see my mum was dressed as Cruella DeVille and Brian was sporting a rather fetching Superman outfit. I reached for my camera and snapped a photo of them before panning round the room to capture everyone else. Linda, or should I say, Snow White, was oblivious to me because, as usual she had her head in her phone, messaging George no doubt. He sometimes came along with her but I think he was still quite frightened of us, so he usually found an excuse to stay away.

Next to her, the boys all turned and gave me the thumbs up. It was a great picture of the three of them. Jake and Callum made a great dynamic duo with their Batman and Robin outfits (Callum had finally won

the 'who would be Batman' argument.) while
ael made a handsome Indiana Jones. Jake and
ichael had become inseparable and they made a
great team. Michael had endeared everyone to him on
his first meeting by already knowing everyone's
names and little details about them. He's one of those
people who always sees the best in people and is kind
and genuine. It was impossible not to like him and he
always brought a sense of fun to the group. Callum
adored him too which was one of Jake's main
concerns.

I'd been worried that it would be difficult for Jake,
trying to juggle looking after Carol and Callum while
also developing his relationship with Michael. For a
lot of people it would have been awkward but Jake
was open with everyone and managed to make time to
be there for everyone in his life without hurting
anyone's feelings. It helped that Michael was so
understanding and supportive of the situation.

Things had really changed for Callum too. Mainly
due to the night he turned up at fat club with his
mother in tow. She needed friends, he'd announced;
good friends to look out for her and we were the
people he'd chosen. She'd been treated to the usual
amount of teasing, and turned up the following week
for more. She was gradually coming out of herself and
seemed more relaxed around us. It was Sophie who'd
taken it upon herself to make sure that Carol was
always invited and included in whatever we were
doing. They'd become firm friends; not that Carol had
any real choice in the matter.

Carol appeared in the kitchen doorway, looking
slightly shy as always. She looked stunning in her Cat

Woman outfit.

"Carol, move over to the boys and I'll take your photo." She smiled and put her hand gently on Callum's shoulder as Jake slung one arm around her and the other around Michael. I was amused by their unconventional little family.

"Marie?" Sophie sidled up next to me – looking super cute in her Lara Croft outfit – and looped her arms casually around my waist.

"No!" I answered automatically.

She rested her head on me and looked up at me with big eyes. "But you don't know what I'm going to say yet."

"Fine, what do you want?"

"Why do you think I want something? Maybe I just came over to give you a hug and wish you a happy birthday."

I smiled at her and raised my eyebrows.

"Okay fine, you know me too well! It's just that Jeff finishes work at five and I wondered if it's okay for him to come over?" She'd been seeing Jeff for a few months now, after deciding to try her luck at speed-dating again and never making it past the front desk of the hotel.

She'd quickly become besotted with him and it brought out her vulnerable side. I lived in fear of her getting her heart broken but for now she was ecstatically happy and they made a cute couple. I'd always liked Jeff but I was wary of him now. If he ever hurt Sophie – even unintentionally – he would have me to deal with. That would be awkward if I was overly fond of him. He'd have me and the rest of them queuing up to take a swing at him if he didn't treat

Sophie right.

"Go on, then," I told her. "The more the merrier!"

"You're the best, Marie! I love you!" She planted a big kiss on my cheek, making me squirm to get away from her.

"Anne! Look this way and smile..." She turned away from the oven and I got a shot of her in her Marilyn Munroe number.

"Are you finished? The sausage rolls are about to burn!"

"Yep, I'm all done!"

I was missing someone. I walked into the living room and found Harry hovering over the sound system and having an argument with Sophie about which CD to put on next.

"Sorry," I said interrupting them. "I need a quick photo."

Harry's Incredible Hulk outfit didn't quite suit his personality but he looked good anyway. "When's it cake time?" he asked. "Just so we can make sure to have a fire extinguisher on standby!"

I managed a sarcastic laugh.

"When is the food ready?" Sophie asked. "I'm going to fade away in a minute."

"I'll find out." I wandered back into the kitchen and looked over to where my mum and Brian had been talking, but Aunt Kath had taken Brian's place and I snapped a photo of them. Poor Aunt Kath was dressed as a Dalmatian to go with Mum's Cruella outfit. Mum had so much fun with the planning of my party. Brian had asked her to make the costumes for everyone. She'd been over the moon and had been on cloud nine ever since.

I spied Brian through the kitchen window, standing alone outside, on the deck. He had a strange look on his face, like he was deep in thought. My stomach flipped and even though I loved having my whole gang of friends and family around me, I was also looking forward to them all leaving and being alone with Brian.

He turned and caught me looking and gave me a weak smile. I walked out to him and instead of pulling me to him like he usually did, he just took my hand, looking concerned.

"Your mum's driving me mad," he told me seriously. "I'm sick of her."

He turned away from me and looked out over the garden. I felt the colour drain from my face and nausea swept through me. "I'm sorry. I'll talk to her. I'll get her to stop. Really, Brian, I didn't realise it bothered you. I'm sorry."

"It won't work. We both know what she's like and telling her to stop isn't going to help."

I felt like my whole world was about to fall apart. Brian was the only person who'd I'd ever known who I didn't have to worry about my mum's behaviour with. He'd always just accepted her and he'd told me to do the same. I'd let my guard down and stopped worrying so much about what other people thought of her. For the first time that I could remember I'd enjoyed her enthusiasm about my birthday. Had I been so relaxed that I'd missed Brian losing his patience with her?

"Brian, really, she doesn't mean it. Can we just talk about this later? I can sort it all out."

"No," he said firmly. "I'm sorry."

"What?" I couldn't believe this was happening. Everything had been perfect. "Brian, I can fix this—"

"There's only one way to fix it, Marie." I was confused when he looked me solemnly in the eyes. Then he was on one knee and holding out a ring.

"What's going on?"

He smiled cheekily. "The only way she'll stop nagging me is if you marry me."

"Brian! You want me to marry you so my mum will stop bothering you?"

"Yes, that's basically it."

"Not because you love me?"

"Nope! And not because I can't imagine life without you and want to spend forever with you. Nothing to do with any of that; just to get your mum off my back. What do you say?"

I couldn't think of anything to say. I was wearing a ridiculous puffy dress, with ringlets in my hair, rosy cheeks, a toy sheep hanging from my apron strings, looking down at Superman who was asking me to marry him.

"My knee's starting to hurt," Brian whispered through a grin.

"Marie!" I turned to see Sophie at the window. "Put the poor man out of his misery will you!"

There was a row of faces lined up at the kitchen window watching us.

"It'd be a bit embarrassing if I said no now, wouldn't it?" I said, turning my gaze back to Brian.

"You'd better say yes then!"

"Yes then!" I said, beaming.

"Just to save me from embarrassment?" he asked.

"Yes."

"Not because you're madly in love with me and want to spend forever with me?"

I shrugged. "Maybe a bit of that as well."

"Is that a yes?" Jake called as Brian picked me up and swung me around.

"It's a yes." I laughed at the array of faces grinning at us through the window. "It's definitely a yes!"

THE END

Made in the USA
San Bernardino, CA
12 October 2018